MOLOCH

OTHER WORKS BY HENRY MILLER
PUBLISHED BY GROVE PRESS

Black Spring
Quiet Days in Clichy
Sexus
Plexus
Nexus
Tropic of Cancer
Tropic of Capricorn
Under the Roofs of Paris
Crazy Cock

INTRODUCTION BY MARY V. DEARBORN

MOLOCH

OR, THIS GENTILE WORLD

HENRY MILLER

GROVE PRESS   NEW YORK

Published by Grove Press
A division of Grove Press, Inc.
841 Broadway
New York, NY 10003-4793

Published in Canada by General Publishing Company, Ltd.

Library of Congress Cataloging-in-Publication Data

Miller, Henry, 1891–1980
Moloch / Henry Miller ; introduction by Mary V. Dearborn.—1st
ed.
p.   cm.
ISBN 0-8021-1419-9 (alk. paper)
I. Title.
PS3525.I5454M57   1992
813′ .52—dc20   92-10327   CIP

Manufactured in the United States of America

Printed on acid-free paper

Designed by Kathy Kikkert

First Edition 1992

1   3   5   7   9   10   8   6   4   2

INTRODUCTION

And the Lord Spake unto Moses, saying, Again, thou shalt say to the children of Israel, Whosoever he be of the children of Israel, or of the strangers that sojourn in Israel, that giveth any of his seed unto Moloch; he shall surely be put to death: the people of the land shall stone him with stones. . . . I will set my face against that man, and against his family, and will cut him off, and all that go whoring after him, to commit whoredom with Moloch, from among their people.

—LEVITICUS 20:1–5

The dawn of 1927, perhaps the most tempestuous year of his long and tempestuous life, found Henry Miller sharing a cellar on Henry Street in Brooklyn Heights with his second wife, June, and her Lesbian lover, Jean. June had convinced Henry to quit his job in order to fulfill his destiny and become a writer, but he did little else but hang about the gloomy apartment, he later wrote, "like a stranger." Thanks to Jean's artistic efforts, the dingy basement apartment walls were decorated with murals, and the ceiling was painted purple. In the middle of the kitchen they set up "the gut table," around which they gathered for marathons of talk. Miller, the son of an obsessively fastidious mother, later described the conditions in which he lived:

> Bed unmade all day; climbing into it with shoes frequently; sheets a mess. Using soiled shirts for towels . . . washing dishes in the bathtub, which was greasy and black rimmed. Bathroom always cold as an icebox. . . . Shades always down, windows never washed, atmosphere sepulchral. Floor constantly strewn with plaster of Paris, tools, paints, books, cigarette butts, garbage, soiled dishes, pots. Jean running around all day in coveralls. June always half-naked and complaining of the cold.

That winter they burned chairs and other furniture in the fireplace for warmth.

Money was in short supply. Jean, who wore men's clothing and two left shoes, took to the manufacture of puppets and later expanded her line to include death masks. When these items failed to bring in the needed cash, she attempted to hire her body out for medical experiments. Jean and June then seized eagerly on Henry's idea of selling blood, but were disappointed when they were turned away for being anemic.

Above and beyond these entrepreneurial activities, the two women provided for household expenses primarily through gold digging on a grand scale, frequenting what Miller called "nothing but dives and joints, nothing but pederasts, Lesbians, pimps, tarts, fakes and phonies of all description." June brought men back to the tiny apartment and entertained them while Henry sat in a little shed behind the house, freezing, listening to the gay sounds that penetrated the thin walls. June's behavior had always been erratic, and her days and nights disordered, but she seemed to become quite mad as her involvement with a decidedly seamy bohemia and the underworld grew more intense. Then one night, after days of vomiting, June confessed to using drugs. Trapped in this lurid and unsanitary universe, broke and tormented by the cold, torn between love and jealousy, his manhood under assault from all quarters, Henry, unsurprisingly, showed little inclination to write. He spent his days hanging around in the streets and panhandling in pool halls, speakeasies, and burlesque parlors. In April an old acquaintance and nemesis, Jimmy Pasta, got Miller a job with the Parks Department, and it had a tonic effect on him, restoring a small measure of order and respectability to his otherwise tumultuous and degraded life. One week later, however, his temporary peace of mind was shattered when he returned home to find June and Jean had run away together to Paris. In a howling fit he smashed up what little furniture was left in the apartment.

Destitute and humbled, Miller moved back in with his domineering mother and ineffectual father. Within two months, however, June had returned without her lover, and the Millers were back in business as husband and wife. June insisted on moving to an elegant apartment on Clinton Avenue in Brooklyn—one they could ill afford—in a neighborhood of luxurious mansions and brownstones. She also insisted that Henry immediately quit his job—to write. It was from a writing table in the comfortable Clinton Avenue apartment, looking out over a pleasant garden with two trees, that Henry began work on *Moloch*. The peculiar circumstances surrounding the genesis of the book made for anything but ideal working conditions.

June had scraped together enough money to open a "cellar dive" called the Roman Tavern in Greenwich Village. It was not the Millers' first foray into the nightclub business. Two years earlier, building on June's extensive experience as a "hostess," they had run a small subterranean establishment on Perry Street where bootleg gin and the company of June were the only commodities for sale. The Roman Tavern operated along similar lines with similar meager profit margins. It was here that June met a man in the fur business who would identify himself only as

"Pop." And it was under Pop's patronage that *Moloch* would be written.

June had managed to convince Pop she was an aspiring literary talent, and he agreed to pay her a weekly stipend so that she could write a novel. The only stipulations were that she should show him a few pages every week and make herself available to discuss the intricacies of the creative process with him.

The actual writing of this novel would, of course, be undertaken by Miller, with June acting as liaison. The unusual arrangement had its literary and emotional difficulties. Writing to order was not Miller's forte, and he had already experienced problems in trying to produce stories for magazines with names like *Breezy Stories, Droll Stories, True Story,* and *True Confessions.* Then too, for a writer who would one day elevate "manly writing" to the status of a personal crusade, sustaining a voice that was supposed to be June's for the length of an entire novel would be no simple matter. In fact, Miller wrote later, "Every time I sat down to write a page for (Pop), I readjusted my skirt, primped my hairdo, and powdered my nose." Further complicating matters, Miller was not blind to the obvious possibilities of the relationship between June and her patron and suspected all along that his wife was giving Pop "value for value, and had been from the very beginning."

Nevertheless, Miller took on the project. The writing was fitful, and the weekly quota of pages hung heavily over him. But the regularity of the grind instilled a new sense of discipline in the budding author, and he was pleased to discover the finished manuscript came to nearly four hundred typed pages. What is more, Pop, the audience of one, liked it so much that he threw in a bonus trip to Paris for purported authoress June, along with enough money for nine months' expenses.

We can only speculate as to the refinement of Pop's literary tastes and the wisdom of his judgment, but the novel Miller produced at his behest, to today's critical eye, leaves much to be desired. *Moloch* is intriguing as a piece of Miller juvenilia and as a first attempt at autobiographical fiction by an extremely autobiographical writer. But its prose is spotty and uneven, almost uniformly stilted and awkward, and the narrative voice is inconsistent and frequently obtrusive. Yet *Moloch* offers some tantalizing rewards.

The story Miller sets out to tell in *Moloch* is based on his years at Western Union and the disintegration of his first marriage. Some of the more interesting parts of the novel are concerned with the day-to-day operations of the telegraph company. Miller held a position of modest importance at the Park Row branch office in Lower Manhattan. (In his later novels and in statements about his life he would represent his job as that of "employment manager," but we should remember that Western Union was a personnel company, and that every Western Union worker who was not a messenger was in some sense in the business of managing employees.) His duties consisted of hiring and firing messengers at a time when the company was experiencing enormous turnover problems, and the pace of his day was hectic.

Dion Moloch, the protagonist and autobiographical hero of the novel, is presented as the idol of everyone with whom he comes in contact—messengers adore him, subordinates seek his company and advice, ex-employees write him long and admiring letters, women lust after him. In reality, Miller's performance on the job was a little on the shady side—he shamelessly confiscated messengers' car fare for his own lunch money and preyed endlessly on the secretaries and female messengers under his supervision. (One of his colleagues, Mike Rivese, who appears as O'Rourke in *Tropic of Capricorn,* later wrote a little-known book called *Inside Western Union,* reporting that Miller was lazy and shoddy in his work habits.)

Moloch's philandering, chronicled at length in the novel, does nothing for his floundering marriage to Blanche, a character modeled on Miller's first wife, Beatrice. He describes the couple's situation as "stranded on the mudflats of matrimony." Their life together is presented as an extended brawl.

But by far the most prominent thematic feature of *Moloch* is its ubiquitous and often virulent anti-Semitism. In his late twenties, Miller systematically went about developing an anti-Semitic "philosophy," taking as his mentors Nietzsche, Herbert Spencer,

Spengler, and Hilaire Belloc. He did "field work" on the Lower East Side and in his old Brooklyn neighborhood of Williamsburg, which he saw as spoiled, dirty, and overrun by Jews.

Yet like many of Miller's obsessions, his feelings toward the Jews were fraught with ambivalence. In the book, Dion Moloch scolds Blanche and his friend Stanley for their anti-Semitism. And there are many passages in which Miller speaks of Jews with open admiration, as when he commends the intellect and independence of Jewish women and proclaims their clear superiority as wives over Gentile women. We must also remember that June, the love of Miller's life, his obsession, his tormentor, was Jewish, and it is not unlikely that some of the anti-Semitic diatribe in *Moloch* was inserted expressly to annoy and torment her.

Of course, Jews are not the only objects of Miller's ire in *Moloch,* and with little effort one can find abundant evidence of explicitly offensive sentiments: references that are sexist ("bimbos" and "sluts"), racist ("niggers" and "tar babies"), homophobic ("faggots"), anti-Italian, anti-Irish, anti-Dutch, anti-Polish, anti-Catholic. Moloch is, furthermore, not above making fun of an epileptic or justifying beating his wife. And—most tellingly, perhaps—he comes off as unrepentantly anti-family, anti-American, and even anti–Western civilization.

There is something almost adolescent in Miller's desire to shock, to *épater le bourgeois* at every conceivable twist and turn, with anything at his disposal, at any price. In fact, the blatant flaunting of his multiple prejudices is only part of a larger strategy that includes a realism carried to the point of ugliness and brutality, a style that will eventually be expressed by the "mature" Miller through a plethora of four-letter words and shocking sexual explicitness.

In *Moloch,* Miller is only warming up, practicing; it is *Tropic of Cancer,* generally agreed to be his first fully realized work, that he introduces to the world as follows: "This is not a book. This is libel, slander, defamation of character. This is not a book in the ordinary sense of the word. No, this is a prolonged insult, a gob of spit in the face of Art, a kick in the pants to God, Man, Destiny, Time, Love, Beauty. . . ."

The choice of the title, *Moloch; or, This Gentile World,* reflects Miller's larger and more systematic rejection of any and all orthodoxies. In turn, it reveals his own somewhat bizarre "orthodoxies" and at the same time dramatizes his own profound alienation. On the literal level, Moloch, "the abomination of the Ammonites," a deity who demands child sacrifice of his adherents, is an implacable and demonic power arrayed against the people of Israel. As such, one enlisted in the service of Moloch is, by definition, an enemy of Israel, the Jewish people.

But for Miller, as it was for the apostolic fathers and the medieval theologians before him, and most probably for the Lutheran ministers whose sermons he was subjected to as a child, "Israel" is also a symbol and figure of something more: of the new chosen people in the new Jerusalem, of the church, of an entire civilization and way of life predicated upon Christianity. With respect to these institutions and values, Moloch/Miller will always style himself the quintessential "Gentile," the ultimate outsider. And Miller's work, above and beyond its strident iconoclasm, becomes, among other things, an extended exploration of the writer's own misanthropy in the face of his (often somewhat desperate) belief in human possibility. In *Moloch,* that lifelong project is only just beginning.

Moloch is Miller's first completed, extant novel. It was preceded by a collection of sketches of twelve Western Union messengers called *Clipped Wings,* which survives only in fragments. Much of the material from this earlier effort, however, finds its way into *Moloch,* including the anti-Semitic orientation and the vaguely repellent portraits of messengers.

In fact, nothing Miller ever wrote was wasted. Everything could be recycled. The ground covered in *Moloch* would be gone over again, more thoroughly in *Tropic of Capricorn* and *Sexus,* where it would receive a typically fantastic, Millerian amplification. For example, what in *Moloch* is characterized somewhat modestly and nondescriptly as the Great American Telegraph Company is transmogrified in the later works into the infamous

Cosmodemonic Telegraph Company of North America. The original manuscript of *Moloch* even bears explicit instructions penciled in the margins in his own hand to indicate that chapter 13 is destined "for Tropic of Capricorn."

The reworking of these bits of life and text is consistent with Miller's early definition of his mission as a writer. Before embarking on *Moloch,* he had committed to paper, in one manic, hallucinatory session, some thirty pages of notes that would constitute a complete plan for his life's work. He would write the story of his life with June and Jean—a colossal tale of love and betrayal, of suffering and violent emotional upheaval. *Moloch* is only a first and very tentative chapter in that story.

Still, glimpses of the later Miller are there to be seen. The preoccupation with sex is already in evidence, although we are spared the accumulation of biological detail. Sex scenes in *Moloch* have a way of either dissolving into fuzzy lyricism or being interrupted or postponed. The reliance on four-letter words and the explicit description of sex acts that would earn him his later reputation as a "dirty book writer" have not yet become part of his technique.

What Miller does discover in *Moloch,* however, is his genre, which is best understood as autobiographical fantasy. He uses himself and his friends as the main characters, and the story that he tells is his own, or at least his own as his psyche remembers it. But if he discovers his form, he has not yet found the voice he needs to sing his song. Both *Moloch* and his subsequent attempt to write about his marriage with June, *Crazy Cock* (originally titled "Lovely Lesbians"), are cast as third-person narratives. It was not until he began to write in the first person that Miller's writing swelled to the epic proportions of his mature style. It is a style based on the willfully extravagant, on the magnificent, the hyperbolic, the overblown, and the *outré.*

It is the liberation of this voice and its boundless energy that are Miller's most significant artistic achievements. In an epiphany described near the end of *Moloch,* he gives us a glimpse of what is to come:

"This world is my world, my stamping-ground. I must run

free, mad-hearted, bellowing with pain and ecstasy, charging with lowered horns, ripping up the barricades that hem me in and stifle me. I must have room to expand . . . vast, silent spaces to charge in so that my voice may be heard to the outermost limits and shake the unseen walls of this cruel universe."

Whatever one thinks of Miller's later work, we can agree with a line from Dion Moloch: "It was written in the first person spectacular. Some of it was in high fettle."

—Mary V. Dearborn

PUBLISHER'S NOTE

THE PUBLISHING OF POSTHUMOUS FICTION NATURALLY presents special problems, and the reader is entitled to know what, if any, editing has taken place. We have earnestly sought to present this novel in as untrammeled a form as possible, correcting only misspellings, obvious inconsistencies, and verb disagreements where no rewriting was entailed. With these minor exceptions, this first publication of this Henry Miller novel is exactly as he wrote it.

MOLOCH

DION MOLOCH WALKED WITH THE DREAMY STRIDE OF A
noctambulo among the apparitions on the Bowery. I say "apparitions" because, as every sophisticated New Yorker knows, the
Bowery is a thoroughfare where blasted souls are repaired for the
price of a free lunch.

Dion Moloch was a modest, sensitive soul attired in a suit of
Bedford whipcord and pale blue shirt, the collars and cuffs of
which were disgracefully frayed.

Though he was in the service of the Great American Telegraph
Company he did not suffer from megalomania, dementia prae-
cox, or any of the fashionable nervous and mental disorders of
the twentieth century. It was often said of him that he was
anti-Semitic, but then this is a prejudice and not a disease.

At any rate, he was not like a certain character out of Gogol
who had to be informed when to blow his nose. He was, in short,

an American of three generations. He was definitely not Russian. His grandparents had fought in the Civil War—on both sides. He had fought in no wars. In point of fact, he was, or had been, a draft dodger. Not that he was a coward, nor a man of high principles, for that matter, like—shall we say Woodrow Wilson? No, it was rather that he was an enigma (to himself) . . . that everything was an enigma.

Two years after the war was over he had arrived at the conclusion that the Germans were right, but it was too late then, of course, to enlist in a cause that had already been lost.

When America entered the war Dion Moloch took it into his head to get married. To be sure, thousands of Americans were similarly moved by the call to arms. This is a phenomenon, however, that chiefly concerns the sociologist.

Despite the fact that the war had been raging on a dozen fronts for several years, and that millions of his fellow creatures, for the sake of a few empty phrases, were being cheerfully converted into so much cannon fodder, Dion Moloch remained the victim of a habit which had begun at an early age. It may seem extraordinary to mention such a detail in connection with the life of this individual when the entire world was convulsed by a holocaust. Nevertheless, this singular detail, trivial as it may seem beside the annals of a great war, had a most important bearing on Dion Moloch's future career.

To put it tersely, our hero could never get up when the alarm went off in the morning.

During the Argonne Drive he had become enamored of a young pianiste who was giving concerts to help make the world safe for democracy. The young lady had a most unpatriotic desire to play the rhapsodies of Liszt, since she had been brought up on that diet in a finishing school at Montreal, but knowing little of the world, and less of Hungary, she was uncertain of the status of her taste. She therefore contented herself with practicing Liszt etudes on a clavier at home.

The assassin who hurled the bomb at the Archduke of Austria also brought these two creatures together. It was left to Providence to unite them.

One morning, when Moloch lay slumbering peacefully, oblivious of the rumble on the Western Front, or all the fronts put together, his mother (for some unknown reason) became unduly incensed by his torpor. Perhaps she had been stirred the night before by some unusual tale of atrocity. At any rate, she had been thinking thus—"If he won't enlist he can at least get a job." The more she thought the more irate she became. Finally, actuated by a sudden blind impulse she hastened to the sink and filled a pail of water. A moment later and she had dashed the chill contents over him.

"Now get up!" she screamed. "You lazy good-for-nothing, you waster . . . *you bum!*"

The last epithet required the complete abdication of her maternal affection.

It would be idle and tortuous to recount the successive steps by which, starting from this simple dramatic scene, our hero finally became enmeshed in the ophidian toils of matrimony. That Rabelaisian escapade forms another volume by itself. Suffice it to relate that immediately upon arising Dion Moloch packed his duds and wiped his feet on the paternal rug for the last time.

Nor does it seem fair to dwell on the fact, though it forms a somewhat colorful note—a leitmotif, as it were, throughout his future marital career—that on the morning of his hurried wedding he was obliged to borrow the price of a haircut and shave. The bride, as you may suspect, paid the marriage fee, a fact which was never entirely forgotten by her throughout their turbulent wedlock.

What seems of great importance, looking back upon his sclerotic past, is that this event, premature though it was, made it necessary for Dion Moloch to find a job.

When we first encounter him among the "apparitions" on the Bowery he has already given three years of his life to a great corporation.

What errand has brought him to this dismal thoroughfare— the Bowery? Is it to get his soul repaired, amid the rataplan of traffic? Or is it the free lunch that has attracted him?

He has just come from the home of a lunatic—one of those self-imposed missions which his position occasionally created and which he found not entirely disagreeable. Intent upon making his way back to the office his attention has been suddenly arrested by a notice suspended over a flight of stairs leading to a gloomy cellar. The notice, printed in huge ocher letters, read:

DEATH ON BUGS

Below these sulphurous words was a canvas whose colors affected the retina as pleasantly as fried eggs. The painter had endeavored, evidently, to reproduce a situation which undoubtedly had poignancy for the denizens of this locality. A recumbent nude with flaxen tresses and flowing hips was shown busily engaged in scratching the tenderer portions of her anatomy. The bed seemed rather to float in the middle air than to rest firmly on the planked flooring. Her consort was depicted stealing about the premises with a squirt-gun. The imbecilic glee he displayed was apparently evoked by the sight of a filthy mattress from which an interminable file of bedbugs issued. (The bedbug is known to scientists as *Cimex lectularius*: a cosmopolitan blood-sucking wingless depressed bug of reddish brown color and vile odor, infesting houses and especially beds. The cockroach is the natural enemy of the bedbug.) Even the counterpane on which the assassin's saffron paramour reclined, after the now classic manner of *Olympe,* was diapered with these cosmopolitan bloodsucking wingless depressed bugs of reddish brown color and vile odor.

At this point a number of things might have happened. Nothing is further from the truth than that, given a certain impetus (as, for instance, this germicide portrait on the Bowery) the hero forthwith reacts in thus and such a manner. The grand metabolistic dynamics of the laboratory worker, which are so impressive in connection with rats and mental defectives, becomes inoperative when a truly human mind and organism is encountered. . . . Possibly twenty-five different courses of action presented themselves to our character. The one impulse to which he was thoroughly immune was to purchase a sample of this rare insecticide. For him the subway blurbs and the garish posters that stood out like a rash along the countryside had no message. His tastes were simple, his wants easily satisfied. Copywriters might rack their brains for another century to come without ever arousing in him that fundamental curiosity upon which the advertising cult of our day rears its ephemeral philosophy of success.

Shreds of thought fluttered like the snapped strings of an epiphone banjo in the gray convolutions of his upper register. True, he did not move entirely in an intellectual vortex. Almost instinctively he reached into his breast pocket and exhumed a leather-covered notebook, wherein he wrote with a neat legible hand these words:

"Read *The House of the Dead* again."

As he turned to elbow his way out of the mass of sweaty flesh that enveloped him like a polyp he was made uncomfortably aware of the odor of sanctity. What that odor is like, someone has remarked, may be imagined from reading the lives of the saints. . . . He paused a moment to survey the stinking proletariat of Karl Marx. Visions assailed him . . . visions of a young immigrant on the second floor of a poem by some Ivanovich or other. The young immigrant was tossing about on the bedsprings, dreaming of bedbugs and cockroaches, haunted by the miseries of his wasting, starved life, despairing of all the violent beauty beyond his grasp. Dion Moloch had an irresistible desire to get up on his hind legs and shout: "Let's all sing goddam!"

Meanwhile his senses were jangled by a weird cacophony. Boss Tweed's progeny of thugs and werewolves choked the Bowery's grimy gullet like clots of phlegm. Dick Croker's penny arcade of lice, lungers, lifers, and hallucinations was at noon of this day in the third decade of the twentieth century a maelstrom of frenetic rhythms. Cranes swinging, bells ringing, horns blowing, gongs clanging, gears meshing and scraping. Crazy, jagged rhythms—like the marriage of the brown derby and the slide trombone. The world of the machine in a tempo of glorified planetary abandon. An orgasm of inorganic lust rising to a crescendo of atomic disintegration. A weird, unearthly chant of a Bowery that had severed its affinity with Dick Croker's dime museum of rotgut and syphilis. A veritable dirge dedicated by Labor to Capital on the ashes of Rosie O'Grady. An amalgamated union of groans supplied by the international workers of the world . . . death rattles contributed gratis by the Salvation Army. Visions of Chuck Connors with a cleaver fighting his way through delirium tremens. Shadows of comets swishing through rhomboidal space into Buxtehude. . . .

What the rabble on the sidewalk observed during this farrago which took possession of Moloch's soul was a modest, sensitive individual of medium height, with the composite features of scholar and faun, wearing a shirt of pale dungaree beneath a suit of Bedford whipcord. A mortal with two legs to his trousers, like any other mortal in the Western hemisphere. Not a pedagogic sadist, like that trapeze artist from the Emerald Isle; not a great Socratic gadfly stinging the thick hide of British philistinism; nor a Slav flirting with eternity in a bath of cockroaches. No, just a man with suit and suspenders . . . *and BVDs for perfect crotch comfort*. A man whose name is un-Byzantine. An American of three generations, a husband and father, a modest, sensitive soul with unmistakable anti-Semitic leanings . . . And yet, employment manager of the Great American Telegraph Company.

HARI DAS WRIGGLED LIKE A WET DRAKE THROUGH THE festering streets of Chinatown. It was noon hour. His greasy, blue-black hair fell in somber ringlets over the military collar of his drab uniform. He looked about him with the eyes of a Martian. The advertisements, plastered like wallpaper on a housefront here and there, reminded him of the wrappers on firecrackers which he had glimpsed in the cluttered shopwindows of Bombay. Pool parlors filled with grimacing, gesticulating figures in shirt sleeves, glimpsed through tiny rectangles of windowpane clouded with grime and grease. A sweetish, sickening odor of decay emanating from the open doors of meat and vegetable stores, loaded with strange, forbidding viands that made a sophisticated appeal to alien palates. Stiff shellacked carcasses of fowl and pigs, some intact, some mutilated and dismembered, hung in the windows like curios in an antique shop. He stared frankly and unconcerned at the stolid forms behind the windows which blinked with grave insolence at the inquisitive world without: grave, imperturbable figures, their yellow mouths glued to long-stemmed bamboo pipes from whose metal bowls thin wreaths of smoke curled up, saturating the air with reek of camel's dung.

It was Hari Das's second day as a telegraph messenger. Removing his visored cap, he examined the batch of telegrams deposited therein. Satisfied that they were properly routed, he sat down on a doorstep and began to munch a banana.

A crowd of ragamuffins quickly gathered. He finished the banana and threw the peels over the heads of the assembled urchins with the cautiousness that Mr. Rockefeller exhibits when, on his birthday, he distributes brand-new dimes.

"Git a haircut!" yelled one youngster.

"Take off that uniform!"

Hari laughed good-naturedly—a rare Burgundian laugh that mocked the famine and pestilence in India. As the self-appointed "Redeemer of Mankind" in this twentieth century he felt that mirth was his most effective weapon. He never hesitated to employ it.

The street gamins swarmed about him like flesh flies. "Get the hell out of here," he shouted, settling comfortably on his elbow as he sprawled lazily over the doorstep. Still the devils persisted in hanging about him. Their gibes were menacing.

"Go on, beat it!" he screamed in a shrill voice. "Or I'll give you a kick in the pants."

Pleased with his ready command of an alien argot, he fished in his inside pocket and commenced the perusal of a pamphlet entitled "An Open Letter to Lloyd George." The extreme elation which he made no attempt to suppress, as he read this alarming manifesto, may be pardoned when it is understood that the reader of the document was himself the author. He chuckled now and then as he reread a felicitous passage, wholly oblivious of the surrounding spectators. If it were possible for a mere mortal to conceive the glee of our anthropomorphic deity upon that day when his miraculous task of creation was ended, when he settled back upon his celestial throne, and gazing abstractly upon his work, pronounced it good, then one might appreciate the unholy joy of this Aryan messenger gloating over his philippic to Lloyd George, Supreme Satanic Majesty.

Occasionally he paused in his reading to fix with the eye of a mesmerist the ornamental figure of a maroon dragon on a balcony across the street. To Hari Das it could as well have been the sapphire tip of Mount Everest, or the proud, stoical figure of Liberty shimmering in verdigris on Bedloe's Island. What gave him pause was the sudden reflection of the ironical situation he found himself in at this moment. The proud inheritor of a great culture, a descendant and representative of the Aryan race, sitting on a doorstep in America, in Chinatown no less, dressed as a menial, regarded as "chandala" . . . an object of curiosity in an alien land.

He reviewed the fruits of his first two months in America: a new slant on sex, a strong sympathy for the Negro, contempt for Nordic supremacy, increasing fears of acquiring a venereal infection (to say nothing of pyorrhea and hemorrhoids), pride in his growing familiarity with the native idiom, with slang and profanity. He thought of his intended studies at Columbia. They seemed far away, and about as useful as a totem pole. What could he do, in America, with a degree of "Doctor of Philosophy"? Get married with it and become a streetcar conductor? Vague, unfinished thoughts of the life he had abandoned occupied him. He wondered listlessly if he would ever go back to India and settle down to the business of driving out the British fleas.

"Hey, you," he chirped pleasantly, "what time is it?"

This query was drowned in an ocean of sneers and guffaws.

Hari grinned, not knowing how else to meet this Gentile world, and stretched leisurely in full view of the public.

Cried a voice: "Say, mutt, what *are* you? Where do you come from?"

The term "mutt," connoting in its restricted sense "telegraph messenger," was unknown to him. But he accepted with fiery exclusiveness the challenge of his origin. Proudly, taut as a bronze statue of Demosthenes, he drew himself up. His black eyes glittered with the keenest amusement as he prepared to "repeat" his maiden speech to the American public. He felt like that great French sot who, in his eloquence, exclaimed: "Take elegance and wring its neck."

"Young roughnecks," he commenced, "you see before you this noon, in this glorious land of equality and fraternity, a representative of the greatest culture the world has ever known. I consider it a privilege, a *rare* privilege"—his "rare" is impossible to reproduce—"to be permitted to answer the question which the young lout before me has just propounded. I am a son of India, you joyous vagabonds . . . a son of that vast empire which stretches from the Himalayas to the coral tip of Ceylon. A nation of three hundred million souls, speaking a hundred different tongues, worshiping a thousand unknown gods. . . . The most precious jewel in the wallet of that predatory monster, the British government."

A few young Chinamen in American dress swelled the ranks of his audience. Toward these Hari flung his ropes of pearls.

"Men of the Orient, I greet you! Followers of Confucius, disciples of the Great Gautama, I have a message for you . . . a message for all mankind, black or white, red or yellow." His teeth gleamed white and strong in the bright sunlight. "Men of Cathay, behold in me the Promised Redeemer . . . the new Savior of the World! O men, nothing surprises me more than the vague, diverse, often contradictory popular conceptions of the coming of Christ. Do you expect the man from the moon to descend on earth and be your ruler? Men of the twentieth century, I think you will have sense enough to recognize this fact: scattered far and wide are the genuine credentials in the Bible, entitling me to the role I aspire to play—'the scroll and the book written within and without, speaking a foreign language, lisping and smattering, publishing peace, and so on and so on. . . .' Even a cursory review of the Bible, with a view to establishing my identity with the Promised One, will convince the skeptic of the force of my claims. . . . The very stupendousness of my task, *that is,* evolving order out of the present chaos, is its simplicity. If I appear to be paradoxical, I am none the less truthful. I do not know how far I shall be able to satisfy the cravings of the world." (Sic!) *"The world has thoroughly disappointed me.* . . . However, the modern Christ does not claim to be infallible. You smile." (A mere oratorical gesture . . . no one understood what he was talking about.) "I am human, all too human. These petty human weaknesses are, however, overshadowed and eclipsed by human greatness, human loftiness inherent in this frail body. . . . *Either I am crazy or the world is crazy."*

This mellifluous exordium was cut short by the approach of Officer Mulligan. That scion of the law grabbed Hari's emaciated arm and squeezed it viciously.

"What's all the fuss?" he inquired savagely.

"He's a nut!" yelled someone.

A swarm of Chinamen in blue and black silk vestments suddenly appeared and pressed close about Officer Mulligan. They seemed whimsically pleased over the prospect of an arrest.

Officer Mulligan brandished his club. "Back up, you slit-faced buggers!"

The sea of yellow faces remained calm and tranquil. No one budged.

"Whaddayagotta say?" A still more vicious squeeze apprised Hari Das that Officer Mulligan was not jesting.

"Wot wuz de *eye*dear? Doncha know yuh gotta have a permit ter make a speech? Wotderhell wuz yer squawkin' about, hah? Gwan and deliver your messages."

The rudeness of Officer Mulligan was exasperating. It smacked of petty British officialdom.

"I beg your pardon, Officer, if I have broken any of the statutes. You may well see, I am a stranger here."

Officer Mulligan gave indications of softening. The fiery young orator softened, too, at the thought of spending another three days in jail. He was not totally ignorant, as he pretended, of American institutions.

Sensing Officer Mulligan's leniency, Hari Das felt impelled to risk a final clause about "free speech." He was immediately rebuffed.

"*Can* that stuff," bellowed Officer Mulligan.

"I beg your pardon?"

"*Cut it,* I said. Doncha un'erstand English?"

"I ought to," Hari replied with affected politeness. "I was educated at Oxford." He allowed the full significance of this to sink into Officer Mulligan's thick-micked skull. Then he continued, after the manner of a rajah settling an ancient score with Anglo-Saxon brigands. "It's possible, Officer, that there are some Americanisms which I don't understand. That's *my* fault, I assure you. A few more weeks, I daresay, and I'll understand your dialect."

"D-I-A-L-E-C-T?" Officer Mulligan handled the word as if it were a stick of dynamite. His brain became active, in its unatrophied area, and corroborative parallels of suspicion began to assemble like the parts of a Ford car under the nimble hands of a gang of mechanics. At the police station there was a West Indian Negro janitor. He had the same suave accent, the polished diction, and the copious jargon of the culprit confronting him. Ergo, this was a West Indian nigger! Still, officer Mulligan was perplexed by the long, straight, black hair, by the aquiline features, by the delicate, sensitive skull of his victim. It dawned on him as he scratched his head that perhaps his knowledge of ethnological differences was limited. Nevertheless, he had to be convinced.

"Where do you come from?" he asked bluntly.

"I am a Hindu," Hari answered with dignity.

"You're not a nigger, then?"

"Not precisely . . . the difference is a specious one."

"Hey, don't try to high-hat me. Come down off yer perch, young fella, or I'll lay this across yer backside, see?"

Hari saw with some misgivings the emblem of the sanctity of the law. He had felt the weight of that emblem two weeks after his arrival in America. He had no desire to repeat the experience. In a few rapt words he made it clear to his inquisitor that he regarded himself beyond all question of a doubt as an insignificant, worshipful atom of society—"a little unused to the free and easy ways of America."

"That's done. We won't go into that," said Officer Mulligan. "You're in the United States now, *remember!* Don't go shootin' off yer mouth too much. . . ."

Hari started to thank him for this gratuitous piece of advice. With high impatience Officer Mulligan raised a large, hairy paw and stuck it squarely in front of Hari's face.

"You've got the gift of gab all right, you black bastard. Now get this! I wanta treat yer right. I'm gonna setcha straight . . . DON'T GO MAKIN' STUMP SPEECHES AROUND HERE ON MY BEAT, UN'ERSTAND? It won't do you no good. If yuh got anything on yer chest, look me up and spill it to me, see? Don't practice on these Chinks. They don't know wotderhell it's all about, *get me?*"

An amused expression hovered over Hari's features. . . . Should he explain his mission to Officer Mulligan, his newfound friend? Doubts assailed him. After all, would Officer Mulligan relish the advent of a black Messiah? He stole a glance at the smooth, hard club which Officer Mulligan twirled so innocently. Associations connected with the club defeated the idea of salvation-mongering. On the whole, he thought Officer Mulligan was a very decent fellow. Further than that, Officer Mulligan had a right to worship as he pleased. Withal he was certain that Officer Mulligan understood his rights.

Now that the difficulties attending the introduction had been smoothed out, he felt like continuing the conversation with this emissary of the law. But, for once, he was at a loss to know just what tack to pursue—the injustice of the British rulers, or Ireland's economic dilemma?

Officer Mulligan relieved him of further cogitations.

"Where's yer messages?" he exclaimed.

Hari dove into his hat.

"Let's see 'em!"

There were eight telegrams, two of them death messages. Hari had been instructed to visit the bereaved Armenian and Greek families first. He mentioned this fact to Officer Mulligan.

"Git along with yer," said that individual with sudden animation. "Yuh c'n chew de fat some other time. You'll be gettin' fired if yuh ain't keerful."

Hari started to elbow his way through the crowd. He was almost on the point of running.

"Hold on," shouted Officer Mulligan. Hari wondered what next.

"Say, you ain't such a dumb bastard. Chuck this job! Come around and see me tomorrow; I'll get you an elevator job. C'n yer run a switchboard?"

Hari thanked him profusely and shook the officer's hand. It was necessary for Officer Mulligan to switch his club to his left hand. Hari looked down at the symbol of the majesty of the law with deference and misgivings.

"Gwan now, git aboutcha bisnis, or I'll be minded to give yuh a polite fannin'."

The way the club was maneuvered back and forth from one hand to the other was astonishing. It made Hari Das shiver with expectancy.

"Come on now, you guys, git along, beat it, scuffle. . . . Shoo!"

Officer Mulligan shuffled along on his beat in a coma. He was thinking of what a fine, upstanding, soft-lipped, educated, black bastard of a heathen that Hindoo was, what a "foine countree" Ireland was before the blimey English got hold of it. Occupied with these thoughts, he ducked into the back door of a saloon and called for a thimbleful of rum.

THE GREAT AMERICAN TELEGRAPH COMPANY HOUSED
its messenger employment department in a low ramshackle
building in the downtown section of the city. On the top floor
was a wardrobe depot; on the floor below a tailor shop, where the
discarded uniforms of the messengers were renovated, cleaned,
and pressed. The tailor-in-chief was the Vice-President's fac-
totum. He traveled all over the United States, instructing his
subordinates in the art of economy, equipping offices with black-
ing brushes, authorizing patches, and so on. He also wrote volu-
minous reports in pidgin English, informing the Vice-President
that the office in Omaha, for instance, on a certain morning of
the year was not opened until 8:15 A.M.; that in Denver he had
found writing tables unequipped with chain and pencil; that the
receiving clerk in New Orleans had dirty fingernails and chewed

tobacco. For information of this sort he received a handsome salary.

Naturally, wherever he went he was welcomed like a leper.

The ground floor of this building was sectioned off into the employment office proper, facing the street, and a dressing room which occupied the rear of the premises. Along the side wall of this rear room tiny cubicles were partitioned off so as to permit the newly appointed messengers to dress and undress. At the rear exit was a table covered with sheet metal on which was fastened a huge roll of wrapping paper and a ball of twine. After a messenger was engaged, and had changed into the uniform, he was obliged to wrap his citizen clothes into a neat bundle and make his departure through the rear exit. If the office he was dispatched to was beyond walking distance, he was allowed carfare. This carfare allowance was theoretical. Usually Moloch reserved it for his lunch money, dolling it out only to "repeaters" who knew of its existence and were cheeky enough to demand it.

The employment office itself was exposed to the public eye. Two enormous plate-glass windows permitted the curious passerby a full sweep of the drama that was constantly being enacted within. Ofttimes it was necessary to send the porter outside to persuade the idlers and vagabonds who collected to remove their noses from the windowpanes. A life-size cardboard figure of a bright, handsome-looking youngster, attired in the full regalia of the service, was placed conspicuously in each of the show windows. This piece of bait served two purposes: it pretended to persuade the idler and the nitwit that in the service of the telegraph company there was ever open a glorious career; it also helped to break down an erroneous popular conception. All messengers, it seemed to say, are not idiots or septuagenarians.

It must be mentioned, in passing, that the rosy-cheeked youngster who had posed for this cardboard effigy (which was on display in every office of the Great American Telegraph Company throughout the United States) was no longer in possession of that bloom and hustle which was so ostentatiously exploited. Through an excess of zeal he had acquired tuberculosis of the foot, and was at this period languishing at home, vainly begging for disability compensation. To be sure, such unfortunate circumstances were not uncommon, nor were they particularly remarkable considering the thousands of individuals who were put through the hopper.

To lighten the burdens of the legal department a "Safety First" campaign had been inaugurated. Large posters were tacked on the bulletin boards in the offices, and on the partitions of the dressing booths, giving the latest country-wide statistics relating to messengers killed, crippled, or incapacitated. To lend a touch of realism, snapshots showing the most prevalent ways in which accidents occurred were often sandwiched in among the statistics. The question of whether or not this gruesome liability roll should be displayed in the dressing booths had been debated for a long while between the Vice-President and the General Manager. The Vice-President had a theory that these announcements acted as a boomerang. Perhaps the Vice-President had been given this impression through reading Moloch's monthly report of "resignations and dismissals." The report showed that no less than ten percent of the force resigned after working less than a day. To the Vice-President this was an inexplicable situation. Perhaps the latter had really convinced himself that the telegraph company offered a career to the messengers in its employ.

Moloch returned to his desk after the razzle-dazzle of the Bowery in a fever of excitement. He had left the office toward noon to make an investigation. One of the messenger force had gone bughouse.

It was now going on to three o'clock. The day was warm and sultry and he was perspiring freely. His discomfiture was made more acute by the pungent, acrid odor of camphor and Lysol escaping from the dressing room and the wardrobe depot. Moreover, he was annoyed to find so many applicants lined up on the benches, waiting for him with that stolid patience which one so often observes in the anteroom of a charity bureau. He looked at the clock impatiently.

Opposite him at the big, double desk sat his friend and assistant, Matt Reardon. Reardon was incompetent, recalcitrant, and temperamental. Moloch had given him the job out of friendship. It was apparent that Reardon was excited about something.

"We just had a helluva time here a few minutes ago," he said breathlessly.

Matt had an endless string of anecdotes, none of them particularly beguiling.

"Hold it, Matt . . . later. I've a lot of work to plow through first."

Matt glowered rebelliously and turned sour. Moloch was forever squelching him, as if he were the office boy and not the assistant employment manager.

"And look here," Moloch fired, without the least regard for his friend's injured feelings, "tell Lawson to get rid of that gang out there. This place looks like a waxworks exhibit!"

"*You're* making this place an Eden Musée, not I," thought Matt, as he rose, sullen and dispirited, to carry out instructions. He was bitterly opposed to Moloch's high-handed way of doing things. He had a dozen arguments up his sleeve, but none of them were worth a damn. He was tired of arguing; they did nothing else but wrangle the whole day long. And in the end, Moloch always had his way. Moloch could be one god-damned son-of-a-bitch, when he wanted to. . . .

Matt Reardon approached the railing which separated the applicants from the office staff, and began telling off the youngsters one at a time. He puffed away at a cigarette as he disposed of one batch after another. "Make it snappy!" he growled, chafing over the tedious drift of each appeal. About a minute and a half was allotted to each plea, followed by a brusque "Tomorrow morning at eight sharp!"

"Say, Matt, what the hell's the matter with you, anyway? Didn't I tell you to let Lawson take care of that? What's he here for?" shouted Moloch, suddenly observing Matt's tactics.

Matt grumbled and got off something about Lawson taking all day to do a trifle. "Besides," he went on, "I think we ought to show these kids a little courtesy. They're not asking for a handout. They want jobs."

"Who's running this joint?"

"Aw, hell, don't be a crab," said Matt coaxingly. "Do you know you're getting to be an old crab? I say," he cooed, "you missed something funny. You got here ten minutes too late."

Moloch's irritation was increasing. "Well, get it off your chest . . . what was it?"

"Ah, *can that!*" said Matt. "Listen a minute, like a regular guy, will you? I had a guy in here after you left—see? I spotted him right away. At first I didn't say much to him . . . let him fill the application out in the usual way. Every now and then I'd throw out a harmless question. He was leery of me all right, I could see that, but after a while when he saw how damn nice I treated him he didn't know what the hell to think. Anyhow we chewed the fat a while, about this and that—Christ, I dragged in everything I could think of except what was on my mind. . . . All of a sudden I says to him, 'Let me look at your throat.' He jumped when I said that, but I passed right over it and mumbled something about having his tonsils removed. What I was after, of course, was to get a good look at his tongue."

Moloch smiled a caustic smile. Matt always thought he knew so god-damned much. He was like a young intern.

"Sure enough," Matt continued, "his tongue was all scarred."

"Ah . . . the hell with it," blurted Moloch. "I don't give a damn about the rest of it."

"No, wait a minute—let me finish. . . . What was I saying? Oh, yes! Listen, are you following me? As I was telling you, I was kiddin' him along nicely, pattin' him on the back and tellin' him what a good egg he was. . . . Jesus! it was a shame to do it! Well, anyhow, I'm talkin' to him in a calm, even voice—just like I'm talkin' to you now—and suddenly I pop this at him: *'When did you have your last fit?'* Boy, you should have been here! He flies up in the air and grabs the application out of my hand . . . tears it to bits. I keep one eye on him while he makes for the door. I'm not sayin' a word, mind you. . . . Instead of goin' out I see him comin' back towards me wavin' his hands and shoutin' at the top of his voice—'It's a lie . . . it's a lie.' With that his lips began to twitch and he went into a spasm . . . one spasm after another. Then his fingers grew rigid and he seemed to claw the air like.

And with that, b'Jesus, he doubles up and keels over. God, it was weird! For half an hour he was stretched out on the floor, foamin' at the mouth. . . . You know, Dion, I must have just touched the button. It was perfect!"

"He isn't lying around in the back somewhere, is he?" said Moloch.

"Hell no! I got rid of him all right. But we had one bitch of a time bringing him to. There were about twenty kids in here, and Christ knows, they were falling all over one another. Mrs. McFadden fainted. She's no damned good, do you know it, Dion? We ought to get rid of her. . . . I thought we'd have the cops in on us. Jesus, the whole place went kerflooey. All because I asked him a simple question! Listen—all I said was: 'When did you have your last fit?' Just like that. That's all."

Moloch looked at his assistant with unmitigated sarcasm.

"Of course you never expected anything like that to happen, did you? *No!* You know what I think of you, Matt? I think you're one crazy bastard yourself. You had one hell of a good time, I can see that."

Matt feigned remorse. Inwardly he felt very pleased with himself. He felt that he had missed his calling.

"Well," said Moloch after a pause, "I suppose I ought to be thankful you didn't put him to work." He assumed a sly, malicious grin. "As Twilliger says, we can't afford to have epileptics falling on the subway tracks and getting all cut up. By the way," he added, "do you know the difference between the sham and the true epileptic?"

Matt Reardon shook his head.

"Well, it's this way, Matt: one always manages to fall in a safe spot; the other isn't so careful."

"Anyway, they both block traffic," Matt responded.

Moloch laughed. So did Matt. It was a hell of a good joke. Moloch knew it wasn't true. Matt didn't.

"Oh, I forgot to tell you—I've got a letter here for you," said Matt suddenly. "From the Egyptian . . . *that nut, Sarwat.*"

"Sarwat? Sarwat?"

"Sure, you remember the bird. Here, read it. I wanted to laugh my head off."

He made no apologies for opening Moloch's private mail. Moloch took the letter and read:

Washington, D. C.

Esteemed and Most Honourable Sir:

I must write and let you know what sorrow's hand has done in my heart, and it grieves me very much to overburden you with my internal pains, but I feel extremely gratified to know that you are a rare and gracious soul.

Here I am; a wrecked ship dashed and broken into pieces, by the huge rocks in the wide, dark, and rolling ocean of America. My dear sir—I have often heard people speak highly of this country, that its imaginary beauty had infatuated me, and drew me hither from the calm East, very vehemently.

Very shortly after I had landed here, I found what I have taken for granted is but a mere poetic sentiment; and the magnificent and gigantic mansions of hopes were but dreams and foundationless. I am very much disappointed, Mr. Moloch. There is a quotation of a Persian poet that runs: "And there must be a humanitarian soul in which you have to deposit your pains and sufferings, and in which you will find a balsam to relieve your ulcerated heart." And this is the reason why, Mr. Moloch, I am daring to write this to you today explaining in the first place my warm love and great wishes to see you, and then explaining my sentiments and impressions.

You know I left New York City, as I was unsuccessful to earn the means of my livelihood there. I found myself lost among the crowds of the Materialistic rush in the very busy streets of the Western Metropolice. Then I have carried my knapsack of travel in the psychological attitude of Jean Val Jean the hero personage of "Les Miserables" by the French "Hugo" and stepped forward hither with the absolute hope to earn easily the means of my living, but to my ill luck and

misfortune I found all of Washington is like what I have
previously had an introduction.

What a pity! A man like me, unable to eat his bread in the
alleged garden spot of the world. That is a great disaster.
Whenever I think of the existing circumstances in this great
country, the lines of "Longfellow" run into my memory:

> (Something, something done,
> has earned a night's repose.)

And I also think of America according to Shakespeare's words
in Hamlet:
"Something is rotten in the State of Denmark."
What can I say more, my dear Mr. Moloch? The flourishing
rose of my hopes had already faded. Conditions are awfully bad
here. Capitalism is enslaving Labour in the midst daylight of the
twentieth century, and Democracy is but a word of no meaning.

He who has money is terribly tormenting he who has not,
simply because he has to feed him, and he who has money is
degraded from his spiritual sentiments. That is the main point of
weakness. That the mistake of society.

I see from afar the magic lantern, held by a mightful hand
from Russia, fixing its lenses on this country to illuminate the
way under the feet of the poor labourers.

> Sooner or later all things pass away, and are no more:
> The beggar and the king with equal steps tread forward to
> their end.

My dear Mr. Moloch, I hope you will excuse my frankness.
It is the sorrow, hidden in the deepest of my heart which had
motivated me to write these few lines to you today, and I
greatly appreciate your "humanity" and "nobility" and
"tenderness."

> Sorrow concealed like an oven stopped,
> Doth burn the heart to cinders.

Kindly write me whenever you have a chance to do so. Advise
me what to do. Shall I be patient, and my patience come to its

limits? Will conditions be continuously bad in the United States as they are now? Is there any hope of the sun shining to kill the dark clouds and enlighten the obscurity? I hardly believe so.

Here is what I am thinking of: I find it a black spot in the white page of my life to come to America, and return back to Egypt with failure, and I would rather die than so do.

My soul is very ambitious, and it is imprisoned within the cage of clay, the body! Shall I release it to enjoy liberty and boundless freedom?

I like to return back to New York, and shall not do so unless I know what my determination there will be. I do not want to be out of work. I want to be employed by you as a sergeant to look after the clothes no matter what long my hours of work will be, as long as I shall be under your direction, and will be leading a sedentary life.

I am sure your heart will sympathize my state and you will resume your endeavorings to put me in some position, and see me settled. I want to be employed by you as a messenger and do any other inside work. Do help me, please.

I shall come back to New York when you will be able to put me in such a work and send me a word to report myself to your kindness.

You may also communicate with your friends if they may let you know definitely that they will employ me in a decent vacancy. Don't care much about the people as I have no faith in them. I have only a very unshaking faith in you. You are the only man I adore and worship. You will be able, yourself, to solve my problem. I am sorry to trouble you with this long letter, but you remember when "Diogenes" the Greek philosopher of the old and goneby days, was wandering through the streets of Athens, bare footed, and with a lantern in his hand, to find the man.

I have wandered, and for a very considerable time, to find the man in America, and I have in you, the true man.

Don't hesitate to help me as much as you can. I want you to employ me as a sergeant, or elsewhere in a decent work. Rate of living is very high, and I am unable to afford being out of work

for such a long time. I cannot exist. Read this letter again.
*Read it over in your spare time and write an answer please. I
don't want to remain here. I like to come back to New York to
see you frequently. Help me to be settled there.
Is Shukrullah still working as a messenger? It is a shame. I
have taken a very long time from yours. I must close. With very
good wishes and kindest regards I beg to lay under your feet my
most respectful homage.*

Your obedient servant always,

Sarwat.

Whilst Moloch read the last few paragraphs to himself, a
rotund figure, streaming with perspiration, strutted in like a
Rhode Island bantam and waddled over to another squat little
figure seated at the switchboard.

"Hello, Dave!" he clucked. "Any excitement around here
today? How is that boss of yours, Mister Moloch? Is he broke?
I may want to borrow a few bucks from him."

Dave, the squat little figure with the paunch of a Brahman,
gave an appreciate smirk and nodded furtively in Moloch's direction. "He's got another funny letter. . . ."

"Come here," yelled Matt Reardon, suddenly spying Prigozi.
"The big cheese has a letter from one of his admirers. . . . Read
him that first paragraph, Dion . . . you know, that bit about 'the
internal pains—what sorrow's hand has done in my heart,' and
so forth."

"You here again?" Moloch exclaimed, glancing up at Prigozi.
"Why don't you find some other place to hang around in for a
change?"

"I like this joint. There's atmosphere here."

"Camphor balls, you mean," Reardon observed.

"Psychopaths! That's what I mean," yelled Prigozi, getting
into form. "You're a pack of nuts . . . the whole lot of you! Think
the messengers are goofy, don't you? Get a lot of fun analyzing
'em, eh? Let me tell you birds something . . . these messengers of
yours are the only normal ones in this lousy joint. I'll modify

that—excluding Mister Moloch's pet freaks, say. Cripes, Matt, you make some awful blunders, but that boss of yours sitting there so complacently"—he looked scathingly at Moloch to see if he were taking this in—"he's the worst amateur psychologist I ever met. Spends a half hour talking to an applicant, and thinks he can read him like a book. I'll bet he's hired more nuts than . . . well, little Dave over there couldn't do worse, if you gave him a chance. You people give me a pain." (He meant Moloch particularly.) "Think you're conducting a laboratory. Cripes! You're turning this joint into a wet nursery!"

Moloch looked up from his papers—he had been waiting for Prigozi to finish—and remarked quietly:

"I see. Yesterday it was a clinic. Today it's a wet nursery."

"Yeah, and tomorrow it'll be a lunatic asylum," roared Prigozi.

Prigozi rambled on, heedless of the impression he made. He fluttered about like a pigeon as he talked. He was very short, hairy, unkempt, and carried himself with the furtive pseudo-important air of a physician who has made a clean-up handling abortions. A third-year medical student, he was plugging along with a bootleg practice on the side, expecting someday to become a full-fledged psychiatrist. For the present, he was wrapped up in the theories of Freud, Jung, Adler, and their ilk. The year previous he had been an enthusiast on vivisection—cut up something like twenty-three guinea pigs, which he secreted in his flat together with a skeleton, a wife, and a few sticks of furniture.

No one could quite fathom why Moloch tolerated him. Indeed, it was something more than mere toleration that Moloch evinced in his relations with Prigozi. One might be tempted to call it a fascination. What it was that fascinated, Moloch himself could not explain. With the possible exception of Dave, who forced himself to admire Prigozi because they were both members of the chosen race, everyone considered him obnoxious and repulsive. It was Matt Reardon's idea that Prigozi dropped in to show off before the female members of the staff. He attached no importance to Moloch's air of geniality. In his mind, Moloch was angling for something; when he got it, whatever it was he was

after, you'd see—he'd drop Prigozi like hot shot. He didn't admire this quality in Moloch very much, even though Prigozi was
a rat. He had a different conception of friendship himself. Moloch was too damned—well, "callous"—that was the word.

In the office Prigozi never dropped his coarse bantering attitude. It was all a part of his warm attachment to the "boss," as
he persisted in calling his friend Moloch. . . . There was no
denying the fellow's unattractiveness. To say that he was ugly is
to flatter him. His skin was coarse and pockmarked, and as
greasy as if it had been rubbed with lard. His nose, which Matt
Reardon had once likened to a rubber syringe, was a huge
priapic organ covered with blackheads. When he grew voluble
and excited, thick globules of grease seeping from the enlarged
pores clustered about the tip. He was forever scratching his scalp,
which was infected and caused his scant hairs to fall out, leaving
big red rings such as children sometimes exhibit when they get
the worms. His clothes were never pressed, and seldom clean; on
his coat collar there was always a thick layer of dandruff which
lay like a mantle of snowflakes about his sober wattles.

In the midst of his clowning Prigozi suddenly stopped chattering and looked fixedly at a queer creature seated on a bench in
a corner of the anteroom. No one seemed to know how long the
man had been sitting there. Looking at him intently, one had the
feeling that he might go on sitting there indefinitely . . . that you
could hang him up by the coat collar and leave him to cure, like
a ham.

"Call that bozo over," Prigozi ordered in a thick, suety voice.
"Now we've got something to make a fuss about."

"Whoa, there!" Moloch almost shoved the flat of his hand in
Prigozi's face. "Pretty late, isn't it, for a sideshow performance?"
He turned to Lawson, who sat like a Cerberus guarding the
sacred portals. "What's this chap waiting for, Lawson? I thought
Matt got rid of all the applicants?"

"He insists on seeing you personally, Mr. Moloch."

"Well, then, *that's different.*" Moloch brought this out with a
mocking bite, as if it were the Sultan of Morocco who had
requested the privilege of an audience.

Though it was oppressively warm outdoors, the mysterious figure on the bench was dressed like Tweedledum preparing for battle with Tweedledee. Over a pair of dirty flannel trousers he had on a cardigan jacket; also a heavy sweater with a long neck that went up about his ears, and on top of this a ragged ulster which was fastened together with huge safety pins. His pockets were stuffed with old newspapers which he had doubtless collected in the day's journey as he wandered aimlessly about the city streets. In the buttonhole of his ulster was a tiny American flag.

Matt Reardon nudged Prigozi and pointed to the flag. Prigozi sniggered and settled down to observe this set-to with all his critical acumen. The lenses of his spectacles were bottle-thick and gave his eyes the appearance of two ugly fish snouts pressing against a pair of Mazda bulbs.

"Good morning, friend. Can you give me a job?"

This was the first sign they had that the mysterious one was alive, and human. He had walked listlessly up to Moloch, when that individual beckoned to him, and commenced to talk in a subdued, distracted manner, as though he had been unexpectedly pushed onto the stage during an amateur night contest and was a little uncertain whether the monologue he had prepared was just the thing or not. It was a chaotic, maundering flow of inanity that started off at random and kept going like an eight-day clock. Despite the fact that it was afternoon, almost evening, he was under the impression that it was still morning.

"Just a moment," said Moloch solicitously, rising and extending his hand in greeting. "Do you mind telling these gentlemen your name?"

"Luther, sir. Luther Becklein. I'm a Presbyterian. My wife, she was Catholic; we both belong to the Second Presbyterian Church of Hoboken. . . ."

"But I thought you came from Paterson," Prigozi wheezed, pretending that he had misunderstood.

"No, friend. . . ." Luther was as placid as a lake. "I *used* to live in Paterson years ago. We had three nice rooms there on Second Avenue, three *lovely* rooms. Tillie was just five years old then— and smart as a Jew. . . ."

Moloch tittered. "As a Jew, you say?"

"That's right, friend. I have no religious prejudices. I took her out of the kindergarten later and put her in a parochial school. That was when I lost my job with the window-shade people and we had to move to Hoboken. The missus had to take a janitress job, but I used to help her with the dishes and little things. . . ."

"Like rushing the growler, I suppose," Matt remarked in a sedate manner, meaning to imply that such a custom was eminently respectable—quite the proper thing, in fact.

But Prigozi refused to permit the conversation to drift into such channels. He was for dredging at once, to see what lay buried in the rich silt at the bottom. He moved closer to the man and laid a sweaty affectionate paw on his shoulder.

"You said a minute ago, Luther, that you used to belong to the Christian Endeavor Society once. Is that right?"

He spoke in an ominous, threatening tone, as though to convey the impression that such an admission constituted a breach of the law.

But Luther was impervious—to cajolery and threats alike.

Meanwhile, unnoticed by the others, Matt Reardon had invited Moloch's secretary to join the group and report the conversation verbatim.

"Never mind the Christian Endeavor Society," said Moloch, suddenly taking a hand in the pleasantries, and radiating a warm, protective assurance which increased Prigozi's aggravation.

"Is *he* your office boy?" asked Luther, indicating Prigozi.

"No," said Moloch dryly, "he's an undertaker—a friend of mine. He just dropped in to pay me a visit."

While this had been going on, Luther was busy fumbling in his pockets, evidently in search of some object of vital importance. As he emptied one pocket after the other a collection of miscellaneous trifles spilled on to the floor. Among them were two stale ham sandwiches, a pair of pliers, a vest-pocket dictionary, some tacks, three yacht-club buttons which had been polished assiduously, a harmonica, hairpins, marbles . . . God knows what unthinkable gimcracks he might have exhumed if he hadn't fortunately come across the object of his search.

Tenderly he placed a worn-looking gilt-edged book in Moloch's hands. The New Testament!

"They gave it to me at the hospital," Luther began, in his unruffled, habitually detached manner. "I always keep it with me so as I can read a few lines before going to bed . . . *to keep me good.* I don't really need it, friend, because I never did a wrong in my life, but I believe in bein' a good Christian. . . . There ain't nobody can take my religion away from me, ain't that right, friend?"

Moloch nodded.

"You see, friend, everything was all right after I got out of the hospital, only Tillie got wronged up account of her mother's bad example. The judge himself said it was bad for the missus to be sittin' on the coal scuttle all day when she oughter been scrubbing floors. . . ."

"You mean she drank?"

"Exactly, friend." The same placid demeanor—impossible to ruffle him. One might have said "murdered" instead of "drank."

"My wife wasn't exactly a good woman," Luther continued. "About two-thirds good and one-third bad, I guess. Her mother had Indian blood. Nobody could live with her, friend . . . *nobody.*"

"What was her father?" demanded Prigozi, inquisitive and menacing again. He seemed dissatisfied with Luther's obliquity. He was itching, as he expressed it later, to get a "reaction."

"I don't know *what* her father was," Luther offered blandly. "I heard her say once that he was an engineer on the Santa Fe line. But you couldn't believe her much. She told so many lies. . . ."

"I don't care whether he was an engineer or an evangelist," cried Prigozi, in an exasperated voice. "*What nationality*—that's what I mean."

"He was a Pawnee Indian, too . . . *some* of him. I guess that makes her two-thirds Indian, don't it?"

"No, about seven-eighths," croaked Matt.

Luther preserved a solemn exterior as the others exchanged

witticisms about the proportion of Pawnee chromosomes in the Becklein family. The secretary begged them not to talk so rapidly . . . she couldn't catch all that Luther had to say.

Luther was chatting on again about the various jobs which he held before "they" took him to the hospital. He used the word "they" frequently now. It had the validity which Euripides imparted to the "Fates" in his dramaturgic machinery.

"I tried to get a job," he was saying, "but *they* wouldn't let me. Every time I went to look for work, something happened. This last time *they* put me in the hospital for six months with a broken leg. I had hay fever, too. But, look here, friend, I need a job. I'm no drinkin' man. I want to work, honest I do. Why, say—I did a day's washin' for a lady down the street." (He forgot that he was not in Paterson anymore.) "That's enough, ain't it, friend? And I ran errands once. You see, I can't hang shades anymore—my back ain't what it used to be. . . ."

"How are your legs?" asked Moloch.

"The left one is all right, but this here one"—he patted his right leg affectionately—"is kinda stiff . . . from layin' in bed so long, you understand?"

"That's all very well, Luther, but do *you* understand what you would have to do, if I were to give you a job?"

"Yes, sir. Couldn't you put me in an office where they don't have so many telegrams to deliver?"

Matt Reardon broke in: "You wouldn't like a carriage to take you around in, would you, Luther?"

"Honest, friend, I want to work, only . . ."

"Here," said Moloch, slipping a half-dollar into the man's hand. "Take that and get a haircut tonight. See me tomorrow morning. Take a bath, too, if you have time, and leave your overcoat home." He was about to turn away. "And say, friend," he added as an afterthought, "tell me—have you got a home?" It was the first indication he gave that he was talking to a human being.

Luther answered ruefully: "I had one once, but the judge he . . ."

Moloch interrupted him. "Mr. Lawson," he called, "will you

give this man a couple of dollars for me? I'll return it to you Saturday." He whispered the last. Luther seemed to lose interest in the job and walked over to get the money. When he had gone Moloch slipped over to Lawson. "Don't let him in again, savvy?" "Sure," said Lawson. His head moved eloquently. He had a way of being at once profound and lugubrious. "I knew the minute I laid eyes on him that you'd want to say a few words to him. I don't let them *all* in, you know. Only the choice ones." Moloch grinned. "That's the idea, Lawson—*only the choice ones.*"

Returning to his desk, he found Prigozi capering about like Silenus and bleating a babble of strange words—synapses, parathyroids, involutional melancholia, euphorias . . . whatnot. The man behaved like an automaton that had been wound up and would go on muttering outlandish jargon until the spring ran down. He was bending hysterically over Matt, his cheeks hot and flushed, tears welling up, his lips slavering.

"What I say"—he slammed the desk with his clammy fist—"what I say," he repeated vociferously, "is this: you ought to hang that poor bugger up to dry . . . hang him up in the toilet, he won't know the difference. Or say, I tell you what—send him up to Dr. Nussbaum in the morning. I'll tip the old codger off. Cripes, we haven't had a decent case for the last two weeks. Nothing but paranoids . . . and cretins."

Restive because Moloch was paying no attention to him, he threw the remains of a voice to the ceiling.

"Gonna doll that guy up in a uniform tomorrow, eh? You ought to make a wardrobe attendant out of him."

Moloch appeared to be absorbed in his papers.

"I say, *Mister* Moloch! Feelin' pretty good now . . . satisfied with the world, heh? Jesus, but you like to play the good Samaritan!"

Prigozi was now fairly launched on his pet theme: playing the good Samaritan. It was his favorite instrument of torture, for Moloch could stand most any other gaff but being dubbed a little Jesus. He was inclined to look upon his charitable impulses as a weakness. Prigozi understood this thoroughly. What he wanted was to see Moloch reduced to a soft, pulpy, Christian mass of flesh and principles. In the ordinary Gentile he saw no hope of resuscitating the Christ spirit. Moloch he recognized as a Christian "sport," a case of religious atavism, one might say. This callous shell in which Moloch encased his tender spirit could not deceive Prigozi. Oh, no. He knew a real Christian when he met one. And the flesh of a real Christian was ever so much more succulent than a priest's or a pope's.

Moloch listened to Prigozi's tirades for a while with mild amusement. That irritated Prigozi, took the wind out of his sails, as it were. Finally Moloch turned to Matt:

"Look here, Matt, do me a favor, will you? Chase this dirty Grand Street savant out of here. Send him home to his wife and guinea pigs."

"There you go!" Prigozi exclaimed, rubbing his hands like Lady Macbeth. "Now that's what I call a normal reaction. You're not psychotic—*yet,* Mister Moloch." He chuckled as though he had made a quick sale.

"No," said the other, "I suppose my behavior is indicative of nothing more than a mild neuroticism. Take yourself now . . . you're a healthy specimen of the 'normal.' How about it, Matt?"

"Slightly tainted," responded Matt.

"Gwan, gwan!" ranted Prigozi, waving his hands excitedly as if he were shooing away a swarm of horseflies. "Someday I'm gonna submit *my* plan to Twilliger, and then you guys better watch out or you'll be losing your jobs."

This eternal question of normality versus abnormality was intimately linked with the messenger problem. Prigozi had certain unique theories about the status of the messenger boy with which Moloch entirely disagreed. In order to give Prigozi material with which to formulate his theories, Moloch had permitted him to don the uniform for a few months as a part-time messenger. Prigozi found the experience thrilling. His solution to the problem could be boiled down to one word: *Revolution.*

Matt Reardon found Prigozi's ideas stimulating and entertaining. He hadn't an ounce of faith in them, but he made it a

principle to encourage Prigozi in order to take some of the conceit out of Moloch. At the same time he utilized this ceaseless
strife to enlarge his afternoon's recreation. He commenced usually by twitting Prigozi about his various schemes.
"That plan of yours," he said, "what plan is that? You don't
mean the idea of substituting pigeons for messengers, do you?"
"Get out of here!" Prigozi snarled. "Where do you get that
stuff? I know the guy who invented that pigeon stunt . . . that
crazy manager of yours up in the third district, that guy with the
big belly, looks like a eunuch. What's his name again, Dion?" He
snapped his fingers to jog his memory.
"You mean Boylan?"
"Yeah, that's the bloke. He was going to buy up those religious paintings your friend Dun brought over from Europe."
     As Prigozi's ebullience rose his ideas became more dissociated,
and what slight command he held over the English language
threatened to relax and disintegrate entirely. However, he lost
none of his picturesque qualities. In fact, Moloch and the others
derived the utmost enjoyment from these explosions. As a daily
ritual, however, it was apt to become monotonous. In an hour or
so Prigozi would quiet down, become earnest in a rather dignified way (if one could ever believe this possible of him—dignity!),
and converse reasonably and charmingly about the vegetation in
the Arctic regions, or the scientific means of determining the
weight of the earth. But first, it seemed, he had to work off his
grosser indulgences, those mad, lyric extravagances which he
brought with him from somewhere—from the ghetto, possibly.
About his past Prigozi was awkwardly reticent, and out of a
feeling of sympathy and delicacy Moloch, despite the intimacy
that existed between them, never alluded to the subject. Several
times Prigozi had been on the verge of unbosoming, but Moloch's attitude of complete indifference nettled him and forced
him to shrink back.
     Prigozi soon forgot about Boylan and his pigeons in the pur-
suit of his own chimeras. "If you fellows are serious," he went on,
"I'm going to tell you about this plan of mine . . . and I mean it
when I say that I'm going to present it to Twilliger someday." He

cleared his throat and looked about for a cuspidor. "That jackass on the thirteenth floor—" referring to Vice-President Twilliger— "he wants to raise the standard of the messenger force, *don't he?*" Moloch nodded.

"Well, then, he's got to recognize this fact," and Prigozi embarked on a flood of ideas which, when the excitement abated, would land him in a telegraphic Utopia.

Moloch never refused an opportunity to listen to these panaceas. No matter how crack-brained the idea, there were always crumbs of information which he found valuable and practicable. It was an admitted fact that the one problem which all the telegraph companies had never adequately met was the business of providing a reliable, intelligent, and steady corps of messengers. Much energy and invention, not to speak of enormous sums, had been spent for the perfection of mechanical and electrical devices, but the messenger problem remained unsolved, almost untouched. It was more acute now than it had ever been in the past.

In the three years that he had been at his desk, Moloch had been given the opportunity to become acquainted with most of the disturbing factors involved; and, if he had not solved the problem for the company, he had at least effected a radical improvement. The chief obstacle in his path, for he had plans up his sleeve to improve the situation further, was that jackass, as Prigozi called him, on the thirteenth floor. Twilliger, who had been a messenger in his youth, believed that the only solutions of any value were those of his own making, or those which his so-called efficiency experts presented to him for approval. He saw no violation of logic in spending a fortune to reduce the transmission time to San Francisco only to have the message lie at the receiving office for a few hours because of a shortage of messengers. If, for instance, you received a message from California, a sticker informed you pompously that it took less than forty-five minutes to speed this greeting across the continent. Yet that same message might be brought you by a half-wit who had stopped on his way for three-quarters of an hour to watch a ball game—we will say nothing of those messages thrown down the sewer daily by aggrieved youngsters who had discovered that it was impossible to earn the twenty or twenty-five dollars a week on a piecework basis which the newspaper advertisements promised.

When Moloch took over the reins he found that it was customary to hire ten thousand messengers a year in order to preserve a working force of a thousand. Two months ago he had succeeded in reducing this extravagant turnover to almost fifty percent. And there were indications that it might be further reduced. Then along came Twilliger with a mandate to slash wages. "There is such a thing as a healthy turnover!" That was Twilliger's dictum. The very next month they were obliged to hire over two thousand raw recruits. Even this staggering influx was insufficient to keep the gaps plugged. It was like a dam bursting. There was scarcely a veteran left. That was the very devil of it! Twilliger's tactics were such that there wasn't even a substantial nucleus on which to build up a mobile, skeleton force. The very bottom had dropped out. Ads appeared like mushrooms—not only in the metropolitan papers, but in suburban papers, weeklies, church papers, foreign papers, school papers, college magazines. Twilliger would have advertised in Purgatory had he not been a Unitarian.

In conjunction with this frantic newspaper activity, roundup squads were inducted to canvass the schoolyards, playgrounds, lots, pool parlors, movie houses—any place and every place that a boy was likely to be encountered, buttonholed, and appealed to.

But none of these expedients relieved the deplorable mess. The hard labor of three years, the effective welfare and educational work that Moloch had introduced, the confidence in the integrity of the organization which he had gradually instilled—all this evaporated overnight. The Great American Telegraph Company became a good joke. You couldn't pay the ordinary boy to work for it.

Naturally he was interested in any program of amelioration. But he was skeptical, too. "Can anyone supply that jackass up there in his swivel chair with a new set of brains?" That was the thought which shot through his head as he listened to Prigozi. *That* seemed the only solution of any moment now. As for Prigozi, tethered as he was to a skein of psychoanalytical theories, what was he to expect from him? Some Freudian-Marx solution, no doubt, which required a categorical affirmative, a stout libido, and a box of Seidlitz powders.

The "revolution" which Prigozi broached with sound and fury turned out upon analysis to be about as radical as the constitution which the Czar Alexander threw to his groveling moujiks. His plan consisted of a string of half-baked ideas which, assuming their feasibility, required at least fifteen years to work out. His campaign of reform had for its object the education of the general public. His goal was the visionary hope of wiping out the stigma attached to the uniform. Even Matt had to smile as he took in Prigozi's involved explanation for the origin of "these civilized taboos."

"We've heard that junk before," Matt started to say.

"Leave him be," urged Moloch. "We'll give Osawatomie ten more minutes to conclude." Even Dave chuckled at this.

Prigozi appeared crestfallen. "There's no sense in going on if that's the way you feel. I'll draw it up on paper and submit it to you. . . ."

"Don't submit it to me," said Moloch caustically. "Take it up to Twilliger. Maybe he'll make room for you on his staff."

"Rub a little insect powder on it first," jeered Matt. "By the way," he added maliciously, "what's that white stuff on your coat collar?"

Without giving Prigozi a chance to explode, Moloch declared: "I'm serious about that suggestion. I think your plan's cock-eyed, but that doesn't make any difference. Go ahead and show it to Twilliger! Tell him I sent you. . . ."

"Raspberries! You want him to give me a kick in the slats."

Moloch suavely assured the latter that this was a highly fantastic idea. Twilliger had never been known to kick anybody downstairs. "On the contrary," he said, "Twilliger may even consider the plan brilliant. You go ahead and present it. Anyway, I believe in letting every man be his own Jesus."

"G'wan, you bastards! G'wan!" Prigozi was recovering his verve.

At this moment the telephone rang. Matt answered it gruffly, but changed his tone immediately. With his hand on the mouthpiece, he handed the instrument to Moloch, whispering as he did so: "It's the old man—*Houghton himself*. There's a strike brewing."

Moloch listened respectfully but with a growing irritation. He punctuated his silences with a subdued, resentful "Yes, sir. Yes sir!" Toward the end, realizing that his protests were ineffectual, he grew red and stammered a bit. He was trying desperately to control his anger. "Very well," he said finally, "if you insist. But I think it's a great mistake." He slammed the receiver down with a growl.

"What's the trouble?" asked Prigozi immediately.

Moloch looked perplexed, harassed.

"A fine muddle we're in now," he said gloomily. At which Prigozi became positively morose.

"What's up?" piped Matt. Everytime Houghton rang up he thought it meant his job. Moloch was too damned stiff-necked to get along with a gang of polite crooks. He didn't know how to play the game, that was Matt's idea. They'd both be out in the street before long.

"We've got to fire the niggers—that's what!" said Moloch.

"Niggers?" Matt repeated.

"Oh, the Hindus . . . the Egyptians, the whole flock of Oriental students we put on lately."

Matt gave a long low whistle and screwed his face up like a gargoyle.

"I'd like to take Twilliger and hack his guts out!"

"Easy, Mister Moloch, easy now!" cried Prigozi, no longer alarmed over the situation, now that it proved to be nothing more than the dismissal of a few Hindus . . . "black buggers," as he called them.

"What started the rumpus?" said Matt.

"It was that long-haired gazook in Chinatown. Seems he muffed a couple of death messages. Twilliger must have raised hell with the old man. He was screeching mad. 'I want every one of them out,' he says. 'Every damned shine you've got on the force.' There was no telling him anything. Twilliger's got the Indian sign on him. God, though, if I were in Houghton's place I'd show a little fight. It's indecent to back down that way. . . . The worst of it is, the old man's in such a fury he won't let me do a thing for the poor dubs. I haven't got the heart to let them out like a lot of cattle."

"I wouldn't weep about it, if I were you," Prigozi spoke up. "They won't starve to death. Let Providence take care of 'em. These black bastards are a lot of crybabies—*that's what I think!*"

There was more than a grain of truth in Prigozi's indictment. The only ones who showed any guts were the Chinese students. The others were merely children for whom Moloch acted as a wet nurse.

Matt broke in suddenly. "Didn't old man Houghton say something about a strike?"

"Christ, yes! I almost forgot about the strike. Grab your hat, Matt, and rush uptown to Carducci's office—that's where the trouble lies."

Matt bolted to the door in a jiffy.

"Hold on a minute," shouted Moloch. "The old man says . . ."

"Says what?" yelled Matt.

"You're not to talk too much—get that?"

"Tell the old man to go crucify himself!" Matt dashed out.

"There's a loyal servant," sneered Prigozi. "He acts first and thinks about it later."

At this juncture, the squat little figure at the switchboard got up and approached Moloch with mingled deference and humility.

"I'm going home now," he said. He had been saying this every day for the last ten years at five o'clock sharp. His tone never varied. It was like a servant announcing "Dinner is ready, sir!"

"Did you take your cathartic pill?" asked Moloch.

Dave's face lit up like a Halloween pumpkin. He enjoyed this five-o'clock raillery. For the best part of the day he was glued to the switchboard, calling up the hundred or more offices in the city, throwing out reserve messengers which he called "waybills" after an old custom, and raising hell in general with the clerks and managers for their tardiness in telephoning the absentee and vacancy reports. Dave always kept a worksheet before him, on which he practiced the art of calligraphy. These sheets formed a chronological register of the daily happenings in the messenger department. In the upper right-hand corner of the worksheet he ruled off a little box wherein he made a faithful report of the weather. The inclusion of this meteorological report was no mere idiosyncrasy of Dave's. It was the grand alibi of the messenger department. . . . Dave preserved these sheets with the same fervor that a lama cherishes his prayer wheel.

Another curious habit of Dave's was his custom upon arriving in the morning of sharpening his lead pencils. No matter how many calls came in over the wire, Dave had to sharpen his pencils first. His contention was that if he were to postpone this important task the pencils would never be sharpened. And in Dave's mind it was a matter of the utmost importance to inscribe his characters in a delicate, legible, ornate hand. That was his proud contribution to the messenger service, the record which would remain after he had gone and testify in golden symbols to his industry and thoroughness.

But in every other respect Dave was a rogue, a scalawag. Almost as unprepossessing as Prigozi, though infinitely more humorous, his one ambition was to parade as a Don Juan. There was never any telling on whom his fancy might fall. In his messenger days he had been known to consort with charwomen, burlesque stars, midwives—any woman, in fact, who was sufficiently déclassée and repulsive to attract him. On one occasion his appetite had led him right up to the Vice-President's sanctuary. He had been on the trail of a big Senegambian whose bust bewildered him. Such temerity can only be faintly apprehended when one realizes with what trepidation Dave usually listened to the Vice-President's voice.

But of this, later. Now he was about to close shop, as he expressed it, and in accordance with time-honored tradition had brought over the "slate" for Moloch to glance at.

"You know there's a strike brewing, Dave?"

"I should worry," he replied, grinning from ear to ear.

"But that means you won't be able to take your wife to the hospital tomorrow morning, old man."

"Just as you say, Mister Moloch. She can have it done next week." He spoke as though it were a plumbing job and not an ovarian operation.

Prigozi's professional ardor was aroused.

"What's ailing your missus, Dave?"

Dave blushed, hemmed and hawed, looked confusedly at the two, and finally stuttered:

"*You* tell him, Mister Moloch. I can't use those big words like you can. What did you call those tubes again?"

"You mean the Fallopian tubes?" snapped Prigozi.

"Yeah, that's it. How do you spell that?"

"What do you want to know that for? You'd think your old woman was going to a spelling match instead of a hospital."

"Aw, I know," said Dave, grinning and blushing some more, "but I want to spring that word on Navarro." He turned to Moloch. "You know how Navarro looks at you when you pull a jawbreaker on him?"

The three of them laughed heartily. The operation was a success in advance. . . .

"You'd better be running along," Moloch advised. He looked up at the clock with sly humor.

"That's right," said Dave. "I'm working overtime."

He laughed uproariously at this feeble crack.

"Look here, Dave," said Prigozi, collaring him forcefully, and shaking him as though he were a dead rat, "you go straight home tonight, understand? No chippy-chasing in the subway or I'll break your neck. That wife of yours needs attention. Having your ovaries removed is no joke."

Dave summoned a tragic air. "You said it!" he observed.

Dave was about to go.

"Oh, Dave . . . before you go!" Moloch made a few mysterious

passes. Dave sidled up to him with a sheepish expression.
"How many?" he said.
"Oh, five will do."
"Here, take ten," said Dave, hauling out a wad of filthy greenbacks.
"Don't spoil the boss!" exclaimed Prigozi. "You'll never get it back, you know."
Concluding this ceremony, Dave paused and bowed his head. It was Dave's way of registering profound thought. "I want to say something before I forget it," he announced sententiously. "Between you and me, I think messenger 785 has an 'effective' mind."
"What makes you think he's defective," said Moloch. He understood quite well that this was Dave's method of showing his appreciation for the privilege of lending his boss a few dollars.
Dave never noticed the grammatical correction, but sailed on blithely; there was more than a hint of braggadocio in his comments.
"Why, I noticed he always carries a book under his arm. It's written in Italian. He says it's a classic."
"Well, there's nothing wrong in that, Dave."
"Maybe not, but when I asked him if he understood Italian he said, 'No, but I like to read it just the same—it makes me feel better.'"
"What was the name of the book?"
"I think he said *Inferno* . . . is that right? Is there such a book?" He laughed apologetically, showing all the yellow stumps in his mouth.
Prigozi nabbed him by the sleeve and pointed to some red lettering on a narrow cardboard strip which Moloch had tacked on the railing for the applicants to study while they waited to be interviewed:

DO NOT ABANDON ALL HOPE YE WHO ENTER HERE

"Do you know what that means?" he asked.
"No," said Dave, "do you?"

"Well, read the *Inferno* and find out. Damn it, Dave, you want to get wised up. You can't go on being an ignoramus all your life."

"Aw hell!" grunted Dave, with a deprecating air, and trundled off like Florizel the Fat.

With Dave's departure the two were left alone. The rest of the staff had disappeared. Moloch had formed the habit of remaining in the office for an hour or two after closing time, waiting for something to happen. His adventures usually began after five o'clock. Generally, one of his cronies dropped in for a chat. Sometimes a gang appeared and swept him out of the office like a cyclone. Frequently this period was taken up by the eccentrics whom he put to work and watched over with a cruel interest. With these he held long consultations in which he dipped freely and morbidly into their private life, gave hygienic advice, regulated their marital conduct, interpreted their dreams, allayed their discontent, studied their phobias and obsessions. Occasionally he borrowed money of them, which he repaid with interest. Or, he might accept their invitation to dine, or go to a show. If he thought there was an opportunity of philandering, he made it his business to call on their wives. . . . Some of the messengers were females. These he subjected to a rigid scrutiny when they made application for work. The addresses of the good-looking ones he kept in a memorandum book. When things got dull, he looked through these addresses and began calling them up— those with a star after their names first. Usually he was rewarded for his thoroughness.

The results of these observations and experiences he recorded with elaborate, painstaking efforts in a loose-leaf journal which he kept at the office. This journal also contained typewritten excerpts from the works of those authors whom he admired with an almost idolatrous fervor. The job of transcribing this material he entrusted to his secretary. It could hardly be said that he was unaware of the effect which these disclosures produced upon the mind of the clever, prurient virgin who acted as his secretary. She accepted the task with the serenity of a censor. Moloch awarded her the interest that a breeder might spend on a prize heifer.

Anticipations arose of utilizing the notebook as a springboard from which to plunge into a sea of more satisfying vicissitudes. Meanwhile the loose, heavy yoke of marriage chafed. This fever of activity which consumed him, and drove him from one escapade to another, offering him knowledge, excitement, sexual gratification—what was it but a partially recognized rebellion against the stagnating influences of wedlock? He was unhappy with the woman he had chosen. She too was unhappy. They lacked something (was it vigor or understanding?) to repair the prosaic damages of erosion.

Moloch got out the battered-looking journal and began to scribble in it. Prigozi amused himself by snooping about—examining applications, mulling over the office correspondence—maintaining, as he did so, a running fire of sardonic comments concerning the slipshod practices employed.

Moloch's grim concentration disturbed him. It was an affront to his ego.

"Humpfh!" he grunted. "What's the item tonight—*Luther?*"

"No!" said Moloch, hoping to thwart any further inquiries by the inflection of his voice.

"When are you going to write that book? You have sufficient notes there to write *The Decline and Fall of the Roman Empire*. . . . Hullo!" he chirped, looking up. "Here's the reason for the decline now."

Hari Das entered. He was in civilian clothes, and hatless. His glossy jet-black hair rested with luxuriant ease upon his slender shoulders. There was a serene, jubilant air about him. His manner verged on boldness, though it contained no vestige of the brash, aggressive qualities peculiar to Prigozi. Neither was it born of secret arrogance. A lofty indifference to the world—that more nearly approximated it.

This, then, was the "nigger" that Twilliger took exception to . . . old man Houghton's "shine" . . . the self-appointed Redeemer of Mankind in the twentieth century!

Hari Das was lighter in color than most of his Indian confreres, and by all odds the most attractive. Women, who are better judges in these matters than men, declared him to be

astonishingly handsome. Almost unanimously their first exclamation of rapture proclaimed the charm of his perfect, gleaming
white teeth. Perhaps that was why he laughed so frequently and
so easily. It was a pity that he had ever condescended to don the
hideous uniform of our Western garb. In his own regalia, as a
member of the warrior caste, he presented a quite different front.
One might easily visualize him in the role of member of Parlia-
ment, parrying suavely with the constipated intellects of the
upper House—juggling them like so many billiard balls. . . . In
a cheap, ready-made suit a forlorn element creeps into this picture, for which he is not responsible, and which has as little to do
with his personality as the frames one sometimes sees about a
masterpiece.

"I came to tell you," he began, and lapsed therewith into an
amusing and wholly spontaneous account of his trials in Chinatown. The spotty, errant emphases he employed, in conjunction
with his simple gestures, imparted a peculiar and altogether
charming note to his utterances.

It was noticeable that although he had been introduced to
Prigozi two days previously, when he first stopped into the employment office (Prigozi having introduced himself), he seemed
to be only slightly aware now of the other's existence. He observed the amenities by a grandiloquent wave of the hand.
Whereupon he proceeded to ignore Prigozi completely. Whether
this was a sign of contempt, or in line with his royal indifference,
it was difficult to tell. Prigozi, of course, was irritated by this
jeweled disregard. His blatant self-assurance, his flamboyant insolence, all the muddy arrogance of the fellow was swept off the
board, as it were. To his extreme surprise, he eventually found
himself listening respectfully and, as the tale proceeded, growing
more and more overawed.

Hari Das had dropped in, as he explained to Moloch, simply
to pay his respects before going off. He had no apologies to make
for his conduct. He saw nothing reprehensible in his tardiness.

Moloch said nothing about the color line. In his most affable
manner he alluded to the importance that was attached to death
messages.

His remarks made little or no impression upon his listener. "In India one takes his time, and when one is already dead, of what use is it to hurry?" said Hari Das. Brushing swiftly over "this Anglo-Saxon absurdity," he gave free rein to his impressions of Western energy and futility. What, he asked, was the ultimate value of these extravagant sacrifices in the name of speed?

Prigozi, who had been roughly revising his concepts of the weak-kneed Hindus during the course of this disquisition, thought the moment opportune to introduce a little dynamite. He had been aching to observe the reaction which the word "nigger" would induce. He drew his bow and shot the arrow home.

The two men looked at Hari Das with that absurd air of vacuity which people display when viewing the fragments of a precious vase which has slipped between their fingers. Moloch was furious, but said nothing. Indeed, it was too late to say anything. Prigozi had said everything that was necessary—and a few things that were unnecessary.

A tiny throatful of laughter, that had the chink of broken glass, broke from the disdainful lips of Hari Das.

"In India," he exclaimed, "I am a problem. In England I am an educated nuisance. If the Americans choose to make a *nigger* of me, very well—let them! I do not care a damn. My difficulty is an economic one, not an ethnologic one."

"Bully!" cried Prigozi, throwing his restraint to the winds.

A twinkle of amusement, that was also a reproach, flashed in Hari Das' eyes.

"Let's get out of here," suggested Moloch.

Prigozi and Hari had taken to behaving like two statesmen who flatter each other assiduously after a prolonged session of profanity and vituperation. There was nothing to be gained by permitting these two to continue. Besides, he was only too familiar with Prigozi's views. He knew his opinions on everything—from theories of "magic and religion" to birth control and conditioned reflexes. What he wanted was an intellectual debauch with this Nietzschean Oriental.

"How about going to the Olympic?" said Prigozi. The fact

that "Mister Moloch" had the price of a burlesque show in his pocket made him almost certain that this innocent suggestion would be adopted with alacrity.

"No, no burlesque for me tonight," said Moloch impatiently. "Here—take this, if you need some coin," and he thrust a five-spot toward Prigozi.

Prigozi refused the money, not from reticence, but because he was unwilling to be shunted off in this manner.

"Come along, then, damn you!" said Moloch, ushering Prigozi out.

Hari Das had gone ahead and was waiting for them in the street.

As they emerged from the office, Prigozi mumbled something in Moloch's ear which caused the latter to voice a vigorous dissent.

"Well, then," said Prigozi, unabashed and abandoning his furtive gestures, "how about that secretary of yours? Can't we manage to seduce *her*? She looks as if she's itching for it."

Again Moloch shook his head. "You forget that I'm a married man," he said facetiously.

Prigozi shrieked. "I always told you you were a god-damned hypocrite, Mister Moloch!"

Then, as if inspired, he took to dancing. Moloch wheeled slowly as Prigozi gyrated about him, observing the way the other's fingers drooped and quivered, ever so delicately. He wondered if Prigozi had ever seen Toscanini, or performed a surgical operation.

A few pedestrians stopped to stare. Hari Das meanwhile leaned against a lamppost and studied the headlines of the *Evening Journal*. He got a great kick out of the headlines. . . . He never read what was printed below.

IN THE SUBWAY HARI DAS RECEIVED AS MUCH ATTEN-
tion as if he were Genghis Khan suddenly come to life. Moloch
was as far removed from the usual cares of an employment
manager as an igloo from the equator.

They were not intoxicated. In the first place, neither Hari nor
Prigozi had touched a drop when they entered the café after
closing the office. Moloch had taken only a few glasses of gin, but
those "few thimblesful" had produced the illusion of a rutilant
Bakst curtain closing slowly over a drab backstage scene whose
realism was not of the theater but of life, life as it is known to a
Pirandello.

On this warm Crimean screen of velvet a cutback, translated
from memory, bathed in vivid stews of color, and aching with
promises that had never been fulfilled, projected itself. He be-

came insensible of the clownish behavior of the man Prigozi standing beside him at the bar.

Indeed, Prigozi himself, the brass rails, the rubicund figure in the white apron whose back was revealed in the fantastically soaped mirrors—the entire imminent reality had melted into a snug, superheated bedroom. There was about this room the same befouling disarray, the same vile odors which we associate with the bottom of a birdcage. He saw again the woman called Blanche, before she had gone through the mock solemnities of the conjugal rite; she was lying on a crazy quilt in a crumpled silk dressing sack, green as the troubled Atlantic. Her lips exuded a flavor of burnt coffee and buttered cinnamon toast. Her armpits were dark, darker than the deep olive of her neck and shoulders. He buried his head in one of the fragrant hollows with a long, deep kiss that left her quivering under the slow-curving caress of his body. Her long chestnut hair, electric with ardor, perfumed with vitality, enveloped him and tantalized him. He found himself climbing under the counterpane, his tongue sputtering with entreaties.

"I feel so ashamed," whispers Blanche, as she lies languidly among the heaving pillows, pop-eyed with fright and expectancy. The word "marriage" is on her lips. He erases it with swollen affirmatives, almost stifling under the thick blankets. The distorted red patterns of the wallpaper are swimming in endless vibrations of heat.

In the midst of this reverie Prigozi nudges him. "What's come over you?" He nods toward the bartender.

Moloch pays, gives Prigozi the change of a five-dollar bill, and dismisses him. He manages it so easily now. Not the slightest embarrassment.

"We're going home," he says, grasping Hari's arm.

In the subway Moloch feels called upon to explain his behavior. "I had to get rid of him, Hari. He gets on my nerves sometimes. He's like a bad breath. One can stand so much and then. . . ." He made a moue and looked around as if he wanted to expectorate.

Hari Das thought this frankness commendable. It was so un-

Oriental. Moreover, he was beginning to perceive great possibilities in this friendship.

"I must tell you something about Blanche before we arrive," said Moloch, apropos of nothing. "She may seem like a nightmare at first . . . somewhat inhospitable, understand? However, you mustn't let that disturb you. It's just her way. She's really a fine woman. A little nervous, perhaps . . . has a worried look. Probably some glandular disturbance. A splendid musician, though."

Hari Das tittered. Then he took a broken comb from his pocket and ran it through his greasy black hair.

"You know you'd make a wonderful Messiah, Hari? A veritable strap-hanging Savior, by George!"

Hari threw back his head and yawped.

"Our women adore Saviors, Hari," Moloch continued. "Particularly when they're handsome. By the way, you don't suffer from delusions, do you? You don't hear voices . . . or anything like that, you know what I mean?"

Hari accepted this as another one of Moloch's little jokes. He enjoyed these sallies hugely.

"I should hate to believe you were setting up as another little Gandhi," Moloch confided. "You're too amiable to be another tin Jesus. Besides, this country is full of them."

Hari's response was lost in the scuffle attending their exit from the subway. They had only a few blocks to walk from the station. Hari appeared to be fascinated by the variety of churches they passed in review. He craned his neck to gape at the gargoyles which leered at the empty streets. Just before they reached the house he stepped to the gutter and blew his nose with two fingers.

Moloch was pondering meanwhile on the reception they would receive, praying that his spouse would make a pretense at civility. Devil take her! He meant to enjoy the evening despite her malingering.

He pushed the button and assumed an air of sangfroid. An extraordinary greeting took place.

"Good evening!" he brought out blandly. "*Mrs. Moloch?* This is *Mister Moloch* . . . friend husband. Dropping in for a little friendly bite. Sorry we're late. . . . May I introduce my esteemed friend, the late Maharajah of Lahore? Swami—*my wife!*"

He made a low bow to smother his hysterical laughter.

Hari saluted the woman with his usual grace. Blanche grasped the proferred hand stiffly, looked him over as if he were a rare guignol, and stepped back with a tight-lipped expression to admit them.

"The mansion," said Moloch, beaming expansively, as if to communicate a moiety of his geniality to that hatchet with the canary-bird mouth. Blanche looked on with undisguised disgust as he prattled away.

"HOME!!! The sanctuary of repose. A cozy hearth, old friends, old wine. . . .!" He spread his arms in the Shakespearean manner. "And above all, the good wife who awaits with eagerness the husband's homecoming." He turned his back on his wife. "Well, Hari, not such great shakes, the place, *what*? A little untidy . . . no servants, you see. Blanche hasn't had a chance to do any housecleaning this week." (He said this to intercept her apologies. His manner conveyed the impression that he was rendering her a favor.) "Believe me, Blanche here is a really excellent hausfrau when she chooses to be. To be or not to be—that's our great domestic problem, isn't it, old battle-horse?"

Blanche, who was neither "an old battle-horse" nor "an excellent hausfrau," had daggers in her eyes. Her fingers were ten convulsive talons. They were by no means the well-kept digitals of a paramour. The nails were short and tough. Splendid independent finger movement—for the Hungarian rhapsodies.

"Excuse me," she said, turning to Hari, "my husband is drunk, I see." Her voice was bitter as tansy.

Hari flung both arms up. "Not at all, not at all," he protested. "I shouldn't be here if I thought he were drunk."

Blanche perceived that she had two monsters to deal with.

"Well," she said, "drunk or sober, I suppose you two want something to eat."

Moloch was undaunted. He grabbed Hari's coattail.

"Now isn't that thoughtful of Blanche? Didn't I tell you she was a cherub?" He turned to Blanche. "Of course, my dear

. . . *of course* we want something to eat. We came home expressly to have dinner with you this evening." He gazed at her ecstatically. Then he lowered his voice, affecting a new tinge of irony, if irony it could be called. "And where is our darling child this evening . . . *that jewel of your loins?*"

Hari Das could no longer restrain himself. He had done his best, up to this point, to show discretion, to appear aloof and disinterested, as though this fantastic colioquy were taking place on the planet Neptune. He looked at Moloch helplessly. Moloch answered his appeal with a comical expression that beggars description, and turned the hydrant on Blanche once again.

"The supper is not ready, you say?"

She hadn't said anything of the kind.

"Too late?" He simpered. "My, my! What difficulties life places in our path! Well, Hari, the maharanee has spoken. It's bacon and eggs for us, I see. Well, well, our old friend, bacon and eggs. Too bad, too bad!" He wagged his head with gross solemnity.

The apologies that Blanche endeavored to make for her husband's conduct gave Hari Das an insight into the private life of his newfound friend. He listened with such grave sympathy, with such a *respectful* mien, that Blanche soon found herself apologizing for more than she had intended.

"I never know when he's coming home," she rattled on, intoxicated with the variety of her husband's peccadilloes. "He doesn't even bother to telephone me. Sometimes he walks in on me like this with a gang . . . yes, a gang. And then he has impudence enough to get angry with me for not waiting on his rowdies hand and foot." She stamped her foot feelingly. "As though I could ever welcome his queer idiots."

"Queer idiots?" Hari repeated after her.

Moloch spoke up. "I told you Blanche was a gem, didn't I? That's just her way of making you welcome. She means to say that you're a gentleman—you're not a bit like the other roughnecks. . . . Why, my dear Blanche, I should say you *are* entertaining a gentleman. My good friend, the maharajah, has royal blood in his veins. You've got to have royal blood to be a maharajah—

isn't that so, Hari? Just the same, he's not above eating bacon and eggs, are you, Swami? And Im' not above making them for you, either. Swami, spill a little Hindustani while I prepare the feast. But let the talk be as excellent as the bacon and eggs!"

He dragged the two of them into the kitchen, shoved his wife into a chair, and commenced rattling the dishes in the pantry. He had forgotten to remove his hat. It was tilted over one eye.

"Now, Hari," he bubbled, emerging with a frying pan which he flourished like a short-order book, "you tell friend wife all about the famine and pestilence in India."

Blanche made a contemptuous grimace and adjusted her skirt.

Friend husband started to caper around her with the frying pan.

"Oh, Moon of My Delight! Gaze upon this jewel of———*

"Does your husband act this way . . . er . . . frequently?" Hari asked. He was at a loss to label Moloch's conduct without giving offense, but he also wished to absolve himself of all share in this brutal baiting.

Blanche answered in a subdued voice, "Most of the time I think I'm living with a lunatic."

"Poltroon, my dear, poltroon!" Moloch put in.

"He has no sense of decency, no respect—for me, or for anything. He's a vulgar, coarse fool."

She sat there stolidly, making no further attempt to prolong the conversation. It was the attitude of a dumb brute waiting for the ax to fall on its neck. A sort of grim, pathetic, God-help-me air about her. Even Moloch was touched.

He made an attempt to kiss her which she frustrated by giving him a vigorous push.

"You can't undo your mischief with a kiss," she hissed. "Leave me in peace, that's all I ask of you."

This outburst pained Moloch beyond words. He was like the criminal who hears the words of the sentence that is being pronounced but is dreaming all the while of the day he went fishing

---

*Editor's note: A line of text is missing from the only known existing manuscript.

thirty-seven years ago—how beautiful the stream looked in the splashing sunlight, the melody of a bird, his own innocent dreams. . . . What he wanted to say was this:

"Forgive me, Blanche. I'm a wretch. Christ! I don't want to go on hurting you, but you make me behave this way . . . with your coldness, your suspicions, your . . ."

Instead, he asked her in a weary voice if there was any mail. "Is there nothing from Burns?"

She shook her head passively.

"Nothing?" he repeated.

"There's this," she answered in a dull voice.

He looked at the envelope incomprehensibly. The handwriting was unfamiliar. He tore it open. Another envelope was inside, folded up within the letter. He looked at it vacantly. There was printing on it:

SHRINE CHURCH OF OUR LADY OF SOLACE
CONEY ISLAND, NEW YORK

It was about the annual novena to our Lady of Solace in preparation for the feast of her ANNUNCIATION. . . . "Dear Friend: During this solemn nine days' prayer, Our Lady of Solace, who is never invoked in vain, will be petitioned for favors including spiritual needs, the sick and infirm, prosperity, positions, success in undertakings, happy marriages, the welfare of expectant mothers, vocations, and whatever else may be desired by those who seek Our Blessed Mother's help."

He flung the letter aside without finishing it. "Somebody's playing a prank," he thought. Now he noticed another envelope, much smaller than the others, with four rows of dotted lines:

KINDLY BURN A VIGIL LIGHT!

For a Novena **$1.00**

"Bah! The dirty rascals!" he muttered. "I wouldn't give them a nickel, not even if they promised to get me out of Purgatory."

No one paid any attention to his mutterings. Blanche tried to make herself inconspicuous by busying herself with the cooking. Hari was rummaging through the books which were heaped on the china closet.

Moloch collapsed in the easy chair which had been dragged into the kitchen. Anything he had any use for he kept in the kitchen. It was the only room in the house he cared to live in.

His thoughts returned to Ronald Burns out in North Dakota. Why the devil was Burns so silent? He missed those huge bundles of mail which used to pass between them. Ten pages of enthusiasm for Dreiser, an essay on *The Bomb,* reams about Dostoevsky . . . almost a little book on *The Idiot* alone. . . . What *was* the matter? Had Blanche come between them? Had she been writing Burns about him . . . spreading calumnies?

One can bear so many things if only there is one in the world to call a friend.

He thought of that line in the Egyptian's letter: "There must be a humanitarian soul in which to deposit your pains and sufferings. . . ." God, that was a scream when he read it. But it was no joke! Ronald Burns had brought him the one friendship that he cared about. And now that was dissolving, apparently.

Ronald Burns was a musician and a litterateur. For three months he had shared the glories of existence with Dion Moloch and his wife. His return to North Dakota left those two individuals where he had found them—stranded on the mudflats of matrimony. For a time they had bobbed blissfully in the deep swift tide of companionship; then the tide had ebbed and they were left in the mud, stuck like scows.

Was Blanche in love with Burns? Moloch was ready to believe so. Was Burns in love with Blanche? That was more important. It made no difference to him what happened between the two so long as their friendship was not destroyed. If Burns wanted his wife— excellent! Come and get her! He could think of no happier solution of his difficulties. But if Burns wanted her, why then had he returned to North Dakota? Was he afraid to face the truth? Was it fear of hurting *him*? Had they no eyes, these two? Couldn't they see he had stepped out of the way to give them free room?

The marginal notations, and the long list of words piled up in the back of each book which Hari Das discovered in browsing among Moloch's slender collection, brought forth a series of critical appreciations that dissipated Moloch's retrospections. Of a sudden Hari Das gave a loud exclamation of joy and astonishment. With reverent fingers he clasped a worn volume and pushed it under Moloch's nose.

"Now," he cried, "now I know you cannot be an utter scoundrel!"

"So he had already accepted me as a scoundrel?" thought Moloch, somewhat cooled by the other's effusiveness.

Hari thumbed the book eagerly, examined Moloch's penciled notations, smiled, applauded silently. He skimmed through it with such feverishness as to make one believe he expected to find a treasure at the end.

"You do recognize beauty," he exclaimed. "I can see that!"

His words startled Moloch and roused him to a pitch of unbridled enthusiasm.

"Stop!" he cried, getting up from the easy chair. "We can't rush on this way. I want to say something to you. I can't let your words go unchallenged."

He was a bundle of excitement now.

"You were speaking about beauty. Yes, there is a little of it left in me . . . a little that my wife never sees."

He spoke of himself in a brutally detached way. Blanche, their marriage, the cluttered kitchen in which he paced feverishly (like a tiger whose cage is not only irksome but too small to turn round in)—all this he seemed to dismiss with a wave of the hand as the detritus of another incarnation.

"Yes, Mukerji . . . Mukerji!" he pronounced ecstatically. (It was a volume of the latter's that had precipitated this outburst.) "Yes, Hari, *there* is beauty to ponder on. Great soul-spluttering beauty! There is a man who should have been trumpeted forth ages ago. He makes India vivid, palpable—and yet ethereal, in her holiness. When I put down that book I wept. . . . Oh, you may shout and rave about your Mahatma Gandhi squatting on his emaciated legs and mumbling economic profundities larded with Vedanta fiddle-faddle. But I tell you, Gandhi may sit on his carbuncled can for another generation to come and never approach this poetry, this sublime beauty of Mukerji's that stirs me. . . . I don't know why I mention the man Gandhi at all. He annoys me, that's the truth of it. A sort of dry, statistical Christ, forever on the verge of departing this life and forever being resuscitated by his ridiculous fasting and praying. With one foot in the belly of the eternal, he lectures the world about putting its house in order. My God! All that damned nonsense about non-cooperation and spinning wheels! No, give me Mukerji every time. Those Indian nightfalls of his—'descending like an avalanche of soot.' The Taj Mahal's 'sigh fixed in marble.'

"Do you remember, Mari, that description of the humble door of a peasant bathed in the violet light of sunset? Or that unforgettable glimpse of the Ganges when he plunges into the tepid waters to hold discourse with the holy man? Imagine, if you will, two Baptist persons floating down the Mississippi with nothing on but tights. Can you picture them stirring up a wet fervor over the Old Testament?"

Hari Das broke into a loud guffaw.

"Unfortunately," Moloch continued, "for most of us India has no more reality than an opium dream. When the feeble Mahatma sets up his caterwauling with a throatful of statistical disclosures he gives the world a distinct shock. Who wants to know about the millions of Untouchables, the forty-nine warring sects and tongues, the endless scheme of castes and fakirs, of filthy caves and whoring temples? No, the world prefers to believe that India is not only a land, ninety percent of whose population is continually on the verge of starvation, a land ravished with cholera and scurvy, but something more, something beyond and above all the confusion of massacres, vice, legislation, and crass ignorance. When the swollen white bullocks of Siva have vanished, when the drum-tight paunches of the Brahmans have disappeared, together with their learned tracts on the digestive organs, what remains of India will still constitute, I feel, a nickelodeon of mystery, horror, and fanaticism. India will always be the place where religion forms the prime daily constituent of man. The sons of India will never permit religion to become the cheap, fractional thing with which the European is content. In their hands it will remain forever a peculiar, intangible earth-product, a something that will outlast our 'struggle-buggies' and 'wind chariots,' the loudspeaker and the high forceps. Ten thousand years hence, when the world will have been made sick and safe for democracy, and every Jake has his Annie, the dawn will still come up like thunder out of China 'cross the bay. *And down the virgin flanks of Mount Everest there will stream rivulets of sapphire!* In that respect your cosmic loafers prophesy correctly. Then, indeed, shall we be able to dispense with town cars and Grand Opera, with elevators and subways, with concrete factories and Babylonish architecture, with barbershop chords and contraceptives that don't contracept. . . . Upon my word, there'll be nothing left of this modern world but a stench. There won't be left a bottle of ketchup, or a Bromo-Seltzer!"

How much further Moloch would have pushed his imagination the Lord only knows. Blanche had been signaling him throughout this harangue to sit down and partake of the meal, which was ready at the beginning of his speech. Her manner, as she pushed the hasty meal before them, was that of a keeper in a lunatic asylum. She detested these discussions which never got one anywhere and which always ended in the larder being cleaned out. None of these "savants" ever thought of bringing so much as a layer cake along. They came equipped with looking-glass theories, speeches all wool and a yard wide, and—enormous appetites. If they addressed her at all it was only to ridicule her in some sly manner.

Blanche wondered therefore very justly what manner of individual the swarthy gentleman might be who sucked his bacon and eggs like oysters on the half shell. . . . She had not long to wait.

Hari Das had listened patiently to Moloch in order to be assured of the same courtesy when he took the notion to flap his wings and "bombinate in the void." First of all—with what seemed like Oriental suavity—he extracted a calling card from his wallet and laid it gravely on the table. Moloch picked it up and scrutinized it:

"Dean of the Oriental Academy? Hm! And where is this institution located, if I may ask?"

Hari stifled his mirth. "The Academy, I am sorry to say, is not yet a physical fact. So far I have only the cards, as you see."

"Well, that's an auspicious start," said Moloch, with comic gravity.

Blanche sniggered openly.

"My friend," Hari went on, "it is one of my ideals to organize in this Western hemisphere an institution similar in aim and feeling to that universal seat of learning which Tagore has established at Shantiniketan. I wish to break down the stupid prejudices which divide your world from mine. I want to see in America—because, in the last analysis, America is the only place to try such an experiment—a university where every culture, every people, will receive its due. I want to abolish forever that circular hypothesis of Greco-Roman origins. The Chinese must have their share of glory, and the Arabs; we must recognize the great contribution of the Slavs, the Negro races, the Jews, the Malayans . . ."

Moloch wondered especially what it was the Malayans had contributed to the great stream of civilization, but he held his tongue.

In estimating the task which confronted the founder of such an institution never once did Hari Das touch upon such prosaic requisites as money, advertising, football teams, or such perquisites. Did he expect this eclectic institution to flourish without an Alumni Association? What would take the place of football and regattas? *Religion?*

Almost as if he divined what was in Moloch's mind, Hari announced with the utmost seriousness: "It should be the duty of every educated American to know and appreciate the other great religious teachers of the world. Jesus the Christ is not the be-all and end-all of religion! The life of Jesus, as described in your Bible, what is it but a repetition of the incidents that occurred in the life of the great Gautama who lived over five hundred years before your Savior? . . ."

"Excuse me for interrupting, but he's not *my* Savior!" said Moloch.

Hari smiled tolerantly and continued.

"Take such unique occurrences as the immaculate conception, the temptation by the Prince of Darkness, the slaughter of the innocents by Herod: these are not isolated Christian myths! Consider the familiar parables of Jesus: the parable of the Prodigal Son, and of the Marriage Feast at Cana . . . why, they were known to the Hindus and Buddhists of the pre-Christian era. The rituals of the Catholic Church—have you any idea how many of them have been borrowed from Buddhism?"

Here Hari Das made a digression to explain to Moloch and Blanche (for she was listening, too, with some amazement) the manner in which Pythagoras came by his knowledge of the doctrines of pre-existence and transmigration of souls, of ascetic observances and vegetarianism, of the virtue of numbers, and the idea of the fifth element, which was unknown in Greece and Egypt at that time. "Ether as an element," said Hari, "was known only among the Hindus then."

"Good stuff, Swami!" chirped Moloch. "Some of our pundits trace everything back to Greece and Rome. Our traffic regulations, for instance, we borrowed them from the congested days of the Roman Empire. The Street Cleaning Department gets no end of brilliant ideas from the archaeological surveys made in Crete. Take our open-work plumbing—you might think that a German importation. No sirree! We copped that idea from the ruins of the Palace of Knossos. . . . As for myself, I think the most important item the Greeks gave birth to was tragedy."

"Even that is a myth," Hari exclaimed, ignoring the Nietzschean invitation to the dance.

"No doubt," said Moloch dryly.

"You see," Hari began again, "in the Occident, because of your falsified traditions, your emphases are on the wrong things. The vast contribution to civilization made by the Oriental peoples, a contribution that is extremely more important in the

ultimate than any Parthenon, Roman laws, or Attic tragedies
. . . this great contribution which flows from Egypt, China,
Africa, India, Japan, has been either deliberately minimized by
your pedants or else respectfully forgotten so as not to affect the
continuity of that beautiful Greco-Roman hypothesis.

"We read in your books endless panegyrics on Plato and
Aristotle, on Euclid, Aesop, Pythagoras, and Hippocrates, but
there is never any mention, unless I am woefully misinformed, of
the fact that we were the first teachers of plane and spherical
trigonometry. In the science of numbers the Greeks never even
approached the ancient Hindus. Take the simple, practical science of arithmetic. It would have been impossible without a
system of decimal notation, would it not? Who gave it to you?
The Arabs. And where did the Arabs get it? From India. . . .
What is plane geometry after all but an elaboration and extension of the Vedic formulae for the construction of sacrificial
altars! As for music, the scale with the seven notes was known in
India centuries before the Greeks had it; it was built up from the
chanting of primitive Vedic hymns . . ."

"Whoa, whoa!" cried Moloch good-naturedly. "Soon you'll
be telling me that the theory of relativity is an anachronism."

Thus the conversation proceeded, while the icebox was stead-
ily drained of jams, fruits, cheese, of all the edibles that Blanche
had been holding in reserve for future meals.

Stimulated by Moloch's sly encouragement, Hari Das tram-
pled joyously on things sacred and profane in the Occidental
world. Moloch applauded generously, and when the former ran
short of material supplied him with ideas. They were in perfect
agreement that without Cascara America would perish of consti-
pation; that halitosis was a scourge second only to leprosy.
America: the land of stop and go! Big Ben: the workingman's
idol!

Blanche was a basilisk, heavy-lidded, blinking indignantly.
The warm blood rose to the back of her neck and clotted her
thoughts and impulses. A dull rage thickened her tongue; it hung
in her mouth like a crape.

In due course Hari got around to our national heroes. He had a severe prejudice against Lincoln because of the Gettysburg Address.

"Either Pericles anticipated Lincoln," said Hari, referring to the famous funeral oration of the Peloponnesian War, "or we must believe the Great Emancipator to be a plagiarist."

"God," cried Moloch, half in earnest, half in jest, "if you're going to take Lincoln from us too"—he scratched his head vigorously—"you may as well summon the angel Gabriel. That's the last ditch! I didn't mind seeing Washington go. In his pajamas he was nothing, you might say, but a British realtor with a strong propensity for the wenches. Franklin—he had to be exposed, too, as a bibulous, whoring son of a chessplayer who liked nothing better than to loll about on the sidewalks of Paris with immoral Frenchwomen. But when it comes to Lincoln . . . hang it, there ought to be something sacred in this democracy of ours. A plagiarist, you say? Tch! Tch! Tch! And he knew such good jokes. . . . But then the Civil War was too big a joke for him, I guess."

"Tell me, you're not holding anything up your sleeve against Robert E. Lee?" he added as an afterthought.

Hari appeared mystified.

"What? You don't know Robert E. Lee? Man, he's the only figure in American history that no one can throw dirt at. Beside him General Grant was just a horny gaffer given to smoking cheap cigars. As for General Sherman—well, to put it politely, he was a common, low-down Jack the Ripper. When he finished marching through Georgia there wasn't enough vegetation left for a plant louse to cling to. All our national heroes—Webster, Brigham Young, Barnum, Buffalo Bill, Jesse James—they were all tainted. There isn't even a good word to be said for that pathetic washboiler Carrie Nation. She wasn't an epileptic, but she heard voices too."

These names were as familiar to Hari Das as an almanac of Polynesian deities, or Lydia Pinkham's remedies for women's complaints.

Blanche had been listening to all this nonsense with a polite sneer. Several times she had been on the point of blowing up.

Finally, she got up, made an inarticulate reference to her husband's diseased mind, and signified that she was retiring.

"So early, my zephyr?" Moloch tauntingly placed his hand on her shoulder to detain her. "I had something to say to you concerning our friend here."

"*Your friend,* if you please. . . . You're not going to ask me to fix a place for him, I hope?" She made the feeble excuse that she was expecting her mother.

"You never dropped a word about that, Blanche."

"Oh, *didn't I?*" She turned to Hari as if he were a judge before whom she was pleading a case. "He goes about in a trance when he's home. You'd think I was a piece of furniture instead of his wife."

"Come, come," said Moloch, "Hari doesn't want to hear that nonsense. Look here, why can't Hari sleep with Matt? I'm sure Matt won't mind."

"How do you know he won't?"

"Because they're great friends already, isn't that so, Hari?"

The latter was perplexed and exceedingly uncomfortable. He begged them not to inconvenience themselves on his account.

"Tut, tut!" cried Moloch. "It's a pleasure."

More fruitless words were exchanged—with dagger thrusts and cobra venom. Nevertheless, Moloch was determined to have his way.

Hari Das derived a somewhat malicious enjoyment from this wretched, absurd squabble. Instinctively he aligned himself with his host, not because there was more justice on that side, but because the Hindu view of women made Blanche appear in his eyes as a sinister example of the fruits of that Occidental evil called feminism. He said nothing, but if one could read his thought it was that a sound thrashing would terminate a lot of unnecessary argument.

Outside a searchlight was spraying the trees and walls with violet rays. When it had finished spraying the earth it tilted upwards and swept the firmament clear of stardust.

Moloch glanced at Hari. His skin barely sufficed to cover his bones; his complexion had paled until it became the color of urine.

When there are girls and boys in a classroom it is trying for the teacher to say "Lake Titicaca." No one takes this lake seriously. It sounds absurd—and a trifle suggestive. Moloch felt the same way about this situation. He wanted someone to extricate him.

Blanche slipped off quietly to clasp her dreams. Her gesture was akin to the shrug of a dance-hall woman tossing aside a novel by Maxwell Bodenheim because "it starts off dirty."

Toward dawn Hari slipped into Matt's bed. It was not necessary to disturb Reardon since he was not there to disturb. In the telegraph game one meets with a large variety of experience. Very likely Matt had put the kibosh on the insurrection uptown, and then, highly satisfied with his efforts, had gone to a prizefight with one of the operators. After that a drinking bout and a Turkish bath. Or an all-night session in a black-and-tan. Matt would arrive bright and early in the morning with a swollen head and a fitful desire to spend the rest of his days in the South Seas. . . .

Moloch tarried a few minutes before retiring to glance at Hari's pamphlet entitled "Merry Christmas Greetings to the World!" It was written in the first person spectacular. Some of it was in high fettle.

"I restrain myself lest a stray casual remark develop into a volume. I do not expect to be appreciated all at once. Of this, however, I am convinced, that only the rarest among men have been foreordained to understand me. . . . The rest are merely humanity on their way to ordination. . . .

"I boast of my system being fluid, gaseous, capable of evaporating. This is the highest rational system ever yet propounded. The sensations embodied in my 'Aphorisms' are a tiny fragment of the vast firmament of my philosophy, and exhibit the state of chaos out of which will order be born, to which I shall willingly, proudly, stand Godfather; it is the state of Inharmony out of which shall Harmony be born, to the divine rhythm of which the world shall dance for the pleasure of the Master-Artist. . . ."

"The Master-Artist"! Moloch mused awhile on megalomania. The Master-Artist was already snoring deeply. His "Aphorisms" were floating like toy balloons over the surface of his dreams. He was no longer aware of such mythical realities as corns, bunions and "Charley Horse." He walked in deep meadow grass through the valley of the moon, and the smell of clover was as incense to his quivering nostrils.

"With a proper diet, clean linen, a soft pallet, he'll get over this Messianic complex. I suppose it's up to me to play Joseph of Arimathea. . . . Ho hum!" He yawned, stretched himself, and lit a cigarette. Ideas gathered, the species of ideas which strangles sleep, and which seems next morning to be more than mildly aberrant. He pictured himself in a Quaker meeting, passing the hat around for his friend, the Master-Artist, who has just finished lecturing on "The Religious Aspects of Procreation." As an entrepreneur his success is established. The hat is full. If this gag can be repeated, it it can be pulled on the Christian Scientists, well . . . the telegraph company can go to hell then. The Master-Artist has no idea what a gold mine awaits them. Once California is reached. . . . California: the land of golden whales. California: where a new cult is born every day. He's glad he was born an American. America: the land of opportunity, where the rich grow richer and the poor poorer. If necessary, he'll change his name . . . Mordecai Brown, Impresario!

In the upper stratum of Chinese society a favorite method of committing suicide is "to take gold leaf." Death is brought on by the gold leaf obstructing the glottis. Similarly, the web of cocoons that Dion Moloch spun brought about a suffocation of ideas and he became deliciously drowsy. The last impression he was conscious of was the racing extra in the *Evening Telegram*: "Original wins in the fourth!" It proved to be no more stimulating than those books which are omitted from the Index Librorum Prohibitorum.

BLANCHE HAS BECOME HABITUATED TO SPEAKING OF
herself in the past, as if she were a piece of secondhand furniture.
Her mind and spirit have become as angular as her face, which
has now acquired an equine aspect. She exhales the atmosphere
of a Protestant church. She is not only morbid and suspicious,
she is colorless, inflexible, poor-at-heart.

It is easier for these two to quarrel than for a preacher to say
Amen. Fortunately, they are seldom left alone. When Moloch
does come of an evening, which is rare, he always finds visitors.
Not that Blanche is responsible. She seldom sees anyone. She
doesn't believe in friends.

Riding to work mornings, Moloch frequently reflected on the
sad state of affairs. His life with Blanche was so absolutely different from anything he had visualized. He almost gave a start
when his mind fell back to the days of their courtship. Was this

the same Blanche? This the passionate, impetuous woman whom he took to matinees, with whom, under cover of darkness, he committed nameless indiscretions?

He thought with premeditated satisfaction of his secretary, a slim, eighteen-year-old virgin whose skin had the mossy bloom of a magnolia. Each evening, as he dozed in the fetid atmosphere of the subway, he planned anew her seduction. Hers was not the platitudinous beauty of a Jewess, that excites the perverse curiosity of a drummer and arouses in her Gentile sisters the itch of envy and despair. Men thought of Marcelle rather as the frail respository of a forgotten charm, the sort of charm that one discovers in a vase at the museum.

It was a pity, he often told himself, that he could not have married the girl he loved. That was so long ago, his first love . . . his only love. (Do we not all speak that way of first love?) He no longer thought about it sanely.

This first love was no pale Mona Lisa, of legendary charm. Cora was a buxom, two-breasted Amazon. He never thought of her without a sharp pang at the remembrance of her firm, upstanding breasts, full as an Indian burial mound—and her breath, warm and milky.

At seventeen Cora was like an Arctic summer. She looked out at the world from cold, porcelain eyes that shimmered like blue icebergs under the play of boreal lights. In ten years Cora had paled into a fragile memory, a memory of a tight bodice and a sassafras peruke. He could never permit himself to think of Greenpoint without a vicious tug at his heart. Maujer, Conselyea, Humboldt Streets; the streets that Cora once had trod. These streets, forlorn now, were consecrated to HER. If the truth were known, he had even kissed the flagging of these very streets. Late at night, of course, and in a moment of terrible anguish.

The period we speak of was in the first decade of this century. Young men in long trousers were not ashamed then to hold parties in which they played at "Post Office" and "Kiss the Pillow." They even formed clubs so that they might meet at one another's homes. Nor were they abashed to call themselves "the Deep Thinkers." Had it not been for such diversions Moloch would probably never have kissed this goddess whom he worshiped with all the pathos and chivalry of an adolescent. For months he has contented himself with taking a long walk every evening after dinner. He does this in order to kill time, because it is impossible for him to fathom how he will go on living unless Cora acknowledges her love for him. And how is she going to do this since he is afraid even to speak to her? He does not think of using the telephone, or inviting her to the theater. He would tremble too violently if he heard her voice, if she sat next to him in the dark. No, these things require a courage that is beyond him. He prefers to take a long walk so that at the end of an hour he may find himself, as though by accident, directly beneath her window. He fears to linger there more than a minute lest the door open suddenly and one of her family, perhaps a younger sister, espy him and make fun of him.

Just the same, his secret is known. The other members of the club (thick-skinned, all of them) have taken to spoofing him. When they mention Cora he blushes terribly and stammers. They fail entirely to perceive what a goddess she is. In their vulgar way, they know her only as a robust, athletic figure, sparkling with life and joy. It amuses them, in an indecent way, to see this girl whom they have played with on the streets and in stables and alleys regarded as a Vestal Virgin. She is good to look at, excellent company, kisses divinely, but shucks! She isn't the only girl in Greenpoint. There is Ethel Tilford, and Violet Munson! What's wrong with them?

One evening they decide to make a man of Moloch. They get him drunk. They saunter out, twelve young blades, full of kümmel and Rhine wine. They make a beeline for Maujer Street, where Cora lives. It is hardly necessary to drag Moloch along. He is up in the van, shouting and gesticulating. "A capital idea," he brags. "Let's give Cora a serenade!"

In front of her home they stop, drag Moloch into the middle of the street, and perform a mystic ceremony. Their shouting and laughter is enough to wake the dead. But no one appears at the window. Not a shade is drawn.

"They must be out," thinks Moloch. Emboldened by the

thought, he mounts nimbly to the top of the stoop and delivers a speech.

His speech is mad, fantastic. He spews it out with volcanic energy. Everything that he has kept locked in his breast pours forth. He plunders the skies to hurl jewels at her feet.

A tumultuous applause bursts from the louts on the sidewalk. They have never heard anything more hilarious. Moloch stands aces high. He will be the next president of the club. . . .

And Cora—where was she during this mad outburst? Was she in bed, dreaming of becoming a ballet dancer? It were better had this been so. But Cora is kneeling at the window in her night-dress, listening to every word of this crazy buffoon. The darkness of the room hides her from sight. She cannot see him, either, but his words make her shiver. He must be mad to love her like this. What are they laughing at, the fools?

She vows never to let him know that she cares for him so. *"So?"* she asks herself. Up till then she was unaware that he meant anything to her—in this way. "Why has he never said anything? Is he afraid of me?" She is delighted with her powers, and clasps her bosom with a strange, possessive joy. "Oh, Dion," she murmurs, "if you only knew, if you only knew." She hugs the shadow of her lover. Her knees are dimpled from the pressure of the carpet. Quivers shoot up and down her spine.

It is tragic, this senseless frustration life deals. Cora is beyond question the woman Dion Moloch should have married. She has everything to offer him: love, health, beauty. God, how he knows it, too! He loves her so much that he wants to crawl to her on his belly and invite her to use him as a footstool.

"This will never occur again," he tells himself.

How truly the heart speaks in crises like this! Later, when he wants to love, when there is every reason for him to flower again, his heart is strangely empty. He no longer thinks of Cora, unless some accident has precipitated her memory. He does not realize, in such moments, that he has given himself to her irrevocably. Such gifts are impossible to repeat.

But, to return. . . . The club is holding an affair. It will be the last racket run by "the Deep Thinkers" for some time. Several of the fellows are going off to college. Moloch is one of them.

There is nothing of an unusual nature about this gathering. The atmosphere is hardly more tense than at any time in the past. The same simple incidents are repeated. Not a shadow of the deeper life to come mars their pleasures. All is joy. Youth is having its day. The morrow will be like any other. Not one among them doubts his capacity to meet the future.

Moloch, too, shares this fatuous belief. But he has reason to feel confident. He should exult. Has not Cora been unusually kind to him this evening? She has eyes for no one else, it seems. Oh, he will go off to college and make a name for himself. And when he returns . . .

"What's this? She's asking for me? For *me*?"

Young Dion Moloch gets up and threads his way through the noisy, chattering group. The room is whirling. He doesn't know what to say to her, nor how he'll behave when he finds her in the hall. All evening he has been waiting for the moment when it will come his turn to invite someone outside "to get a few letters." That she should call him . . . no, that he never expected.

In the few steps that are left he already sees himself as a swashbuckling figure. Women are clamoring for him . . . can't wait till they are called. Great guns! What is this magnetism he possesses?

The face that Cora turns to his in the dim light of the hall is the most beautiful sight in the world. One glance at her and he has lost all that bravado. Not a word is exchanged.

It is up to him to kiss this divinity.

Cora stands ready, her head just the least bit tilted, her arms hanging limp. Her bosom is heaving. It makes him tremble uncontrollably. He has never been so close to her, not even in his dreams.

Without knowing how he finds her in his arms. Their lips touch. The feel of her flesh staggers him. His sensations are so acute, so unique, he wants to scream. He has never held a woman in his arms. He imagines there is a certain amount of struggling to be gone through—what is called "putting up a fight." But Cora is swaying limply in his arms. There is no resistance. He is certain she is clinging to him; he can feel her grip tightening.

He no longer fastens his mouth to hers; he seeks her ears, her eyes, her throat. She groans as he does so and repeats again and again: "Oh, God! Oh God!" He no longer cares what he says, what he does. Get at her! Conquer her! Devour her!

He is lost to everything.

Now he leans her against the wall, pressing his full weight against her, stroking her hair, uttering her name with hoarse vehemence. His violence terrifies her. To be the target of such passion!

"He must love me tremendously . . . !"

She, too, does her part—returns pressure for pressure. Her lips are parched and bruised.

"God help me for what I am thinking!"

There is no help for it . . . she permits him to fasten himself upon her and crush her. "Oh, what can this come to?" She wants time to think. She tries to appeal to him.

Oh, God, what is he up to now?

His hands are clutching at her, straying over her body. His movements become convulsive. There is something bestial about him. . . .

There are things no gentleman ever does to a lady, not even in a moment of passion. One does not play with a woman's body as if it were a guitar.

Dion Moloch buries his face in his arms and leans against the wall. Nothing but dry sobs fill the hall.

Shortly after this episode his father gives him money to enter college. It is too late. There is a different ordeal in store for him.

The money which his father can scarcely spare young Moloch squanders on a woman who is almost old enough to be his mother. *He is hooked.*

Cora seems so far beyond his reach that he no longer hopes. The sweet, mysterious, painful world of sex opens. Pauline is a mother to him—and a concubine. She needs someone to cling to, someone who will appreciate the sacrifice she desires to make. Dion Moloch accepts her with open arms. He attaches himself to her body as a tick does to a cow.

The thought that he is making a greater sacrifice nourishes him.

Pauline has a frail, consumptive child. This child, George, is only a year younger than her lover. At night she kisses George tenderly, and tucks him in bed. Then she kisses her lover also, and steals into bed with him. In the morning George finds her sleeping peacefully.

Months pass and Moloch is almost ready to believe that he is happy with his mistress. He has found a job, a paltry one, to be sure, but it enables him to keep her. George has been shipped to a sanitarium. It is better with George away. There is no longer any need for dissembling. George will die soon, anyway. Pauline knows that. So does Moloch.

When Pauline breaks the news that she is with child her lover's attitude is one of keen disappointment. In a mistress pregnancy is an unpardonable sin. Pauline's lover interprets this accident in the usual masculine way: it is a trap! The idea is strengthened because it corroborates the opinions of friends and advisers. No one has been able to see any good in this absurd relationship. "It will never work"—that is the unanimous verdict.

Poor Pauline! No one has ever made the least attempt to probe the depths of her affection. It is concluded, because of her age, that she is a schemer, a succubus. A woman of her years has no business to fall in love with a child! How many harsh things were said of her!

On top of this George passes out. Grief overwhelms Pauline. Now she has neither son nor lover, for Dion is hiding away.

Pauline wonders would Dion refuse to see her if he knew George was dead. She does not rush to act immediately on this idea. She surveys it from every angle. Her life and happiness are at stake. A false move and Dion will be lost forever.

Carefully now she tries to piece together his character. First of all, does he love her? She is not misled by his running away. She understands his fear. Men have run away from her before.

Supposing it is only pity. Supposing it is her body—simply that. What then? What then?

These questions drive her frantic. Meanwhile she's got to

think about burying George. And there's a bastard under her belt. . . . That also has to be disposed of. But how? How?

She looks about the room with terror-stricken eyes. His books are still scattered about, plaguing her with memories of quiet, peaceful evenings—so many of them—spent just with him. Mechanically she gets up and examines the titles of the books. She hasn't the faintest idea what it is all about. The titles baffle her. His mentality is the one thing she has left unexplored.

An hour later her mind is made up. She is at the telephone, calling Dion's home. Her voice is faint and timid.

"Please tell Dion that George is dead. Yes, that's all. He will understand."

At breakfast next morning Dion is given the message.

"What George is that?" asks his father.

"George? Huh . . . just an acquaintance. You don't know him."

He sips his coffee and goes on reading the newspaper. The news affects him, but not in the way Pauline had pictured. He is sorry for her, if it is true. But is it? Isn't this possibly just another trap?

A week later Pauline becomes panic-stricken. She is absolutely convinced of her lover's faithlessness. He has become a monster in her eyes. She'd like to strangle the bastard in her womb. She'll strangle him, too, if she can lay her hands on him. . . .

Day after day, as soon as dark approaches, she stations herself outside his home. A loaded revolver is in her bag. And every evening, after a forlorn, fruitless wait, she returns to her room and takes the revolver out of her bag. Distracted, beside herself with rage and grief, she toys with the weapon and practices by taking aim at herself in the mirror. . . .

Will she have the strength to pull the trigger? Her fingers are weak with fear and dread.

"This is no solution," she whispers to herself. "God, he *must* come back! He can't leave me alone like this."

She throws the gun aside and weeps.

A guardian angel must be watching over this lover of hers, preserving him from harm and from a fate that he would be unable to cope with. He hasn't the slightest suspicion of Pauline's doings. If someone were to tell him about the revolver he would laugh. "She'll get over it," he repeats to himself. He grows more and more hardened each day, more and more disgusted with himself.

If we had been with Pauline and Dion one evening in early summer, just a few weeks before these dramatic events, we might have had an inkling of the tortures which brought about this determined resolution on the part of Pauline's lover.

It was a very warm night and Pauline had complained of a stifling feeling. They decided to take a ride to Coney Island. As they listen to the band concert at Luna Park they are entertained by a slack-wire performance high up above the artificial lake. Boats filled with merrymakers shoot down the steep incline and smack the surface of the water. The woman with the parasol slides dexterously above the blare and confusion. She seems to float in the air, like the opening notes of the *Tannhäuser* Overture. Presently they get up and saunter over to the dance pavilion. He thinks it would do Pauline good to exercise a bit.

As they come abreast of the pavilion he begins to doubt whether, in her present condition, it is the wisest thing to cause her this exertion. Little does he realize the ordeal he is to go through.

On the very steps of the pavilion, watching him breathlessly, is Cora.

She watches him fully a minute before he becomes aware of her presence. Cora takes Pauline in with one devastating glance. She notes the way the woman hangs on his arm. No words are necessary to convey the intimacy of these two. All the ugly rumors that she had given the lie were true, alas. *Dion was living with this woman.*

"The strumpet!" she thought. "Taking a boy for her lover." Ugh! It was abominable. She could forgive him if he had taken a woman off the street, but *this* . . . She notes the dejected way he drags along. "Ashamed of himself, is he? Well, he ought to be! She's old enough to be his mother."

Dion has averted his eyes. He knows that he is under fire.

"Christ! How long will it take to get by her?"

He squeezes Pauline's arm so as to hasten her steps. He is like a soldier being drummed out of the regiment. There is no room in his mind for anything but the disgrace which shackles him.

To pass Cora without a greeting is out of the question. He *must* lift his face for just an instant, if only to nod to her. . . . If only Pauline wouldn't cling to him so. He might pass her off as an aunt. A wave of disgust passes over him as he thinks of her figure. How much does it show?

God, what a cruel predicament! (He is thinking of himself.)

At last he can put it off no longer. Another step and it must happen. His temples are hammering, his tongue is dry and thick. He knows what an ass he is. Nevertheless, he tries to appear calm.

His lips form a hollow, noiseless salutation. He thinks he is saying "How do you do," as if he were a gentleman out strolling with a lady of his acquaintance . . . as though it were the most casual greeting ever. His spine stiffens as he makes a slight bow and doffs his hat.

It all happens so swiftly that Pauline almost fails to notice the gesture. They walk in silence for a few paces. Presently Pauline asks in a pleasant voice, "Who was it?" Then, noticing the color in his cheeks, "Why Dion, how you're blushing!" He begins to stammer. "Tell me," she begs, drawing him close to her, "who was it?"

He implores her not to look back. "I'll tell you in a minute. Am I really blushing so? Pshaw! I thought I was over that nonsense. I don't see why I should be blushing. What the devil! Who was it, you say?"

By this time Pauline was eyeing him gravely. There was no escape. And yet, he didn't wish to hurt Pauline. This business with Cora was done for. Was he still blushing, he wondered.

"Look here, Pauline, don't go thinking a lot of fool things. It's nothing at all—just a girl I knew once. A pretty kid, but nothing much to her. Once I thought I liked her a good deal . . . ah, but that was ages ago. I forgot about her long ago. . . . Funny we should bump into her down here, though." He shut up like a clam.

His "ages ago" did not deceive Pauline. She detected in this expression about as much sincerity as one attributes to the slips of a slack-wire performer. And just as one's heart leaps to his mouth at every purposive slip of these performers, so her fears assailed her in spite of his assurances. One can sometimes carry these assurances too far. The air was heavy with danger. However, she told him nothing about her fears.

It was much later—after she had put the revolver away permanently—that she understood his blushes. They imparted meaning to her fears.

LESLIE'S PARENTS HAD JUST RETURNED FROM A SUC-
cessful carnival tour. They had been away eighteen months. The
time which elapsed between greetings had been sufficient to
transform a hobbledehoy into a raw, brass-lipped youth whose
affection had soured and whose obedience was a mirage.

Leslie's mother was a loving, trustful creature whose devotion
had been imposed on, first by her husbands, and then by her son.
Her first husband was a railroad man who beat her in her cups.
He died during an attack of delirium tremens. Leslie had only a
vague remembrance of him, but it was a memory that he cher-
ished. He had absolutely no use for his stepfather, a stranger
whom his mother had married in order that she might later
reform him.

This individual had failed in the first flush of his career as a "con" man, and after serving a term in the penitentiary, married Leslie's mother; thereafter he attempted to repudiate his past by eking out a precarious living "playing the grifts and the grinds." As a boy Leslie accompanied these two in their wanderings over the face of the earth; there was hardly a civilized country they had not traversed. Speaking of his experiences, Leslie always referred to his people as circus folk, a vague description which permitted the credulous to glut their fancy. Pinned down, he spoke more definitely, as the whim dictated, of lion tamers, equestrians, acrobats, and so on. The fact was, he was ashamed of his folk. Not of his mother so much (he recognized her helplessness), but of his stepfather.

In the last three years he had been left behind to acquire a less desultory education. Alas, his education was already in advance of his years. The placid, sterile, surrogate form of instruction of the schools proved unpalatable to him. At fifteen he knew more about life—the vital aspects of it—than the spinsters and eunuchs whose desiccated, bankrupt emotional vitality makes them regarded by our age as the fit mentors of youth.

During his parents' last tour he had kicked over the traces and taken a job. *A job* is incorrect. In the course of a year he had held over a dozen jobs. He had what employment managers and entrepreneurs recognize as personality. To sell himself was so simple a trick that he became enamored of it. A fit of malaise was sufficient to make him surrender his job—there was always another around the corner. He had no more difficulty securing recommendations than a bank president has in slipping into a silk-lined tuxedo jacket. Just as he had been fascinated by the gaping yokels under the carnival tent, so now he longed to probe the rich gullibility of hornswoggled employers.

Moloch put him to work in the spirit of a pickpocket engaging a confederate. He wasn't the least taken in by Leslie's "savoir faire." "Play the game," he warned him at the outset, "or I'll give you a thrashing." And forthwith he proceeded with diligence, at every turn of the road, to undermine Leslie's conceit. Never for a moment did he allow Leslie to believe that he was anything but a convenient (and submissive) tool—one that he could dispense with arbitrarily at an instant's notice. In these matters he was a despot.

There was another sort of training going on, however, that acted as compensation and eased the chafing which smarted Leslie's spirit. Moloch introduced him to the companionship of such exiles as Herbert Spencer, Winwood Reade, Kropotkin, De Gourmont, Nietzsche, Latzko, Ambrose Bierce. . . .

And so Leslie gradually came to behave with the conviction that he was employed by a god, a very warm, human, personable deity who was accessible and with whom he could be as intimate as a sympathetic older brother. He saw his savior as a sturdy immoralist, a dispassionate liar who cared deeply about the larger truths, a skeptic among fanatics, an iconoclast who destroyed from a sheer superabundance of health and strength. . . . He imitated—sometimes disastrously. A fierce hunger gnawed him to break his fetters and test his eagle wings in truly empyreal realms.

The aunt to whose care he had been confided was the only relative the family possessed. Leslie's mother was not without misgivings concerning the wisdom of sheltering her son under her sister-in-law's roof. Aunt Sophie was a woman approaching forty, rather plump, and unmistakably gross and sensual. Her husband had died soon after their marriage and left her in the predicament of proving her charms to the world. She had a meager talent which she leased for a pittance to the services of the Jewish stage. Her life was hectic, disordered, and without a foundation of any sort. The remnants of an intellect with which she confronted the exigencies of life were salvaged from the swamps of adolescence. Her movements oscillated between the satisfying of her appetites and the meretricious arts of the theater. Incapable of attracting a permanent consort, she converted her boudoir into a lupanar. In this flourishing atmosphere Leslie sprouted like a weed. Here he found such treasures as *Aphrodite,* the *Satyricon,* and *Flossie,* gifts which had been deposited by her whilom admirers. The pernicious influence of this premature initiation into the splendors of an antique world his Aunt Sophie supplemented by making him privy to her scandalous amours, occasionally exploiting him as an instrument to abet her passionate intrigues. Later he became the turbid spring at which she slaked her unquenchable thirst.

It was to dispel the premonitions of impending disaster that Leslie's mother had taken him to task, in a gentle way, one morning shortly after her arrival. She was amazed at the flagrant disrespect her son exhibited toward his aunt. There was in it a great deal more than the mere defiance of rebellious youth; a painful intimacy obtruded and buried its corruption in her heart like a canker. She observed with grief that her son had thrust her out of his heart, that he reveled in the possession of vile secrets, oppressive and suffocating in their turpitude.

"Leslie, you must come and live with us," she remonstrated. "Your father has been anxious about you."

"He's not my father," Leslie replied with bitterness. "He's a dirty kike. I don't want to hear anything about him."

"Shame, Leslie, shame! What a way to speak. Is that the way you have learned to behave in my absence?"

Harsh and ugly as these words appear, they were not the first that his mother had listened to. Hitherto she had made excuses for these outbursts. She attributed his vehemence to jealousy. But the word "kike" rankled. It lent an unfamiliar interpretation to his hostility.

"My father wasn't like him, you know that. You say he used to beat you. I never saw it . . . maybe I was too young to notice. But he treated *me* all right. That kike—the only education he ever gave me was in crime."

"Why do you use that word? I'm a Jew just as your step-father is. You're a Jew, too, though you're proud of your drop of Gentile blood. Don't be a silly little boy. I don't like to speak of such things—I know how much you love your own father—but Leslie, my child"—"child" irritated him beyond words—"your father wasn't half as good to me as . . ."

"Well," he snarled, "he wasn't a jailbird. His worst fault was drink. You could have stopped that. Instead of complaining about him you should have trained him differently. At least he didn't make his living trimming a bunch of poor suckers. That bum would steal the pennies off a dead man's eye!"

"Leslie, I forbid you to speak this way about your stepfather. If he ever heard of this he'd beat you within an inch of your life."

"Oh, he would? Let him try. I guess I can handle myself against a tub of fat like him. . . . Tell him what I said. I'm not afraid of him—*anymore.*" (The beatings he had received reminded him that he had yet to establish his supremacy.)

His mother became conciliatory. She recognized his father's sullen obduracy, the futility of combating him with threats.

"Why have you become so bitter against your own people?" she asked. "Haven't I brought you up to be a good Jew? Have I ever said anything against the Christians like you're talking now about your father . . . your stepfather, I mean?"

"You bring me up like a Jew and you two masquerade as Christians—because it's better for your business. Is that being a good Jew? Besides, I'm only half a Jew, and from now on I disown that half. It's only a religion anyway and I can choose what I like to believe in. . . . I don't believe in anything—*but I won't be a Jew!* Nobody takes me for one, so why should I pretend to be what I don't want to be? I'm not taking your religion away from you, Mom, but I want to be free to lead my own life, to think as I please, and believe what I please. I've been doing a lot of reading . . . *and thinking*"—an afterthought— "since you left. My ideas are changed."

"I'm sorry that they haven't improved, Leslie," said his mother sadly. She had been intending to speak to him about the strange books she had noticed in his possession. She feared they were corrupting him.

"Who has been giving you these books?" she asked. She knew they were not of his own choice.

"Moloch," he answered.

"Moloch? who is that?"

"My boss."

"Don't you say *Mister* Moloch?"

Leslie smiled disdainfully. "It ain't necessary. I'm his friend. We pal around together."

"I should like to meet this man. What can he find so interesting in a boy like you? You're hardly out of your short pants.
You're not a man yet." Leslie glowered at her. "Oh! I know you
think you are."

Leslie ignored the thrust and swept on enthusiastically about
his employer. "That's just it, Mom. He doesn't treat me like a
boy. He trusts me and lets me into his confidences. Why, I know
all about him. When I'm with him I feel as if I were a man, too,
just like him. He's my idea of a real guy."

"What a way to speak about your boss. How old is he?"

"Aw, I don't know. He must be thirty or forty. He's married
and has a kid . . . a pretty little girl, and *bright*—you ought to
hear her speak. He treats her great. Gee, if I had a kid that's the
way I'd like to bring it up. You never see him get angry with her
or scold her. He talks so sensibly to her . . . that's the way he is,
Mom. He treats every one the same. He's a prince!"

Several times during the course of this panegyric his mother
restrained her emotions. She wanted to laugh, at first—his ideas
were so diffuse—and then, impressed by his sincerity and earnestness, the passion of his avowals, a new feeling surged up in
her and put a catch in her throat. Was she being dispossessed so
soon? She had hardly come to know her boy and he was being
snatched away. Already the worship which she had always
counted on, which warmed her and sustained her in her secret
trials, had been transferred to this being who was strange to her
and whom she feared instinctively. The influence of this man
whom she had never met, who in the space of a few months had
taken complete possession of her boy, filled her with trepidation.

"Bring him here," she said quietly, betraying no sign of her
disquietude. "I want to talk to him. I want to see what he has to
say about you."

"I'll bring him tonight, Mom. He wants to meet you, too. I
didn't tell him anything about—" he refused to sully his lips with
the name—"about *him*. I'll bring Marcelle along, too, that's his
. . . she's his secretary. You'll like her. I'd take her myself if
Moloch wasn't . . . ." He stopped short, aware that he had said too
much.

"So that's the kind of man he is? Runs about with his secretary—and takes you along to chaperon the party? I see now. Oh,
I thought there was something like that. And what does his wife
say to this, or doesn't he tell her about his secretary?"

Leslie reddened to the ears and stammered: "He isn't in love
with his wife anymore. They never did get along. Anyway, she
doesn't understand him. You've got to see him, Mom. I can't
explain it to you. He isn't what you think. Wait till you hear him
talk . . . I know you'll believe in him."

"So that's it! You can't excuse him yourself, but you know
that *he* can convince me. He's a smooth talker, eh? If he tells you
white is black that's the end of it. You believe him. Oh, you poor
boy, you can't see any further than the end of your nose. You
don't want to believe in your religion any more; it isn't good
enough for you. But you fall down on your knees and worship
this profligate who lends you his crazy books, who lets you share
his harlot. . . ." She forgot herself completely. A spate of ugly
epithets slid from her tongue. Having nothing concrete to fasten
on she drowned her hatred (there was no longer any disguising
it) in a flood of calumny.

Leslie grew white with rage. He couldn't believe his ears. His
own mother talking this way, hurling these dastardly insults at
Moloch. It was idiotic. It amazed him. Such fury! Such violence!
Why? Why? What was Moloch to her? She didn't know a thing
about him, except for the careless remark he had dropped. At
that, he hadn't said what was on his tongue. He remembered now
distinctly—he had checked himself in the nick of time. Supposing
she had struck on the truth? How could she be sure? People
ought to have proofs before they spoke so hastily.

His mother ceased raving. Her impetuosity frightened her, as
though she had listened to the speech of some lunatic. She was
ashamed, too, but her pride stifled any admission of it. Nevertheless she was adamant.

"I won't have him here, Leslie," she said, with muffled anger.
"Don't you dare to bring him without my permission."

He grew insolent. "I wouldn't think of bringing him here after
this explosion. Do you think I'd stand by and see him insulted?

Not much. If you want to know something, I'm clearing out. Talk about your harlots and adulterers—do you think I's blind to Aunt Sophie's . . . er . . . er . . ." He didn't know just how to describe his aunt's behavior in a pithy term.

His mother recoiled. "My God," she thought, "what have they done to my son? Where has his innocence fled?" She entreated him to stay, to give her a chance to show her affection. Oh, he needn't worry about his stepfather. She'd keep him in his place. She'd do everything for him to make him happy, but he must not go away. "My arms are aching for you," she cried. "You've been away from me so long. I should never have let you go. Oh, Leslie, Leslie, forgive me. I did not mean to hurt you. Bring Mr. Moloch here. You will see, I shan't say anything to offend him. We will be good friends. Do ask him, Leslie, do. Only don't leave me." She began to sob and weep bitterly.

He was affected. "Come, Mom," he whispered, "don't carry on like this. I won't decide anything today, but I can't go on living with that sl—" The word almost slipped out of his mouth. He had started to say "slut," but he felt his mother shiver and restrained himself. "You know what Aunt Sophie's like," he added. His mother knew too well what he meant. . . .

"Foul whore!" she cursed under her breath as Leslie turned to wipe his eyes.

At the close of business that day Leslie suggested to Marcelle and Moloch that they take dinner with him at his aunt's house. To clinch their assent he added that there was a barrel of sacramental wine in the cellar.

Leslie's determination to "clear out" was grounded in the belief that Moloch would take him in. He avoided mentioning this idea to his mother partly from a desire to pour oil on the troubled waters and partly because there was a doubt in his mind that Moloch would acquiesce. Moloch had been insisting right along that Leslie go to live with his parents.

Leslie seized this occasion to open a serious discussion with Moloch. He would have preferred to talk to him alone but he had a fear that Moloch would not consider it important enough; the invitation was therefore extended to Marcelle also. They thought it a capital idea—Moloch because he was strapped, and Marcelle because she was weary of defraying the expenses.

"What are you going to do about Blanche?" Marcelle inquired.

"You say that with such solicitude!" Moloch sneered. "One would think we had a real problem to contend with. Call her up, Leslie, and . . . put a little color into it this time. Make it plausible."

Marcelle objected to this strenuously.

"I'd rather speak to her myself than listen to these abominable lies. Can't you be kind to her, at least?

They wrangled for a few minutes, and then Moloch turned to Leslie again.

"Go ahead, do as I say. What's the use of starting something new? It's too late in the day to be developing a conscience."

Leslie obeyed, but as he hung up the receiver he said gravely: "That's the last time. I'm through with that dirty business. Why don't you get a divorce?"

Moloch threw him a withering glance.

"Oho! Moralizing now? The next thing we know, little Leslie will be joining the church . . . or will it be the synagogue, Leslie?"

The boy was stung in a tender spot. He glared savagely.

"Go easy," murmured Marcelle. "You've hurt him enough today."

Moloch ignored her. "You're not ashamed of your Jewish blood, are you, Leslie? I wouldn't be. That's where you get your originality . . . and your moral promptings. Don't think that for a minute that you're a hundred percent rotten. Give the Jewish blood a chance . . . there's where your salvation lies."

Leslie hung his head and flushed crimson. He detested Moloch now with his whole heart. No one could bruise his so—not even his stepfather. He preferred a beating to this vindicative tongue-lashing.

In a few minutes, however, his good humor was restored. He had an opportunity to observe Marcelle wincing under the scourge of Moloch's retorts. "God," he said to himself, "I wish I could say things as cruel as that . . . and not mean it."

* * *

It was one of those sticky, sultry nights when the heat seems to coil about the body like a woolen fog. Up in Leslie's flat the heat was oppressive. The walls looked moldy and the upholstery had a mildewed appearance. Moloch amused himself, as Marcelle scraped a meal together, by running through the family album. He thought Aunt Sophie looked like a cream puff. "What is she," he asked, "a Lapp or a Croat?" Leslie screwed up his face in the way one does when he recognizes a bad odor. "What does she do on the stage?" asked Moloch. "Her legs are fat and adulterous." Leslie tried to explain. He had often asked himself the same question.

"She missed her calling," said Moloch. "She should have been a matron in a comfort station."

He snooped about, examining objects that interested him as if he were in the Egyptian wing of the Metropolitan Museum.

Leslie uncorked a demijohn and together they sampled the sacramental wine. A mood of relaxation followed. Moloch permitted himself a few pleasantries.

"What a glorious life—for the priest; porterhouse steaks, Havana cigars, a short trip now and then to the bawdy house or the convent, an earful of smut behind the curtain . . . no wonder they look sleek and contented. They always remind me of the hindquarter of a calf. . . ." He downed another tumblerful of the sacramental wine and slipped Leslie a huge wink. . . . "Drink ye *all* of it!" Down went the wine, making a pleasant gurgling sound as it swished down his throat.

Marcelle had removed her stockings. She was still complaining about the heat. "Lower the lights," said Moloch, as they sat down to the table. "And, say, can't you give Marcelle a kimono? She's dying to slip out of her dress."

Leslie jumped to his feet, Marcelle protesting.

"Very well, then, let her stew, Leslie."

With the progress of the meal, and a few drafts of wine, Marcelle reconsidered. She wanted to be coaxed.

"But supposing your aunt returns suddenly . . . ?"

"She won't," said Leslie promptly. "And what if she did? You're not going naked." He looked to Moloch for support.

"Of course!" Moloch chimed in. "Don't be stupid, Marcelle. Make yourself comfortable." (He was in his suspenders.) "Here, have another glass of wine."

"All right, then," she assented timidly. "Where can I undress?"

Leslie showed her to the bathroom and handed her a piece of silk.

Marcelle loitered in the bathroom listening to the droning of Moloch's voice. Moloch had stumbled into a nest of reminiscences.

Leslie wondered when he would get the opportunity to speak to him privately.

"Another time I remember a peculiar thing happening to me," Moloch was saying. "It was a night similar to this . . . frightfully close. I was at the beach with a girl—I don't remember how or where I picked her up. We were buried in the shadow of a giant Ferris wheel. There was a peculiar fascination about—the way it swished slowly and majestically through the suffocating blanket of humidity. An insane desire took hold of me to rip off my clothes and plunge into the surf. I mean this seriously. It wasn't just an idea that you toy with and dismiss after you've had your fill of it. This was an obsession that I had to fight against with all my strength. Each time I got to the point of jumping up and carrying out this impulse one of the big carriages on the Ferris wheel would come sliding out toward the rim as though to make a nose dive into the sea. You could hear the occupants gasp and shriek when it started on its terrific lunge into space. I suppose my mind was diverted, for an instant, each time this happened by the notion of what would take place should these merrymakers suddenly be hurled to death by that twisted piece of steel. And that led me to thinking about God. No profound thoughts, mind you . . . just the ordinary lazy speculations about a frowning giant, with long whiskers, floating on his throne, over a heap of beautiful clouds. I thought to myself—*old man,* if you actually do exist, there is nothing I envy you except, perhaps, your memories. In three seconds, no doubt I went through five hundred pages of history. For an endless time I lay there, hypnotized by the incessant purring of this enormous, senseless contraption. The young lady in my arms was slightly peeved because I didn't ask her to do things which I knew she would refuse. And then— golly, it must have been right on top of us!—an accordion suddenly broke loose. It had just the effect you might expect if you suddenly saw a comet swing out of its orbit—and you had nowhere to run."

The narrative was interrupted by Leslie, who had succumbed to an inexplicable seizure of hysterics. Tears rolled down his cheeks; he held his sides to prevent them from bursting under the violent paroxysms of mirth.

"What's wrong, kid?" said Moloch. He failed to perceive anything explosively comic in his anecdote. . . . "I hadn't finished telling . . ."

"Don't! Wait a second," sputtered Leslie. "Don't go on just yet."

Marcelle returned and put out the lights; then she went over to Moloch and sat in his lap. In the sudden gloom the latter accidentally slipped his arm through the loose sleeve of her kimono. Her flesh was soft night and powder smooth. She made no attempt to change her position. Gently and quite casually he opened her kimono and clasped his hands about her dimpled form. She offered no more resistance to his embrace than a violet crushed between the leaves of the *Heptameron*. Their lips met and matched the silence of the dark. In a few seconds Marcelle straightened up taut and commenced talking in a rapid nervous staccato.

It was so very black in the room the instant after the lights went out that Leslie was not sure of his impressions. Nevertheless, he felt uneasy, strangely excited, as if the ether had communicated the intoxication of this silent union.

Marcelle begged Moloch to continue his tale. . . . "Why did you laugh so, Leslie?"

"That accordion!" he gasped. "Don't let him go on . . . please. I can't stand it!"

They waited again for him to subside.

"I swear he never heard an accordion," Leslie ripped out after a valiant struggle to control himself. "He got that out of a book, or else he made it up. I swear it never happened. *Not an accordion!* Never, never!" He threatened to erupt again.

"Oh, damn the accordion!" said Moloch. "Let's have some canned music."

Marcelle scrambled to her feet. "Let me look, will you, Leslie?"

Leslie lit a match while she knelt down to go over the records. As he did so, he peered defiantly through the partly opened kimono at her violet-tinted breasts. His hands trembled so that he dropped the match. It flickered out quickly and he was obliged to fumble for another, availing himself meanwhile of the sudden blackness to rub against her body. The touch of her thigh made him glow all over. He quivered with premeditated ecstasies.

"Just one dance," he whispered stealthily.

Marcelle rose instantly and left his side. She too trembled. In the same manner the islands of the Pacific, just before they slip from under the light of the sun, seem to glow with a dying zeal and tremble under the avalanche of extinction.

The floor space in which Marcelle and Moloch simulated the execution of the dance was an irregular clearing, a rather circuitous lane studded with chairs and other objects against which they bumped cautiously, and with the speed of snails.

Leslie flung himself on a divan. He was absorbed in following the tantalizing movements of these two. With effort he could distinguish vaguely their welded forms, but he chose instead to lie back with eyes closed and listen to their heavy, irregular breathing, or the awkward scraping of their feet, drugged with desire. At times he had a feeling that they were not moving at all. Then the breathing grew heavier; the very atmosphere of the room became vitalized with their shuddering transports. He felt completely overpowered.

The touch of Marcelle's thigh stuck to him. It phosphorized his senses. How had it affected her, he wondered; and immediately after he had formulated the thought came regret that he had taken so little advantage of his opportunity. It was useless to believe that she would give him a chance. If she did, it would be from pity. He didn't want any of her god-damned sympathy. But wait . . . just let her get too gay, and then see. She'd be coming to him yet, with a tale of woe . . . asking his sweet advice. He'd give it to her—and something more! Christ, couldn't she see what Moloch was after? It sickened him to see what an idol she made of her Dion. Walking into a trap with her eyes shut—that's all she was doing. . . . He wished Moloch had chosen another night, another place, to perpetrate his seduction. That's what it was. Not a damned thing else! He could actually feel that something was going to happen. It was in the air.

They were perspiring freely, Moloch and Marcelle.

"Anything cool to drink around here?" asked Moloch.

"Yeah . . . water!" Leslie answered.

"You're a hell of a host."

"Run out and get something. It's my treat." It was Marcelle who said this. She dashed to the bathroom to get her purse.

Leslie detected the gleam of two slim white legs as she swished hurriedly past him. He was sorely tempted to reach out and grab her . . . grab her anywhere. It made him sore, the two of them coming here and using the place as if it were a house of assignation. It wouldn't be so bad if they showed some regard for his feelings, but—Christ, he was no better than a louse.

He took the money she offered unceremoniously and stuffed it in his pocket.

"How long do you want me to stay?" he said bitterly.

"Don't be smart!" Marcelle came back at him like a spitfire. "You come right back . . . I'm dying of thirst."

"Are you sure you're merely thirsty?" he fired as he slammed the door.

"What a dirty little cad!" Marcelle felt her way to the armchair where Moloch was sitting, quietly puffing at a cigarette. He flung the butt on the floor and stamped on it. Then he seized her and carried her over to the divan.

"Please don't let him find us here," she murmured. "He's such a nasty little devil."

His lips, glued against the marble of her bosom, responded with meaningless yum-yums. It was apparent that he cared little whether Leslie found them in this position or in the morgue. His feelings were comparable to those of a husband who sees his wife departing up the gangplank, and by a violation of natural law also sees himself on the terrace of the golf club, sipping a gin rickey.

A parched zephyr invaded the stifling chamber. The tang of sea air, faint but unmistakable, permeated Marcelle's disheveled hair. . . .

To be spiteful, Leslie returned promptly. He knew the location of their bodies but it was impossible, coming in from the brilliant light of the street, to unravel the twisted skein of flesh.

"What would you do if you two had to get out of here suddenly?" The tone of Leslie's voice was a rich mixture of malevolence and glee.

"Why, I guess we'd go to the park," said Moloch indifferently.

"What's ailing you?" said Marcelle, disengaging herself. "You know, Leslie, you're nothing but a filthy little brat! . . . If we get on your nerves, why don't you go downstairs and pick up someone. Get it out of your system! Don't be mooning all night . . . and plaguing us to death. We know you're suffering from adolescence."

"You might try writing to Beatrice Fairfax," said Moloch, his voice velvety smooth.

Marcelle tittered. "Yes, that's a bright idea, Leslie."

"Go to hell—the two of you!"

"What—on a hot night like this?" Moloch proceeded calmly to open the bottles. "Get a corkscrew, will you, Leslie?"

"Is there anything else you'd like?" He suggested an article of convenience usually associated with bedrooms.

"Now, Leslie! Don't get nasty! You're losing your poise. Remember what I told you on another occasion. This is a free country. If you don't like it here, you can get out and try some other place."

"Oh, have some regard for his feelings," Marcelle pleaded. "We shouldn't expect too much of him. He's just a child."

At this Leslie was in a fair way to burst.

"A lot of control you people display!" he blurted resentfully.

"I can turn you out, if I want, do you know it?"

"The perfect host!" cried Moloch. "Have a drink, kid, it'll cool you off. When you dance with Marcelle you'll need a barrel of poise. Try to control yourself. . . ."

Marcelle spoke up quickly. "No, thanks. No more dancing tonight for me. It's too beastly hot."

"All right, then. Let's finish this stuff and take a stroll in the park."

"I hope you two enjoyed yourselves," Leslie moaned.

"Of course we did, kid. Of course, we did. . . . Er, next time, make it sour wine. I can't go this sweet stuff!"

"You managed to get away with a few bottles, I notice."

"Out of politeness, kid . . . sheer politeness."

"Well, next time don't be so damned polite." He turned and commenced to stalk out of the room. "I wish to hell I'd never met you two," he flung at them over his shoulder.

"What a tantrum!" exclaimed Marcelle.

"Leslie! How about a nice little carousel ride?"

No answer.

The heat was less intolerable down in the street. Marcelle hung on Moloch's arm. They walked in silence for a few blocks.

"Must we go through the park?" Marcelle asked suddenly.

"No-o-o-h . . . it's a shortcut, that's all."

"I'd rather talk to you, Dion."

"Can't we talk in the park?" He wondered what disturbed her now.

She was hesitant. He knew very well what she meant—why did he pretend? She was disgusted with herself sometimes. The park seemed as indecent as a menagerie.

She struggled to screen the nakedness of her thoughts. "It's just this, Dion—we hardly ever seem to talk anymore. You used to tell me so many things; you don't confide in me anymore. You never have time to say anything to me . . . oh, you know what

I'm talking about. . . . You're not a good comrade, that's what I mean."

"Come, come!" he protested. "You know that's not true. Heavens! All day long, in the office, I look at you and I'm aching to walk over and throw my arms around you. We seldom have a chance to be alone anymore."

This was not precisely the passionate language she had expected to awaken. It seemed to her that he was growing deucedly prosaic.

They came upon a deserted bench.

"Sit down," he urged. "You're in no hurry to get home, are you?"

"Only a few minutes, Dion. You've got to get to work on time tomorrow."

"Don't remind me of tomorrow," he muttered, and drew her familiarly to him.

"Don't . . . please, *not here,*" she implored. She tried to wrestle free, but he held her in a vise.

"Marcelle, you're driving me crazy, do you know it?" He kept kissing her lips and neck and shoulders. "Why not—here? God, you're ravishing!"

When they floated up from the bottom of the sea they found an equally preoccupied couple parked alongside of them.

"Let's go," said Marcelle. "We can find another bench."

They sauntered off in silence. Instinctively they left the path and cut through the heavy grass. Moloch walked with head down, burrowing into seedy abstractions.

"Why don't you say something to me?" she asked, after a space.

"I can't," he answered hoarsely.

They stopped dead (as if someone had given a signal) and faced each other. Her bosom heaved expectantly. . . .

"My God, Dion! Can't you behave?"

He pushed her roughly against a thick oak.

"You're hurting me . . . stop it. Listen to me—you're crushing me."

"Be quiet," he muttered fiercely. "I'm *not* hurting you."

He leaned against her insolently, savagely. With furious hands he clutched her convulsively. . . . She was gasping.

"You *must* stop it!" She lowered her voice until it resembled a heart throb. . . . *"I'm afraid, Dion. . . ."*

"Oh, come on, then." He sounded sullen, vengeful. She felt as though he was dragging her along by the scalp.

"You'll get us into trouble," she said softly.

"I don't give a damn!"

"But, listen, dear . . . supposing we were caught here? What would Blanche do?"

"That's right—think of all the ugly things."

"I can't help it. You remember the last time. Do you want one of those filthy perverts to catch us again?"

The thought of that shameful episode made him wince.

"Oh, I guess you're right, Marcelle. . . . I lose my head— sometimes." He looked about him helplessly. . . . "God, is there nowhere we can go?"

They walked on again, each striving to find the solution to this riddle, neither coming to any conclusion.

Finally, with the timidity of a squirrel burying its treasure of nuts, Marcelle hid her bosom in the prism of shadow cast by the upholstered facade of the museum.

So far she had remained inviolate. . . .

Like a butterfly in the palpitant tomb of its chrysalis, Marcelle fluttered and yearned with nubile wings for the miracle of the advent of dawn. In the surrender of a caress she looked for the swoon which would bring about her deliverance.

The shroud which enveloped her struggling pinions had the rigidity of a cathedral's vaulted ribs. . . . She lost herself in the ecstasy of brushing against the delicate-tinted panes now suffused with the faint flush of dawn. The voice of her lover was drowned in the tumultuous peals of shattering chords. His lips were the edges of raw wounds which shrieked unspeakable horrors, whose agonizings mingled with the suffocating smolder of caromed organ notes. . . . At that moment when, galvanized by gusts of devastating energy, her delirious ardor seemed about to burst the taut filaments of her being and engulf her in a chaos of deliquescence, a thundering diapason sounded, the barrel vault was riven, and the temple of her spirit laved in a rutilant flood of light. Her wings, which were meant for flying, proved incapable of such sustained effort. Tremors, like the mournful echoes of a flute, capered over the moistened silk of her wings. The languor of ten thousand moody nocturnes invaded the hollows of her loins and draped her crumpled form in quivering curves.

The sacrifice of which Marcelle had dreamed—inflamed by virginal fantasies—had been consummated under the spell of that lunar deity, the goddess Astarte. Instead of a hundred bulls, the fabled hecatomb of antiquity, the offering had been herself, "her plowed divinity." Her silhouette, fugitive and palpitant, had wandered in the course of the ceremony, from the tenebrous depths of the lawn, in which it was hidden, to the flake-white exterior of the museum.

In the violent emergence of reality, she caught a vision of her new self: a shuddering, tripled horror surmounting a granite plinth. Touched with moon madness she gazed with frozen fear to behold the dismal goddess Hecate, who it is said guards the crossways of life—whose worship it is also said is associated with the shades of the dead, with ghosts, and with sorcery. . . . From her feet issued serpents; serpents were entwined in her hair. And in her hand she bore a lighted torch.

THE ALARM WENT OFF PROMPTLY AT SEVEN-THIRTY.
Moloch turned over and pretended not to hear. Blanche went through the usual morning's efforts to rouse him but it was useless. He piled the covers over his head and rolled up like a ball.

"Are you going to take a day off again?"

Warily he stuck his head out of the covers. "Call up and say I'm ill. I can't go to work today. . . . I'm all in. Let me sleep another two hours—that's all."

Blanche detested these lies. He was always forcing her to make excuses for him. Rather than get up and telephone, he'd sacrifice his job. . . .

As soon as he learned that she had phoned he was a different being. In a jiffy the blankets came off. Out of bed he sprang, frisking about in his nightgown, making grotesque faces at her, singing snatches of operatic aires. . . . *Sing?* He had lungs of leather, now that a holiday was decreed.

"How about some bacon and eggs, Blanche?" he inquired cheerfully. He smacked his lips. They were rather thick lips, excellent for the purpose. "I can smell the victuals frying in the pan. . . . And get a big loaf of Jewish bread—corn bread—a couple of pounds. Don't come back with white bread or I'll slit your parsimonious throat." He made a queer guttural sound in his throat. He had acquired the knack from long practice; it derived from "burlesque." At the same time he drew his hand slowly across his throat. "From ear to ear," he mimicked, supernally pleased with his droll behavior.

Blanche was anything but delighted over this unexpected holiday. She realized sadly how long it would take him to find another job. Every time he took a day off she went through tortures for fear that he would be seen by someone and reported to the officials.

"Am I to buy theater tickets while I'm out, or are you going off somewhere by yourself, as usual?"

"Anything *you* like, honey."

As she put her hand on the doorknob, to go, he added hastily: "No, don't let's go to a vaudeville show today. I'm fed up on vaudeville. . . . Perhaps I'll stay home and do some writing."

"Remember that you have a job," she threw out. "Don't go starting a book again." She slammed the door to emphasize her malice.

Don't start a book, eh? Why not? That was the very thing he did want to do. Why couldn't she leave him alone to do as he pleased? He might finish one if she were a little more tolerant, a little more interested in what he was doing. . . . Always worried about "the job." Christ, would she ever let up on that subject? She'd have him dig ditches rather than see him idle for two weeks. For her part, he could tackle anything—so long as the rent was paid and she had the price of another hat in her pocket. He asked himself, what did she do with the money she earned giving piano lessons? He never saw any of it. She expected him to get along on five bucks a week; had it all figured out; so much for carfare, so much for lunch, so much for tobacco, etc., etc. How about a good cigar once in a while, or a burlesque show, or a trip to Luna Park? Not that he gave a damn much, but it was good to put your hand in your pocket once in a while and feel a couple of bills there. He was sick of borrowing lunch money every day, or getting Dave to take him to a show. . . . How many books did they buy in a year; how many times did they go to a concert, or take in a lecture? Pfooh! No wonder a man ran around nights with other women. He needed recreation. That was it . . . recreation.

They ate breakfast in customary silence, dividing the newspaper between them. He started to warble once, but she made such a wry face the words died in his throat.

"I'm going for a short walk first," he announced, after he had finished his second cup of coffee.

"For inspiration, I suppose?"

"No, to pick up a Jane. That's what you wanted me to say, wasn't it?"

"Don't hurry on my account. I won't be here when you get back. I wouldn't think of interfering with your . . . er, writing."

She gave him a cadaverous smile and started to collect the dishes and pile them in the sink where they would remain until the next meal.

"The hell with you," he thought. "For my part, you can go and drown yourself."

She went into the next room and began to pound away on the fourteenth rhapsody of Liszt. "Go ahead, pound away," he mumbled to himself. "Break the damned instrument."

If anything could drive him crazy, it was Liszt. "That Wurlitzer composer! That charlatan with lecherous vigor!" That's what came of studying music in a convent . . . *Her Sister Dorothea!* Another George Sand. . . . What wouldn't he give to shove a big cigar in her mouth and give her a sound slap on the tenderloin! A pack of women lovers—all of them. Someone ought to call in the Society for the Suppression of Vice!

He donned a sweater and cap and started down the street. There was a snap in the air. Things looked bright and inviting.

A flock of sparrows flew in and out of the church belfry across the street. It was a somber, stately street they lived on. Houses of worship on every block. So utterly respectable, their neighbors! Wouldn't think of slipping outdoors without a necktie. . . . Rows and rows of brownstone houses, with massive doors and iron-barred windows. Every few doors a physician—with good old American names. "Dr. Edward Mitchell Swan": five dollars a visit—homeopath, pince-nez, "How is Granny?" . . . The neighborhood had a quieting effect, nevertheless. His mind commenced to show signs of working peacefully. He began to reminisce.

Fine! Perhaps he really would go back, after a while—not end up in a burlesque hall. He'd show her he meant business. . . . If only he could get her out of his mind! She loomed up on his cerebral frontiers like some nasty carrion bird. "My vulture!" he thought, and smiled a feeble smile.

He walked along thus, pondering on queer incidents in his past, stopping now and then to inspect an interesting facade, thinking about the women he had failed to make, and wondering all the time, in the back of his head, just what he would sit down to write about. That was the pity of it . . . so much hectic gadding about, so many friends who seemed created for the sole purpose of pestering him to death. All manner of useless inroads on his precious time. Nothing accomplished.

The soliloquies he conducted in the street, or in the subway, or in bed nights, when his mind raced like a millstream—he could capture none of these when he sat down before a blank sheet of paper. What extraordinary confabulations he held with himself! "Get it down, get it down!" he repeated aloud, clenching his fist and waving it mechanically. . . .

For some time he had been walking along in this abstract muddle but partially aware of his environment. Suddenly it came to him that he was following a familiar route. He was heading toward the old neighborhood, where he had spent his youth. The prospect delighted him. It happened to him a number of times, when he let himself go, that he found his steps directed toward that dear old neighborhood with its quaint tumbledown shanties, its gas tanks, its ferry slips, and a squalid, teeming ghetto life.

He emerged from a maze of crooked, woebegone streets onto the broad highway of Bedford Avenue, which smiled in its melancholy senescence like a snaggle-toothed courtesan. What was it about Bedford Avenue that tickled him so? Not the upper reaches, mind you, where the dour bourgeoisie dwelt in smug, stiff apartment houses, where they went for an airing of a Sunday afternoon in swallowtails and plug hats. (Yes, they still wore plug hats on Bedford Avenue—but only on Sunday afternoons, after a swill-fest and a turn in the Men's Bible Class.) . . . No, that wasn't the part he cared about. Down near the fountain, where the avenue first broadens out and begins to take on dignity—that was the section.

But what in the name of Lucifer were they doing to his Bedford Avenue? Each time he went back to it, it got worse. It was like a venerable patriarch who has but one frock coat in his wardrobe which he brushes carefully before going out for a walk. And despite his care, now and then a button falls off, or the elbows shine, or it begins to fray at the cuff. But the lines remain. Nothing can alter that. You can see it came from a good shop, that it's substantial. You don't have to look at the label to make the discovery. The way it hangs—*that tells the story!*

It was something like that with Bedford Avenue. . . . The "sheenies" could come, stick a funny little star on the steeple top, and christen the church a synagogue. They could take an old brownstone front, and with renovations make it into a cozy little fur shop, or a Parisian millinery store . . . any damned thing you want! But the form was there; the lines remained. Nobody could take that away. . . . It was idle for anyone to deny it: New York belonged to the Jews. Everywhere you went, there were Kosher signs, garish mansions for banquets and weddings, delicatessen shops with pastrami, sturgeon, "lox," smelly cheeses and wursts hanging in the window . . . and coleslaw dressed with a vomit. In course of time comes the dentist, and puts a little white sign in his window: "Painless Dentistry." He lies. There was only one such benefactor in Brooklyn: "Painless Parker." . . . And in the wake of the dentist comes the chiropractor, the masseur, and the music teacher—bleating like stuck pigs for a crumb of business. Whatever, whoever it was, it made no difference. They were all making a living, advertising themselves, getting pupils or patients, selling their nostrums and their indigestible comestibles.

Why did he detest them so, these long-suffering and (as every one admits) perfectly harmless people? They didn't damage the country, did they, with their merchant ideas and their bogus intellectual life? No, not that exactly, but—to put it succinctly, *"they smelled bad."* One doesn't like to harp on distasteful subjects, but that was precisely the case: they smelled bad! They were like the disgusting creatures Virgil mentions: they soiled everything. Where they were, life was coarsened, cheapened, vulgarized. Sacred or profane: a human life, a discarded vest, a woman's virtue—everything was smeared with a price-mark. . . . It wasn't only Bedford Avenue, the entire metropolis was worm-eaten.

If you pressed them hard enough they admitted it themselves, these wandering ones. Try it sometime. Get them in a corner. Just rub their noses in the dirt, and then ask them for a little plain talk. "Out with it, blatherskites! Own up, shitepokes! Who's responsible for this mess?" Watch them whine and whimper, offer flimsy excuses: Russia, the pale, pogrom-makers, the whole category of bromidic absurdities. Press them a little further. . . . "Who's asking you now to use dirty handkerchiefs? Is there any law against clean linen in this country? Why do you insist on throwing your refuse into the street? Haven't we given you garbage cans . . . don't we collect your dirt for you every day?" . . . Oh, they'll give you an answer to that, too. Argue themselves black in the face. In the end, they'll admit it: *"they love dirt!"* It's just as natural for them to be filthy as it is for the Germans to be tidy, for the Irish to be poor, and the Catholics ignorant. "It must be in the blood," he told himself. The poor, lousy, mangy devils! Just the same, he could never get used to it. If he could only bawl them out publicly, or clout their fat behinds with a barrel stave! Whew!

At the fountain he loafed awhile, enjoying the fine tingle of spray, musing, smiling quietly as some funny little incident out of his boyhood leaped to mind. He recaptured an image of himself walking along the street with Dr. Carmichael on his arm. They were going to the Clymer Police Station to notify the sergeant that his wheel had been stolen. What a stinker Carmichael was! Was there a more cantankerous principal in all Brooklyn? Always holding out for decorum, the veriest stickler for propriety. Pretending to be outraged when he found them playing tag in the toilet. Never gave one a chance to explain. But what fun it was, slamming those toilet doors, climbing over the partitions, turning all the spigots on. . . . Perhaps they did wreck the joint, but what of it? Boys will be boys. And what did it matter, in the long run, if a few toilet seats were broken? Misdirected energy, that's all. . . . But you couldn't tell Carmichael that. The old crab didn't have a friend in the world, unless it was his battered skullcap. Fancy an old fusspot like that walking through the cold corridors. A pious peacock, with his nose in the air. Garbed in the same old pinhead suit . . . a Presbyterian monitor with a paunch, and chronic catarrh. They used to say he was "nuts" on the Latin teacher, that he got her to stay after hours and help him with his office work. Office work, raspberries! Maybe that's why he used to visit the Latin class so often, letting on that he did so in order to keep his hand in; asking foolish questions about Julius Caesar, the Lupercalia, and Vercingetorix. And that simpering way he had of droning his Latin. Trying to make us believe he was cultivating our ears so that we might appreciate Cicero's noble cadences. . . . Worse than a priest at it! Then making us translate at sight, saying he would try it himself, too, when all the time the old geezer knew the book backwards. A sly old fox he was, keeping one eye on the nefarious practices of Catiline and the other eye on her nibs, perched on the high stool with a brilliantine smile, applauding him whenever he said something clever— something *she* called clever, for no one else could detect his cleverness! (Unless one could call it clever to expatiate for a whole period on the pooh-pooh theory of language.)

Well, the Jewies settled his hash. . . .

"Wouldn't you boys like to do some extra reading so as to become more familiar with your Virgil?"

Sammy Mankowitz speaks up instanter. "I can't. I gotta help muh fader in der store."

"But wouldn't you like to pass with honor, Master Mankowitz?"

"Naw . . . I jes wanna pass. I'm goin' in fer dentistry soon as I'm tru."

"How about you and you," he asks, feeling out the Gentiles in the class.

"Me eyes are weak." . . . "I'm taking music lessons." A bagful of excuses. Not a damned soul interested in the rites of the Lupercal, or the *Lives* of Plutarch. He shakes his head pathetically. "It's a different generation, Miss Dillon." That's all he says, and closes the book. As Carmichael closes the door behind him Izzy Lefkowitz blows a snotter.

"Is that nice?" tweets Miss Dillon. "I want the boy who made that horrid noise to come right up here."

Silence.

"I'll give the young gentleman who was guilty of such misbehavior just three minutes to stand up and offer me his apology."

More silence.

"May I leave the room, Miss Dillon?"

"Yes, Mr. Wright. I'm certain it wasn't *you.*"

She taps the desk impatiently with her ruler, hoping that the culprit will be man enough to announce himself and spare her the injustice of punishing the others along with him. She waits a few more minutes, then looks at her watch. "Very well, we'll all stay after hours and conjugate irregular verbs. We'll do that for the rest of the week."

Master Lefkowitz murmurs under his breath: "You big hunk of cheese!"

"What are you mumbling so for?" she demands fiercely, almost certain that he was the culprit.

He whines piteously: "I gotta help me fader."

Moloch laughed softly as he reflected on Izzy's trickery. Izzy

was true to form: anarchic, and without honor. When they fell
into a trap the herd instinct asserted itself. They fled then into the
arms of Karl Marx, Bakunin, Kropotkin, and hid their long
noses in the sands of Anti-Semitism. Thenceforth, until the sweat
glands have exuded the last drop of soul-quaking panic, they
espouse with the full vigor of their stribilious temperament the
philosophy of work. This lasts until the philosophy is annihilated
by discussion.

But aren't they intellectual, you say. To be sure. They have a
dry intelligence which condones deceit, which elevates cheating
to the point of supreme virtue. Fool! That's what they have
intellects for. It takes a stupid goy to recite his paternosters, to
try for a hundred percent when sixty is all that is required to pass.
. . . But they produce some great men, some rare geniuses, do
they not? Admitted—but why the soft pedal when it comes to
talking about imbeciles, cretins, hydrocephalics, crooks and
thugs, cadets and whoremongers? . . . Every great scientist, every
great author, every great leader of the world has been a Jew—
sometime or other!

Meek and humble, you think? Because you see them plodding
along on Canal Street, or East Broadway, with their heads in
their beards? Not a bit of it! Get him alone and every Jew will
admit his superiority. The world couldn't get along without
them. They're a leaven in the body politic—it's that tosh you'll
hear. . . . Who wrote your Bible? Who gave you a Savior? Who
produces your motion pictures? Who underwrites your operas
and symphonic concerts? Who conducts them? Who writes the
world's masterpieces? Who discovered Salvarsan? Who orga-
nized the needle trades? Who gave us the eight-hour day? Who
supplies the teaching staff in the public schools? Who is at the
bottom of this infernal, ceaseless agitation for more sewers,
brighter lights, bigger theaters, gayer neckwear, shorter skirts,
sheer hose, furs in summer, municipal golf courses, public baths,
Catholics for the White House, emancipation for the Negro, and
so on and so on? Come to find out, there are only a few things
they overlooked. Lacunae: Shakespeare, Goethe, Milton—a few
odd names like that; a building here and there: St. Peter's or the

Taj Mahal; the world of premodern painting. God knows, was Rembrandt a Jew? One can't be sure anymore. Not when a Jew is elected mayor of the holy city; not when they tamper with the father of *Parsifal* and the author of *Jean Christophe*. If this nonsense continues, one may soon expect to hear Bernard Shaw announcing his Semitic lineage. . . . However, there are one or two we may be fairly certain of: the Buddha and Confucius. But this is strictly without reference to the *Jewish Encyclopedia*. . . .

A throng of children were coming down the street with books under their arms. Lunchtime. Down the avenue a little farther Moloch came upon the Amphion Theatre, the old Amphion where he had sat in the gallery with his mother to see *Way Down East*. Someone had slapped the Kosher label on the Amphion, too. Rudolph Schildkraut playing in some schrecklichkeit or other. Posters heralded the coming of a female cantor from Abyssinia, a fat tar baby with platyrrhine nose and blubber lips. "There you go. Dig 'em up out of Africa, Mesopotamia, Tibet, perhaps Alaska, too. Soon the American Indian will be robbed of his ethnologic mystery. . . ."

Was there ever a people who lived so successfully in the aura of the past? It has been proposed that they try assimilation. No go! Like a cold-water cure for excessive public itch. They don't want to be assimilated . . . much too good for that. But it was going on just the same. There was Donald Fleming and his second wife, Rhoda, a comely Jewess from the ranks of the intelligentsia. They were trying it out—this shopworn solution of the Jewish problem. That is, Donald was doing the assimilating and Rhoda was taking the punishment. When Rhoda's parents came to visit, they stood in a corner modestly, like a brace of portmanteaus, or a pair of inoffensive candlesticks. On these occasions Donald would generally find a pretext to absent himself, claiming an engagement at the Chess Club. More Jews there. One didn't mind playing chess with them. But living with them? That was another matter. . . . Not that Donald became an anti-Semite. Oh, no! On the contrary, no one defended the Jew more stoutly than Donald Fleming. He was too stout a defender.

One suspected that he was a little silly on the subject. After all, the Jew is fairly well able to defend himself. He's been doing it now for how many hundreds of years. A Gentile is always a mere tyro at the game. . . . Anyhow, when Fleming got up on his hind legs and began to brag about the Jews he filled one with irritable questions.

So it went. Five of his friends married to daughters of Israel. All getting along famously. No divorces, no plate-throwing. Why? Apparently their wives weren't mere bedmates, hash-slingers, booby prizes. They discussed things together: books, politics, the marriage question, the miracles of Saint Patrick, chess problems, the hundred and one subjects which the ordinary Gentile usually takes to the saloon or the billiard parlor. These Jewish wives showed no reluctance, no finical squeamishness in making the home usurp the attractiveness of the beer parlor. . . . Neither did they mess around the house all day and complain of backaches when the husband returned. They went out, and found jobs for themselves, took up plastic dancing, batik work, music lessons, attended free art schools. In other words, they refused to mold themselves into ornaments for hubby to stick in his nose. They lived their own lives, and they fused well. . . . Take Blanche now. More talent in her than in any of the Jewesses his friends had adopted. What did she do with her gifts? Nothing, absolutely nothing. She knew less and less each day. It never occurred to her to open a score of Stravinsky, Schoenberg, Ornstein, Honegger. They didn't interest her. She played the same things over and over—the things she had learned at the convent. Technique: perfect. Presentation: according to Hoyle. Ideas: none. Soul: less than none. He had a feeling that the piano was wasted on her; the washboard would serve better. She had all the motions: proper wrist movement, full pauses, good legato—everything but inspiration. If Sister Dorothea had played an arpeggio thus and so, she did likewise.

He remembered once buying her a ticket to hear Ornstein. She came home raving like a Shakespeare of the madhouse. Fragments of conversation recurred to memory.

"What's the matter, was he too original?"

"*Original?* I call it cheap."

"You didn't like him, then?"

"He ought to be prohibited from playing anything but his own compositions."

"Yes, and I daresay you'd get the censors after him for that."

"He's just a flashy Jew, that's all. A vaudeville kike."

"All right, call him a Jew. He doesn't mind. But he made you sit up, didn't he?"

"He made me furious, if that's what you mean."

"Well, that's something. Your playing wouldn't cause a commotion in an igloo."

Perhaps that was unkind, but it was coming to her . . . and to her god-damned Sister Dorothea!

Moloch rambled along leisurely, keeping a weather eye open for a clean lunch place, growing more and more intoxicated by his introspections as he penetrated further into the old neighborhood. Whatever became of Eddie Carney and Tom Fowler? And sober-faced Gus Mills? The names evoked recollections: a strip of cobblestoned street (the old cup-shaped cobbles that the trucks rattled over) with a narrow asphalt band along the curb for cyclists. Bob Ramsay in front on a dizzy high-wheeler and Tom Buckley right behind on a classy low "Columbia" leading the pack on their way to the Island of a bright Sunday morning. In the name of the Holy Catholic Church he'd like to know what had become of them all? Sing Sing, or the Supreme Court bench?

The past rose up warm and misty. How bright and promising the world seemed then! Nothing to do but go out in the street and play; when it grew dark, run upstairs and tackle Hans Christian Andersen. And what a wonderful day Saturday could be! In the morning bustling about, cleaning the silverware and washing the windows for mother. At one o'clock he and Stanley (it was Stasu then) standing on line outside the Novelty, waiting to nab a seat in the gallery for a dime. He could never forget those vaudeville shows, nor that big Hunky, Bob Maloney, the special officer in a Confederate uniform, who stood outside the theater and kept the gang in line. Big square shoulders he had, and cauliflower ears. To look at him, hard as nails; but when he smiled it was all

golden. And that heavy rattan he carried! When they went upstairs and waited in the gloom and stench for the orchestra to
appear it always seemed an age. There was such a pitch to the
gallery; it made him breathless at first. Suddenly Bob Maloney
would rap on the gallery rail with that wicked rattan. "Hats off!"
he'd bellow . . . wouldn't he put the fear of Christ in them!

He halted in front of a vacant store, arrested by a blatant sign
whose ugly letters proclaimed it a RESCUE MISSION. He chuckled
as he peered through the dirty windowpane and scanned the huge
letters on a banner over the altar that had been erected in the rear
of the shop:

WHOSOEVER BELIEVETH IN ME SHALL NOT DIE BUT . . .

He gazed fondly at the walls and puzzled over the familiar texts
and warnings posted conspicuously for the sinners to heed. He
seemed to be searching for one in particular. Yes, there it was,
that peaceful admonition: "Don't spit on the floor."

It all came back clearly—the night he and Matt Reardon
sailed in for a lark and almost got converted. Almost! If it hadn't
been for an attack of hysterics. He'd say to Matt furtively: "Read
that one over there." And Matt would repeat the words under his
breath, adding something vile and nasty. Then Matt: "Look at
that one over yonder," whereupon he (Moloch) would invent
some abracadabra to go with the sign. . . . Suddenly a big bass
voice booms out: "Miss Powell, you make ready a song!"
("Make ready to leave," whispers Matt, bending down and hiding his snoot in his cap.) . . . "Come now, who'll testify?" roars
the big bass voice again. The voice of a sea lion, the effrontery of
a labor leader; great big hairy paws (like a blacksmith's), a funeral parlor suit and a forehead like Herbert Spencer's. . . . "Let
us all go down after the meeting and call on our bereaved sister,
Mrs. Blatchford. Let us go down together, in a body, after this
beautiful HYMN NUMBER 73—and all take a look at that beautiful
face. Come, brothers, let us stand while we sing HYMN NUMBER
73: 'Lord, plant my feet on the higher ground.' As I was saying
a moment ago, when I saw that steeplejack climbing up there like
a huge spider, painting our new steeple bright and pure for us,

the words of this dear old hymn rushed to my lips: 'Lord, plant my feet on the higher ground.' " The hymn over, a thin squeaky voice from the back pipes up: "I praise God for his savin' and keepin' power!" An antiphonal chorus from the four quarters of the room hurls back "Amen! AMEN! HALLELUJAH!" The walking delegate in the funereal suit booms again: "He purchased you with a price, brother . . . the price of his own precious blood shed on Calvary. . . . Someone else now . . . someone come. Plunge in! *Someone else!*" Another voice, timid, quaky: "You know, folks, I'm not much for testifying. You know I generally keep my mouth shut. But there's one verse very dear to me, very comforting. I believe it's Colossians Three: 'Stand still and see the salvation of the Lord.' . . . Just stand still. Just keep quiet. Brothers, sisters—that's the hardest thing I've ever tried. And I never *have* succeeded. Try it sometime. Get down on your knees, and just try to stay there for ten minutes thinking of HIM. Try to listen to Him. Let HIM speak. Don't *you* be making suggestions. Listen for that still small voice . . . just see how hard it is. AND TRY TO KEEP YOUR MOUTH SHUT. Let God talk! Give *HIM* a chance to say something!" (Matt nudges him and points to something directly overhead: "Jesus Loves You.") He stuffs a handkerchief in his mouth to muffle the convulsive mirth. Again that stentorian appeal: "Sister Powell, you get ready another hymn." (Matt whispering: "You get ready to be crowned!") . . . "Before we take a last look at the face of Sister Blatchford's dear son, let us sing one more beautiful song, my favorite: 'What a friend we have in Jesus.' I guess we all know that by heart, don't we?" (Matt muttering amiably: "I'll tell the cock-eyed world we do!") . . . "Oh, men, MEN—if you're not washed in the blood of the Lamb it won't matter how many books your name is registered in down here. Don't put HIM off. Tomorrow it may be too late. Come to HIM tonight. . . . All together now: 'What a friend we have. . . .' " Thus the song and dance continued for an hour or so, until it got time to "go down and take a last look at that beautiful face." The two of them were in convulsions. The entire congregation—sinners, repentants, Colossians, snot-nosed Pharisees, gay cats and cracked sopranos—stared. Such stares as are worn by the statues of Egypt's "Petrified City." But there came an end at last, even as Pontifical Dick exhausted his store of mealy objurgations. The final exhortation came: "Yes, Brother Pritchard, you put out the lights." . . .

"Yes," thought Moloch, "Brother Pritchard, put them out, please. And put out the sight of these hideous rows of human derelicts testifying to a greasy hat-passer for the sake of a slim handout and a flop for the night. Put out the lights that we may forget the corrugated-metal ceiling and the bughouse walls screaming "Jesus Loves You" but "Don't Spit on the Floor." Yes, Brother Pritchard, you put out the lights, and Sister Powell, you make ready a song!"

Turning away from the Rescue Mission, he plunged into a side street and before long found himself standing before a dignified, time-bitten edifice separated by a well-trimmed lawn from an ivy-covered rectory. It was out of the gaunt, massive doors of this old Presbyterian Church that he emerged one June day in a velvet Eton jacket, his curly head capped by a creamy tam-o-shanter with a pompon attached and a snow-white feather peeping out of the band. Down the broad stone stoop they trooped, a flock of noisy boys and girls decked in Sunday finery, ready for the first leg of their grueling march up Bedford Avenue. It was that Anniversary Day that put the spell of Bedford Avenue upon him. That day its broad thoroughfare was thronged with cheering, smiling crowds; flags fluttered riantly, bands played, and the somnolent, staid brown fronts played their grave, sedate role. Afterwards came the ice cream and soda water, and the award of a calfskin Testament with name engraved in letters of gold.

What a funny little youngster he must have been! A little sissy, no doubt, with his Eton jacket and a white feather in his hat. But then, it was not altogether his fault; he was not responsible for the ensemble.

What happened that day, after he left the church and started walking home with the New Testament under his arm? What was that Jew-boy's name that he had the argument with? Funny, it completely escaped him. Anyhow, he could recall that he knocked him down, and left him curled up under the fruit stand on the corner of Grand Street and Driggs Avenue. Later that day Eddie Carney bumped into him. He thought a heap of Eddie Carney then. And Eddie had said: "Didn't think it was in you, kiddo," and shook him heartily by the hand. . . . After that little episode he was one of the boys; he could go anywhere with them—cook chippies in the lots, help the gang in a stone fight, break windows in the tin factory at night, or knock down showcases in front of the clothing stores on Grand Street.

He sauntered along South Third Street, staring at the fire escapes alive with bedding, iceboxes, geraniums, whatnot. Sea cows distributed their flowing buttocks over cane seats at the curb; some held laborious conversation with their neighbors across the street; some found stimulating amusement in dandling their brats. Most of them appeared to have contracted elephantiasis, or suffered from prolapsis of the womb. All of them had big udders oozing with contented milk. . . . One creature in a fur coat (a specimen of the porpoise family) fumbled with her little boy's trousers as he waited impatiently to relieve his bladder. He stood brazenly watching the performance as the fond parent placidly shook the urine out of her coat sleeve. He was not afraid of embarrassing her. That was impossible. For a moment he was inclined to admire this imperviousness. Should he go up to her, tap her on the shoulder, and say: "Madam, have you no toilet in your house?" He would like to say just that, in a suave, offish manner, as though he were inviting her to join him in a plate of wheat cakes at the Ritz-Carlton. . . . What made them foster this gutter etiquette? No use asking them, of course. No matter what neighborhood they overran, this gutter life opened up, flourished and burgeoned. If it was summer, they floundered about in fish-eyed ataraxia with nightgown and carpet slippers, wading through swill like ducks slipping through lily pads. As soon as the brats were able to toddle they were trained to piddle at the curb and discharge their mucus with two nimble fingers. Milk bottles were thrown from second-story windows and smashed to bits in the middle of the street. With nightfall evil-looking felines took possession of the street and nibbled at the putrid refuse that clogged the arteries of traffic. In spite of the foul, nauseating vomit of the streets, babes were brought down and suckled at the breast. And marvel of marvels, they blossomed like the rose! *Those contented udders most likely . . . !* How does one explain it? Is it possible that the stench of offal revives tender memories of a distant land?

The Children of Israel. God's chosen people! Is it these Disraeli referred to when he said: "The Jew cannot be absorbed; it is not possible for a superior race to be absorbed by an inferior"? Moloch reminded himself (to use an idiomatic expression of the ghetto) of the Jewish prophets: Isaiah walking naked through the streets of Jerusalem to show the inhabitants that the Lord would strip her bare; Ezekiel eating dung and wearing a rotten girdle as a sign that their city would decay. All of them uncouth in appearance, unclean in garb, existing on roots and wild honey, sometimes browsing on grass and flowers; skipping about in the mountains from rock to rock like goats. . . . And Moses, the animated Kosher sign of Israel, peeping at the hind parts of the Lord!

Down Havemeyer Street that was broadened to make an approach for the Williamsburg Bridge. Crowded now with pushcarts creaking with nondescript freight. Here one can purchase anything from coffeepots and bedchambers to Ford parts. He walked gingerly beneath the awnings, fearful lest a bucket of swill be emptied on his head or some stray lice drop off the gray feather bedding flaunted like bunting everywhere. "An industrious people, verily. A thriving people: harmless, law-abiding, gregarious. Give their children all. . . ." Bah! He spat in disgust. "Take them away. Take them back to Zion City, O Lord. Lead them out of this wilderness of pushcarts and catamarans. . . . And give every circumcised son a clean linen handkerchief for keeps!" He strode brusquely through the pushing swarms, elbowing his way clear, thrusting his nose toward the fleece-lined clouds to get a whiff, if possible, of unpolluted air.

Depressed by the melancholy transformation of the old neighborhood, and furious with God's vermin whose coprophilous tendencies he regarded as the cause, he returned to Bedford Avenue and boarded a crosstown car.

The ride was somewhat of a relief. Immediately as they swung into Kent Avenue, and passed in review the old Broadway Ferry (which was running again), his mood changed. Peering eagerly through the old wooden gates at the fresh river life, his mind surged with glittering memories. Once again he saw the sturdy brewery wagons clattering through the open gates, and a teeming pedestrian life marching in through the swinging doors of the cafés that gilded the corners. Visions of silken mustaches dripping with cool foam, of an old-fashioned slate scoreboard over the free lunch counter, telling where the "Brooklyn" stood. Animated discussions by men in straw hats, perspiring under loud plaid suits, weighed down with heavy watch chains that were draped like Armenian letters across the solar plexus. And the horsecars at the other end of the ferry line—how they swayed and bobbed when you jumped aboard! A big coal stove in the center of the car fending off the cold with its ruddy glow. Those were the days when blizzards came and smote the city hard.

He was still dreaming about the ferry, and the golden, mellow days of the Nineties, when out of the corner of his eye he caught sight of two giant gray cruisers swinging at anchorage in the basin. A huge steel coaling dock, with lacy network of bars and girders, appeared and vanished. Beyond it all were the skyscrapers, looming up like rugged sentinels in a turquoise haze. Finally, old Wallabout Market, lying just beyond the grease-streaked waters of the creek; separated by a comfortable distance from the odors of decomposition by which the creek is identified.

Somehow, amid the ceaseless change, the market survived. Not a building ever seemed changed, though doubtless here, too, subtle metamorphoses took place. Row upon row of low red-brick storehouses, bulging with produce, abubble with hand trucks, crates, and gunnysacks. There was something archaic about Wallabout Market. Perhaps it only seemed so, but the impression created was that of permanence, durability. It was as though Peter Stuyvesant had laid his heavy hand upon it, and defied the dago and the sheeny to remove it.

WHEN MOLOCH ARRIVED AT HIS HOME THAT AFTER-
noon he found Sid Prigozi planked on the doorstep, waiting for
him. The fellow looked the same as ever, possibly a trifle worse—
unkempt, greasy, hatless. His features were stretched in a sickly
smirk that was intended as a badge of welcome.

"Well, well, *Mister* Moloch!" at the top of his voice. "If I ain't
glad to see *you.* I thought you were sick in bed. . . ."

"You knew damned well I wasn't."

"Aha! The old stuff, I see. Taking a day off again, eh? What's
up now?"

Moloch tried to put an end to this jabbering with a sneer.

"Christ!" he ripped out. "Do you have to visit me every time
I take a day off? Do you suppose you contribute anything to my
happiness by dropping around this way?"

Prigozi had been sitting on the stoop like a bird of prey during

these greetings. He got up now and commenced to dance about
his friend Moloch, rubbing his hands and making India-rubber
faces as he spoke. Throughout this strange performance, as he
shot one remark after the other, he kept surveying the other from
head to foot in no complimentary manner.

"So I spoil your vacations, do I . . . *Mister* Moloch?"
That *"Mister"*! It was like a dentist's pet drill. . . . There were
times when Moloch wanted to run at the mention of it.

"Come on inside," he said quietly. "We can talk better in
there."

"No, why should we go inside?" shouted Prigozi, in his
squeaky, high-pitched voice. "You're ashamed to talk to me in
public, are you? You don't like me to dance in the street in front
of your home, eh? All right, we'll sit down here on the stoop. I'll
try to behave like a minister." He paused. "Now tell me, Mister
Moloch, just what ails you? Tut, tut! Don't tell me there's nothing wrong. I know there's some dame behind it all. Out with it
. . . who is she?"

Moloch laughed, but not so contemptuously as he endeavored
to. "Always a skirt, heh? Go on, hand me one of your windy
psychological spiels."

"There you go! Didn't I say so?" Prigozi bounced to his feet
and started to pull a jig on the stoop. . . . "Out with it! *Confess!*
Don't try to pull the wool over my eyes. . . . You've got a mild
euphoria today, I notice; you look pale, a little haggard around
the eyes."

"Oh, let up! I haven't any euphoria, and I'm not disturbed
about a woman." He stopped, and reflected a moment. "Look
here, if I told you the truth, what then?"

"Well now, that all depends. The truth, you say? Do you want
me to tell you something, Mister Moloch? . . . THE TRUTH ISN'T
IN YOU! You're a confirmed cheat. You even lie to yourself. You
may be telling yourself this minute that you're truthful with me,
but if we were to go into it, the chances are we'd discover that
you were humbugging again. However, I'm listening."

"If you could conquer the illusion that I'm a patient of
yours . . ."

Prigozi interrupted. "This sounds good to me. I'm staying on for the rest of the day. We've got to run this down, whatever it is. . . . Oh, don't look so glum about it. I don't invite myself to dinner very often, and when I do, you'll recall that I usually pay for the meal."

Moloch was thinking of the reception Prigozi would get. Blanche usually handled him like a third rail.

"I dropped by, Dion," said Prigozi, dropping his bantering and worming, "because I wanted to have a serious chat with you. I knew you weren't ill. Tell me frankly—can I help you in any way? What's bothering you?"

Moloch slapped him brusquely to hide his affection.

"I don't understand you," he said. "Can't a fellow take a day off without exposing himself to your infernal investigations? You want to know why I stayed away today. Well, look here . . . don't laugh! I'm going to tell you the truth: I thought I wanted to write . . ."

Prigozi melted. It was not precisely what he had expected to hear.

"Hang it all," he said gravely, "why don't you stay home and write? I don't mean for you to quit your job, but for God's sake, stop running around nights with Marcelle, and Betty, and this one and that one. Give yourself a chance. I believe in you!"

"You mean it?" A shyness suddenly seized Moloch. "Do you mean to say that you think I can write?" Before Prigozi could answer, he continued: "Wait a bit; let me explain. I know it sounds ridiculous to ask a question like that. One ought to know, I suppose, whether or not he can write. But I tell you, I'm all at sea. I can't get started, for some reason. Someone, or some thing, is forever getting between me and my impulses, robbing me of my energies. . . ."

"You mean Blanche, I guess. Don't misunderstand me. Not that Blanche deliberately prevents you from doing what you wish, but . . . well, damn it anyway, why do you permit her to get in your way?" He dropped his voice a peg. "Am I hurting you? I don't mean to say anything offensive."

"You're not. Go ahead. I'm glad you mentioned it. I've got to talk to someone about it. You're not so far off the track."

Prigozi seemed at a loss to know just how to help Moloch along. It was seldom the latter honored him with his confidences in such matters. With other things it was different. His appreciation was so intense that he grew flustered and said things of no consequence, things he never meant. . . . There were other indications of his embarrassment. He turned red as a beet, his eyes became watery, his lips trembled and twitched as though he were making a proposal of marriage.

"By the way," he inquired, "what did you do with yourself today? You haven't told me yet. The burlesque?"

"Hell no! Why do you suspect that? Perhaps I went to the Aquarium."

"People don't go to the Aquarium, Mister Moloch, to see belly dancers. Tell me, how was Cleo today?"

Moloch smiled. It was a rather wan, pathetic smile.

"I don't blame you," he said. "However, get this straight: generally I invent the burlesque shows! Sometimes I do it to get a rise out of people, sometimes to indulge my sense of the grotesque. Often it's intended as a subterfuge, if there are women about, to make the conversation spicier, to help me establish a more intimate footing without wasting a deal of valuable time. Understand?"

"Serious, Dion, I don't. There's something queer about such behavior. But then, that's neither here nor there. Where were you then, if it was not the burlesque?"

"Had a long walk."

"That all?"

"Isn't that enough? I've been out ever since breakfast; strolling about, thinking, mooning, vegetating." He went into a lengthy exposition of his state of mind. The other listened gravely. When Moloch talked to him in this earnest, rhapsodical fashion all the windows of his soul opened. Nothing his friend might ask of him could prove too great. He was almost ashamed to confess it to himself, but it was so—for Moloch he was prepared to make a greater sacrifice than for anyone he knew . . . including his wife.

"I don't have to tell you, Sid," Moloch was saying, "but that job of mine saps me dry. They should have a YMCA secretary, not me. Someone whose feelings are encased in an oyster shell. I'm too soft. How I come by this Jesus Christ foolishness licks me. . . ."

"The old man thinks the world of you, Dion."

"I know it. He told me only the other day that I stood aces high. But on top of that he gives me a lecture for being too big-hearted. He knows I'm always in the hole."

"Do you ever get any of it back—this dough you're handing out so lavishly?"

"Damned little. I'd be a fool if I expected it to be otherwise."

"This generosity is admirable, Dion, but you ought to do a little more for yourself. What do you expect to do—die in harness?"

"I know, I know. What do you want—a row of spare-time novels? I tell you, when it comes five o'clock, I'm licked. The company's got me, body and guts. And when I get home, there's Blanche. Do you know what it feels like to sit down at the table with a totem pole?"

"How about Edda?"

"How about Betelgeuse? That's how much I see of Edda. Damn Blanche! She has a trick of maneuvering the kid out of reach that makes my blood boil. You'd think I was a contamination!"

"You think an awful lot of Edda, don't you?"

A look of anguish sped over Moloch's countenance. Prigozi's words were like a torch that set his thoughts aflame.

"By God!" he swore. "There are times when I feel like murdering her."

He had forgotten all about Edda in his hatred for Blanche.

"It's a rotten shame," Prigozi remarked. "I'm not thinking of Blanche. _Edda_ . . . that's who's getting a raw deal."

"I know it." Moloch's voice softened. It became quavery. "No one in the world could make me behave this way except Blanche. This quarreling and battling, I detest it thoroughly. Why, we fly at one another for nothing at all! The other night, for instance, the two of us were lying in bed, she in one room and I in the other. Neither of us could sleep. Finally we sat up in bed and began to insult and abuse each other. As I tell it to you now it seems hardly believable that two intelligent people could let themselves go in such a fashion. We stormed and raged like two maniacs. What oaths! It was horrible. . . . Well, at last we got to such a pitch that we jumped out of bed simultaneously and went for each other's throat. . . ."

He paused here.

"I'll tell you something. Do you know what I believe? Sometimes I believe that she *wants* me to strike her!"

"Do you—ever?"

"Y-e-e-s . . . I have. I won't deny it. I defy anyone in my predicament not to. . . . She stands there, egging me on, daring me to touch her, accusing me of the vilest things . . . what am I to do? If I remain silent and glower at her, or if I try imploring her to stop, she commences to scream. And how she can scream! I imagine everybody in the neighborhood must be awakened. And what insults! She piles them up like cordwood. Eventually she adds one too many and then, bang!—my fist shoots out automatically. That very instant I regret it, but it's too late. Even a saint couldn't stand by idly and tolerate such abuse. . . . Anyway, last night when I hit her she just dropped like a sack . . . there wasn't a groan out of her. You can imagine my state of mind. I was conscience-stricken."

Moloch paused again. Prigozi didn't have a word of comment.

"With the rumpus the kid wakes up. She cries for Blanche. All that tumult in the dark, and then the sudden quiet . . . it frightened her stiff. I was frightened myself, and filled with loathing. What a way to bring up a child, I thought. I wished to Christ that I was dead! Of course, I looked after Blanche immediately, picked her up, talked to her soothingly, bathed her face, tried to smooth her hair. . . . What hurt most of all was that she never said a word. No reproaches. Not a word. Nothing. She just looked up at me tenderly and put on a brave smile. Her eyes opened wide and stared into mine. And the strangest thing was there nothing in them but trust, and pity perhaps. 'Jesus!' I said to myself. 'This will never happen again!' "

He laughed hysterically. A thought occurred which filled him with shame, which seemed to mock the fervor of the words still fresh on his lips.

Why was it, he asked himself, that at such moments he also experienced a feeling of elation, a curious abortive longing to repeat the drama, as though that brief interval of tranquillity, when he held his wife in his arms and spoke to her tenderly, was compensation for all the misery and degradation that preceded it?

"Excuse me," he said aloud, "I didn't mean to laugh."

Prigozi's face was twitching like a frog's leg under the scalpel.

"Don't say any more," he urged. "I didn't know things were quite so bad. I feel sorry for Blanche . . . damned sorry. She's to be pitied. You can't subject a sensitive being to such treatment indefinitely. She'll break. . . . And frankly, Dion, I don't think she's as bad as you paint her. She must have some good qualities or you wouldn't have married her. Perhaps it's not too late to patch things up."

Moloch made no answer. He resented Prigozi's remarks. What was the matter—was Prigozi stupid? Why did he, Prigozi, insist on holding *him* responsible? Hadn't he just explained the inevitability of circumstances? *Of course* Blanche wasn't so bad. He knew the extent of his exaggerations. But how could one preserve an attitude of impartiality in such situations? This was no struggle between nations. It was a civil war, an internecine struggle that would leave both vanquished at the end. . . . "Patch things up!" He detested the phrase.

"I know you have decent feelings occasionally," Prigozi was saying. "But what a muddle-head you are! It's strange," he continued, as though speaking to himself, "how a man's intelligence deserts him in matters like this, where his life and happiness are so vitally concerned."

He paused to allow the full weight of his words to sink in.

"This wrangling between man and wife isn't one of the riddles of the Sphinx, you know. You bundle it in mystery, as if it were the doctrine of immaculate conception. It's a very complicated mess now, I grant you, but it originated in very trivial offenses

. . . on both sides. What you want is a microscope—to examine what's under your nose. Don't go muddling around, searching for glandular disturbances. Your wife's endocrine system is probably like a railroad wreck. For that matter, so is yours. Don't think for a moment that you can go to a psychiatrist and have your domestic problems solved. If they had a panacea the courts would have been closed long ago. They're no better than bald-headed druggists selling us hair restorers. . . ."

The sight of Blanche coming down the street put an end to Prigozi's divagations. Edda slipped from her mother's grasp and ran to greet her father. He caught her up in his arms and tossed her in the air.

While Moloch hugged his child warmly Prigozi was left to exchange the icicles of convention with Blanche.

Blanche, strange to say, adopted a more cordial attitude toward the latter than was her wont. She wore the receptive mood of one who had just left the Turkish baths and is atingle with pleasant aches to which she has not yet grown accustomed. Perhaps she was relieved to find her husband home early. She expressed her tepid satisfaction by sub-acid reactions to their remarks, which, in the first flush of politeness, conveyed a cordial awareness of her existence.

Generally she was bored by the Chinese character of their discussions: reference to books she had never read, a grand hullabalooing of theories and principles which she could scarcely understand. These long-winded discussions usually caused her to question the sincerity of her husband. How thoroughly did he evaluate Prigozi's vaporings? To her chaste ears their language sounded wild, heretical, subversive of all she held true and sacred. Particularly their investigations in the field of sex. Her husband's bland confessions amazed her, and wounded her deeply. Carried away by a clinical ardor, they omitted nothing. Like two Peeping Toms they observed and made note of every detail, no matter how trifling, no matter how disgustingly intimate. Her feelings, if she gave way to analysis at all in the midst of these frightful discussions, might be compared to those of a virgin being examined through the keyhole of sexology. Never,

during these discussions, were any apologies offered for in-
delicacy of thought or speech. On the contrary, it was quite
obvious that her stubborn refusal to participate served them with
a splendid pretext for prolongation of the stupid baiting that
usually marked these discussions. She could hear her husband's
voice saying: "Get in this, Blanche . . . there's nothing personal
about this."

"Nothing personal"—that was the rub. She was so much
wood, in his estimation. A log, if you like, to throw on the fire,
to provide fuel for their fiery debates. It was despicable of them,
of Dion particularly, since he who should have been her protec-
tor evinced the greatest satisfaction from her discomfiture. As for
the other, he was just a nosy little Jew. All that drivel about
Freud and Jung, the diseases of Krafft-Ebing, and so on—
weren't they simply devices of his to unload his own salacious
thoughts? He made her tired going about analyzing people five
minutes after he was introduced to them. Why didn't he stay
home and practice on his wife? What business had he snooping
into *their* affairs, stirring up trouble, leaving absurd problems
hanging in the air, like the odor of depilatories which linger in the
bathroom for days. His grin (like a slightly soiled napkin) when
he departed seemed to say: "There now, I've shown you what a
mess you've made of your lives; try and patch it up, if you can!"

A visit from Prigozi was in the nature of a cyclonic force which
threw them out of their natural orbits and left them sitting disconsolately in a litter of debris to face the ghastly uncertainties
of the morrow. His vehemence warped the furniture of her mind,
paralyzed her desires, deformed her spirit.

The most exasperating part of this mockery was her husband's
attitude: forever defending this miserable, filthy creature; constantly attempting to convince her that Prigozi was filled with the
purest intentions, that he was the one true friend that they had
in the world. Persuading her to drop her antagonism . . . calling
it a piece of ill-disguised anti-Semitism. (As though he weren't a
Jew-hater himself!) Why, she had never heard the term until
Prigozi introduced it! What did she care about the Jews, as a
race? She simply didn't want any dealings with them, collectively

or individually. It was no concern of hers what became of them. If they wanted to establish a Zion in Palestine, let them! All she cared about was that they leave her alone, stay out of her home.

It was apparent that Blanche was doing her best to act civilly toward this intruder.

"I suppose you'll be staying for dinner?" she asked. Her tone carried the reverse English that one puts on the ball when pressing a mother-in-law to stay for a weekend.

A note of cordiality crept into Prigozi's voice.

Sure, he would stay if she wanted him to. He meant, by these words, that she should be sincere. "The woman has no right to hate me like she does," he said to himself. "Certainly," he repeated aloud, "I'll stay."

Blanche turned to her husband. "Have you any money?"

"Oh, don't bother to get anything on my account." Prigozi protested. "I'll take potluck, if it's all the same to you people."

"That means *I* won't eat," said Blanche. Her words fell blunt and harsh.

"You people never mean what you say," she added by way of explanation. "I don't mean you especially," she directed to Prigozi, noticing his pained expression. "But that selfish—" pointing to her husband—"he'd gorge himself and wonder later why we didn't eat anything." She requested her husband to get some meat.

"I'm sorry, but I'm broke," said Moloch limply.

Prigozi immediately offered to run out and get something. "Don't you want to come along?" he said.

"No, I'll wait here," Moloch answered. He had dropped into a moody vein.

The door had no sooner closed behind Prigozi than Blanche flared up.

"Why must you always embarrass me? You invite your friends to stay and then you chase them out to buy things for us."

"I didn't ask him to stay. You did."

"*I did!* Just as I expected. If I hadn't asked him you'd accuse me of being inhospitable. No matter what I do you find means of ridiculing me."

"Blanche, for heaven's sake, be reasonable. How often have I told you these people don't want any fuss made over them? Why did you let him go, anyway? I wager there's enough here to feed ten people. You probably did it to make him uncomfortable. I know your petty tricks!"

He was getting overheated, adding up his indictments. He went at her more vigorously.

"Do you suppose for one minute that I'm treated in this shabby way when I visit my friends? God damn it! Whenever anyone comes here I've got to make apologies for you."

Blanche acknowledged that she was not the least ashamed of her behavior. "At least," she retorted, "I do things openly. I guess your friends appreciate that!"

"Look here," he said, "I know you don't like them. I don't ask you to pamper them. But is it necessary to act so cold-bloodedly? Can't you be tolerant? Take *your* friends, for example. Do I treat them the way you do mine?"

Blanche said nothing to this for the reason that she was too busy adding up her recollections of his behavior in the presence of her friends. She was trying to assure herself that there might be one whom he hadn't made overtures to, one whose affections he hadn't stolen.

He mistook her silence for self-chastisement, and threw in a piece of suet for good measure.

"Now, do you wonder," he remarked, "that I don't come home more often?"

"So that's it?" she exclaimed with a rush. "Then it isn't your work that keeps you away. . . ?"

"Must you start that again? What are we to do—lock horns for the rest of the evening? How you love to air your grievances when I bring a friend to the house! Do you suppose they like to sit around and listen to your complaints? Why don't you drop it? They don't believe you, anyway."

Blanche brought the frying pan down with a bang.

"And why don't they?" Her voice rose shrilly. "Why don't they believe me?"

He looked at her in amazement. What a trifle to fly into a rage about! In another minute they would be rehearsing the comedy of the insulted and injured. Or it might take a short turn, with the slippery ease that Chekhov manifests in his short stories. An incident out of the early days of their wedlock came to mind. . . . They were eating dinner. A remark was dropped that displeased her. In the twinkling of an eye they were rolling on the floor, wrestling in dead earnest. Fleming was there. He didn't know what to make of it, but he had presence of mind to pull her skirt down. He seemed to be more concerned about her modesty than the danger she was exposed to of having her skull cracked.

The gleam of a carving knife which Blanche was brandishing lifted him out of the past. Blanche went at him full tilt.

"I'll tell you why they don't believe me," she hissed. "It's because you're always making me out to be a liar."

He took the knife from her hands. She looked at it blankly. She had the expression of one who has been victimized by an obsession, and suddenly finds himself released.

"For God's sake, Blanche, don't carry on so. If you must say these things, say them later, when . . ."

"When your friend leaves . . . I know."

"No, I wasn't thinking of that at all, Blanche. I was thinking of Edda. It isn't right, you know, to talk this way in her hearing."

"Oh, it isn't? You're funny! How careful you are not to let her hear anything bad about you. Do you ever think of her when you're tramping around nights with your women friends?"

"Stop it!" He went up to her threateningly. "I won't have it! You're an insane fool, do you know that?"

"Am I, huh? Go and look at yourself. See what a maniac you can be."

He slunk down in a chair beside her and buried his head in his fists.

"What's the matter, Mamma?" Edda cried from the next room, where she had been playing with her toys.

"Go in and play with her for a while," said Blanche quickly. She regretted her sharp words.

He went in to the child with a crestfallen air, like a penitent approaching the altar.

"Why do you fight so, Daddy?" Edda put her arms about his neck and kissed him.

He held her with one arm, his other hand brushing a tear away. "We weren't fighting," he said soothingly. "I was just playing with Mother. We were acting."

"Were you? That's funny, Daddy. Act with me, too."

He put her down gently and sat on the floor. "Come, dear, let's make believe Daddy's a pony." He crouched low so that she could climb upon his back. He felt her little arms around his neck, choking him. He wished to Christ someone *would* choke him.

"You ought to come home every night, Daddy, and play with me. Mamma says so, too."

"I will, dear, I will," he mumbled. He couldn't stop them, the tears were streaming down his face. He put his head on the floor and jiggled her up and down with slight body twists as he choked down the sobs that rose to his lips.

"That's the way, Daddy! Keep it up, keep it up!" The child was delighted with the attention she was receiving. . . . "How little she asks of me," he thought.

In the midst of their romping Prigozi returned.

"Where's the old man?" he asked.

"Inside, playing with Edda."

If Prigozi had put his hand on a live wire he couldn't have expressed the shock more effectively.

"*Well!* So that's what he's up to?" He was rubbing his hands again in the old way. "Playing the fond parent, now, eh?"

Blanche gave him an indignant glance and turned her face away. Prigozi strode inside and tried to join in the romping. But Edda would have none of him.

"Go away," she cried. "I don't want you."

The child's outburst stopped his impetuosity. He tried insinuating himself. His attempts were ineffectual.

"I don't like you," she persisted. "Go away."

Moloch tried to chide her. "That isn't the way to talk to the man, Edda." But she was obdurate. It was obvious that her hostility was genuine and not the ordinary whimsical petulance of a child.

"There's no use," said Prigozi falteringly. "She doesn't like me; I wouldn't try to force her, if I were you."

Puzzled by the child's frank dislike, he returned to the kitchen dejectedly. "Is it because I'm a Jew?" he wondered. He dismissed the idea immediately. "Why, she's a mere tot." His mind rambled from one thing to another. "Children are easily frightened by ugliness," he said to himself, and the next moment he found himself reviewing the tragic end which came to the dwarf when he looked for the first time in the mirror upon the occasion of the Infanta's birthday. Possibly his thoughts were thus directed by the sight of a mirror hanging on the kitchen wall. It was one of those imperishable, yet wholly dilapidated articles which often outlive the owner. It was pockmarked with blemishes, and gave back a thoroughly distorted image.

Prigozi got up, nevertheless, drawn to it no doubt by its very hideousness, and gazed into it as if it were the mouth of a crater. He rubbed his beard reflectively. It was impossible to conceal the fact, even to himself, that this which he beheld was not the face of an Apollo. It was more like a pile of refuse.

He sat down again, with a lugubrious air, and allowed himself to be absorbed watching Blanche stir about. She made a great deal of fuss but seemed to get nowhere. Nor was there any attempt on her part to engage him in conversation. For a while he pretended to be interested in drumming nervously with his ungainly fingers, but soon even that pretense was removed by the increasing despondency of his mood, and he simply went slack all over, his big, tousled head slumping forward on his chest and rolling about disconsolately.

Blanche cast a glance in his direction now and then, but her interest was more like that of a detective keeping an eye on his prisoner. "A dirty kike," she repeated to herself, over and over.

Could she have read his mind, she would have found the man Prigozi in strange agreement with these sentiments.

He had hoped so earnestly to be a real friend. He had hoped, I say; but his hopes were lost in the discovery of something he had always known—the fact that he was nothing more than a freak, a morose, flyblown creature with Semitic blood in its veins.

DURING THE COURSE OF THE MEAL, WHICH PRO-
gressed with glacial smoothness, the bell rang. It was Stanley
Miravski. He greeted them with one word: "Hullo."

"Throw your cap inside," said Moloch.

Stanley grunted, and held himself stiffly erect on a high-
backed chair against the wall. He didn't care to pull up his chair,
thanks . . . he'd stay right where he was. "I'm satisfied here," he
drawled in his brusque way. His manner conveyed that possibly
the others had not been so successful in putting themselves at
ease.

Despite the severity of his face, the extreme homeliness, there
was something eloquent and arresting about the man. Stanley
was a Pole. It didn't take one long to discover that. It was not his
accent—he had none. His language was a rude American, with
a pronounced Brooklyn twang. One might localize it still further,

and call it the "Fourteenth Ward." To some it sounded droll, titivating. Blanche thought it quite unique. Prigozi was annoyed by it. The sluggishness of it awakened in him the sensation of holding intercourse with a torpid mind.

"I've been doing a lot of reading lately," Stanley commenced. He employed no preliminary flourishes. To put it in his own language, he didn't believe in fiddling around the bush. As nobody attempted to contradict a statement of such a highly personal character, he placed his cap on the table and continued. . . . Somehow, it's rather hard to describe what it was precisely about this individual that created the impression, but he had the air of a Spanish grandee. An enlivening contrast: the brusque, military pose, with the left hand firmly grasping the knee as he leaned (almost deferentially) toward them, and those queer Brooklyn solecisms leaking from the pencil line of his lips. Semi-profile, his head was a fine replica of the Duke of Alva's. Seven generations of cruelty and arid intellectuality had gone to mold the sallow mask whose single touch of color was a thin smear of black beneath the nose.

Stanley was infected by his own enthusiasm. It was unusual for him to talk at any length, unless his scorn was aroused; then he hammered the piercing edges of his words with a mallet of gold. But it was apparent, as he went on, that Prigozi's mere presence was sufficient incitement. He seldom glanced in that direction, but when he did, his face would lift into a frozen sneer. His ancestors, handy with the cleaver, ever busy with pogroms, had perpetuated this characteristic in him.

"You hafter read this here writer, Swift," he was telling Moloch, in his inimitable drawl. "If you're looking for irony or scalding invective—" He paused here in imitation of Dr. Munyan, to raise a lean forefinger. . . . "He knows how to call a spade a spade. And when Jonathan Swift gets through with the human race there's nothin' left but dandruff."

"Dandruff?" roared Prigozi. He laughed so heartily his fork dropped in the milk pitcher.

"Yes, DANDRUFF,' " repeated Stanley.

Prigozi ignored the belligerent tone and continued to laugh. It was a relief for him to break the ice.

"Say, what's the matter with this gazebo?" asked Stanley, as Prigozi's merriment increased instead of subsiding. "You're sure he's not laughing at me? Otherwise I'd lam him in the puss."

Hearing this, Prigozi sobered up.

The telephone rang in the hall upstairs. Moloch jumped. "If it's for me," he said, as Blanche was about to answer, "remember—I'm ill. I can't be disturbed. . . . No matter how important they say it is."

Blanche came down in a minute.

"It's for you. They said it was important."

"Damn it! Didn't I just tell you . . .?"

"I can't help it. Whoever it was said the message couldn't be entrusted to anyone but you. *It was strictly personal.*"

He marched off at once. Perhaps it *was* important. Perhaps there was something of the feminine gender involved. He fully expected to hear a woman's voice when he picked up the receiver.

"What's up?" said Prigozi, remarking the solemn expression Moloch brought back with him.

The effect of this inquiry was to cause the other to flop into his seat. The three of them looked up expectantly. A sigh, neither heavy nor affected, broke from him.

"You act as though you lost your best friend," came from Prigozi.

"He's thinking up a lie," Blanche stated bitterly.

The last remark brought about a response.

"Our good friend Hari Das has kicked the bucket!"

Exclamations, astonishment, a nervous exhilaration.

"Yep! That's the news. Telegram from Atlantic City. Forwarding remains of Hari Das, unable locate relatives or countrymen, signed Reverend somebody or other."

"What are you going to do?"

"Me? Nothing."

"Can't you get in touch with his friends . . . his Hindu friends?"

"I don't know that he has any," said Moloch.

"You don't seem to care very much," Blanche observed.

"Care? What do you mean? He's dead now."

"Well, aren't you going to look after his body?"

"I certainly am not. With death my interest in Hari Das ceases."

"Do you hear that?" says Blanche, addressing the others. "He means it, too. Now you can see what his friendship means. A short time ago he was ready to kick me out in order to make room for his friend, Hari."

"It does seem rather cold-blooded, Dion," came from Prigozi. Stanley felt called upon to throw in a word or two.

"That's like him, sure enough. He's all for himself."

To Moloch the situation was becoming amusing. Why the sudden interest . . . *in a corpse?*

"Have you all had your say? Don't hesitate to relieve your feelings. Before you become prostrated, however, let me get a word in edgeways. . . . Who looked after him when he was alive? Who fed him and put a roof over his head? None of you weeping willows! You hadn't much use for him, then. . . . *You, Prigozi* . . . you talked a lot about letting them shift for themselves, these Hindu bastards. My sympathetic little wife here treated him like a scavenger . . . she was afraid that the neighbors would catch sight of him blowing his nose in the gutter. He was a boor . . . he laughed too noisily. And he didn't bathe often enough to suit her royal highness." He looked at them scornfully. . . . "Suddenly he's converted to a cadaver. Immediately tears, lamentations, eulogies. Can't do too much for him . . . *for the corpse.* Listen, you fatheads . . . I'll give you the corpse. Have a good time with it! I don't like dead bodies . . . *they stink!* I don't even intend to buy a floral piece, what do you know about that? And by the way"—he bent his gaze on Blanche—"how did you expect me to finance his burial?"

Blanche was confused. "Why . . . er, I didn't know," she stammered. "I thought you might borrow . . ."

"You wouldn't need to do that," Prigozi threw in. "We could

get up a collection. You wouldn't want him to be buried in Potter's Field, would you?"

"Why not?" Moloch exclaimed. "What does it matter how he's buried? He's more of an encumbrance now than he was before. But society shows more ingenuity when it comes to getting rid of stiffs." He turned to Blanche again. "If you have some money around here that's not in use, I'd like to borrow it to get some of my suits out of hock. Hari has one of my best suits on his back . . . or did have. I suppose they left it on him. . . . Well, that's a gift to the worms."

The sudden demise of Hari Das served to remind Stanley of the reason for his visit. He had come to borrow a suit.

"I want to hock this for a few days," he said, touching the sleeve of his coat. "We've got a big mock for a landlord, and he wants to throw us out. If I can lay hands on a few berries we can stave him off for a week or so."

It was natural for Moloch to assume that Stanley was out of work again. Stanley had a propensity for changing jobs.

"No, it ain't that," came his glib reassurance. "I've been taking days off lately, and we fell behind. That's all." Then, as a supplement—"I felt like writin', do you see." This information was vouchsafed in a manner calculated to excuse any dilemma.

Moloch had a mental image of Stanley engaged in this toil. His *romances*—that was the label Stanley affixed to his efforts—were usually labored over in the kitchen. The washtub was his desk. It was necessary for him to nurse his creative instincts under these conditions for the very practical reason that the rest of the ménage was too noisy. He had five children, and they were uncontrollable unless he threw a shoe at them, which was always sure to occasion a row with the wife. He had therefore learned through bitter experience that it was more expedient to retreat to the sanctuary mentioned.

Gazing at the snot-green walls of the Miravski demesne, Moloch had often told himself that Stanley must indeed possess a strong poetic gift to concern himself with "romances."

Similar thoughts evidently occupied the others.

Prigozi, in his gauche way, was endeavoring to efface the poor impression he had made a few moments ago. "What are you writing?" he asked, sympathetic yet not craven.

"Nothing you'd be interested in."

"How do you know?"

"Well . . . I'll be brief with you. You like this here guy Dreiser, don't you?" Stanley wore the polite inquisitorial frown of a Torquemada.

Prigozi was obliged to say yes. But he proceeded at once to qualify his admission. "I think some of Dreiser's stuff is mere journalism, but then, you take a thing like *Jennie Gerhardt*—now *that* was superb!"

"Superb! I guess you mean *cheesy*. Now it just happens that I read about fifteen pages of that book once. You want to know what I think about your Theodore Dreiser? I chucked that piece of superb literature down the sewer . . . yeah! What have you to say to that?"

Prigozi's answer was a barnyard cackle.

"Talk about your superb writers," Stanley continued, "say . . . did you ever hear of Pierre Loti?" The emphasis he put on the name should have been a warning to Prigozi that Stanley was offering him a god to worship. Stanley had a bad habit of asking people if they had ever heard of so-and-so (like Pliny, Juvenal, Petrarch, etc.) when he really meant, what do you think of them?

Prigozi was not unfamiliar with Loti. He started to give an account of his reading. "Well, I thought *The Icelandic Fisherman* a very beautiful tale. . . ."

"Never mind telling me what *you* thought. I'm goin' to tell you what *I* believe."

"Where his favorites are concerned Stanley regards himself as an authority." Moloch put in diplomatically. He threw Prigozi a horse wink.

But Stanley was implacable.

"You pipe down!" he commanded. "I'm gonna tell this egg something about literature. Not about journalism—get that?" He fixed Prigozi with a look of severity. "And when I say a thing, I don't modify it. I don't say *some* of his work is good. With me

a man's work is either good or bad, and that settles it. If he's
rotten, I drop him. If he's good, he's good all the way through.
I don't believe in this half-and-half business. . . . Now this here
Loti, mind you, he's a chap I admire. He don't go in for a lot of
petty details, with a Kodak under his arm. He ain't tryin' to be
another Zola. And I wouldn't compare him with that boilerplate,
Theodore Dreiser . . . or that smart aleck from *Main Street,* Mr.
what's-his-name . . . Lewis, yeah, Sinclair Lewis. Who the hell
wants to read his junk, anyway? Where does he come off to hand
us these long-winded spiels? Does he think he's another Tolstoy?
He takes himself too damned seriously, that guy! Anyhow,
America's no country to write about. There's no romance here.
What's a man to do—sit down and write about the eight-hour
day? Now this chap, Loti—he didn't break his back turning out
a best-seller every year. He took his own sweet time. He breezed
along with the French navy, saw the world, made love here and
there. . . . I tell you, he was a regular guy. Nowadays, to be
literary, a fellow thinks he must be either a hobo or a homo. Loti
was a man of the world, and a gentleman! He wasn't obliged to
go to the library and do research work before he sat down to
write a book. Take that book of his called *Jerusalem.* Could Mr.
Sinclair Lewis or Theodore Dreiser ever write anything like that?
Why, it ain't in 'em! If they can't write about dirty underwear
and weak-kneed factory hands they're lost."

As Stanley paused here the others exchanged glances. There
was in these glances a sort of silent understanding, such as sometimes takes place among the members of a jury, which did no
discredit to Stanley.

"But what I was goin' to say is this. There's one book of his
called *Disenchanted.* I don't know what you'd call it, but I say it's
a magnificent *ro-mance.*" Nobody had ever been able to convince
Stanley that it was more euphonious to stress the last syllable of
this precious word.

"I agree with you," Prigozi burst out, to the amazement of the
others. "It was quite good."

"*Quite* good?" All the vitriol that Stanley's glands could com-
mandeer was poured into that word "quite." "Say, you never

read anything better in your life! *Quite* good! What a patronizing gink you can be! The next thing you know you'll be comparing him to that French Jew with the horse face. . . . What's his name again, Dion?"

"You mean Anatole France, I guess."

"Yeah, France . . . that's the bird. France was his pen name. I suppose you call him a fine writer, heh? Such a wonderful scholar, preening his wings all day in an ivory tower . . . tryin' to make believe he was a Socialist, too. Jeez! he makes me laugh. He never did a hard day's work in his life. Some woman kept him— that's what I heard. There's a lot of frogs like him dabbling in literature just to kill time."

Prigozi had been making several abortive attempts to swallow a forkful of spaghetti during the airing of these critical denunciations. For a time he had put on his best airs, but as the conversation grew more hectic, his table manners began to show symptoms of degeneration. It was noticeable that whenever he made an unsuccessful attempt to interrupt Stanley's flow he would revert to the practice of scratching his head with his broken nails. He became so excited, finally, that he was seized with a violent fit of coughing and choking. It was sheer nervousness, together with a frantic desire to jump into the fray with two feet. For no good reason he was now playing with his handkerchief (diligently picking his nose with it), heedless of the fact that one end of it was almost in his plate. Only when he caught Stanley staring at it did he realize the nature of his absentmindedness. He was amazed, when he thrust it back in his trousers pocket, to observe how soiled and crumpled it looked.

Stanley made no attempt to conceal his disgust. It was impossible to get him to go on with Pierre Loti . . . and *Disenchanted.* He beckoned to Moloch. "Come out in the hall a minute; I've got something to say to you in private."

Outside, Stanley whispered in his ear; "Say, why don't you chase that kike home? I can't talk with him around. Get rid of him, and let's play a game of chess. . . . And say, don't forget the suit . . . I need it!"

Moloch hadn't the least intention of acceding to Stanley's

plain-spoken request, more especially when he noted the wretched, woebegone expression on Prigozi's face. Nor did he wish to give Stanley any opportunity to take up the cudgel on his own account, as Stanley would upon the least provocation. So he took refuge in talk. . . .

The cataract of words that Moloch unleashed in his mad scramble to restore the semblance of a sufferable equation resembled rather the soliloquy of a drugged Hamlet than the smooth patter of a host concerned with the incommensurable amenities of the dinner table. He began in the grandstand manner of a filibustering Congressman who ingloriously works the law of association of ideas to death in the first three hours of his endurance contest. Blanche looked up now and then with an approving eye as he let fall a few well-turned phrases. It was so seldom they held anything like polite intercourse that she had almost forgotten how well he could speak when he chose. With his eyes fastened on Prigozi, he made a scrupulous effort to exorcise the demons of suspicion he was certain haunted that individual's febrile brain; at the same time, he made plentiful allusions to things that he and Stanley had in common so as to effectually throttle any dinner-table pogroms that worthy might take it into his head to perpetrate.

It was a funambulesque exhibition sans parasol. To race with deft, sure steps, to grease his way through rather than ponder on equilibrium—that seemed the safest measure. And as he raced . . . he opened fire ("Are you ready, Griswold?" said Admiral Dewey at Manila Bay) with an account of the throes of authorship, the memory of his morning's psychic state still warm and powerful. Thence he launched with hermeneutic zeal into the mysteries of phallic worship, inspired by the recollection of church steeples; it was the profusion of these which had first fired his imagination when he set foot out of doors, en route to a destination then unfixed in his mind. Noticing the look of agreeable confusion in Prigozi's face, yet apprehensive lest Prigozi make an attempt to take over the reins (with an upholstered explanation of the euphorias), he retracted his meanderings and got back to the sparrows in the belfry. He held to the sparrows just long enough to touch upon current theories of heredity, ringing in a brief mention of the work of that famous monk (whose name he had forgotten) who had established his theories through the medium of sweet peas . . . he thought it was sweet peas, possibly it may have been sweet Williams. Knowing that Prigozi would like to say a few words at this juncture about the experiments of Brown-Sequard, he mentioned the name himself, thinking as he passed rapidly on to the next subject how cleverly he had spiked that imp's guns. Several alternatives presented themselves after the sparrows had been left to roost in the belfry: he could go on and dwell fulsomely on the varying aspects of life as it was lived in Brooklyn, the street life, particularly (for instance: Myrtle Avenue, the liver of old Brooklyn)—or, he could give twenty-one reasons why the use of Brooklyn as the locale of a novel was an aesthetic as well as a commercial blunder. But he was not so sure at this point (halfway along the line of the second alternative, though still fiddling around with the tag ends of Brown-Sequard) whether one of the two warring factions would not remember some outlandish title of a book to hurl at him and confound him. By this time, you see, he had definitely committed himself to holding the floor until he felt perfectly safe in relinquishing it, and then only with laurel chaplet wreathed about his noble brow. But, at the last moment, after exhausting every crumb of miscellany that he had stored in connection with sweet peas and Brown-Sequard, he decided on a wholly different tack. . . . It was possible that he was boring his listeners. An anecdote . . . a dash of cold water! He had none in mind when he made this resolution to dilute his speech, but in glancing down at the table-cloth (the patch in front of Prigozi) an incident from some Russian tale filled the breach.

Of course, no one was being bored. The three of them were flabbergasted. Had he turned psychopomp and conducted them on a tour to Hades they could not have been more thrilled. What prompted this strange access of eloquence? Each one invented for himself a thoroughly personal, plausible explanation. Stanley, for example, was convinced that it was all a result of his whispered suggestion in the hallway—this was Moloch's erratic

way of shoving Prigozi out, by talking him out of the house.
. . . However, to get back to the anecdote. What was it but a
rather pointless, long-drawn-out affair, in the true Russian style,
about a moujik who was inordinately parsimonious, even as
moujiks go. It occurred to him, after he had used the word
"parsimonious," to add that modifying phrase "as moujiks go,"
because he had forgotten, in his haste to make them laugh, that
moujiks are not celebrated for their parsimonious qualities. But
it went over quite unnoticed. . . .

"You may think it absurd," he was saying, "this use of tablecloths in a peasant's home; it was that way in the story, and I
assume the author knew what he was talking about. Briefly, it
seems that after this peasant had thought of every possible economy which might be effected . . ." Thus the story progressed until
the point was rammed home. The point? Oh . . . that the table-
cloth did double duty. "Fancy," he wound up, "the sensation of
sleeping on dirty tablecloths, of tossing around all night on dry
breadcrumbs!"

At this point his audience broke out in a rash.

Said Stanley bluntly: "I don't believe that yarn at all."

Moloch accepted the several reproofs with good grace and was
off again, like an old corsair, for deeper waters. He had some
unexpected nonsense on his chest about his grandfather's appetite for metaphysics. He narrowed it down to a matter of cosmogony. The grandfather had some curious views about the
constitution of the universe.

But Stanley could contain himself no longer. "Haven't we had
about enough of this twaddle?" he said.

Blanche pushed her chair aside with a decisive gesture and
informed them that she was off to bed. "I'm sure you won't miss
my presence," came her chill voice. "I really can't contribute a
thing about . . . er, *cosmogony.*" She mouthed the word as though
it were as meaningful as "sesquipedalian."

They permitted her to leave without remonstrance. Then Stanley took the floor again.

"Speaking of philosophy"—he looked down at them like the
muzzle of a six-shooter—"I was reading about a character the

other day in the newspaper. Some character! A philosopher, too, in his way. From what I could gather, he prided himself on the fact that he had never killed a man unless it was absolutely necessary. 'I gave every man a chance,' he told the reporters just before leaving the death cell. It appears, however, that few people had availed themselves of this chance he talked about. He had killed something like twelve or thirteen men in cold blood. . . . At the last minute they tried talking religion to him. First they shoved a priest onto him; after that, they trotted out a Methodist preacher. But this guy had his wits about him. He told them all to go plumb to hell. 'I'm a self-respecting atheist,' he says to them. 'I never had any need for a God so far . . . guess I won't need him where I'm goin'.' They weren't frightening him with any bogeyman stuff about the hereafter. 'If you guys want to do something for me,' he tells them, 'buy me a Corona-Corona and the last edition of the newspaper.' It seems foolish, but a dying man's requests are generally listened to. They brought him what he wanted. . . . He walked to the death chair without assistance, sat down calmly, lit the Corona-Corona, and turned to the last page of the evening paper, where an advance illustration of his execution was depicted. Then he looked at them as if they were a bunch of imbeciles and said: 'Go ahead . . . shoot the works!' . . . Now a chap like that I call a thoroughbred. He had the courage of his convictions." Whereupon he appended a few caustic remarks about the great scoffers of literature who repent on their deathbeds and die with a crucifix in their hands.

Prigozi clanked like a radiator. Voltaire, Ingersoll—he had a half-dozen names on his lips.

"I mean the whole shooting match," said Stanley.

"When it comes to being an absolutely heartless, conscienceless rogue, you take the cake yourself," Moloch threw in.

Stanley was not at all displeased over this broadside. He accepted the declaration as an encomium.

"Admitting that there may be some truth in what you say," he replied, unable to suppress a broad grin, "did I ever tell you about the time I was working in the Navy Yard, and they sent me to Washington to petition Secretary Daniels? No? Well, that's a yarn you've got to listen to. Talk about nerve—I was chock full of it in those days."

A soupçon of encouragement, and Stanley was down the stretch.

"It was after I got fired at Ellis Island this happened. I spoke Polish fluently then. All in all I was pretty capable of holding my own. This job at the Navy Yard was a regular lead-pipe cinch. Night work: not a damned thing to do but look wise. The other lads used to pass the time away playing cards, telling dirty stories, and stuff like that, but I got tired of that in short order and soon began to avail myself of the idle time by doing some scribbling. It was nothing very much, what writing I did, but it gave me excellent practice. I used to compose long letters, witty ones, too, even if I say it myself. At least, those dubs thought so. Before I mailed them I would pass them around and give every one a chance to laugh his head off. Often I conveniently forgot to post the letters . . . because they were generally addressed to fictitious individuals. I would sit down and write on whatever subject happened to interest me at the time, and when I was through, I'd stick a phony name at the top: 'Dear Frederick,' or 'Dear José'. For sheer devilment, sometimes, I'd rake up queer-sounding names, like Moscow Fife or Melchoir Svengali. It didn't matter . . . nobody knew the difference. Well, after this flapdoodle had been going on for some time . . . oh, yes, I forgot to say that I also invented ingenious answers to my letters—just to make things more plausible. Anyway, after a time I became quite a figure around the Yard. It was conceded that I was rather a brilliant chap, a little eccentric, perhaps, but *ambitious.* When I had been there about a year—I had been keeping a close mouth, understand, about the past—the fellows asked me one day if I wouldn't represent them at the capital: they were petitioning Secretary Daniels for an increase. I told them I'd think it over. . . ."

He cleared his throat and lit a Turkish Trophy.

"I figured, you see, it would be more diplomatic on my part to show some hesitancy rather than snap at the proposition immediately. Meanwhile, you can bet your boots, I began to prepare a speech which I intended to deliver to this here Secretary Daniels. Sure enough, one day a gang of them walked into my cubby hole with a list of names for the petition. 'You're the man, Stanley,' they said, and gave me a hundred-dollar bill to defray the expenses. I blushed and stammered as though I were overcome with emotion. I had expected it to happen right along, of course. Anyway, I shoved the hundred-dollar bill in my pocket; it was a brand-new bill, smooth and thin as a wafer. To this day I can feel the way that bill slid into my pocket . . . so easy, and me saying all the while, 'Sure, I'll take the first train out in the morning.' "

"I can well imagine the rest of the story," said Moloch slyly.

"Keep your shirt on. You *don't* know what happened. This isn't an O. Henry story. I'm goin' to tell you about it." He sniffed and looked at Prigozi pompously. . . . "When I left the office that evening, as I was saying, I felt like a drum major. Everybody in the Yard had stopped in to shake hands with me and wish me luck. It was Stanley this and Stanley that. You'd think I was Hamilcar Barca. . . . Naturally, I felt pretty jubilant. I was quite a youngster, then, and this here trip to Washington seemed like a pretty important piece of business to me. (You know how Lincoln felt at Gettysburg!) Leastways, I knew I'd have to come back with an O.K. or take a back seat forever afterwards. The peculiar thing about it was (it first began to dawn on me after I had accepted the money for the trip) how difficult my mission was going to be. I thought I'd get by the Secretary's door all right, but after that, what? That pretty little speech I had prepared . . . holy smokes! I was positive then and there it wouldn't go. I realized all of a sudden that it was the sort of speech a schoolboy might make on graduation day: it was full of rhetorical flourishes, allusions to Plato, Mark Antony, and Napoleon—I don't know whether I had down Napoleon or Nelson—on board the *Bellerophon*. Even Pontius Pilate was dragged in . . . I don't know why, except that I admired him a great deal . . . always thought he got a raw deal. But that's another story. . . . The more I thought about that speech, and all the cuts I'd have to make, the more depressed I began to feel.

There was none of the smart drum major in me after I had walked a few blocks and some of the conceit had evaporated. Between you and me and the lamppost, I felt like a flat tire. I says to myself: 'This ain't gonna be a matter of writing a grandiloquent epistle to someone who don't exist.' No, Secretary Daniels was flesh and blood, and from all that I had heard of him, he was no soft-boiled egg. In the midst of my gloomy misgivings I happened to pass a saloon. Without giving the matter a second thought, I turned instinctively and pushed through the swinging doors. It was an A-1 joint! It was like a house of mirrors: what a blaze of light! And a cheap Wurlitzer going full-blast . . . some tipsy bozo feeding it nickels all night. It looked good to me, gave me a new lease of life. The bartender—I mustn't forget to tell you about him—proved to be a well-educated chap. Later on I learned that he was a Harvard man. He didn't boast about it. All in all I took quite a fancy to him. I liked the cut of his jib. . . ."

Really warming up to Stanley, Prigozi spilled over: "He wasn't just a smart aleck, eh?"

"Now you're talking. No, he was a modest, unassuming cuss who knew how to mind his own business. What's more, he knew how to pour a drink!"

"A Harvard man, you say?" came from Moloch.

"Yeah. . . . Don't interrupt me, I forget what I was saying."

"You were talking about pouring drinks."

"That's right. . . . It was like this: at the start I told myself to take it easy. After all, I wanted but a glass or two to collect my thoughts. I had some of my own money in my pocket—enough for all the drinks *I* wanted—so I drained a few small beers. You could get a swell glass for a dime . . . big schooners, you know. For that matter I guess a dime'd get you a scuttle of suds in those days. . . . After I had downed a few schooners—I switched at the bartender's suggestion—I noticed my mind wasn't getting any clearer. The bartender was asking me every few minutes to have one with him. I wasn't exactly befuddled . . . a little tight, maybe. Anyhow, I know I wasn't drunk. This bartender chap—he was so damned polite, such a suave, well-spoken cuss, I didn't have the heart to refuse him. So I had another one or two—maybe three or four with him . . . *on* him. Along about there I remember a discussion taking place at my elbow. A couple of dudes in spats and butter-colored gloves commenced a palaver about evolution. One of them was studying for the priesthood . . . can you make that out? A genuine dude, too! He was telling his friend what a fraud Darwin was, how it was all a theory, and damned weak in the major premises, or some crack like that. I saw the bartender prick up his ears, and pretty soon he gives me the high sign. 'Ask that sky pilot,' he said, nodding toward the divinity student, 'ask him if he ever heard of Ernst Haeckel.' He didn't want to be embroiled . . . guess he was afraid of losing his job. So he eggs me on—'Go on, tell them about the morphological evidences; give 'em a little spiel on embryology'—and he keeps winking slyly all the while. I don't know what led him to suppose that I was an evolutionist, but I tackled them just the same. I couldn't say much about Haeckel for the simple reason that I didn't know a hell of a lot about him and his morphological evidences . . . not *then,* anyways. But I handed them a great line about Huxley. (I used to read Huxley for breakfast!) Say! Before I got through with my argument, they walked out on us. Well, I just looks at the bartender and he looks at me, and then we laughed like hell. "Have one on Thomas Huxley,' he says good-naturedly, and fills up a couple of big schooners. We downed that quickly enough, and then I popped up: 'What about having one on Ernst Haeckel?' So it went. We had a few more on 'embryology' and 'morphology' respectively, and by that time I was pretty well tanked. . . . Mind you, for two years I had been on my good behavior . . . never touched a drop in all that time. And just when I needed my wits, bango! I fall off the water wagon! But while I was falling off the water wagon I didn't take it so much to heart. The truth of the matter is, I never gave the trip to Washington a thought. After a while, of course, I had emptied my vest pockets of all the loose coin I had on me. Eventually I fished out the hundred-dollar bill. That was rich! I pulled it out like a man who has been doing that sort of thing for years. The bartender was taken back. You know what he said when I slapped it on the bar?

He says: 'Hadn't you better let me take care of this till the morning?' Pretty decent of him, hah? 'Aw, hell,' I says, 'that's just a piece of easy change I picked up in a poker game this afternoon. Easy come, easy go, you know.' And I slipped him a friendly smile. . . . Well, he paid me out in fives and tens, and there were a lot of singles, too, I recall. To me it felt like a helluva big wad—big enough to choke a horse, as they say. We had another drink on the house, and then I lit out. Boy, what a load-on!"

He lit another cigarette: a Mecca. They were better than Turk-ish Trophies, Stanley declared.

"When I got outside the joint the first thing I saw was an old-fashioned horse cab with a big Sambo perched on top of the thingamajig and a long whip in his hand that would cut a boxcar in two. 'Hey, buddy!' I called. 'Come 'ere. Drive this gentleman to Coney Island!' He pretended not to hear me, but I ran after the bloody gig and jumped in. How the hell I managed it I don't know . . . just to show this bozo I meant business I shoved a couple of Hoya de Monterez through the little box at the top and repeated: 'Coney Island, Sambo. . . . All aboard for Dreamland!' We started off at a trot. In a few minutes I was sound asleep. When I woke up I was still in dreamland. 'Dis yeah's Coney Island, boss,' the nigger kept repeating, as though I were going to argue the point with him. . . . So it was, b'Jesus! We were on Surf Avenue, and a big mob milling around on the sidewalks. I gave the cabby a five-spot and told him to keep the change. Then I takes a look around me. Cripes, the place was one big razzle-dazzle! I was still under the weather, but what you'd call awry-eyed. I felt bully . . . wanted to tell the whole cock-eyed world to blow up and bust. . . . Now that I had arrived, I wondered what the hell to do with myself. I guess I was standing there half an hour—maybe it was five minutes (time didn't mean a damned thing to me)—when a dizzy blonde with a sailor hat grabs me by the elbow and says: 'Lonesome, honey?' My first impulse was to sock her in the eye, but she kept on talking so quietly and gently (and she was nothing but a bum) that before I realized what was what we were ambling down Surf Avenue together, arm in arm, as though we were on a honeymoon. 'Let's go somewheres and talk this over,' I suggested. Seeing as how she had hooked on to me so cleverly it was rather embarrassing to try and give her the slip right there in that big crowd. You can never tell what a moll like that may be up to. She might take it into her head to say I had insulted her. I wasn't taking any chances . . . not in my condition. She said she knew a nice quiet little place not far away, so I let her steer me.

"Two minutes later we were sitting inside a swell café with a sprinkle of soft lights and rubber-heeled waiters gliding around with heavy silver trays. There was more crystal than you could shake a stick at. Even the saltcellars glittered as if they had been polished especially for us. . . . I wasn't slow in noticing that someone had set a big bottle of wine in front of us . . . yellow wine, tasted like cheap champagne. 'How did that get here?' I had sense enough to inquire. 'Why, honey, you ordered that. Dear me, what a weak memory you have!' I bawled her out good and plenty. 'Weak memory hell! You're a god-damned liar,' I shouted. . . . 'I never ordered a toothpick.' 'Easy, honey, easy,' she smiled. 'You don't want to be carried out, do you?' There was such a mean emphasis to her words that I piped down at once, and decided to act like a good sport—until I got my bearings, at least. After all, what was a bottle of wine? Shoot another five: that was the way I looked at it. . . . Well, to make a long story short, I shot the other ninety-five. Some more wine, a shore dinner, champagne and cognac, a box of good cigars for the doorman, a few toys for some sick relative she mentioned, and a little change for herself so as she wouldn't starve to death in the morning. Man, I never thought a hundred dollars could go so fast!

"But that was only the beginning of my troubles. . . . When I got back to my own neighborhood in the morning I was ashamed to go home. So I went into a saloon on the corner and tried to brace myself up. I was determined, one way or another, to get to Washington and see Secretary Daniels. . . . But it was no go. I couldn't for the life of me think of a way to raise the carfare, let alone the incidental expenses. Would you believe it, I hung around that saloon for three days, making short trips at intervals to borrow a few bucks from this fellow and that in the neighborhood. All the time, too, I wondered what the hell my wife would be thinking. It got so that I grew afraid to look at a newspaper for fear there would be headlines about me. . . . On the afternoon of the third day who did I see coming into the joint but a lad from the Navy Yard. Jesus! I wanted to pass out! 'Well, Stanley, old boy,' he chirps up. 'what the hell's come *over* you?' I must say he acted pretty decent about it. I was so damned mortified I couldn't get a word out. . . . 'Look here, you,' he said all of a sudden, and all the friendliness went out of his voice, 'I'll give you until tomorrow morning to get on the train and present that petition.' He didn't have to tell me twice. I knew he didn't mean maybe. Believe me, I sobered up presto! Fifteen minutes later I was down at my aunt's house; twenty-five minutes later I left my aunt's house with seventy-five bucks in my jeans. I didn't look for no saloon, neither, I'm tellin' you. I bought a clean shirt, got my suit pressed while I waited in my BVD's, and went straight to the depot. . . . I was in my berth and asleep before the train pulled out."

"Did you make your speech?" cried Prigozi and Moloch in unison.

"Did I? You should have been there. . . . It was all impromptu, but it went over big. I forgot all about Pontius Pilate and the *Bellerophon;* I forgot everything I had once memorized. . . . When I walked in and told the Secretary who I was and where I came from, he gave me a peach of a reception. I must say he treated me like a prince. No ceremony . . . not a bit of it. The first thing he did was to hand me a fat cigar. Then he tells me to sit down and make myself comfortable. I was still a bit shaky, kind o' rocky, you know, and almost afraid to put the cigar in my mouth for fear it would fall out. . . . 'Mr. Daniels,' I commenced—but he wouldn't hear of me starting right in that way. He made me sit there for a while and chat with him. I guess we talked about nine hundred different things . . . *everything but increases.* Then, when he saw I was feeling easy, and had lost my stage fright, he says: 'Now, my young man, just what brought you down here to see me?' When he said that, I let him have it—the whole works—straight from the shoulder; no filigree, no fussing and fuming, no fireworks à la Daniel Webster. Just plain dollars and cents. . . . When I get through, he stands up and grabs my hand (with some warmth, I thought). 'Mr. Miravaki,' he says (funny how he remembered my name!), 'let me congratulate you. You're a credit to the service. A clean, intelligent, level-headed young man, yes sir! You may depend upon me—I certainly shall see to it that this petition is heeded.' . . . I took the next train back, and soon after we got what we asked for. . . . And that's that!

ONE BALMY EVENING AFTER THE OTHERS HAD GONE,
Dave and Moloch were going over the slate together. It was
about six-thirty and Dave was complaining of being hungry. His
having an empty feeling in his breadbasket was just force of
habit. Dave was the sort of gink, as we have hinted before, who
did everything on time.

"Take it easy," said Moloch. "We have loads of time."

"I know, but I want to get it off my mind."

"Get what off your mind?"

"The chow," said Dave.

Moloch condescended to humor him. After all, it was Dave's
party.

"I think we're gonna have a great time," said Dave shortly.

"Say, what are these bimbos like? You haven't told me a
damned thing about them yet."

"Grade A, take it from me," and Dave chuckled. "I got pretty good judgment, you know."

"What nationality?"

Dave shrugged his stomach. "Search me! What's the diff? You'll get plenty of excitement."

"That's fine, Dave, but how about the lingo? Do they talk United States?"

"Betcha life. Good as me."

While Moloch reflected on this happy circumstance, Dave went to the rear to clean his flask. He was back in a jiffy, beaming with satisfaction.

"Smell this!" He held the flask under Moloch's nose.

"How about a little snifter right now, Dave?"

"Anything you say, D. M."

"Atta boy, Dave. Remember now, don't mister me tonight. We're old pals from the car barn. You worked the rear end, and I was up front."

Dave cackled. "Gee, you think up some funny ones," he laughed, pouring out a stiff hooker.

They took a drink and looked cheerful. Dave commenced to show signs of extreme thought. You could always tell when that happened by the way he wrinkled his brow.

"What's eatin' you now?" said Moloch.

"I was just thinkin'. . . ."

"Yeah, I noticed that."

"No kiddin', D. M. Here's what I was wonderin' about. If we're gonna pull this motorman-and-conductor gag, you'll have to cut out the big words. You know what I mean?"

Moloch smiled. "I thought of that long ago, Dave. What are we talkin' now? Ain't this good enough for them?"

"Sure! I'll tell the world," said Dave, looking more like a Billikin than ever. "But c'n you keep it up?"

"Just keep the flask replenished and . . ."

"Opp, bopp . . . there you go!"

"Whaddaya mean?"

"You just got off a fifty-cent word."

"Jesus, did I? Say, you're on to me, ain't you? Step on me if

I make another crack like that, will you?"

"Supposin' I'm in the next room mushin' it up?"

"I never thought of that. Dave, you're a hot sketch, on the level. You certainly think fast. . . . How about another little drink?"

"No, save it, I wanta feed my face."

They got up and put out the lights. Then they went around the corner to a German beer saloon to get some pig's knuckles and sauerkraut.

"Let's order a big stein of beer," suggested Moloch. "Somehow this rye don't quench your thirst."

"*You* order one," said Dave. "I can't mix no drinks. Doctor's orders."

"Forget it. Have one on me. It won't hurt you this once. You're as healthy as a pig. Come on, none of your shenanigans."

"I know, but . . ." Nevertheless he drank it.

They ate hurriedly (from force of habit) and laughed a whole lot doing it. A couple of steins and they were just getting to the right pitch. Dave was chock full of curiosity about the nudes on the wall. "Is that good art?" he asked in a low voice. "Nix," said Moloch, but he soon gave up trying to explain his point of view. Why rob Dave of his preconceptions?

"Whaddaya say we move along, D. M.?"

"Righto. Where didja say they lived?"

"Greenpoint."

"No? Why didn't you tell me that before? Holy Good God! *Greenpoint!*"

"Whatsa matter? Too far?"

"No-o-o. I wasn't thinking of that. . . . Let's walk across the bridge and get some air."

"Do we hafter do that?" said Dave, looking uneasy.

"Why not? It'll do you good. What you need is exercise." He grabbed Dave's arm and bent over him solicitously. "Let me look at that belly of yours again." He rubbed the little round paunch vigorously. . . . "If you don't watch out, Dave, you'll be kickin' off one of these fine days. You're fallin' away to a ton, know that?"

Dave was awfully touchy about his health. Hence the cathartic pills and the liver salts.

"I try to keep my bowels open," he offered apologetically.

"*You try!* Did you ever play handball?"

"Whaddaya want do—kill me off?"

"What the hell! Wouldn't you rather kick the bucket than carry that tub around with you for the rest of your natural life?"

Dave stopped dead and looked up quizzically.

"Let me ask you, D. M.—are you serious or are you jes' tryin' to scare the daylight out o' me?"

"Here's what I think, Dave. You oughta cut out this Christian Science nonsense."

Dave looked at him in astonishment. Moloch went on.

"Those C. C. pills, or whatever the hell you're taking—they don't work anymore, don't you know that? Your bowels are workin'—through suggestion. Keep on takin' those pills and in six months they'll be paralyzed."

Dave stopped again. "Have a heart, D. M. I'm apt to keel right over here if you go on talkin' that way. . . . Let's change the subject."

They were passing a United Cigar store. Dave dragged Moloch inside, grabbed a handful of Optimos, and pushed them in Moloch's fist.

"What the hell, Dave, I won't smoke all these tonight!"

"I should worry! Stick 'em in your pocket. You never know when we might need 'em."

Moloch pretended to be overwhelmed by this show of generosity. He expected Dave to do the honors.

"Here, smoke one yourself," he said, trying to shove one in Dave's trap.

"Nuthin' doin'," said Dave. "Luckies for me . . . look at me teeth."

He displayed an irregular row of stained fangs.

"Fierce!" Moloch commented and looked away.

They were walking through City Hall Park. The benches were full of bums parking their fannies after a day of sloth and despair. Some of them were sprawled comfortably on the very steps of the City Hall, a thin layer of newspaper protecting their weak backs. A spanking breeze had set in from the ocean. It wafted a delicious smell of clams and mud.

Moloch poked his nose up and inhaled a strong dose of ozone.

"I could go a shore dinner tonight," he remarked.

"Geez, you must have a tapeworm," said Dave.

"No, I got a feeling of ro-mance," he answered. "Nothing would suit me better now, Dave, than to sit out on the end of a pier with a stein in my hand and some music playin' off in the distance, and a lot of little Japanese lanterns swaying up above. . . ."

"What brought this on, the beer? You forgot sumpin' in that cute little picture, didn'tja?"

"What?"

"You ain't fergettin' the molls, are yuh?"

Dave scratched his head, pushed his hat comically over one eye, and put on the expression of a man trying to solve a crossword puzzle.

At the Brooklyn Bridge Dave insisted on boarding a car. It was an open car. They sat up front with the motorman.

Dave held his hat under his arm. "This breeze is great, ain't it?" he said as they got to the top of the bridge.

Moloch was busy peering down through the steel latticework at the swift-running tide below, eddying and swirling in great inky blotches. A tiny tug was dragging a string of towboats up the river.

"There's only one Noo York, ain't there, D. M.?"

Dave asked this this with his eyes strained toward the Battery. Moloch wondered what kind of impression this awesome panorama inspired in Dave. He looked at him intently. Dave's fat little rubber neck was still craned toward the towering peaks poking their soft nozzles through the smoke and haze of the peaceful canyons downtown.

"Didja ever think of taking a Brodie from the Brooklyn Bridge?" asked Moloch.

"Yeah, *I don't think!* Did you?"

"Oh, sometimes." He let out a delicious yawn, and slouching

down in his seat, nonchalantly stuck his gunboats up on the front of the car, which got the motorman's goat.

On the other side they jumped off and walked to Borough Hall, where they caught a crosstown car.

"What street do we get off at?"

"She said India Street."

"Where's that?"

"I dunno. Somewheres near the end of the line, she said."

"Some ride."

"Ain't it? Tell me, D. M., where in hell can you get as big a ride for yer money as Noo York?"

"How do you know?" growled Moloch. "You've never been anywhere else, have you?"

"That's right, too. Well you oughta know . . . you've been around a lot."

"Take it from me, Dave, this is the lousiest place in the world. You don't realize it until you get away from it."

This observation brought on a heavy silence. Dave looked as if he were sizing up the world through a kinetoscope. Suddenly he turned to Moloch and assumed a confidential air.

"I wanta ask yer somethin', D. M.," he said seriously. "I'd like to know what I could read to . . . to improve my mind."

Moloch was flabbergasted. Dave might as well have asked him to hand over the seven sacred seals. He intimated that Dave was trying to spoil a pleasant evening.

"No, I'm serious," Dave continued. "You see, I'd like to improve my education. I started to work when I was twelve."

Moloch glanced at him skeptically. "Hm!" he said. "I've got to ask *you* a question, Dave. . . . What would you do with an education, anyway?"

"Aw, be serious, will yer?"

"I am," said Moloch. "Don't you know that an education is unnecessary—if you want to get ahead in the world? That's what you want it for, don't you?"

"Sure, what else could I do with it?"

"Precisely. Now look at old man Houghton, and that jackass on the thirteenth floor. Did they have an education?"

"They musta had somethin' else," Dave admitted reluctantly. He brightened up suddenly. "Anyways, D. M., I've come to the conclusion that if you wanta succeed in life either you must be educated or you must be a good crook. . . ." He was going to continue but Moloch choked him off.

"Now you're talkin' horse sense, Dave." He slapped him heartily on the back. "Dave, I'm gonna tell you somethin': we're too god-damned honest for this world, do you know that? We're never gonna be rich as long as we lead this Sunday-school life. Look at Morgan, Rockefeller, Astor, Vanderbilt, Gould. . . . How do you suppose they got rich? Savin' it up?"

Dave looked considerably cheered by this piece of information.

"Gee, I'm glad to hear you talk like that," he said. "I thought maybe you thought I wuz talkin' through muh hat."

In a little while Dave opened up again. This time it was to explain to Moloch how tough it was to be born a Jew.

"Forget it!" said Moloch. "You're gettin' along, aincher?"

"Yeah, but . . ."

"I don't want to hear any buts. Think of something pleasant. . . . You never told me how you landed these tarts we're gonna see. Where did you pick 'em up?"

"Didn't I tell yuh? Gee, that's funny." He thought a minute. . . . "It wuz a cinch. You shoulda been with me. I hopped into Child's one day last week fer a bite; I no sooner gets inside than I pikes a gal I knew onct . . . someone I met a long time ago at the Roseland. She wuz workin' as a waitress. I goes right up to her. 'Hello,' I says, 'how did *you* get here?' 'Well, well,' she says, 'where you been all this time?' I told her I worked around here. It didn't take me three minutes to date her up. And then I thought of you. . . . I asts her: 'C'n yer git a friend?' 'Why not?' she says, and that's all there was to it."

"That sounds great."

"Don't it? There's no trouble if you work it right."

"You said it."

The car was rumbling over the bridge at Wallabout Creek. The sullen stream was streaked with floating islands of grease, and a stench as of sixty-nine dead horses filled their nostrils. Dave held his nose with two fingers until they got out of the zone.

"Reminds me of old times," Moloch reflected aloud.

Dave perked up and smiled.

"I wuz born around here m'self," he confessed.

"*What?* Do you mean it?" Moloch grasped Dave's hand and wrung it heartily. "Pull out that flask," he commanded. "We've got to have a drink on that, Dave."

"What, *here?*"

"Sure, you're not gonna wait till we get to Greenpoint, are you?"

"Yeah, but . . ."

Moloch reached into Dave's back pocket and extracted the flask. "Who's gonna stop us, heh?" As he held the upturned flask to his lips a soft gurgling sound escaped. Dave watched him, fascinated.

"Now tell us, where did you hail from—the North Side?"

"No, the South Side—Lee Avenue."

"That so? I was raised on the North Side. . . . Do you remember Pat McCarren?"

"Do I? Ask me another."

"Remember the battles we had when the two gangs fought it out in the lots?"

Dave grinned all over. "Look at this." He held his finger to a deep scar over his right eye. "Got that with a can one day."

"Great! Great!" roared Moloch. "So you're from the old neighborhood, too. Well, well."

They put their arms about each other's shoulders and sank lower into their seats. Neither said a word for some time. They just sat contentedly, gazing out on scenes of bygone days. The car took a sharp swing at Broadway Ferry.

"Those were the happy days," sighed Moloch. "That was when New York was a gay, spanking dog of a town, eh Dave?"

Dave shook his head. "Do you remember the Haymarket?"

"Which one—Brooklyn or New York? Aw, the hell with that. Do you remember the Girl in Blue?"

"You mean Millie de Leon . . . at the Bum? Say, I'd give ten bucks to see her again. Remember how the sailors used to run up the aisle to grab one of her garters . . . do you remember that?"

"Don't make me laugh. And Pat McCarren parading up and down like an undertaker from Larry Carroll's saloon to the Bum and back again, with a mug on him like a Jesuit. . . . By the way, did you go to Houston Street last week?"

Here the conversation became rather technical. The burlesque season had just opened and there was quite a long-drawn-out controversy between the two as to the merits of the stock company which flourished at the National Winter Garden.

Finally Dave relapsed into a moody silence. Moloch puffed away contentedly on his cigar. When he looked at Dave again he thought the latter was becoming glum.

Dave explained that he was "thinkin'."

"I can't figure out, D. M., why a fella like you goes to a burlesque show anyhow."

Moloch received this in silence.

"It ain't that you look like a priest . . . it's the books you read. The two don't go together, do you understand me?"

"I sure do. You mean my mind's too good?"

"Sumpin' like that. . . . I wuz lookin' at that paper-covered book you had with you last week. I couldn't read a page of it without a dictionary by my side, and then I don't think I'd make it out. Geez, it wuz dry. I thought it wuz a book on science, or somethin' like that."

"Oh, you mean *Ulysses*," said Moloch.

"That's it. I couldn't pronounce the name. What does a guy write a book like that for that nobody can understand—except a few educated people?"

Moloch agreed that this was one of the mysteries of the universe. "But there was a lot of dirt in it, Dave. I think you missed something that time."

"Is zat so? Then why the hell does he put all those jawbreakers in it for?"

"To keep it out of the hands of children, I guess. . . . Say, watch out, we must be near India Street now. This looks like Greenpoint."

Moloch started to say something about Boccaccio and Rabelais. Dave only had time to gather that they too contained a rich mixture of filth and obscenity when he saw a sign reading India Street. He tugged Moloch's sleeve. They hopped off and looked about them. It looked like the fringe of the pale in a Polish city.

"What's that?" Dave exclaimed, pointing to a mast going by the end of the street.

"Why, that's the river, Dave. Great, eh?"

"I'll say so. All yer gotta do here is stick yer head outa the winder and yer c'n see tugboats goin' by fer breakfast. Not such a terrible dump after all. Yer c'n get some fresh air, b'Jesus!"

Dave got out his address book and began to check up on the house numbers. "We're right," he said, tugging Moloch along. "Don't forgit, on our way home tell me about them books. I wanta read 'em."

"Fine. Don't forget to ask me."

There were more "don't forgets." Dave suddenly remembered that his name should be Brown for the occasion. "Don't forget: *Dave Brown.*"

"All right, *Brown.* Call me Morgan . . . Danny Morgan."

Dave commenced to cackle again.

"What's the matter?" asked Moloch. "Morgan's a good Irish name, ain't it?"

"Yeah, but you ain't Irish."

"The hell I ain't. Who's gonna prove it?"

"All right, D. M., but not *Danny* Morgan. . . ."

"Why not? What's wrong with Danny?"

"It don't fit you. Wait a minute," he begged, "or I'll laugh muh guts out. Look here, D. M., we don't wanta look phony."

"Geez, what a fusspot you can be over a name. What's the difference what name I take? We'll be drunk inside of fifteen minutes."

"That's all well and good, but . . ."

"But what? You and your buts again. . . ."

Dave bent over and whispered: "We don't wanta get arrested."

"*Arrested?*"

"Sure. For givin' false names."

"*W-h-a-t?* To a coupla Polacks? Go on. Chase yourself. You're getting frightened."

"Wait a minute, D. M. Take it easy." He lowered his voice. "You know where we are?" He blinked as he said this. "This is a tough neighborhood. . . ."

"The tougher it is, the better I like it. . . . Watch me kiss the cross after the party's on a while."

Dave clutched Moloch's arm frantically.

"For Christ's sake, D. M., don't do a thing like that. I gotta go home wid the same mug."

Moloch laughed. "I'm only kiddin'," he said. "Don't stand there like a pigeon."

"You're sure?"

"Positive."

"You had me worried. I never know when to take you serious or not."

They arrived in front of the house. Dave went first up the low stoop and struck a match in the vestibule to read the names.

"I had you frightened, eh?" said Moloch, as Dave glanced from one name to another. Some bells had three and four names under them.

"Before you push the button, Dave—I want to tell you something that happened to me around here about ten years ago. . . . You don't like to get in a jam, you say. Well, listen. One night I went to a dance somewhere in this neighborhood . . . it all comes back to me now. I got a terrible jag on, and so I went outside to get the air. I see a big mick of a cop coming along, so I gets friendly with him. I don't know what I said to him, but I guess he didn't like the way I talked to him. Maybe I said something about religion. . . . Anyhow, the more I tried to excuse myself, the worse he got. I never saw such a dumb bastard! But that's the way they are. . . . Anyway, the first thing you know, he grabs me by the collar and starts choking me. Then he hauls off with the other hand and clouts me right in the puss. Wow! I guess I saw daylight. . . . Now that's what I call mean . . . *tough.* If we see any of those birds hanging around we clear out . . . right?"

Dave pressed the button and remarked casually: "What pleasant subjects you bring up!"

The latch clicked in a moment and they pressed their combined weight against the door. Dave whispered a final warning in Moloch's ear: to avoid the subject of wives.

"I promise," said Moloch lightly. "By the way, how is she now?"

Dave made an unnecessary clatter on the rough wooden stairs and answered:

"My sister's fine now . . . just a touch of tonsilitis. . . . Are you following me, Morgan?"

"Right behind you, Brown, old man," and Moloch let out a big guffaw.

Two malapert sluts, as Congreve would call them, leaned over the banisters and warbled a jocund greeting. The blonde one wasn't so bad but the other one, the one in the black satin dress, she was terrible. Oddly enough, she was the one Dave had arranged the party with. Dave wanted to swap horses right then and there, but Moloch was too fast for him. He sized up the situation immediately, and before Dave had a chance to finagle, he threw his arms around the blonde as though he had known her all his life.

"Wot a warm baby this bird is," said the blonde, plastering a slobbery kiss on Moloch's lips. She got a good whiff of the liquor. "Whew! Where did you get it?"

He motioned to Dave. Dave was frankly disturbed. As they laid their coats on the bed—they were asked to make themselves comfortable right away—he conveyed in an undertone that there had been a mistake about the girls. "You picked the wrong one, D. M."

"Like hell I did. You mean *you* picked the lemon. Don't try to crawl out of it." Unconsciously he was raising his voice.

"Not so loud," cautioned Dave. "You work her for a while and afterwards we'll switch."

"Not while I'm conscious, Dave."

The two clucks followed them into the bedroom.

"Say, wot are you boys arguin' about?"

"He wanted me to be sure and take him home early," Moloch confided.

"Swell chance," piped the runt in the black satin dress, giving Dave a big squeeze.

"Wot's the matter?" said the blonde, who had a little more acumen than the other. "Is his wife waitin' up fer him?"

Dave looked imploringly at his companion.

"That guy?" said Moloch. "Why, he's got a half-dozen wives waitin' up fer him. He's a regular sheik, ain't that right, *Brown*?"

Dave offered the blonde the flask. She threw back her head and took a good swig, then passed it over to her friend, who was already sitting like a bunch of bananas in Dave's lap.

"Am I heavy, kid?" she asked.

Dave made a wry grimace behind her back. "Naw, you're as light as a feather," he replied.

Someone suggested starting the victrola. Moloch assisted the blonde in cranking the machine. He leaned all over her and almost broke her back.

"Hey, you!" she cried. "Shove off! Wot do you take me for, a horse?"

He offered a polite apology which seemed to baffle her.

"Say, wot wuz dat last woid?"

"Why, that was French for *very chic*." He smiled affably at her.

"You talk Polish, too?"

"No, just French . . . and English, sometimes."

"Quit cher kiddin'."

He grabbed her roughly and commenced to dance. Dave sat by as though a tombstone had fallen on him and crushed him. He got a kick just watching Moloch wiggle the blonde around.

"Wot's the matter with yer friend?" asked the blonde.

"He must be drunk already," said Moloch.

"I'll shake him out of it," she said, freeing herself from his embrace.

The disk was grinding out "The St. Louis Blues." In an instant the tall blonde baby was standing before Dave, hardly moving her feet but managing to make the rest of her body compensate.

With eyes rolling heavenward, shoulders twitching, knees bending slightly forward, she unlimbered a drowsy, frankly crude muscle dance. Dave's eyes opened like two saucers. She snapped her fingers under his nose, raised her skirt a little higher, and settled down to a slow, steady roll that caught Dave in the pit of the stomach.

"Take her away," he cried, putting his hand over his eyes and peeking through his fingers.

"Where did she get that movement?" Moloch inquired, studying her as if she were a trick seal. Dave ventured to suggest that they introduce her to the manager of the National Winter Garden.

"That dump?" she said scornfully.

Then she stationed herself in front of Moloch, who had taken a cigar from his pocket with the intention of enjoying the performance in comfort.

"Want to see some more?" she asked.

"Sure," he said, "but give us something rough this time," and he looked over at Dave for approval.

"Something like this?" She made a few Arabian passes with her navel.

"Lady, don't do that!" begged Dave. "Oh, lady!"

Moloch calmly lit his cigar and proceeded to blow the smoke in her face as she writhed and twisted her loins.

When she had finished he remarked: "Not bad, kid, not bad."

"How can he sit there like that?" said Dave. He pointed to his companion, who was puffing away on his cigar as though a prandial interregnum had been declared at the six-day bike race.

"For life's pleasant retrospections nothing like a cigar," Moloch reflected aloud, carelessly flicking the ashes on the carpet as he spoke.

"Wot is he?" asked the blonde. "A reporter?"

"No, he peddles dope," said Dave.

"GOOD NIGHT!" chorused the two females in unison.

The party had the gamy flavor that was peculiar to the dying days of the Roman Empire. It was hard to believe that a couple of stupid Polacks could provide such merriment. When they weren't dancing, or mushing it up in a corner, or leaning against the mantelpiece, they were telling dirty stories. Here Dave's natural lubricity showed to mean advantage. Occasionally even the blonde one signaled thumbs down. No one blushed because there wasn't any time for blushing. Things happened too fast. And when the flask gave out, as it did immediately, the two malapert sluts proved their sportsmanship by dragging a case of kümmel up from the cellar.

Every once in a while Moloch would sing out: "Hey, Brown, hadn't we better think about getting back to the car barns?"

When the women got maudlinly stewed they began to tire of the smut and take a romantic turn. The blonde demanded a recitation . . . "somethin' decent."

Moloch obliged by standing on his hands with his feet propped against the wall. In that ridiculous posture it suddenly occurred to him to intone the opening lines of Virgil's *Aeneid* . . . *"Arma virumque cano,"* etc., etc., for about ten lines. Here he lost the continuity, and with true poetic license, jumped to that magic line *"Rari nantes in gurgite vasto."* Enchanted with this, he kept repeating the last two words—*"gurgite vasto," "gurgite vasto"*—until the blonde yelled for him to come up for air.

Dave was lolling on a settee, with his tongue hanging out like a St. Bernard's, trying to imitate the sonorous roar of Virgil's *gurgite vasto,* but never quite succeeding. The runt in the black satin dress put an end to his Latinizing by squirting seltzer water over him. Everyone laughed but Dave. He was thinking of what his wife would say when she saw his bedrabbled appearance.

As no one could read his thoughts the conversation flowed along just as if there had been no seltzer water squirted over him.

Said the runt in the black satin dress: "Vat vere you spikkink—Spahneesh or mebbe Grik?"

"No," Moloch replied, "that was just a little Tagalog I picked up in the Philippines. You liked it, hah?"

"I like it better ven I could understand de woids."

"No you wouldn't, kid. Poetry is better when you don't understand the words."

The blonde had lost all interest in poetry. She was doing her best to entice Moloch to lie down beside her on the daybed. "Put your arms around me, kid, and squeeze the guts outa me," she begged.

"I can't, honey, I'm hungry, honest I am. Can't you dig up a few sandwiches?"

Dave tittered at the mention of food and thought to smooth over Moloch's tactlessness by dilating on the subject of tapeworms. But the blonde was hard to ruffle. She had taken quite a fancy to Dave's boss and wasn't going to permit a little food to get between her and the object of her affection.

While the Lithuanian miscarriage prepared the sandwiches in the kitchen, Moloch and Dave were entertained by an impromptu exhibition that revealed the blonde's superb muscle control. Dave, who was perched like a rubber doll on the settee, glutted his greedy eyes until, exasperated beyond endurance by Moloch's composure, he jumped up impulsively, clutched the blonde's white thigh like a turkey leg, and fastened his yellow teeth into it. The girl screamed with terror. Dave let go with a whine and groveled at her feet, begging forgiveness.

Moloch laughed inordinately and gave Dave a vigorous shove with his feet which sent him sprawling on his back. Dave looked like a turtle that had been turned over. His eyes were bloodshot and terror-stricken. He had never bitten a woman before.

"Get up, you dirty little bum," cried Moloch, pretending to be furious with him. "This is no Billy Sunday show," he added savagely, yanking Dave to his feet. "Now apologize to the lady."

Dave wondered if a mere apology would clear him. The blonde was evidently impressed by his earnestness, although it took quite a few drinks of kümmel to restore her equanimity. However, the episode was finally forgotten and they were soon seated in convivial mood in the kitchen, surrounded by slimy green walls, munching cheerfully on caviar sandwiches and pickled herring.

After her third sandwich the blonde sighed and remarked that her appetite had flown. A polite inquiry into the cause of this regrettable condition revealed the fact that on her way home that evening she had witnessed a terrifying spectacle. It seems that a man, evidently respectable, well dressed, had suddenly decided to commit suicide . . . right before her eyes. Just as the subway train pulled into the station he had jumped from the platform and landed under the wheels. He was ground to a pulp. Later they found his head lying a few yards from his mangled body. She was unaccustomed to the sight of severed heads.

"I think it's dreadful," she said, working herself up into a frenzy. "To think that he went and did it right in front of my eyes. I can't eat a thing when I think of it. It takes all my appetite away."

Moloch offered his sympathies. "The big brute, he ought to have been more considerate . . . the idea, committing cusensyrup before my little tootsie had her dinner. I'm damned glad he had his head cut off, the big bum! He didn't have any sense, anyhow."

The women looked at each other in astonishment, uncertain whether to laugh or grow indignant. Dave came to the bat, however, with a brand-new quip from the Olympic. A merry little jest about Santa Claus, in which someone got a fine new set of false teeth instead of a lavalier.

Then Dave felt a song coming on. He suggested that they try a little close harmony. Everyone felt agreeable. The decapitated trunk lying on the subway tracks was forgotten, which was fine because it would have spoiled the quartet.

Dave had a funny falsetto. The girls thought it was lovely. "Let's sing 'Sweet Genevieve,' " Moloch suggested. He didn't care a rap what they sang so long as everybody felt happy. "Hadn't we better swab our throats with a little kümmel first?" He filled the glasses and gave the blonde a friendly pinch under the table.

"We don't know that song," she said, getting up and putting her arms around his neck. "How about 'Meet Me Tonight in Dreamland'?"

Dave sounded off, timid and quavery. The girls giggled a bit, but it was only a flurry. In a minute they had their heads together and were yodeling in dismal earnest:

"Where love's sweet dreams come true, ooh, ooh . . ." When it came time for the second verse everyone was delighted that they had all ended upon the same note. This time the blonde opened the barrage with a sour whine that was meant to convey deep pathos. Her adenoids served to tauten the deep pathos.

God knows how long the harmonizing would have continued, but after the fifth attempt, someone knocked at the door and in a gruff voice bade them all jump in the river. The blonde was for ignoring such incivility, but Dave kept remonstrating that he intended to go home with the same mug. His paramour finally grew hysterical with laughter and they forgot all about "Mammy Jinny's Jubilee."

During a brief interlude in which the girls excused themselves to run to the lavatory, which was down the hall, Dave pleaded with Moloch to make a break.

When the girls came back Dave and Moloch excused themselves and went searching for the lavatory also. "A big day tomorrow," said Dave, trying to break the ice. He knew they were going to have a hell of a time to tear away from the two females.

The blonde glued herself to Moloch. "Ah, no! You're not going now," she pleaded. "You can stay for the night, kid; nobody's gonna put you out."

"He's gotta go," said Dave solemnly.

"That's right, kid. We gotta be at the car barns in a couple of hours," grinned Moloch, as he tried to release himself from the frantic clutches of the blonde.

"Gee, and we were havin' such a swell time, too," the other moaned.

"I hate to do it, ladies, but we gotta go," Dave repeated.

The girls followed them down into the vestibule and they stood there awhile in the dark, leaning against the doorbells.

"Jesus, they were steamed up," Dave exclaimed when they emerged from the vestibule. "Look at my collar, D. M. I'm just a wet rag!"

"Well, you had a good time, didn't you?"

Dave grunted and fussed with his tie as if to restore a portion of his respectability.

"That blonde was no slouch," Moloch remarked as they strode up the street toward the car line.

"She was mine by rights, D. M."

"Well, you know where to find her now. I saw enough of her."

In a few minutes a crosstown car came along. They sat on the rear seat this time. Soon Dave began in his quavering falsetto: "Meet me tonight in Dreamland, under the silvery moon, meet me tonight . . ."

Suddenly he broke off and slapped Moloch's knee.

"Wasn't that funny when the guy rapped on the door and bawled hell out of us?"

"You didn't act as though you thought it funny then," Moloch retorted.

"I thought we were in for a good beating."

Dave didn't forget to remember about the books. He started off by inquiring about Shakespeare. "Somebody told me there was a lot of dirt in his plays. Is that on the up-and-up, D. M.?"

"Yeah, Shakespeare got away with murder. But you wouldn't like him."

Dave ignored the last remark. "Funny," he said. "I never saw any rough stuff in *Julius Caesar.*"

Moloch promised to take Dave to the 42nd Street library someday and show him what he had missed.

"I'm willin' to go blind if I can get the real goods, D. M."

Moloch thought that was splendid of Dave. "I'll make a scholar of you yet, you little smut-hound."

"And how about the Bible, D. M.?"

"I'll show you the Bible, too."

"They won't kick us out if we ask for the Bible?"

"Shucks! Where did you get that idea? Tell 'em you're doing research work."

Dave was still a little leery about this proposition. He expressed the idea that they might recognize him for a Jew and become suspicious.

"What the hell, Dave, you've got a right to read the Bible. You're a citizen, ain't you?"

"I thought maybe you had to be a Catholic or a Protestant."
Even Dave had to laugh when he got through saying this.
Religion seemed to fascinate Dave. He was curious to know
how many religions there were in the world, and which was the
best one, the most liberal.

"One is about as bad as another," Moloch confided. Suddenly
he turned on Dave and said: "Say, I'm beginning to think you're
an atheist. Don't you know anything about your own religion?"

"Only what the rabbi tells me. He puts me to sleep."

"A fine guy you are! I'll bet you don't go to the synagogue
more than once a year."

"Ah, hell!" said Dave. "It's too dry. I'd rather go to the
movies. If it wasn't for the old folks I wouldn't bother to go even
on Yom Kippur. That's how much I think of religion."

Moloch chided him some more about his lack of faith and
suddenly Dave burst out: "What's the diff! Who knows what's
goin' to happen to us when we croak? Them geezers don't know
any more about it than we do. Am I right?"

"Who do you mean . . . *them geezers?*"

"The rabbis . . . *you know,* the greasy beards, the matzoths.
Where do they get that stuff about the hereafter? It's a lot of
bologna, if you ask me."

"Dave, you're not such an awful dub after all."

Dave grinned and lit a cigar. He was all out of Luckies. They
rode along in silence for a while. Moloch took off his hat to enjoy
the breeze.

"D'yuh know you're losin' your hair?" Dave observed.

Moloch rubbed his head to corroborate the statement.

"I know you can stop it, D. M. Maybe it'll sound funny to you
but I got a lot of faith in it."

"I'll bet it's Glover's Mange Cure."

"No, this is an old Norwegian remedy a fella told me about.
His family used it for years and you oughta see the head of hair
he's got."

"Well, spit it out."

Dave explained that it wasn't kerosene oil or pigeon fat or any
of those things. Just plain boiled urine. (He didn't say urine

. . . he used a more familiar Anglo-Saxon term.)

"Well, that's new to me, Dave. How does he explain it?"

"I don't remember what he said now about baldness. I know he said it was good for that, too. He was talkin' at the time about rheumatism. You know, rheumatism is supposed to come from too much uric acid in the system. Well, urine is ninety percent uric acid, or thereabouts. I don't remember exactly. Anyway, when you apply the uric acid on the outside it affects the uric acid on the inside. It's like a double negative, you see. One wipes out the other . . . just like electricity."

"That certainly is clear enough. The next question is, Dave, where do we get the uric acid? You haven't any uric acid you don't know what to do with, have you?"

Dave hawhawed and got red as a beet. Moloch hummed "Sweet Genevieve." It came time soon for Dave to hop off.

"Will you be in early?" asked Dave, as he stood on the running board.

"Sure, same as usual."

"Get in early, will you, D. M.? The old man's liable to call up tomorrow morning. He asked for you three times last week."

"What did you say?"

"I told him what you told me to say: that you were in the back."

"Every time?"

"Yeah. And I forgot to tell you this. The last time he called up and I told him what you said, he said: 'You might suggest to Mr. Moloch that he transfer his desk to the lavatory' . . . and he hung up."

"All right, Dave. See you bright and early."

Dave hopped off. "It's almost daylight," he yelled as the car started forward.

RETIRING BESIDE THE CATALEPTIC FIGURE OF HIS WIFE,
Dion Moloch at once sank five fathoms deep into a splendorous
sea of unconsciousness.

His dream was of such a quality as we experience only in the
trammeled depths of a profound stupor. It commenced with a
nightmarish vertigo that sent him hurtling from a dizzy precipice
into the warm waters of the Caribbean. The waters closed over
him but failed to suffocate. He felt himself swirling down, down,
down in great spiral curves that had no beginning and promised
to end in eternity.

During this ceaseless descent a bewildering and enchanting
panorama of marine life unrolled before his eyes. Enormous
sea-dragons of legendary awesomeness wriggled and shimmered
in the powdered sunlight which filtered through the green waters;
huge cactus plants with hideous detached roots floated by, fol-

lowed by sponge-like coral growths of curious hues, some sullen as ox-blood, some a brilliant vermillon or soft lavender. Out of this teeming aquatic life poured myriads of animalcules, resembling gnomes and pixies, streaming up in bubbles like a gorgeous flux of stardust in the tail-sweep of a comet. Gradually the successive scenes were bathed in a mist which reminded him of Debussy's unresolved chords and shattering vertical harmonies. The roaring in his ears had given way to plangent, verdant melodies; he became aware of the tremors of earth, or poplars and birches, shrouded in ghost-like vapors, bending gracefully to the caress of fragrant land-breeze.

Stealthily the vapors rolled away and he found himself trudging through a mysterious forest alive with screaming monkeys and birds of tropical plumage. To his astonishment he discovered a quiver of arrows in his girdle and a giant golden bow over his shoulder.

As he penetrated deeper and deeper into the woods the music became more celestial, the light more golden, and the earth beneath his feet became a carpet of soft blood-red leaves and twigs the color of burnt orange. Overwhelmed by the stifling beauty that surrounded him, he swooned away. When he awoke the forest had vanished and it seemed to his befuddled mind that he was standing before a pale, towering canvas on which a simple pastoral scene of classic dignity had been painted. A mural such as Puvis de Chavannes has given us out of the grave, seraphic void of his dream life. The sedate, sombre wraiths of the canvas moved with a measured, dreamlike elegance that made our awkward earthly movements appear grotesque. Without realizing quite what he was doing, he stepped into the canvas and followed a quiet path which led back toward the retreating horizon. A full-hipped figure in a Grecian robe, balancing a faience urn, directed his footsteps toward the turret of a castle which was dimly visible above the crest of a gentle knoll. He followed the undulating hip until it was lost in a dip beyond the distant knoll.

Arriving at this spot he was dismayed to observe that the maid was no longer discernible. But his eyes were rewarded by a more mystifying sight. It was as though he had arrived at the very end of this habitable earth, at that magic fringe of the ancient world where all the mysteries and gloom and terror of the universe are bottled up and await the rash intrusion of a swollen adventurer. About and around him was a vast enclosure whose limits he could only faintly apprehend. Before him rose the walls of a fabulously hoary castle whose ramparts bristled with spears. Pennants wrought with miraculously diabolical designs fluttered ominously above the crenellated battlements. Fire-eating monsters, repulsive and licentious-looking, leered at him from the battle-scarred portals of the castle. A sickly fungus growth choked the broad sweeps leading out from the terrifying portals. The gloomy casements were bespattered with the remains of great carrion birds which gave off a most nauseating stench of putrefaction.

But what awed and fascinated him most was the gruesome color scheme of the castle. It was a red, but like no red he could recall. The walls nearest him, indeed, had a warm bloodlike hue, the tint of rich corpuscles emerging from a knife wound. And yet, it was not exactly such a tinge but rather as though a layer of rich Carolina clay had been compounded with it and given it a glazed, carnal sheen.

Beyond the frontier walls loomed more spectacular parapets and battlements, turrets and spires, each receding rank steeped in varying shades of this murderous dye until it seemed to his terrified eyes that the whole monstrous spectacle was a butcher's orgy, a Caracalla fantasy, dripping with gore and excrement.

He averted his gaze for a moment for fear he would swoon; when he looked up again with trembling lids the foreground had lost some of its odious appeal. Instead of the poisonous fungus and the scabby carcasses of vultures, he saw a rich mosaic of ebony and cinnamon shadowed by deep purple panoplies from which cascades of cherry blossoms slithered and arranged themselves in billowy heaps on the chequered court. A few yards from where he stood there was a resplendent couch festooned with royal drapes and pillows of gossamer loveliness. On it his wife reclined languidly, as if anticipating his arrival. . . . It was not a wholly familiar Blanche, though he recognized her tiny mouth at once. He waited expectantly for an inane tweet-tweet. Instead there issued from her columnar throat a flood of contralto notes which sent the blood hammering to his temples and made him buoyant with the madness of youth. It was only then that he became aware of her nudity, of the vague splendor of her loins and bosom.

He bent over her to lift her in his arms, but recoiled with horror at the sight of a dun-colored spider crawling over her breast. His fear amused her and she commenced anew a deep vibrant melody that bewitched him. But the sight of the foul spider crawling unmolested over her gleaming white body filled him with loathing and he ran like one possessed toward the castle walls. . . .

As he reached the forbidding, menacing gates, encrusted with preposterous scarabs, a strange thing happened. The huge rusty hinges groaned and creaked, and by some magic connivance, the towering gates swung slowly open and admitted him.

Inside the portals a narrow path led straight to a spiral staircase that wound dizzily about a flaming turret. He fled precipitately up the iron steps, growing more frightened and breathless as he climbed frantically higher and higher, never seeming to reach the top. Finally, when it seemed that his heart must break with the exertion, he found himself at the summit. But the ramparts and battlements, the casements and turrets of the mysterious castle were no longer beneath him. A black volcanic waste unfolded, a waste furrowed with innumerable chasms of bottomless depth. Here nothing of plant or vegetable life could be seen. Petrified limbs of gigantic proportions, carbuncled with glistering mineral crustations, sprawled supinely in this brackish void. Gazing more intently, he was amazed, and then terrified, to discover that in this phantasmal waste there existed a spark of life. It was a slimy, crawling ophidian life which contented itself with winding and unwinding huge coils about the petrified remains of a forest.

Then suddenly he had a presentiment that the towering steeple up which he had climbed in panic was crumbling at the foundation, and that he and this immense spire together hung teetering over the edge of the cataclysmic waste, threatening at any moment to be dashed into shattering annihilation. Presently the profound stillness was broken. Faintly there came the sound of a voice—a human voice. Possibly it was Blanche enticing him again with her throaty warbling. He forgot for a moment the imminence of the pit, the scaly reptiles waiting with heavy-lidded eyes for his certain downfall. As though his very salvation depended on it, he strained every nerve to recapture the tones of that faint human voice. Suddenly it rang out again with a weird moaning accent, and then quickly died, as if it had been choked down deep in the sulphurous abysses of the slimy void. His support was lurching violently, describing great swooping arcs that ceased miraculously just when the inevitable seemed inescapable. The voices rang out clearer. They were human—as human as the laughter of hyenas. Shrill lunatic screams, blood-curdling oaths and epithets . . . the piercing, horror-laden cachinations of the mad.

And then the rail against which he was leaning gave way. He was flung out into space, catapulted with meteoric velocity into the shrieking Bedlam. Leprous claws, and talons covered with verdigris, reached out and stripped the tender flesh from his hide as he continued on in his swooning flight. Down, down, down he shot, his beautiful frail body a loathsome dripping carcass of ribboned flesh. His bones felt as if they had been mangled by unicorns.

And now he was no longer hurtling with terrifying speed through the interminable void, but shooting down a paraffin incline which was supported in space by gigantic columns of human flesh, formed in an inextricable pattern of latticework. The chute, he could see, emptied into the cavernous maw of a decapitated ogre who champed his teeth with fierce delectation. Only a few hundred yards to go and the cruel gaping orifice would open for the last time. Another instant and he would be enmeshed in those frightful tusklike fangs . . . the monstrous jaws would be crunching his polished bones into pulverized bits. . . .

But at the very moment of his doom the monster sneezed. The explosion snuffed out the universe.

12

A TWELVE-HOUR SLEEP HAD REPAIRED THE RAVAGES OF
the previous night, the night spent in Greenpoint with Dave.
Moloch found a note lying in the top drawer of his desk. It was
from his new secretary, Valeska.

The office was crowded with youngsters waiting to be interviewed. It promised to be another terrific day. He glanced at the
note impatiently, put it down absentmindedly, and looked at the
sea of faces that swarmed up close to him. They reminded him
of curious aquatic sports whose flattened snouts rubbing rest-
lessly against the glass tanks in the Aquarium provide amusement and edification for the sightseer. His thoughts were divided
between the answer that he would be obliged to make and the
arithmetical problem of filling the vacancies that appeared on the
slate. It was a terribly late start he had made, and the mob
beyond the rail was impatient. He read the note once again.

"I'm going to hold you to your promise tonight. You must take me somewhere—I don't care where, *but tonight!*"

"Later, Valeska . . . later," he begged.

Valeska was nettled.

"But you'll go?" she pleaded hurriedly. She appeared to be desperate about it.

"I'm not sure," he mumbled. A perplexed look came over his face.

His perplexity was well founded. Only that morning he had promised Blanche to raise a sum of money so that she might have an abortion performed. He hadn't the slightest idea, when he made the promise, how he would raise the money. No matter whom he thought of it seemed hopeless. Debts, little ones and big ones, old ones and new ones, confronted him at every turn. There wasn't a soul whom he had overlooked. He got out an address book and skimmed through it; opposite every name there were figures. They ran from two dollars up to three hundred. These latter sums, running up into three figures, he no longer regarded as debts. A debt was an obligation one intended to meet some-day.

Toward the middle of the afternoon Valeska made bold to broach the subject of the note.

"Look here, Dion," she said, with strange determination, "you simply *can't* put me off tonight. I don't care what you had planned, you're going out with *me!*"

"But Valeska—" He leaned as far forward as he could and murmured: "Can't we make it tomorrow? I've got something *very* important to attend to this evening."

Valeska refused to countenance the thought.

"Tell me what it is," she whispered. "Perhaps I can suggest a way out."

"Wouldn't do any good," he replied, looking more than ever perplexed. He looked at her again, baffled, wondering if she could help in any way. There was only one way she could help, he knew that only too well.

She gave him a strong look of encouragement. "You don't

need to keep anything from me, Dion. Can I help you? What's disturbing you?"

He told her the whole business—falteringly, apologizing at intervals, and blushing now and then like a schoolboy. She seemed neither surprised nor aggrieved.

"Must you have it immediately?"

He grasped at the straw she proffered. "Absolutely!" he replied.

He looked at her so straightforwardly she never doubted him for an instant. "Well, then . . . how much?" she asked.

He dissembled further, not so successfully this time—at least, he thought not.

"You don't mean that you want to . . . er, that you'll get it for me?"

"How much?" she repeated. Her voice had grown a little harder.

"At least a hundred . . . I guess." He had no precise idea of what was needed. When he promised Blanche faithfully that he would raise the money for her he hadn't the slightest hope of carrying out his promise. A hundred dollars seemed like a sensible sum now. It was a round figure and it sounded to him, as it rolled off his tongue, just the appropriate sum for a professional fee. No doubt it could be managed for less, but he was not supposed to be a connoisseur in this realm. The last time Blanche had managed everything herself. He never knew what she paid. All he remembered was that it was a sanguine affair. He resolutely shut his mind to further speculation. It left a bad taste in his mouth. The very thought of those filthy butchers on Henry Street made his blood boil. . . .

Valeska put an end to his reflections.

"Meet me at six o'clock and I'll give you the money. Return as soon as you can. I'll be waiting. A hundred's all I can manage . . . not a cent more. However, you won't need to worry about returning it immediately. When I need it, I'll ask for it."

He was about to thank her profusely but the look she threw him made him change his mind at once.

"You don't need to think I'm playing the good Samaritan," she sneered. "Let's not make any pretenses."

When she left he tried to apply himself to his work. Questions presented themselves. He wondered where she was going to raise the dough. "Tonight, tonight!" What the devil was that all about?

"Christ," he mumbled to himself, "I hope the old man doesn't get wind of it." And who was going to foot the expenses for this little expedition? "Hell," he said to himself, "I guess there's no need worrying about that. If she can raise a hundred as easily as that, she can raise a few more."

He knew he wouldn't have any trouble getting away from Blanche. Once he showed her the money he could do what he liked. But what the devil did Valeska want of him? That's what bothered him most. . . .

In a dancing trough in Harlem they were playing "The Circassian Walnut Waltz." Ebony giants in emperor green were clinging fast to pale, skinny things smothered in lace and pearl smoke. The hall was one huge mirror of banjo eyes floating in a sloe gin fizz.

Moloch and Valeska were jammed together at a little table wedged in among many others. A magnificent, barbaric jazz deafened their ears. They were forced into such proximity that Valeska's knees had no freedom of movement except between the vise of his muscular legs. Floods of rain-drenched melodies poured forth from the powerful epileptic figures on the dais. From the sluggish, drugged couples on the floor a peculiar aroma emanated, as from the marriage of camphor and patchouli. Notes like deep wounds gushed over them in founts of dragon blood.

Valeska pointed to the leader, a hypnotic topaz clown. Her bosom was heaving, her shoulders twitching in response to the frozen thuds that reverberated from the traps.

"Have another drink?" Moloch was in an ecstasy himself.

"Get some gin," she begged. "I can't drink your rotten

booze." She slipped him a bill under the table.

They sat there electrified, unable to take their eyes off the weird figure who directed the swaying group on the platform. He was no great mogul with his men, this leader. No panjandrum of stuffy concert hall, wielding an airy baton. A smooth, slippery dynamo, rather, charging the sentient ether with shuddering violet rays of ecstasy. His eyes had the mossy glaze of two oysters on the half shell. Wrapped in a tarnished skin, like a strong cigar; a Mumbo-Jumbo in a full-dress suit. Wearing a lyric smile.

"Sour music with a vengeance," chuckled Moloch.

"I love it, love it!" Valeska ripped out with becoming passion.

A nigger, dancing lightly, brought the gin, and as he poured the drinks his feet kept moving, shuffling, working with the music.

Valeska looked up at Moloch with frank admiration, her lips slightly parted, luscious-looking, warm as the tip of Ceylon. Someone said of a great tragedienne that her eyes were like a drowsy flame. So were Valeska's. She wore a pale yellow gown that was almost transparent; it matched the faint bronze of her skin. It became her admirably, and she knew it.

"I want to do as I please tonight," she said, squeezing the hand that rested on her knee, that burned her like a branding iron. "You didn't tell me what happened when you got home this evening." She made a little pout, as though she were ruffled by his thoughtlessness.

"You haven't given me a chance! God, you look wonderful, do you know it?"

"Say that again!" She gave his hand another squeeze. He felt her limbs trembling between his own. "Now tell me," she went on as if nothing had happened, "wasn't Blanche curious about the money?"

He smiled blandly. "Naturally!"

"Well, what did she say? Don't make me drag it out of you."

"Oh, I gave her another one of my fifty-seven cock-and-bull stories." He topped this off with a gulp of gin which twisted his face into a wry grimace.

Valeska's gaiety seemed at the point of evaporation. "I suppose I'll be listening to them, too, someday," she added with a pensive air.

He was enjoying the flavor of the place too much to permit himself to become annoyed by her pensive mood. Women were always talking about the end. There was time to develop that theme later. Just now—he looked at her tenderly, raised the glass to his lips again, and threw a glance above her head at the colorful throng on the floor, huddled in grotesque embraces. They were being jostled and pushed about by a turbid mass of glistening humanity. The voluptuous tide lapped against the frail tables that formed a cordon about the dance floor. The reek of perfume and barbaric crash of sound almost whipped them into one another's arms.

"Come on and dance," he whispered hoarsely.

She closed her eyes and permitted him to crush her like a sheaf of wind bending before a storm. He murmured something in her ear, over and over. The words fell on her ears like a torrent of liquid fire. Whatever barriers had existed between them were beaten down like chaff. . . . They were gyrating in the midst of a turbulent mob whose civilized veneer had been checked at the door. Above the raucous din rose exhausting trombone smears and the libidinous wail of the saxophones. "Hold me tight," whispered Valeska, "hug me, squeeze me. . . ." Her pleas were like the snarl of an exasperated bitch.

Here and there were a few white faces, women sheathed in silk, with gleaming arms and necks, men in dinner coats—just a sprinkling of pale faces in a grotto of wide-eyed, expectant blacks. Dusky limbs and bodies flashed and poised, and flashed again in a frenzied ritual of eccentric gestures. With bland, sylphlike motions the leader distilled a blare of vertiginous fanfares: barrel-organ tunes, orchestrion studies, ocarina solos. The sourish, velvety tones of the clarinet were lost in a sonorous snuffle. Jazz reared its anonymous bestial voice.

The dance ended spectacularly in one final discordant wail. Valeska and Moloch sat down to drink and stare intoxicatingly at each other. Suddenly the lights were dimmed and a stocky mulatto in full-length saffron tights appeared.

"She has the refined grandeur of a murderess," cried Valeska, quoting for Moloch's approval the words of an immortal Frenchman. Her eyes were flashing, her entire body alive with the vigor of an unrestrained imagination. They sat back and watched this "murderess" with the brass bellows as she paused for a space at each tiny table to do her stunt, and then pass on.

"Mah daddy rocks me with one steady roll;
Dere ain't no slippin' when he once takes hol' . . ."

With repetition of this verse at each glutted table she threw in a few suggestive movements and held out her hand like an organ grinder. Valeska extracted a greenback from her purse in readiness for her coming. A dazzling spotlight accompanied the movements of the saffron tights as the "murderess" passed from table to table, repeating the performance, shoving greenbacks down her flaccid bosom. Meanwhile the epileptics on the dais kept pouring forth an explosive mixture of trip-hammer rhythms that affected the very chemistry of the blood. With nervous, angular pulsations they shook out a gorgeous fretwork of counterpoint, like vague theorems of watered silk. Glittering clusters of lapidary chords, following upon one another like the incessant beat of a tom-tom, disclosed gusts of wind and fading sounds, fluffy clouds of silk with flowers, skeletons in décolleté, athletic robust limbs swelling with sap and blood. There was a fury in their eyes, at the climax, like dark hot coals, and in their cavernous flapping mouths the thick blood beat.

The mulatto's performance ended on a split in a parrot-blue spotlight.

"You should have brought me here before," murmured Valeska, breathing heavily. A riot of sensations deluged her in quick succession. The cheap gin permeated her guts. She was like a house afire.

Her eyes roamed over the boisterous groups. They brimmed with unfeigned admiration.

"They're real, aren't they?" she said excitedly.

"Real?" echoed Moloch. "I'll say so! No neuroses, no inhibitions, eh?" It seemed to him that he had darned few himself.

Valeska had expected a different response. "Do you find them attractive, that's what I mean," she asked. "Could you make love to them—to one like that over there?" She pointed to a tawny female with straight black hair and aquiline features who reclined in the arms of a ferocious-looking buck.

"*He* seems to find her attractive."

Apparently Moloch was unwilling to commit himself. Valeska had broached an idea that was not at all new to him. There were Negresses he had glimpsed on the street, not necessarily pale ones, either, who proved more enticing—some of them, at least—than any white woman he could think of. He had even followed them on occasion, wondering if he could screw up sufficient courage to engage them in conversation.

He realized that Valeska's enthusiasm was not a mere expression of idle rapture. She was fully aware of the dark blood in her veins. At times she became morbid about it and shrunk out of sight like a leper, or she would ask him at the most unexpected moments (when they were riding in a bus, or dancing in a public place) if he wasn't just a little bit ashamed of her.

This unwonted ardor of hers, this curious medley of exultation, of savage pride and ostentatious affection, made him slightly uncomfortable. He looked her straight in the eyes as she went on to accuse him of discarding his habitual frankness. Her eyes were smoldering; they leaped ahead of her words, inflaming his senses, making him sick with desire.

What was she going to do—start a scene? Was it the cheap booze talking, or had she dragged him here purposely to reveal her inmost self? She was pretty well oiled. He hoped she wouldn't go blotto . . . not in this Eldorado of lust.

Another entertainer had taken the floor. "Get the words of this, Valeska." As he spoke he detected the big buck with the woman Valeska had pointed out ogling the latter wickedly. He nodded toward the amorous couple and whispered: "You have an admirer over there."

Meanwhile the performer was crooning:

"Ah wouldn't be where Ah am,
Feelin' lak Ah am,
Doin' what Ah am,
Ef you hadn't gone away. . . . "

When the entertainer had concluded Moloch nodded toward the big buck again and said: "Let's call him over, what do you say?"

"Splendid!" she answered. "And you take his woman, eh?"

The music opened with a crash of carbolic tartness. He reeled among the swirling figures in a shaft of cobalt blue. In the middle of the floor stood a big Ethiopian with a red sweater. He acted as master of ceremonies. His nostrils, the color of roast veal, were distended and quivering. His ears had the puffy quality of a frankfurter skin. He glowered ferociously at the reeking bodies, taut and tingling, which brushed by him in all directions.

Moloch kept his eyes riveted on Valeska. Now and then he stole a timid glance at the dusky creature whose body was fastened to his with the impersonality of a brassiere clinging to the redoubtable bosom of a courtesan. Two splotches of rouge overlaid the deep cinammon of her cheeks. As she moved, with tigerish grace and vigor, the clanking of her crude adornments accompanied the violence of her gestures.

"Are you nervous, honey?" she inquired. At the same time she increased the convulsive movements of her loins.

Moloch forgot about Valeska entirely. He had a dry, indescribable sensation in his palate; his temples throbbed madly. He clasped his hands about her back and strove to imitate the careless freedom of his more primitive associates. "Your hands are hot, honey," she murmured, resting her cheek softly against his. This simple gesture so completely unnerved him that he lost the power of locomotion. He stood still and crushed her to him, his lips fastened to her odorous throat. *There was nothing repulsive about it.* The fragrance of her body exhilarated him. The warm blood tingled in his veins and gave him the illusive strength of a stallion.

"You've got to keep moving, honey," came the voice of the

creature panting in his arms. Out of the corner of her eye she surveyed the bouncer in the red sweater.

They moved in closer to the voodoo workers on the platform. A brass whine, like a little child's fear, yammered MOM-MER . . . MOM-MER! The brazen impudence of the cornet smote his ears and sent a chill down his spine. From the trombone came exasperating mocking glissades which made him tighten his steely grip on the fluttering form that shivered in his arms. She looked up at him and sang with burning lips:

> *"Not on the first night, baby,*
> *An' mebbe not a-tall!"*

Whirling in and out among the reeking, glistening figures, flecked with quixotic shadows, he pushed her before him savagely. The maddening, hurried flurries of the strings swept them away into a limbo of insensate lust. From time to time, in breathless interludes, the musicians leaned forward over the edge of the platform, the full moon of their faces wrinkled and creased by huge steeplechase grins; brusque jets of creosote spilled over the heads of the revolving figures.

"Well, how was it?" asked Valeska, trembling and breathless, as he rejoined her at the table.

"Like nothing that ever was before." He wiped the beads of perspiration from his forehead.

"Want to try it again?"

"Hell, *no!*" he stammered. "I'd go hermantile." He suggested leaving.

Nevertheless they stayed. They stayed until the last horn brayed its last. When the lights went out it was on a scene of utter pandemonium.

"I wonder what the hour is," he remarked, as he led Valeska to the cloakroom. It had just occurred to him that his wife had a serious engagement with the doctor in the next few hours. Perhaps she'd expect him to go along with her.

Valeska was singing to herself, staggering all over the place, oblivious of everything but her own pleasurable sensations. He grasped her arm, not too gently, and looked at her wristwatch.

Just then the performer with the full-length saffron tights came along. She was full of gin and song. She began to hum:

"Ah looked at the clock and the clock struck six;
Ah said, Now daddy, do you know any more tricks?"

He listened indulgently, flung a wrap over Valeska's shoulders, and started to carry her up the stairs. Valeska clung to him as if he were a fireman rescuing her from the burning flames. "Love me, Dion, love me," she murmured, kissing him with an ardor that he found impossible to match. A few grinning bucks passed them on the stairs, offering silent congratulations, happy because they were happy.

A string of cabs were lined up at the curb. It was an everyday dawn in Harlem: drab, dingy, streaked with tenement cornices. A bevy of sawdust dolls, some white, some brown, some black as the royal prostitute of the Apocalypse, bounced out upon the chalky streets of Bedlam. They teetered at the gutter, stacked like a deck of cards waiting for a new deal. Thought Moloch: "Me for the laminated queen of diamonds gleaming like a bunch of carbuncles under the blue arc light . . . or that tall venereal flower in the buttonhole of the ace of spades whose mug is so wonderfully damasked with eruptions!"

As they flung a last glance out of the cab window out came the Great-I-Am, with his starch-front hierarchy, marching splayfooted down the Avenue. Mr. Mumbo-Jumbo (in full-dress suit and celluloid collar) walking home to the "Paludal Ooze Blues." Under his right arm he carried a black funerary case containing a breath from the plagues of Egypt.

13

And there came one of the seven angels which had the seven vials, and talked with me, saying unto me, Come hither; I will shew unto thee the judgment of the great whore that sitteth upon many waters; with whom the kings of the earth have committed fornication, and the inhabitants of the earth have been made drunk with the wine of her fornication. So he carried me away in the spirit into the wilderness.

The Café Royal on Second Avenue is an insignificant paste jewel in the lap of a great whore. Men and women congregate there like bluebottles. If it were a Gentile establishment the waiters would not be so proud of their soiled aprons; they would retire once in a while to shave and bathe. But if the congregation were less like the progeny of the maggot, and the waiters more immaculate, it would not be the Café Royal. That is why the great literati of America inhale the aroma of the place with deep drafts, and bury their seed in its rich manure.

Abraham Lincoln at Gettysburg said: "It is altogether fitting and proper that we, the living, should do this. . . ." Without caring a hang what Abraham Lincoln said at Gettysburg, Prigozi and Moloch were met by appointment in this sawdust rendezvous just below the beltline. They were well plastered when they met. Which, too, was altogether fitting and proper. For they had come to dedicate a portion of their grief to the memory of the dead.

Prigozi was sepulchral. His eyes were two tapers burning in a crypt. He spoke in a broken voice that issued from the bowels of the earth. When he laughed (which he did occasionally, to relieve the gloom in which he was smothered) the reverberations sounded like the punctuated squeals of a sow getting her throat slit.

"You're going mad," said Moloch.

Prigozi grinned sheepishly from behind his Mazda sockets.

"Listen, Sid, you've got to brace up. Do you hear me, you've got to brace up!"

A wan smile illumined the cadaverish expression. The man looked as if he wanted to puke up but couldn't. His brain was working like a dynamo. No matter how much he drank it kept on whirring smoothly, piling up ideas, ideas that would haunt him tomorrow and the next day, and the day after.

At four o'clock that afternoon his wife had died of childbirth. For hours he had stood outside the operating room, absorbing the punishment the doctors were meting out to her. The incessant piercing screams had conveyed better than words that a murder was going on inside.

Behind the massive doors he knew there were cool, muscular men in long white robes mutilating her body. He knew they were working silently, swiftly, with glittering instruments that were swallowed up by her shuddering white body.

A tall young man with spectacles was bending over the inert form of Sarah Prigozi, his blood-soaked fists moving with furious diligence to extricate the twisted mass of flesh imprisoned in the narrow pelvic cradle. The prostrate figure offered no resistance. The screams had given way to a drawn-out moan that rose and fell with insane monotony.

Presently the moaning ceased. It was the end, Prigozi told himself.

It was. The battle was over. The shapeless, battered pulp of flesh fell out. Quietly the nurses gathered up the instruments. They were bathed in a vivid red glow.

Prigozi left the bodies of his loved ones in the hospital to be washed, packed with excelsior, and laid out for a long sleep.

Leaving the hospital he remarked to himself with a strange calm that but a few hours ago he had brought a healthy, budding, live form to them which they had exchanged for two dead ones: a big one, and a little one. The little one didn't even resemble a corpse. . . . That, he told himself, was what the practice of obstetrics amounted to!

"I never broke down," he explained to Moloch, "until I got home and saw the empty flat. Then I cracked. Jesus, I went wild! I wanted to go back and murder the doctors. But all I did was to run out into the street and bellow my lungs out.

He looked around him helplessly with the eyes of a man who can see nothing but the four walls of his cell, and is victimized by the thought that in six hours and twenty-five minutes he will be strapped to a chair and given a dose of embalming fluid.

Moloch started to pour another drink, changed his mind, and placed his hand affectionately on the other's sleeve.

Prigozi burst out: "Come on, act natural! You can't do anything. Let's stay here and talk. Call some of these Jew bastards over, if you like, and pull their beards." He banged his fists mechanically against the tabletop; his voice grew shrill and then hoarse.

"We've got to do something, that's all there is to it!" He kept banging away with his fists. The knuckles were red and bruised.

His violence attracted the attention of an elderly gentleman with a goatee seated at a distant table. The gentleman left the group he was with and walked over.

He gave Prigozi a scrutinizing look. "My God! What's happened to you?" he exclaimed.

"Meet Dr. Elfenbein," said Prigozi in a lifeless tone of voice. Moloch rose to his feet and glared at the intruder. "You'd better run along . . . leave us!" he cried.

"He's all right," said Prigozi. "He's a friend of mine. He's no doctor—he's a dentist."

He uttered the words without raising his eyes. He sat humped up, like a sack of potatoes, still banging away with his fists.

Dr. Elfenbein gave the two of them a hasty glance and made a move to retreat. A group of vaudeville artists at the adjoining table were taking it all in. The performance was as good as a rehearsal to them.

Prigozi now rose to his feet unsteadily. He put his arms about Dr. Elfenbein's shoulders and pushed him gently into a seat.

"Everything's fine, and we want you to stay and enjoy the funeral party," he croaked.

"The funeral party?" Dr. Elfenbein tried to get up.

"Sit down!" Moloch shouted. "He says he wants you to stay."

"Tell him about the two stiffs, Dion. He's never seen a stiff in his life. . . . Tell him about the instruments."

"Sure! Sure!" said Moloch. "If that'll make you feel any better, Sid."

Dr. Elfenbein showed plainly his amazement and alarm. Moloch frowned severely. Once more the dentist fastened his eyes upon Prigozi. He looked into a pair of drowning eyes. Big flakes of dandruff rimmed the man's coat collar. Some mud had caked in his hair.

Prigozi's glassy eyes stared straight through Dr. Elfenbein, straight through the outer wall of the café. He saw a chiseled epitaph in letters of fire.

Moloch called the waiter and ordered a big spread. Dr. Elfenbein protested that he had no desire for food. Moloch insisted.

"This is Sid's party and you've got to eat with us. After the funeral comes the eats."

The funeral had not taken place yet, naturally, nevertheless the two of them persisted in referring to it as a thing of the past.

Dr. Elfenbein smiled apprehensively as Moloch buried Prigozi under an avalanche of vile raillery that had to do with Lutheran Cemetery.

"You see, doc," said Moloch familiarly, realizing that Prigozi was as receptive as a stone monument, "my relatives always insisted on patronizing Lutheran Cemetery because . . . well, for one thing, it was a custom in the family, and then, too, it wasn't so expensive. They served wonderful food and drink at the brewery nearby, I remember that distinctly."

He swallowed some stale Vichy to clear his throat.

"These relatives of mine had a fine comprehension of the meaning of that saying 'All the labor of man is for his mouth!' So, when they had wept themselves dry, they ate and drank. I was only a little chap, then, and it was my lot to finish the beer they left in their glasses. It had a flat, brassy taste, but I was too young to be a connoisseur. I licked it up just the same. . . ."

Dr. Elfenbein listened stoically. He felt that he had a lunatic on his hands, if one could judge by his expression.

"After a few drinks the conversation always veered back to the corpse. I must say that they always had a kind word for the dead. 'Poor old soul,' someone would say, 'he's better off than we are.' And, as if by the way of proving it, everyone would thereupon take a good swig. And so it went, doc—guzzling and swilling it—until someone would break out in song, one of those dismal, sentimental ditties that the Germans like to sing en masse."

He started to hum "The German Fifth" . . . "When we march we don't stand still . . ." Then he leaned forward, beaming with pleasure at the recollection of those warm, cozy funeral parties next door to the cemetery, as it were. The doctor's trim goatee was almost in his mouth. Indeed, the doctor had a vague misapprehension that Moloch might commence to chew his goatee. He was an insane devil, this loquacious goy.

However, Dr. Elfenbein managed to preserve his composure.

"You enjoyed your funerals, then?" he remarked, lost for an appropriate comment.

"Of course, doc! I never could understand why people object to attending funerals. Funerals never depress me. My own, of course—that's a different matter. Ho, hum! 'God giveth, and God taketh away.' That's a fair break, ain't it? Of course it is." At this juncture the waiter returned with a tray full of dishes. "Who's going to eat all this?" Prigozi exclaimed. He was stupefied by the proportions of the banquet.

"Haven't I just been explaining the etiquette of the funeral? Shove it down, you'll feel better. Don't sit there like a poor rabbi who has neither congregation nor slaughterhouses!"

Dr. Elfenbein gave a start. He disliked such allusions. There was absolutely no need to mention slaughterhouses. He thought Moloch's mind about as putrid as pork. At the same time he forgot that he had just finished a meal at the other table and fell to—like a priest of the tabernacle.

Moloch maintained a ceaseless flow of talk. His topics were one and all depressing; yet he contrived to infuse a hilarious note. Prigozi acted as though he enjoyed the situation because there was nothing to life anymore but to enjoy oneself.

After a time Dr. Elfenbein, to whom most of the conversation was addressed, found it necessary to register a protest. He felt decidedly uncomfortable. Moloch had just gotten off a string of abusive epithets and had now taken to ranting about the Jews. Dr. Elfenbein had no desire to see a rumpus started.

"My dear man," he exclaimed, "aren't these expressions a little too strong?"

"My dear man," came the mimicking reply, "an editor once said the same thing to me after he had read my manuscript. " 'My dear sir,' I said to him, 'your words are an insult. *A little too strong?* My dear fellow, we're not speaking of mustard!' "

Moloch carried on in this vein. Prigozi pricked up his ears. He was glad the doctor was getting an earful. He loathed these little Jews who tried to put on dignity by cultivating a beard. They ought to get busy and cultivate their intellects.

Just then he caught Moloch's words.

"Why, doc," the latter was saying, "if only two people in the United States felt as I do about these bastards there'd be an insurrection. Hang it all, we have no temperament! How can we go on living with these people and remain passive? We ought to get busy with a razor . . . slash off a few slices of this juicy respectability. How about it now, doc, how about it?"

Dr. Elfenbein tried making his head wag yes and no at the same time.

"I'm beginning to understand your extravagances. You're a literary man, I see."

"Literary! That's a lousy word to fling at a man."

Dr. Elfenbein recalled that he had feelings, that those fellings had been insulted—outraged, in fact.

"You might have some consideration," he said softly, "for the guest you invited to your table."

Moloch thought this a highly anemic expression of one's injured feelings. He had been aching for a punch in the jaw. With it all, however, he began to feel sorry for the target of his gibes. He wished he had picked on someone with more guts. What he was after was a free-for-all souffle under the tables, a mouthful of sawdust, and some broken bones. . . . He wondered whether Prigozi was capable of showing any fight. If he thought it would do him any good he was ready to hand him a wallop.

The situation was saved by the dramatic entrance of a very attractive young lady whom every one seemed eager to recognize or be recognized by. Some got up from their seats and rushed to greet her; others waved and called her by name.

Moloch caught the name, Naomi. A beautiful name, he thought. A beautiful creature, too.

Dispatching her admirers like so many couriers, she came directly over to their table and put her arms around Prigozi's shoulders.

"Poor fellow," she murmured—a little ostentatiously, thought Moloch—"what can I say?" Her words of consolation were lost in the clatter of dishes and hubbub created by the actors at the table.

What he caught of her voice sounded ravishing to Moloch. He surveyed her from head to foot. Prigozi was at once eager to introduce the young lady.

"An old flame," he said, and a deep flush spread over his features, intensifying his ugliness. He drew up a chair and begged the girl to sit beside him. They fell into an easy conversation in which Naomi did most of the talking. The other two looked on, content to listen, and thoroughly charmed by her dark voice and vivacious gestures.

When she had expressed all the conventional thoughts which she believed the occasion demanded, she quite suddenly ceased talking. No one knew just what to say. The silence became awkward.

"Perhaps I'm intruding," she said.

"Oh, no!" the others responded in one voice.

"You two," said Naomi, like a perfect coquette, "you *look terrible!*"

Simple and commonplace as this remark was, Moloch was instantly flattered. To be included in such a mark of concern was a tribute. He was at a loss to know just how Prigozi took it. . . . *"An old flame"*? Huh! Impossible!

That Naomi was a Jewess was without question, but it was a type he had seldom encountered before; certainly never in this utter loveliness, never with quite such unique blandishments. She was Oriental rather than Jewish, Egyptian rather than Semitic. Quick to idealize her, he pictured her in his mind as an exotic offshoot from the ancient Alexandrian world, a raven-haired waif steeped in the wisdom of the cult of Aphrodite; nurtured in a foreign tongue pregnant with mystery and ardor.

The effect of her charms upon Prigozi was to alter his speech habits. He talked now with a mouthful of marbles. He thought it improved his diction. No one else gained this impression.

Voices were speaking to Prigozi. They had nothing to say about the Bible (which had formed a prominent part in the conversation), or Christian lunatics, or poets like Stanley, who could jabber endlessly about Ecclesiastes. The voices in him were tongues of flame. "It is better to marry than to burn," they whimpered.

He stole shy glances at Naomi. Her mouth was cherry-ripe, her eyes dark as kohl. Her supple limbs were bursting with vigor. Tremors flew up and down his spine as he thought of Naomi lying beside him, comforting him, weeping for him. . . . He had traveled such a distance, in his thoughts, he was disgusted with himself.

Naomi studied the other two as she carried on a tepid conversation with Dr. Elfenbein. The latter's existence was scarcely noted anymore; he was like a vegetable which one knows is in the garden, but ignores until it is time to pull it up by the roots. Men came over from time to time, intruding long enough to win her smile, or extract a faint promise. Naomi was like a doe which has fallen into a snare and lies waiting with beating heart for the cymbals to crash and the dogs to bark. The glances she received were so many spears aimed at her heart. She was at a loss how to appease her hungry admirers.

Presently Prigozi excused himself and hurried away from the table. Moloch followed him. They went down a flight of stairs to the lavatory. Moloch thought he detected Naomi staring at him. Her eyes were imploring him to hasten back—so he thought.

In the lavatory Prigozi turned and looked at his companion with sorrowful, sunken eyes.

He came to the point at once.

"You want her, don't you?"

Moloch was somewhat taken back.

"Go ahead, take her, but . . . but don't tell her in front of me how much you care for her." His voice was unsteady. "Do you hear?" he repeated, advancing closer. "Don't tell her in front of me. . . . I couldn't stand that."

Moloch tried to feign disinterest. He spoke of Naomi's charms as if he were criticizing a piece of marble.

Prigozi was sinister and preemptory.

"You can't put that over on me, Dion. I don't want her, understand? You've got a chance . . . go and take her before I change my mind."

"Change your mind?"

"Listen! I said you had a chance. So you have, but it's a small one. Remember, in her eyes you're a goy. Better strike while the iron's hot."

"What the hell is he insinuating?" thought Moloch, knowing

that a goy is always five leagues behind when talking to a member of the chosen race.

"Damn it!" he blurted out. "I've a good mind to go back in there and take her off under your nose—just to prove to you that I can pull the trick."

"That's what I want you to do. You couldn't find a better girl than Naomi." Prigozi gave out a deep sigh.

"Look here, Sid, what's the meaning of all this? What are you up to? There's something queer about this."

"Well, what do you make of it?" Prigozi answered readily. "You don't think *I* want her, do you?"

"That's the second time you've asked me that. What's eating you? God damn it! Don't stand there gaping at me!"

Prigozi hesitated. Was it worthwhile making things clear to this goy? In some ways Moloch was just like all the other goyim.

"I want you to get rid of that nigger you're running around with. Does that satisfy you?" he announced.

"The nigger? God, is that all he has on his mind?" thought Moloch. He smiled benignantly. If that was all that bothered Prigozi, what made him so damned persistent about Naomi? What made him talk the way he did?

Prigozi read his thoughts. He was a block ahead of him, in fact. "Let him worry," he thought. Then he said aloud:

"How on earth do you ever expect to amount to anything with that mulatto tied to your coattails? Do you know what I've been thinking about you? I believe you're crazy enough to *marry* Valeska. Man, you're tied up with a she-devil now—isn't that bad enough? What will you do with a darky in your home? You'll be ostracized, do you realize that? You won't have any friends, you understand? Nobody . . . nobody."

This speech struck Moloch as so amusing that he let out a sidesplitting guffaw.

"You're getting worked up about a trifle, Sid. Who said I was going to run off with Valeska?"

Prigozi looked resolutely unconvinced.

"Why, look here," Moloch flew on, "Valeska told me only the

other day if ever I was stuck for a place to bring someone I could use *her flat*. . . . Do you get that? Does that look as if I were going to elope with her?"

It was Prigozi's turn to laugh immoderately.

"You try that some night . . . just try it! Ho, ho, ho! Go ahead, try it! You'll never bring a Jane out of her place alive. You're going to get your throat cut as sure as I stand here. Jesus, you must be a simpleton to believe everything she tells you. Who ever heard of a thing like that?"

He laughed more heartily. Tears came to his eyes.

"Ah, shush!" said Moloch. "Let's go back upstairs and take Naomi out of here. This joint's full of bedbugs."

About fifty years ago a French archaeologist discovered in the city of Jerusalem one of the very few relics of the first temple of the Lord. The relic which Clermont Ganneau discovered was an inscription on the post of the balustrade surrounding the second part of the sacred quadrangle. It read:

"No Gentile shall pass this gate on pain of death."

This pile of magnificence which Solomon caused to be erected, and which, it has been alleged, has ever been of vast significance to the Masons, had a life, as we know, of about four hundred years. The Babylonian, Nebuchadnezzar, demolished it completely, taking the Jews with him into captivity. In relating this historical incident, H. G. Wells adds—"making of them a cultured and civilized people."

Surrounded by spurious descendants of the Babylonian captivity, Naomi sat at the table enveloped in a golden silence which weighed on her fragile tympani like a purple hippogriff. Her figure bore a faint resemblance to the beautiful Byzantine moths in silk and fur who emerge unexpectedly from the foul hallways of Hester and Forsyth Streets.

Outside, a small car with a family of nine in it drew up to the curb. The mother, who was suckling an infant, hastily slung a discolored teat over her shoulder. It was a whale of a teat, full of pap. An enormous udder, like a sack of flour.

The entire family trooped inside. Madeira and Cluny laces jostled against pretzels and pieces of knockwurst. Alaskan seals, with a grandiloquent gesture, swept up clots of sawdust, matted with spittle and salami rind. Satin dresses, cut like an open barouche, made a hissing noise as they swished against tables and chairs. Pitiful old men, venders of shoelaces and pencils, moved like paralytics through the throng of chattering cormorants. It is this same crablike gait one observes on Friday evenings when, worn with toil and suffering, shaken with palsy, they join the procession that pours into the synagogue. On this day of the week, when the people of Israel give themselves up to lamentation, and dream in their beards of that Ark of the Covenant which has never been found, the whole East Side opens up like a festering wound, alive with the maggots of corruption.

"Truly," thought Moloch, feasting his eyes on this guano field of sybarites, "if the Germans are the Chinese of Europe, these wretches are the lice and ticks of mankind."

He asked himself what Naomi had in common with this offal that swirled about her like bloated cauliflower. What affinity existed between her and the evil-smelling crowds who were belched like sewer gas from the subways, who streamed back from the battlefields of toil like defeated army corps?

Naomi's delicate touch, resting on Moloch's arm like an apparition, caused him to take in the presence of an additional member of the party.

This personage had a sad Jewish face of a mystagogue. He was a writer, of dubious fame, who wrote fables in Yiddish for the newspapers. The slugs who frequented the Café Royal pretended, over a bottle of seltzer and a snack of pastrami, to enjoy his conundrums.

This man was a bundle of animation. His hands were continually busy mopping the perspiration from his nose and brow. He was always in a sweat. His mind, too, was in a state of continual eruption. Moloch could not but notice his fingers. They were not the soft, tuberous growths of a tailor (such as Dr. Elfenbein displayed) that reminded him unpleasantly of white lard. On the contrary, they were firm, spatulate extensions that promised to grasp hold of life and wring its filthy neck.

This conundrum, whose fables were as pointless as his finger-tips and mocking as his grinning skull, had the articulated sprightliness of a skeleton dangling in a dime museum. He laughed when there was no reason to laugh, and when he recited an anecdote, or one of his countless fables, the gloom of Egypt settled on his brow.

This sidesplitting cadaver, who went to bed each night with one of the Classics (*Don Quixote* or *Huckleberry Finn*), was in the toils of a devastating passion. Between the hours of five and seven in the evening he wrote love lyrics. They were not written for the daily press, nor yet for book publishers, but to console himself for the folly of his passion. He waited regularly every night until Naomi had retired to her room, which was but a stone's throw from the Royal. Then he would tiptoe to her landing and slip a poem under her door. Sometimes he left a flower, which would wither during the night, and dissipate its fragrance. No word about these gifts was ever exchanged. Naomi read them wistfully, touched by the psalmody of his Hebrew heart, yet unable to fathom the mystery of his ugliness.

This Gorgon, whose love was like the sigh at sunrise of the Colossus at Memnon, excited Moloch by reason of his eclecti-cism. Who would surmise, when he buried his terrible fist in the bowels of the Talmud, or clung like a convert to the sacred skirts of Mahomet, that he intended thereby to caress the face of his beloved with the tips of his rigid wings?

His enthusiasm was like the growl of a cataract. He could gush with equal fervor about the architecture of the Alhambra, the nature of idolatry, the topography of ancient Thebes, or Com-munism among the Incas. At the mention of Moses Maimonides he fell into a rhapsody concerning the achievements of the twelfth century. He enumerated the titles of certain original trea-tises by that great sage, such as "On the Bites of Venomous Animals," "On Asthma," "On Natural History," "On Hemor-rhoids," and so on.

His imagination was like the intestinal procession of the sca-rab, which, while gorging itself for days and nights uninterruptedly, continues at the same time to unwind its unbroken tape of excreta as a reminder of the abdominal prodigies performed in its temple of dung. His rabbinical metaphors were invested with the cloudiness of the pearl. When he touched the real of epistemology everything trembled and glittered. Sinister and hideous to the perceiver, his soul fluttered like an elongated spirit lost in a mirage.

Meanwhile Prigozi had suddenly become interested in a newspaper which someone had left on a chair beside him. This is what he read beneath a flamboyant illustration on page fifteen:

"Since the beginning of the world it has been the recognized duty of man to reverence his dead—to give appropriate expression of his sincere affection and fidelity, by providing a suitable resting place for them, according to the custom of the times.

"It is a comforting thought, as far as consolation is possible, to know that one has done all he can to make the last abode of those who have gone before beautiful and soothing to the eye of the living who come there to reverence their memory.

"Just as nations honor their illustrious dead by providing an enduring monument, so that their names may be perpetuated for all time, it is now possible to do as much for your own beloved dead, and it is in keeping with the progress of the times; other methods belong to bygone ages.

"The directors of this humanitarian movement personally request you to clip the coupon from this notice and send it to the address below, and you will receive a beautifully illustrated book describing this magnificent and imposing edifice that will enable you to get a full, comprehensive idea of its scope.

"Do not confuse mausoleum with cremation. The body of your loved one is not consumed by fire-heat, but is sealed up in a snow-white compartment, same as is done in the finest tombs or private vaults, at no greater cost than ordinary ground burial. Mausoleum entombment is in keeping with the progress of the times, and it is as sanitary as cremation and as sentimental as a churchyard. A mausoleum provides a beautiful resting place and a permanent memorial for the dead, and is a sane and practical mode of burial.

"It provides a place where families and friends may lie side by side in a snow-white compartment, high and dry above the ground, where neither water, damp, nor mold can enter. THE MAUSOLEUM ELIMINATES THE HORRORS OF THE GRAVE, MAKING THE ULTIMATE END ONE OF CONSOLATION AND BEAUTY.

"This edifice, so sacred in its memories, will never be desecrated, as is often the case in abandoned cemeteries. This mausoleum is nonsectarian, and is open to all creeds and religions. For those preferring cremation we will have a few very fine niches for urns.

"The mausoleum will be beautiful and rich in architecture; constructed of granite, marble, and bronze, making it as secure and time-resisting as the pyramids of Egypt.

"You must admit that death is the final victor over all, and you would not bury your family in the ground unprotected by casket or box, but even though you do use a casket or a box it means not much more than leaving them entirely unprotected. "WHEN YOU PLACE THE LOVED FORM IN THE MAUSOLEUM YOU KNOW THAT IT WILL BE IN THE DRY.

"You have the choice of just two things. The one typifying death in darkness; death in the depths; looking down, always down, into the wet grave. The other typifying death in light; death in sunshine and brightness; death in the hope of the resurrection."

Prigozi folded the newspaper and shoved it into his coat pocket. A hideous peal of laughter burst from his lips.

Naomi and Moloch exchanged meaningful glances. The poet excused himself to take a walk.

Prigozi was easily persuaded to leave. On the way home they loitered before a number of dim-lit windows. A sign in a drugstore window, reading "Headquarters for drugs, trusses, and crutches," attracted Prigozi's attention. He was enthralled by it.

"I want a facsimile of that," he shouted, dancing in front of the window and clapping his hands like a child clamoring for a bauble.

Arrived at his door, he turned to Moloch.

"You take Naomi home, but mind you, don't take her in the

subway. It snows chloride of lime there. Psst!" (He put a finger
to his lips.) "That keeps the galoots and buzzards away! Psst!"
Moloch escorted Naomi along Second Avenue in silence. It
was only a few minutes' walk from Prigozi's place to hers. He
intended to rush back to Prigozi immediately.

They passed once more the little Russian bookshop with a
picture of Dostoevsky in the window. It was a veritable Christ
reincarnated in the body of a moujik. Tears dropped languidly
from the sockets of his eyes. Moloch tipped his hat, a gesture
which, rapid and unobtrusive though it was, did not fail to catch
Naomi's eye.

The furnished room which Naomi called her home was situ-
ated on the third floor of an old brick house, above the "European" restaurant. The odor of the kitchen saturated the halls.

He said good night to her at the vestibule and pressed her hand
warmly. She permitted her hand to remain in his. As they stood
there John Dos Passos' gong of a moon came up over Wee-
hawken.

Naomi had extracted a promise from him to call on her soon.
"When you come," she said, "knock softly."

Moloch now strode with rapid steps in the direction whence
they had come. "Knock softly," he repeated to himself, his
shadow already visualized athwart her threshold. He wondered
if Prigozi had slashed his throat in the meantime. This speculation did not prevent him from making a mental note to purchase
a collar in the morning so that he might make himself present-
able. Presently he stepped into a telephone booth. He always
telephoned Blanche when he had a good excuse.

Blanche sounded sleepy and annoyed.

"I've got to stick by him," he reiterated. "Sorry I had to
disturb you."

"You didn't need to telephone," came Blanche's voice. "We'll
get along without you," and she hung up.

"There you go," he mumbled to himself, as if he were the most
righteous individual on two legs, "that's just another cock-and-
bull story to her! The devil take her! Let her think as she likes."

As he approached the corner, the Colossus of Memnon passed

him. His chin was resting on his shirtfront. His two blackjacking fists were hidden in his coat pockets, the one strangling the bull Apis, the other hurling imprecations at the god Osiris. His mustache was moist with cologne water.

Moloch stopped resolutely and turned about. His eyes traveled after the mysterious one. He waited and watched. The figure moved unswervingly toward its destination. It was swallowed up by a vestibule above the "European" restaurant.

Moloch retraced his steps with the utmost deliberation, and took up a post a few feet from the stoop, in the obscurity of a deep shadow.

"We'll give this fly-by-night a few minutes to reappear," he decided, "or we'll investigate."

The thought of a preposterous tale he had been on the verge of telling Naomi at the Café recurred to mind. Had he taken leave of his sense altogether? There were things one could apologize for—such as pulling goatees—but this tale . . . ! He heaved a sigh of relief.

What was the Holy Ghost doing up there so long? Were they holding a tryst?

But no . . . the poet was coming out of the vestibule. Cautiously he placed one foot before the other, treading softly, very very softly, down the stone stoop. He gripped the balustrade with the sweat of his moist palms. In the darkness his form had the appearance of an amorphous mass set in concrete clodhoppers. If one were to come suddenly upon the massive figure of Rodin's *Balzac* of a foggy night one might observe a strange similarity in these two figures. Those who had never seen the *Balzac* under the conditions described often said that he resembled a crumpled Yiddish newspaper. (Why a "Yiddish" paper?) For the same reason, no doubt, that people speak of a "bright Sunday morning"; implying, it is to be assumed, that the seventh day of the week, when it *is* bright, is brighter than any of the other days in the week.

Moloch stood unnoticed during the other's descent, eclipsed by the velvet shadow of the huge stoop. He watched the figure depart and lose itself, as a wraith makes its appearance on a darkened stage only to be quickly swallowed up by the wings. His mind was groping for an explanation to fit this strange episode. It encountered only high, blank walls.

And then a curious thing happened to him. The Colossus of Memnon faded completely from his mind, and perhaps for the fraction of a minute he was lost to the world about him. In a dreamlike state he saw himself again as a big, overgrown child, sucking a lollipop. His skin was very fair, and he had lovely, flaxen curls. Under his arm was a handsome, gilt-edged Testament bound in rich vellum. He was sitting in the belfry of the old Presbyterian Church, repeating like an automaton the words of the Twenty-third Psalm.

But why were the crowds down below muttering and shaking their ponderous fists at him? He grew terribly frightened. The lollipop fell out of his mouth, hit the pavement below with a resounding smack, and was shattered to bits, like a watch crystal. A panic seized him as the crowd surged closer, threatening to pull him and the belfry down.

Suddenly an angel appeared in the sky and swooped down upon him like a hawk. With a tremendous flapping of wings the angel carried him aloft, up into the azure reaches of the sky. When he recovered sufficiently to look into the angel's face, he discovered that it was not a Gentile angel. The angel looked a hell of a lot like Prigozi, except that it had no wens, no spectacles, no blackheads. . . . Who was it said that it is not possible to conceive of an ugly angel? Well, then, whoever it was lied!

Dion Moloch made up his mind to storm the donjon. He stood outside Naomi's door and knocked softly. There was no answer. He knocked again, very softly. He felt something smooth and slippery under his feet. Someone was fumbling with the lock. The door opened, ever so lightly, for just a fraction of a space, and he heard her whisper, "Who is there?"

The sound of her hushed voice coming from the darkness made his very guts tremble. He leaned his full weight against the door and pushed into the room. Her frightened form was vaguely visible in the center of the tiny room. "It's me, Dion Moloch," he whispered hoarsely, seizing her and fastening his mouth to hers. She made no resistance; her head fell back, her body completely relaxed. Thus they stood for several minutes; he released her to close the door. Locking it carefully, he extracted the key and placed it on the dresser.

She was still standing in the center of the room, clad in a flimsy nightshirt, her arms crossed on her bosom in the attitude of a martyr about to mount the stake. He grabbed her again and repeated his advances. She uttered not a word, but surrendered herself to him as in a dream.

"Were you expecting me?" he gasped finally.

He had awakened her from a profound slumber. She had been dreaming, so she related, of a woman robed in white who was carrying a pitcher to a well. The well was fearsomely deep, and looking down into its depths, the woman had seen the reflection of the moon, a slender crescent moon shimmering with opals. "I was still dreaming when I went to the door," she concluded.

"And now," he asked, "are you dreaming now?"

She reclined on a narrow cot, her exquisite figure revealed by the light of the street which managed to beat its way uncertainly through the yellow shade. Placing a robe over her prostrate figure, he knelt beside the bed to embrace her. The touch of his hand stealing lightly over her warm body made her tremble and cling to him. He lay down beside her, flesh to flesh, quivering with spasms of ecstasy. . . . "Naomi, Naomi," he murmured in the darkness. . . .

The brief delirium of utter silence in which they were swallowed was shattered by a rude knock at the door. They heard a voice calling, "Naomi."

Instantly she placed her hand on his mouth and implored him in a panic-stricken whisper to be quiet. "Don't move!" she begged. The fragrance of her breath invaded his nostrils, mingled with his blood, and took complete possession of him. They clutched each other tightly, scarcely daring to breathe.

"Naomi, Naomi," the voice called. "For God's sake open the door. It's only me. Please, please . . . I won't hurt you."

There could be no doubt whose voice it was. Moloch gave a start; a feeling of horror and pity came over him. Naomi continued to hold her hand over his mouth. He could hear her heart pounding.

Meanwhile the voice continued to plead . . . a perfect babble of entreaties, pitched in a low, wailing mode that threatened at any moment to break into sobs, or wild laughter. "Naomi, say something. Don't lie there like a dead one. Speak to me . . . speak to me. I'm going mad!" The voice trailed off into a distaff of gibberish. Suddenly the door trembled, as if a heavy object had been thrown against it. This was followed by groans—mournful, sickening groans, that filled them with dread.

The picture of Prigozi, lying in a state of collapse outside the door, dominated Moloch's mind. It made him writhe and squirm. Naomi clutched him frantically.

"Please don't go," she whispered. Her voice was hushed with awe.

"But he may be hurt. . . ."

The thought that Prigozi may have come there, of all places, to destroy himself filled Moloch with alarm. He pictured himself stumbling over a cold body in the dawn . . . ignoring it as if it were the body of a murdered criminal. . . . And the questions Blanche would ask! All her foul suspicions. . . .

Naomi tried to soothe him. She kissed him passionately, stroked his hair, fondled him and whispered her love in words that burned his ears. But he was immune. Prigozi might as well be lying in bed with them, between them, his sorrowful face upturned, baying to the moon.

"No one will know about us, Naomi. Don't let him lie there. This is horrible. Let me go to him. . . ." In vain he expostulated. She refused to let him move.

"No, no, no!" she whimpered. "You must stay here. He won't die. You'll see—he'll go away. . . . He wouldn't do . . . *that.*" She buried her head on his bosom to avert the sinister shadow of the corpse.

Moloch thought and thought. "If one only knew what had happened to him! He might be shamming. It's not impossible for him to do a trick like that." He pursued this idea further, exhausting every shred of comfort there was in it. . . . To begin with, he asked himself, how was he to know that Prigozi hadn't followed him? On the other hand, supposing he were in distress, supposing he really did take a notion to search for him, wouldn't it be natural for him to come here first? He thought of their conversation in the lavatory, and the strange conduct of Prigozi thereafter. All that lunatic nonsense in the street, when they were taking him home—it was plain enough! The fellow was putting on so as to draw him back again. Prigozi couldn't very well say, "Look here, Dion, I changed my mind about Naomi, I don't want you to take her." . . . It was more simple to put up a ruse, to snare him away.

"By Jove! I have it!" he muttered, and sprang to a sitting position. Naomi sat up, too, and looked at him in bewilderment.

"The hell with him!" he exclaimed. "Let him lie there!" He pointed to the door with a gleeful expression, as though the door constituted a successful barricade against gnomes and goblins. Just then a whitish square gleamed with a faint reflected light at the crack of the door. He put his arm about Naomi and pointed to the object. There was a dark, irregular spot on the sheet of white as though a clot of blood had congealed upon it. Naomi was frightened; then she grew perplexed, and finally, unable to restrain her curiosity, she stole quietly out of the bed and tiptoed to the door. She bent over to examine the object. Moloch kept his eyes riveted to the spot.

She came close to him and held a piece of letter paper before his eyes. The dark spot was no longer there. Between her thumb and forefinger was the petal of a rose.

They lay flat on their stomachs and held the paper under the soft light that penetrated from beneath the window shade. The moment he glanced at the distorted characters Moloch was shocked. It was not that he recognized the handwriting. It would be impossible to recognize such a scrawl. He had seen such chirography before—from the pens of imbeciles and maniacs. His speculations were interrupted by the sound of Prigozi's heavy body rustling at the door. They were startled. They gazed at one another with an expression of dubiety. In a moment came the sound of heavy, firm steps. They heard the wooden stairs creak and groan under the firm, vengeful tread. . . .

Naomi gave a sigh of relief. "It was he!" she exclaimed.

"Of course it was!" Moloch stopped short. "What the devil!" he reflected. "Could she have thought all along it was someone else?"

He looked at her quizzically. Naomi continued to gaze at him with the same evident relief.

"See, I told you not to worry," she observed. She wondered what made him look at her so intently.

Moloch grasped the paper again and studied it carefully. Then he passed it to her to read. Naomi's scrutiny was brief.

"Could he have written this?" she asked.

"He must have written it in the dark. See how the letters run—up and down hill. Certainly he wrote it. He did it as he lay there frightening us with his damned nonsense. Oh, he's a sly devil, that bird!"

"But I can't make it out," cried Naomi, glancing again at the paper.

"You little goose! It's a saying from the Bible."

"Read it, then."

" 'Mene, mene, tekel, upharsin!' " He arched his eyebrows.

"Don't you know what it means? You said you recognized it."

"Certainly! It's the handwriting on the wall that Daniel saw at the Feast of Belshazzar."

"But what does it mean?"

"Oh . . . the goose is cooked, or something like that."

"Fancy that!" said Naomi. "He must be nuts!"

"You said it!"

They lay down to snatch a few hours' sleep.

"You know, kid," said Moloch quietly, after they had snuggled close, "you ought to read the Bible. No kidding! It's a marvelous book. There's everything in it; love, hate, fear, envy, malice, lust, greed, murder . . . everything that makes the world go round."

"What queer thoughts!" Naomi reflected aloud.
"Above all," he went on, "read Ecclesiastes."
Silence.
"Naomi, what's the matter? Aren't you listening?"
Naomi had fallen into a bottomless pit.

WHENEVER THE PHENOMENON KNOWN TO ASTROLO-gers as a "grand conjunction" took place this pockmarked planet became the scene of curious and extraordinary occurrences. The Great American Telegraph Company, for instance, usually responded to this portent by issuing a bonus to its employees.

Thus it happened that Dion Moloch found himself at Cooper Square one evening with several hundred dollars in his pocket. He might have bought himself an extra shirt or a new tie or, like most of the married men in the telegraph company, he might have rushed home to his wife with a bouquet of roses and, holding her hand to his, sat up half the night examining advertisements for suburban homes.

But he did none of these things. He kept the money intact in the right-hand pocket of his trousers. He had other plans. As he set his face towards the North River, whom did he see approaching but his very dear friend Randolph Scott.

"Well, you old bum!" shouted Randy, beaming affectionately.

They exchanged the usual greetings of old friends who have drifted apart and are somewhat ashamed of the fact.

"I wish you had been with me just a few hours ago," said Randy. "Pfui! I saw something that made me turn cold inside."

Moloch was curious. Randy could be upset by the most diverse phenomena. Sometimes he was overwhelmed by the sight of an old building being torn down; or, if it were late at night and a beggar accosted him, he went home blubbering. His latest revulsion was for dressed beef.

Randy stopped short in the middle of his narrative.

"Did you ever stop to examine a dressed pig?"

He made a shuddering grimace.

"Ugh! I saw one hanging in the window a little while ago. Man, you should have seen it! *All suet!* Christ! Do we turn into suet that way, too?"

Moloch let out a howl.

"So that's what's bothering you . . . *suet?*" He roared some more.

Randy looked peeved. "I don't see what's so funny in that. You go and stand in front of a meat store someday. Look at a dead pig for fifteen minutes. God, this one was nothing but fat, and the anus was simply a great big hole that had been cut away with a knife."

"And you're disturbed about how you're going to look when you're dead, is that it? Believe me, Randy, you won't look half so good, I can tell you that."

Randy hesitated a few moments. He was grappling with an idea.

"No-o-o," he drawled, "I don't give a damn what they do to me when I'm dead. I'm just thinking of what we carry around with us all the time—lumps of fat and gristle, blue and purplish veins, gizzards, bile, kidneys, a string of intestines . . . and that ugly damned skeleton. Wow!" He smacked his face soundly. It was a medieval touch, often employed in conjunction with the reading of Jeremiah.

Moloch thwacked him bravely for good measure. Randy coughed in embarrassment—one of those feeble theater coughs which saturates the culprit with the effluence of his own pity.

"It's not age that's getting you," said Moloch heartily, "it's just a touch of neurasthenia, you poor old slob. A little more poetry in your soul, and with that nervous sensitivity you could grind out marvelous stuff. The Germans would lionize you." He gave Randy a stiff poke in the ribs.

" 'Man and Woman Going Through the Cancer Ward'! How do you fancy that for a title?"

"Are you going daffy?" said Randy. However, he was growing decidedly more cheerful. To him cancer was almost as engrossing as insanity.

It was a splendid evening for morbid inquiries. Sepia-colored clouds rent the sky in tatters. The Sixth Avenue "L" structure shrieked with the weight of human freight; it was human freight, all right, because thick newspapers separated one piece of freight from the other.

Presently Randy raised his voice above the din of traffic and, fired with a druid's passion, bellowed in his companion's ear:

"At this very minute people are passing out by the thousands, begging the Almighty to forgive them. The earth is filled with groans and wailing. Children are being torn from their mothers in pangs of childbirth; ships are going down at sea while the multitude listens placidly to radio concerts, safe and snug at home. Destruction and misery everywhere—that's all I can see."

Moloch made an ear trumpet of his hands.

"And I see lovers and mistresses, husbands and other men's wives climbing into bed, snuggling under the blankets . . . Honolulu, Copenhagen, Zanzibar, Stamboul, Nagasaki, Moscow, Dubuque, Hoboken. They're all around us, Randy . . . *everywhere!* If we could only knock the walls down this minute, eh what?"

"You win," Randy exclaimed. "I knew we'd come to that sooner or later."

He put his arms about his friend and licked him with bloodshot eyes. The universe which a moment ago had been an abattoir floating in a crimson lake became a chop suey joint again. (For Randolph Scott!)

Randolph Scott once read, in the pages of a financial journal, that light travels fast until it encounters the human mind. At the mention of lovers climbing into bed through all the gridiron of latitude and longitude his mind traveled so fast that he thought the scientists had made an error when they computed the speed at which light travels per second. It was absolutely ridiculous, to be sure, but after he had violated queens, dowagers, scullion maids, and all the coryphées of the Folies Bergère in turn, his mind was as dry as the inner rind of a navel orange.

"Keep this under your hat," he announced, "but I've been striking some good stuff lately. You ought to get a car, do you know that?"

"Yes?" said the other, thinking of Roxand, daughter of the king of Samarkand, swooning in the mist of centuries.

"Do you still keep a notebook?" Moloch ventured to inquire.

"A notebook? What do I need a notebook for?"

"Telephone numbers."

"Telephone numbers? What . . . with the way these floozies are running around? Wait here a few minutes; I'll get you as nifty a piece of . . ."

"Hold on, Randy! Not now."

"Why? What are you doing?"

"Come along with me. I'm giving a blowout . . . wine, spaghetti, cigarros . . . any damned thing you want."

"What's come over you all of a sudden . . . too much money?"

"Hell, no! I'm paying off a bunch of old debts."

"Don't be foolish! Pay half of them . . . stick the rest in the bank. Come on, I know where we can pick up . . ."

"Nothing doing. You're coming with me. I'm throwing a banquet tonight. Here, it's right down this street. Are you coming?" shouted Moloch.

Randy seemed on the point of accepting, grew suddenly hesitant, and then stood stock still.

"Any women in the party?"

"No."

"No women?"
"No, I told you."
"So long, then!"
"So long!"
Neither turned to look back.

At eight-fifteen, punctual as a Twentieth Century Limited, Dion
Moloch and his thirteen satisfied creditors were moving south
and east in three Yellow taxis. Fourteen theater tickets, marked
A2, A4, and so on, were stacked in his vest pocket like so many
Sweet Caporal soubrettes which youngsters used to accumulate
in the days when Admiral Dewey sailed into Manila Bay.

At St. Marks-on-the-Bouwerie the flotilla turns into the Judean Way. St. Marks, in its somnolescence, is turning a gentle
tutti-frutti. Everywhere letters like music. Everywhere black
snow, lousy wigs, unfurled beards.

Watch this window for slightly used bargains!
Cut rates
Slashed prices
Must vacate

Buy, buy, buy! Poverty walking about in fur coats; match ven-
dors with fat jewels in the safe deposit vaults. Bankbooks hidden
away in tattered trousers. Turkish Baths, Russian Baths, Sitz
Baths, Public Baths. Baths, baths, baths—but no cleanliness.

Signs, placards, posters, electric light displays: the world made
palatable, fashionable, lecherous, odoriferous. Dirty linen, adenoids, catarrh. An irruption of pimples, blackheads, warts, and
wens.

A planet turned inside out, ransacked for trifles. A greasy vest,
this Judean Way, over the fat belly of the metropolis.

Further along, movie houses, clinics, dance halls, tabernacles.
The ghost of Jacob Gordin trudging through the blood-soaked
tundras of Siberia. Natacha Rambova in a Laura Jean Libby
anachronism. . . . *Parisian Love* with Clara Bow.

Still further along . . . "Bridgework, reasonable prices." The

Roumanian Rotisserie tickling the cold storage rump of Leo Tolstoy with the faint notes of a cymbalon. Renovated tenements converted into clean white facades glittering with pedagogical distinctions bulging with amorphous fur manufacturers and their bleating, dropsical consorts.

Messrs. Haunch, Paunch, and Jowl introducing Mme. Bertha Kalich in a morganatic marriage with the Second Avenue Chess Club. Frank Merrill in *The Speed King* . . . *The Golden Cocoon* . . . *Infatuation* . . . the Church of All Nations with Russian letters over the door.

In pillars of fire, threatening every evening at seven o'clock to turn the Manhattan Business School into a conflagration:

THE NATIONAL WINTER GARDEN

From a joke to a national institution! A laugh-exploding burlesque in nine explosions. *Burlesk*: like it was in the good old days.

STOP!!!

Turn to Walter Pater's *Renaissance*. The chapter on Botticelli.

"Besides those great men there is a certain number of artists who have a distinct faculty of their own, by which they convey to us a peculiar quality of pleasure which we cannot get elsewhere. . . ."

We will say no more about this conglomeration of bedlamites, this potpourri of pimps, pugs, and profanities, this melange of sybarites and cormorants. Not another word about acne, catarrh, eczema. Strike out the Kosher sign! These things are anathema to the polite American public. Besides, we are now in front of St. Augustine's Church, trying to break into the long line of ticket buyers that stretches like the lower intestine from Second Avenue to the Bowery, and back again.

A big sign has been slapped under the illuminated cross: NO PARKING. But the wards of Houston Street have long ceased to believe in signs.

The lean Episcopal rector stands on the steps of St. Augustine's Church and wonders if salvation *is* of the Jews. The church is as popular as an alderman without money.

The line moves like a corkscrew pushing into the neck of a bottle. Plenty of time to read the billboards; plenty of time to study Princess Lolo's anatomical modulations. Always a good show at the National Winter Garden. Always a liberal array of photographs. Three Oriental dancers with a string of beads. Soubrettes with a bun on. Hal Rathbun and his bevy of Rosebuds. Dion Moloch and his flotilla of cock-eyed creditors. Everybody's happy. "Ask Dad, he knows!"

An election rig rolls by with a calliope going full-blast. Seated on the front seat, in a convict's uniform, is a life-size dummy. The words of a popular song float out.

"DURCH SCHIECHTE SCILAVERIM ZUM ELECTRIC CHAIR."

Anglo-Saxons would call it "The Wages of Sin."

The line breaks to admit the passage of the buxom prima donna, swathed in 124 rabbit skins. She treads with mincing steps in coy red-heeled pumps.

"Let did lady pass!"

In the lobby two freight elevators with trick doors pump the crowds up to the auditorium. The doors slide open as smoothly as nutmegs scraping over grated glass. Bohunks, sick with anticipation, are dumped out pell-mell. Uniformed attendants are on hand to grab, grab, grab. . . . They are as shy as Tammany Hall politicians.

Moloch is mistaken for a judge, and is obliged to give the usher a tip. He assembles his henchmen with the air of Napoleon returning from Elba. Like the Corsican, devoid of ambition, moving on through the power of destiny. The audience is taken in like so much gathered snot.

A seething inferno of smoke-smothered red lights is the orchestra pit. Standees three rows deep behind what should be Z, for zebra. The Minsky Brothers are dreaming in the box office of adding an extension next season. They dream this every night for ten months of the year.

Pathé News clicks monotonously. Winter sports in St. Moritz; Al Smith posing as a newsboy; Oberammergau players warming up for the *Passion Play*; the President's wife in a set of new monkey furs; the Red Army, menace to the world, marching past the Kremlin; society belles giving *Oedipus Rex* for charity; blue ribbon chow dogs basking in superheated mansions; bathing beauties on floats, convinced that Atlantic City is a Mecca. . . .

Meanwhile the calcimined coloratura singer flings open the grimy window of her dressing room and gazes out over the rooftops and steeples extending limitless about her. Her brain is dizzy. She is debating whether to sing the Bird Song from *Pagliacci* or take the next train back to Allentown, Pa. New York is a filthy hole. Even the snow is dirty. And Signor Gatti-Casazza is a minotaur hidden in the adytum of a rose-scented labyrinth.

The tears of a burlesque prima donna are few, and not so expensive. Tears, expensive or inexpensive, are usually hidden by an asbestos curtain. And on the asbestos curtain, embroidered in letters of gold, is this epitaph:

"THE SHOW IS THE THING" —Shakespeare

Sad-eyed madonnas of avoirdupois, take a back seat! If ye must weep, weep where the Minsky Brothers cannot see. Shakespeare was right after all—"The show is the thing!" Afterwards . . . well, that's another matter. Cut your throat, if you like.

Is this Purgatory, or are we dreaming? Bam, wham, slam, crang-bang! The curtain goes up on a jabberwocky chorus with beery voices and dirty necks. (The Rosebuds, previously mentioned!) Withered, mildewed roses of the dungheap. A barrelful of chipped pewter and cracked mugs. Shapes like corrugated ashcans. All wiggling away for dear life. Four bucks a day and a steady job. (The management requests, dear Rosebuds, that you kindly endeavor to keep the creases from those regions of the abdomen known as the epigastric, umbilical, and hypogastric.)

An 1888 peroxide blonde, suffering from adipose tissue, waggles a wicked hip: front view, side view, back view. Back view— immense! Juicy layers of fat sloshing about like floodtide in a ferry slip. . . . *Ninth encore.* She glues herself to the floor and, with the control of a yogi, slowly, deliberately, mercilessly sets in motion those portions of the human anatomy about which the less said the better. For the 669th time the orchestra leader refuses the proffered chunks of meat. Up front judges, bank clerks, pawnbrokers, pick and shovel men—all busy gulping down oysters. . . .

More two-four flams from the traps and a ground bass of muffled roars like the stertorous last moments of a brontosaur. Thunderous applause licked up by the brass tongue of the orchestra.

Then, on with the dance! The joy is really unconfined, unformulated, unprognosticated. More hoochee koochee. Twenty-five song-and-dance installments to undress a pretty little Grand Street whore. Three-card monte. A medley of wisecracks. Ghostwalking done to uproarious mirth: Dr. Jekyll and Mr. Hyde à la Rube Goldberg. (No one suspects that Ben Ami is playing in English somewhere in the Tenderloin.)

Suddenly a brassy whang zam from the cymbals. A blanket of utter darkness, and then a cold blue spotlight accompanied by weird, exotic melodies from the woodwinds.

CLEO!!! DARLING OF THE GODS! OH MOMMER!

Izzy, the gallery god, downy with adolescence, gangrened with puberty, grips the cold iron rail with clammy hands. Izzy can't take his hands off the blood-red rose that hangs from Cleo's girdle. Someday she's goin' to lose that rose! Someday Izzy's gonna be there when it happens.

She's coming now, Cleo, from the wings. First an arm, snakelike and sinuous, followed by a leg from the Parthenon, and then her head, expressive as a turnip. Izzy's eyes are fastened upon her velvet torso. It swells and heaves like a green ocean billow. Izzy's forehead is a champagne bottle beaded with sweat.

Naked and sexed, Cleo moves like a wraith in a violet light, She is a hundred times more radiant, more vivid, than any dream. The air reeks with the perfume of her armpits. Izzy wants to screech. The molten fluid in his green body is choking him. He puts forth two scrawny arms. He embraces her. He takes her to him and crushes her, like a boa constrictor. The sinews of his muscles are twisted into a rag carpet. He groans with intoxication. His mouth is wide open, the tongue cemented to the roof. Every pore, every cell of his downy, gangrened body opens to receive the drench of ambrosial pollen. Music, flesh, incense: a kaleidoscope of undulating passions flash before him. Keep it up and Izzy will go cuckoo. This rot is too utterly utter. . . .

And all the while not a muscle of Cleo's face moves.

Of an instant, like a discharge of virulent pus, comes a frenetic crescendo from the pit. All of Cleo, from her generous breasts to her gleaming thighs, blazes forth with spasmic violence. Even the mollusks in the audience tremble and gasp before this grand whoop-la that seizes the torso with paroxysmal fury, shakes the cobwebs out of it, and subsides with volcanic tremors.

As the lights flash Cleo flees, drawing her iron filings into the wings. The Rosebuds, nothing daunted by this exhibition, are out front, wiggling hard. A mad stampede to the latrines follows.

Moloch and his troupe bridge the intermission by standing on the fire escape and peering through the dressing-room windows. The shades are up, and the windows partially open. Some one yells: "There's Cleo!" But it isn't Cleo. *"It's some other bum."*

The discussions on the fire escape and in the latrines are similar in character to those that take place daily in brokers' offices, barber shops, and political clubs. The important (!) female members of the cast are carefully sifted and graded, and then classified according to this or that . . . chiefly *that.*

After the intermission an illustrated song is thrown upon the screen. Everyone sings: "In Life's December, When Love Is an Ember". Under cover of darkness the ushers get busy with squirt guns. Now the entire edifice has the aroma of a urinal.

The curtain rises upon a solitary figure. It is the straight man, dressed in a shepherd's plaid suit. He is grave and sedate. He brings a message from the management. In the pose of a poet about to hurl a prologue into the uterus of the beyond he battens his straw hat over his diaphragm with flexible, gem-strewn fingers. . . . "Next week, with the aid of our inimitable comedian,

Hal Rathbun, we will put over a corking good skit entitled 'Pussy Café.' "

Moloch, who has heard this wheeze at frequent intervals ever since the year 1905, is so far lost in ruminations that the remainder of the show becomes a complete blank. He fumbles in his empty pockets. The wad is gone. According to the galumphs who stand up in the pulpit every Sunday and yawp about the hereafter his mind should be easy. He is free of debt. But he doesn't feel easy. He feels sore. To liquidate one's debt is not like throwing one's sins overboard. . . . He decides to walk out of the theater and leave the bunch flat. What the hell! He doesn't owe them anything. . . .

Plunging at once into the stench of the East Side he gave himself up to reflections upon the white-haired matron of the rest room. Old age had given her a fallen womb. He wondered what her thoughts were as she sat in the rocker amid the odors of disinfectants and Woolworth perfumes. Were all women in the chorus diseased? He thought of Randy and his suet complex. A nice question . . . "Do we all turn into suet?" There was a barrel of suet—yes, indeedy—in Hal Rathbun's bevy of Rosebuds. Take all excess fat, roll it into a ball, and you'd have enough fat for frying purposes to last the ordinary housewife a year. How about human fat? Fancy now, a vat of grease, of human grease, always on tap for weddings, banquets, clambakes, and so forth. . . . One of Hal Rathbun's wisecracks perched on the front porch of his brain: "the sewer rat and I." The expression carried no excess baggage with it. Imagine the Governor of South Carolina discussing his friend the governor of North Carolina and saying: "The sewer rat and I." . . . If one were to dally with such ideas the brain might go on a jamboree and land up in the psychopathic ward.

Threading his way toward the Delancy Street Bridge was like going on a rampage with the Jukes and Kallikaks. Washlines and fire escapes made symphonies only in the minds of poets and ultramodern painters. What a trite melodrama! Reginald Pierpoint Rockfeller, the villain, versus the Peepul of these United

States, the meek and lowly, the disinherited, the homeless homers of the brave. To a physician the scene is apt to suggest a warfare between conflicting armies of microbes, with human bodies as battlefields and pestilence as high explosives. For him there is only one remedy: LYSOL.

Dion Moloch experienced a plethora of sensations. Foremost among them was an itching sensation such as is sometimes produced by lying naked on dry breadcrumbs.

Gordon Craig once took Ibsen's *Rosmersholm* and gave it spiritual dimensions. Dion Moloch felt as though he had checked his soul at the National Winter Garden and was now delivering his bones to a charnel house. He tried to resurrect Cleo's priapic devotions. No go. The streets swarmed with maggots, the air was alive with vermin. Here a nose was missing, there an eye stuck out like an abscess. Deformities pegged along, rheumy, bile-ridden, lopsided, and demented. He stepped aside to make way for an idiot. There was a look of agglutinated oatmeal on the face of this overgrown fetus. Moloch shuddered. "An ax!" he cried. "An ax!"

He came to the Williamsburg Bridge.

A blast of the sea air smote him on the cheek. He sucked the ozone into his system with great gasps. The bridge was deserted on the footpath. It looked gray and sanitary. It matched his thoughts. "In the morning," he reflected aloud, "fetid tides of flesh will roll up and inundate this span; the beautiful steel girders will groan and creak with carrion, the entire edifice will crawl with human vermin, be drenched with garlic, sing with business."

The old Fourteenth Ward was waiting to greet him on the other side of the bridge. Night and the stars had settled down on the old neighborhood, it was festooned with melancholy. In youth the homesite may be dilapidated and asthmatic, but never melancholy. His mind now was a whirlpool of recollections. Willy Maine danced a dervish for him. "Crazy Willy Maine." A big shambling gawk with the brain of a tadpole, who used to crawl out on the shed of a Sunday morning, when the folks had gone to church, and exhibit himself in his undershirt. A thoroughly bestial exhibition which horrified the neighbors. "Bijork, bijork!" was the only utterance Crazy Willy Maine could articulate. There he would remain, on the shed overhanging the paint shop, carried away by his obscene divertissement, until his parents returned from church. The street gamins would shriek with hysterical glee. On the sly they fed this ape rotten bananas. Crazy Willy gobbled them up as if they were stuffed truffles. Later he would get an old-fashioned bellyache and scream at the top of his lungs: "Bijork! Bijork!"

Sunday mornings the old Fourteenth Ward usually opened up like a flower pot in Paine's fireworks. By nine o'clock, at the corner of Driggs Avenue and North First Street, things began to happen. Willy Maine wasn't the whole show. Silverstein, the tailor, generally crawled out of his scabby little shanty in his shirt sleeves, his suspenders flapping between his legs, and a pair of newly pressed pants slung over his arm to be delivered to Daly, the fishman. Johnny Paul, maybe, ducked into the saloon on the corner of Fillmore Place with a big glass pitcher hidden under the Sunday newspaper. When Johnny emerged he would wipe the foam off his lips—carefully, as if he were scooping gems into a casket. Soon Father O'Toole would come mincing along, a little bleary-eyed from Saturday night's shindig. "Good morning, Mrs. Gorman," says he, doffing his greasy lid. "Good morning, Father," says Mrs. Gorman very respectfully. Her hubby's drawers are hanging on the line in the backyard. "It's a sin to go to mass without drawers," yells the uxorious Mr. Gorman from the folding bed. "Sure, and it's a greater sin to lie abed on Sunday morning," shouts Mrs. Gorman, flopping about in her bed slippers and disturbing the neighborhood with her County Cork jabber.

By ten o'clock the ward heelers are out in full regalia, and William Jennings Bryan is sure to be the next President. Mike Pirosso is up on the roof, shooing his pigeons away with a piece of bunting stuck on the end of a long swaying pole. If he didn't have his pigeons to look after he'd go nuts tending the fruit stand all day and night. . . . In the old days a man could get along with just pigeons for relaxation. A man didn't have to go to the movies or break his neck getting nowhere in a tin buggy. Shucks! What if he did rush the growler a few times on Sunday? It made him feel good. It made him a public-spirited citizen, a man capable of voting the Democratic ticket.

Moloch had not yet cleared the South Side in his walk. He was making a beeline along Driggs Avenue. His thoughts flew ahead of him like motorcycle police escorting a rubber-tire cavalade. The Novelty Theatre loomed up, full of scars and rhodomontade. He saluted it in the name of Topsy and Denman Thompson. Corse Payton came later in his life, and not at the Novelty. The ten-twenty-thirty god was only a faint image now. The last time he remembered seeing him was at the bar of the Wolcott Hotel, Thirty-first Street near Fifth Avenue (somewhat out of bounds for this matinee idol); he was sipping his hot toddy to stimulate his hepatic cells. Corse Payton always had one unshakable conviction. That was that Shakespeare was the greatest genius who ever lived. To prove it, he would recite at any hour of the day or night Polonius's advice to Laertes.

Corse Payton, Larry Carroll, Pat McCarren: the best sprig of shamrock that was ever worn in Williamsburg's frock coat. When any of this trinity ambled along the thoroughfare there was life. It was years later that the North Side and the South Side became moth-eaten. But in that day men like old man Martin flourished. Professor Martin, if you please! Professor of bugology. Roach and rodent exterminator for the best hotels in New York. Worked single-handed, with a pair of ferrets and a concoction of powders invented out of his own head. When the Professor came reeling along Driggs Avenue, scattering coins, his red nose gleaming like the setting sun, you knew that God had found an answer to the Asiatic scourge. Professor Martin was a big man in a world that teemed with rodents. He commanded a high price. A bit of a blowhard, too, but a damned good spender. He threw fortunes across the bar. When he spoke of cigars, he said: "Yesterday I bought thirty-five hundred Havana cigars, at two hundred dollars the thousand." On Saturday nights he referred to his cigars in carload lots, and less carload. You can bet your bottom dollar there were no pikers in the Fourteenth Ward

. . . except a few Dutchmen. And, as everyone admitted with a smile, the only time that the Germans got ahead of the Irish was on St. Patrick's Day, when the band led the parade.

Moloch hot-footed it from one corner to another. North First Street was simply a broken actor. Not a sign of life. Not even a "Commit No Nuisance" sign, such as Sauer used to have hanging on his property. He stood peering in the basement of Sauer's old store. The familiar smell of leather came back to him . . . queer, big chunks of leather that used to lie curled up on the counter like slumbering Angoras.

He sat down on the curb in front of Miss O'Melio's house, drinking in every detail of the red brick house opposite. On the top floor were the windows he used to wash every Friday as soon as school was out. What a job! All the kids could see him from the street . . . the little pet washing Mamma's windows. From the top-floor windows he was able, once upon a time, to look down on Miss O'Melio's low roof, where she fed her army of stray cats. All the cats in Williamsburg were on that roof at feeding time. What ever put that bug in her head? Is that what happens to a woman when she can't get a man?

And underneath the pussy-cat sanitarium was the veterinary's. Always something going on at Dr. Kinney's establishment. Somedays the whole street smelled of iodoform. He had a fresh, clear vision of a horse pegged to the ground just inside the low archway; a man was sitting on the animal's shoulders, holding a big rag to its nose. When he grew up and went to college he realized that the operations he used to witness in Dr. Kinney's establishment were for purposes of castration. It dawned on him one day as he sat listening to a lecture on Spinoza. . . . "Now a horse," he thought, "hasn't any philosophy to give up. When a horse is gelded his joys and troubles are over. After that his only concern is oats . . . bushels of oats."

Well, and what was *his* concern right now? To get to bed, or prepare for eternity? He made a grimace, got up, stretched, and looked up at the roof of Miss O'Melio's. There wasn't even the ghost of a cat in evidence. After the Williamsburg Bridge was thrown open, and the Exodus commenced, even the cats were ashamed to remain in the old neighborhood.

He walked along morosely, taking his own sweet time. He didn't care a hang about sleep. His illusions, speaking figuratively, were wrapped in a neat paper bundle marked "Fragile." Thoughts about Blanche hovered in the offing; they stood off, these thoughts, at a respectful distance—in the way that mourners behave when they at last comprehend the tremendous grief of those about to witness the body of their loved ones lowered into the deep hole. Down, down, into the slimy pit, down into eternal darkness and worm-eaten corruption.

It wasn't that he felt he had made a mess of his life. It was rather that life had made a mess of him. . . . "He that believeth and is baptized shall be saved." . . . The Bible for you! What had baptism to do with it? One might with equal reason ordain: "Only vegetarians admitted." What about maggots, then? Where would they come off? Or didn't maggots have souls? What sort of soul would Crazy Willy Maine deliver at the Golden Gate? Perhaps there were compartments in Heaven just as in Continental trains . . . first, second, and third class. "Garlic eaters stand on the platform!"

He was passing the old Presbyterian Church. When, as a child, he had memorized the Twenty-third Psalm (it was a little worn-out, that psalm!) he was obliged to recite it to the white-haired minister. The minister used an ear trumpet to catch the words which he knew backwards. . . . "He maketh the lame to walk, the deaf to hear." (Drunkards and harlots given a thorough cleansing.) The thought of that silly old pfoof cutting up didoes with his fool trumpet made Señor Moloch savage. "Put up that trumpet," he shouted, hoping that his voice would carry across the valley of death, "and tell me whether the streets are paved with gold."

Silly stuff, talking that way in the middle of the night, with Williamsburg so silent, Pat McCarren dead and buried, and Larry Carroll's saloon looking like a morgue. But he had an insane notion to ask that dried-up centenarian with the ear trumpet to tell him what happened to all the dead horses that used to swell up and lie in their own filth in the middle of the street until the wagon came and took their bloated carcasses away.... When a horse swelled up, he stank. (Worse than a dead senator!) It didn't matter whether he was a racehorse once, or attached to a brewery wagon. They all stank at the finish. . . .

There was Teves, the funeral director. Just passed his place a minute ago. A nice, quiet little place next door to the Chinese laundry. Teves was always open for a game of pinochle, always waiting for new cadavers . . . for fresh orders, as it were. Sometimes they'd interrupt Teves in the middle of a good hand. It never made Teves sore, though. There were lots of good hands in a pinochle deck. You couldn't expect him to sit tight and say, like Jesus—"Let the dead bury their dead." Somebody had to be on hand all the time to shovel them under. Otherwise there'd be a helluva stink.

At the Bridge Plaza, Moloch borrowed a nickel from a newsboy. The boy didn't ask him for his name and address, nor did Moloch promise to mail him the five cents in penny stamps.

He took a Broadway train, marked "Cypress Hills," and settled down to chew the cud of reminiscences. It was a long ride, with two changes. The changes were uneventful. At the second change he got into an empty car and had his pick of discarded newspapers. He picked up a *Morning World.*

It was customary for him to take a squint each morning at the advertising section because sometimes the newspapers omitted to print the Great American Telegraph Company's want ads. Of course, they always got a rebate for these oversights, what good was a rebate if they had no applicants for "messengers from 16 to 21 on a piecework basis, good earnings, some make as high as $25 a week," etc.?

He took his usual squint. The ad was in all right. That meant a fine crop in the morning. He'd go through them like a dose of salts. . . . *What's this?*

M E N ! ! !
D O   Y O U   N E E D
A   F E W   T H O U S A N D   D O L L A R S ?

NOW AND THEN AS THE YEARS ROLL AROUND TOWARD THE HOLIDAY SEASON SOME OF US FEEL AS THOUGH WE'D LIKE TO DO A RIP VAN WINKLE TILL IT'S ALL OVER. THAT'S BECAUSE OF THE SLENDER BANKROLL. TO GIVE AT CHRISTMAS IS GREAT . . . IF YOU HAVE SOMETHING TO GIVE WITH. IF IT SHOULD HAPPEN THAT YOU NEED A FEW THOUSAND DOLLARS EXTRA THIS YEAR, whether you are

> **Engineer**
> **Foreman**
> **Shipping clerk**
> **Retired business**
> **Labor union leaders**
> **Superintendents, &c.**

or whatever your walk in life, IF YOU WANT TO MAKE A SUBSTANTIAL AMOUNT OF MONEY DURING THE NEXT FEW MONTHS WRITE ME A LETTER OR POSTAL CARD FOR AN INTERVIEW.   **XYZ, World, Downtown.**

"Dear Mr. XYZ," Moloch dictated in his sleep, "Your ingratiating exhortation in today's (yesterday's) *World* almost leads me to believe that there really is a Santa Claus. Who of us has not suffered from a too slender bankroll at Christmastime? Until I read your pleasing expedient in the morning paper I was much agitated by the problem of just which soporific to resort to in order to induce that hibernating condition which you refer to euphemistically as "The Rip Van Winkle." Now I am happy to learn that by merely spending the price of a postcard the secret of avoiding this periodical embarrassment can be revealed to me.

"You ask very pertinently (in capital letters) IF I NEED A FEW THOUSAND DOLLARS EXTRA. I not only need it *extra,* but constantly. In fact, to put it to you plainly—why should we keep anything from one another?—I should say conservatively that a few thousand dollars a year regularly would relieve me of the trying ordeal of writing you for information about some crack-brained scheme or other for peddling Christmas cards or silk hosiery.

"I have never been a retired businessman, or a labor union leader, nor even a shipping clerk, unfortunately. My previous occupational experience is necessarily denominated by that all-embracing caption '&c.' Undoubtedly you are sufficiently astute to gather from this just whether or not I am suited to the proposition of raking in a few thousand shekels in my spare time.

"If so, please let me know when I may be favored with an interview. There is less than ninety days till Christmas, and I don't like the idea of being stuck at the last minute (on Christmas Eve) with a measly seven or eight hundred in my wad.

"Yours for opulence in this world or the next.

"Dion Moloch, Esquire

or

Mr. Dion Moloch

or

Just Plain Dion Moloch."

15

THE SERENITY THAT MOLOCH HAD BEGUN TO MANIFEST of late is proving a source of mystery and irritation to his spouse. This poise, this grip on life, as it were, Blanche unfortunately is capable of attributing only to the appearance of a new star in the firmament of his adulterous brain.

How can we best describe the change he felt coming over him? Certainly it was not a moral improvement. Perhaps the simplest way to express it is that his soul made itself known; he no longer thought of it as an intangible entity inhabiting the body, and deserting it at death. This soul of his suddenly began to take on apostolic dimensions. It required attention, like a plant.

The book he had promised himself to write was completed. The manuscript was now reposing in a drawer of Mr. Twilliger's rolltop desk. It was to remain there for a period until that individual could go through it at his leisure. Neither Twilliger nor

Moloch, at this time, had any apprehension of the fact that this simple-looking document would serve, not many days hence, as a pretext for the dismissal of the erstwhile employment manager Dion Moloch. However, our narrative does not carry us that far. We have no concern with Dion Moloch as job-hunter and temporary lodger in the Miravski menage.

Significant of Moloch's changed attitude is his complete silence about the other sex. It is impossible for Blanche to fathom his motives. If she had consulted him in the matter it might not have proven such a mystery. Valeska had been transferred to a post of importance in Havana as soon as the President of the company got wind of the fact that she was not a pure Caucasian. How the President acquired this delicate piece of information is another story; it is enough to hint that Mr. Twilliger's chief tailor was still proving his ability to earn his salt. As for Marcelle, well—Moloch began to realize that she had never been anything more than a depraved virgin. Her virginity stank, like Father Zossima's corpse. Concerning Marcello's virginity Blanche, of course, affected a complete ignorance. Possibly she never thought of the young lady's virginity in a purely analytical way. As for such an expression—"depraved virginity"—it is doubtful if Blanche could ever regard it as having anything more than a vague literary connotation.

The sullen bitterness of the woman, her morose defiance, the silent, repressed fury whose malignant potency would heretofore have goaded him into desperation—all this he endured now with a calm, pervasive air. He had acquired the habit recently of referring, in a dark way, to his spiritual state, or condition. Blanche regarded this enigmatic nonsense as a religious travesty. She dosed him with vitriolic shafts of ridicule. It was not, as with some husbands who pose before the world as martyrs, a showcase stoicism that Moloch displayed. Indeed, there was nothing of suffering, or of consciously willed forbearance, in his attitude. He was simply possessed by a fantastic exuberance.

In this condition of exaltation he came home one evening to find his supper on the stove. Blanche was not there. He examined the food that had been left for him with an abstract air. Presently there was a knock at the door, and the woman upstairs poked her head through the door. She came to inform him that Blanche had gone to the theater.

He smiled tenderly at her. Was it so, indeed? He seemed over-joyed at the news. Had Blanche gone to see *Androcles and the Lion*? No? He mentioned another. Not that either? The woman repeated that she hadn't the least idea where Blanche had gone. Well, what did it matter? He would go out and purchase a bouquet for her. Perhaps the good woman would sit down a few moments and sip a little port wine with him? It was always well to keep a little port wine about the house for just such occasions as these. He apologized for the absence of anything better than port wine. . . . Ideal weather, wasn't it? Had she noticed the moon this evening? Why did people insist on mentioning green cheese when they referred to the moon? It was more like a mauve scimitar, if you asked his opinion. Had she ever thought about the moon?—that is, in dactylic hexameters?

The woman listened to him as if he were a broken shutter slapping against a stone wall. She had expected a radically dif-ferent tune. If a palliative had been necessary she was there with a harmless little fib or two up her sleeve.

"A man's home is his palace, eh what? God, that supper smells inviting! I should have said 'an Englishman's home.' Come on in. Don't stick your head in the crack like that. You're not afraid of me, are you? How about some wine . . . or a little marmalade?"

The old harridan wagged her solemn, tousled head.

"Well, as you please," he mumbled, and fell to.

He finished the meal hastily. The bottle he had dug up stood on the table untouched. "Drink deep," said the poet, "or taste not of the Pierian spring." He walked into the living room on pads of velvet. The disorder which greeted him was a philosophic disorder. It reminded him of a chapter from *Creative Evolution*. He was accustomed to thinking of this room as a birdcage in which his intoxicated guests deposited their cigarette butts, crumbs of *Streusselkuchen*. But now he thought, "Only a Ger-man can be annoyed by untidiness." He sat down at the piano and crossed his legs. With his left foot on the right-hand pedal he played the opening measures of Stojowski's "Love Song." His technique was rusty. He uncrossed his legs and turned to Czerny's studies in velocity. "Bah!" he muttered disconsolately. "Life is too rich to be squandered in exercises." Anyway, it was getting too late in the day to ever become a musician. He wished someone had taught him a ruder instrument. Somewhere he had once read of artists returning to their cold garrets in the Latin Quarter and silencing their hunger with an accordion. . . . Probably Delineator artists!

He got up and took a seat in a low-cushioned armless chair. Did Blanche ever think of the associations wrapped up in that chair? he asked himself. To tell the truth, he hadn't thought about that chair for three years himself. It belonged to another period—the period called courtship. Marriage dissolves courtship just as vinegar dissolves pearls. (Cleopatra once dissolved her pearls in an effort to swallow a fortune.) A sentimental song from Laubscher's Biergarten came to his lips: "Es War So Schön Gewesen." . . . Try that on your piano when the sands of the desert grow cold.

His fingers were toying with the frazzled edges of an unframed picture. It was done in crayon on a piece of pasteboard. The edges were fat and greasy, like a well-used pack of playing cards. The picture had hung in the one spot so long it had almost lost its meaning. But it seemed a wonderful study now—an eloquent expression of the artist's joy. The peace that hung in the room made the picture dance. The appearance of the room was, as usual, drab. If anything it was a trifle drabber, filthier. But the peace that was in his heart transformed everything.

The young lady who had made the sketch was dead. She had become so thoroughly saturated with the drunkenness of life that she up and killed herself one day. She up and killed herself out of sheer joy. It's the fashion nowadays to deride such tales. It is said "people don't do such things . . . out of joy!" Or some "smart aleck," as Stanley would say, will mention Dostoevsky . . . as though only in Russian literature, among the epileptoid geniuses, do we encounter such . . . such—shall we call it—*bravado*? But Milka had acted in precisely this manner. He turned the sketch over. On the back she had penciled: *"Forsan et haec olim meminisse iuvabit."* That was her idea about everything. Wherever she went, she used to affix as her seal and signature this quotation from Augustus Caesar's prime ballyhoo artist. Perhaps it sounds indelicate to mention this, but it was so—she had even put her signature on the toilet box one day. The sound of gurgling water trickling through the drainpipes—that, too, she had to lend the stamp of her approval . . . the *"Forsan et haec olim meminisse iuvabit."* A great girl, Milka!

He examined the work carefully. There was a great superabundance of vitality in it. He scrutinized it meticulously, as if it were the very first time he had looked upon it. . . .

It represented a female nude, with Nile-green hair, squatting on her haunches. The interstices made by the junctions of her arms and legs were outlined by black triangles, some isosceles, some scalene. The one which a casual observer would notice first was a daring scalene, within the boundaries of which the artist had traced her initials. For the most part, the stuff of which this nude was made was nothing more than the untouched pasteboard. The crayon had been employed most liberally for the highlights and the luminous shadows of her contours, the artist being of the opinion of Mallarmé, whose dictum it was that "to name is to destroy, to suggest is to create." If one looked more closely at these innocent highlights fantastic shapes emerged: the hostile poise of a cobra along the right forearm, a penguin airily traced along the shinbone of the left leg, and an Achilles heel (Milka insisted it was *"Achilles"*) on the visible breast, a great Amazonian breast that seemed chiseled in marble. The nipple of the breast was a bright drop of blood. It was the brightest spot, with the possible exception of the lips, in the entire conception. Despite the railway curves of her crouch, the subject revealed more straight lines than the human figure can be said to boast. One such line was made of the top of the right hand, which might conveniently have supported a card tray, only Milka had seen fit to rest on it a cumulus cloud through which a wild goose was flying. Milka had insisted it was a wild goose, though it was so conventionalized, and had such a rigidity, that everyone said it resembled a roast turkey. However, if the artist saw a wild goose, a wild goose it must have been. . . . The reader must be aware, at this point, that Milke was untrammeled by academic canons. . . . Irritation was likewise often expressed by the liberties that Milka had taken with the right knee of the nude. The knee had been sacrificed to the imagination, owing to the enormous length of the upper leg, which which would have been cramped in the narrow confines of its pasteboard frame. When Milka was taken to task for this desecration, she observed in her quaint way that only a master could do justice to the knee of a virgin. But surely the nude had two knees? Absolutely! (Milka had not borrowed her subject from a Coney Island freak show.) But the other knee was hidden, you understand, and very skillfully, too, by a huge pendant breast which forever threatened to be metamorphosed into a cataract of human gore. . . . There was one other object, in the foreground, which deserves mention. It had no other reason for existence than the artist's will. What it was can only be conjectured. Milka styled it a geranium *without a flower pot.* She never said simply—a geranium. It was always a geranium *without a flower pot,* as if some mystic import were to be attached to the naming of an invisible object. It sounded very much as if one were to say—"Beethoven without a hat."

Supposing you were in the habit of placing your cane in a certain corner of the office, and then one day you were to march in absentmindedly, like a proofreader, and place it in the spittoon. Now the same incongruity applied to this Amazon's breast. It was as importunate as a harelip. . . . As Moloch concentrated his powers upon it his mind raced back to another Amazon . . . a buxom, *two-breasted* Amazon by the name of Cora. There was a time when to have possessed Cora would have meant his soul's salvation.

But Cora is out of the picture. . . .

"Can a man by taking thought add a cubit to his stature?" He pondered that as if the words were stuck under his nose in six-inch Goudy type.

"What shall it profit a man if he gain the whole world and lose his own soul?" Aye, he pondered that, too.

When a man takes to feeling deeply he is apt to let the Bible go to his head; he is apt to forget that the love his wife bears him is a caldron of hate which she delights in heaping anew each day upon his head. For what did her love—*their* love—amount to? It was nothing less than an unholy antagonism that had reached such bounds as to resemble more the celebrated Darwinian struggle than a bed of roses. If his wife embraced him it was only to ask: "Whom do I remind you of now?" If he touched her familiarly, as a husband will, she bristled and said: "All you think of is sex."

In his exalted spiritual condition much of the bitterness had dropped out of his soul. When a person loses the power of sight in one eye the other eye makes up for the deficiency . . . compensates, we say. So it was with these two. What he lost in powers of hatred Blanche supplied. No longer did he get up in the morning, draped in an old-fashioned nightshirt, and dance about her like a zany. It was disgustingly true that very often in the past he had carried on in a gross, buffoonish manner. It was true, also, that he had done so with the express purpose of irritating her. To rid his wife of that devastating glacial stare he had been capable, in the past, of resorting to any licentious prank. Better to see her rage than to withstand the cold, piercing hostility of the women. Sometimes, prompted by an inexplicable diabolism, he would stand before his wife, making abscence grimaces, pelting her with vile epithets that made her wince and blanche. Why? To goad her into behaving like a human being. To befoul her, if necessary, in order to get that "reaction" Prigozi always spoke about. You see, he had already committed himself to that belief that he was dealing with a type of pathologic abnormality. He never defined the type; he was satisfied to call her a "diseased soul." Blanche, in turn, made her own diagnoses. She used the word "hyper-sexed." No matter what the argument was about, no matter what turn the quarrel took, Blanche always ended up with "hyper-sexed." She flung it at him as if it were a red-hot poker. Later, when he had time to reflect, and devoted his attention to analyzing her conduct, he found refuge behind such phrases as "vicious slut," "ingrown Puritanism," etc. And of all the afflictions that humanity was heir to, he was ready to swear that Puritanism was the worst. There was something leprous about that condition of the soul. Its ravages brought a stench to the nostrils. . . .

But this evening all such behavior, all the wanton, vicious thoughts which he was able to summon on the slightest provocation, vanished. He could scarcely wait for Blanche to appear. Never again was she to suffer for any deviltry of his . . . not even if she ridiculed him and taunted him. He looked back upon his cruel, senseless behavior with abhorrence. "By God!" he swore. "This madness must come to an end!"

He reviewed kaleidoscopically the stormy course of their marital career. A conviction began to steal over him that his had been the blame, his entirely. Thinking back to one quarrel upon another, he could put his finger on the root of every one . . . *himself.*

Oh, if Blanche would only walk in now, this very minute, that he might sweep away all her hatred, all her profound disgust, and prostrate himself at her feet. "Blanche," he murmured aloud, "Blanche, my poor little dear, it is I who am guilty . . . I, I, I."

At that moment he imagined himself another Raskolnikov, another assassin waiting for the words of a Sonya: "Go to the marketplace and kneel before the multitude. Go and confess your sins. Speak to God in the public square; pray to him on your knees, so that every one may hear. . . ." He got down on his knees. He made his appeal to the Almighty. No snout-faced moujik ever prayed more lustily. His prayers were woven in the strands of her hair, in the letters of her name.

And, even as he did so, the door opened gently. Blanche stood there listening.

Her first temptation was to laugh. Never had she seen a more grotesque object than this figure, this obscene bedmate of hers, huddled in an attitude of reverence. She had a wanton desire to laugh outright—a spiteful, mocking laugh that would chill the very marrow of his bones. But the prayerful babble from his blasphemous lips, the earnest flood, so unlike the scoffer she had known, silenced her. She heard the sound of her name as she had never heard it before. For the instant she was touched; her hatred was at the point of melting before this devout furnace. But, at that very moment when, overwhelmed by this example of sincerity, she was about to throw herself at his feet and pour out her affection so fiercely withheld, a morbid, blighting suspicion entered her brain. With a blinding radiance the idea flashed through her mind that he was . . . yes, that he was *jealous.*

The knowledge that he loved her increased her bitterness. Her faint lease of gladness was despoiled by the swollen floods of resentment that welled up in her and urged her impulsively to wrest from him the last drop of servitude. . . . Hitherto his jealousies had been the sullen, fitful fires of a vengeful spirit. They were of short duration and but added fuel to the flames of discord. Never had she witnessed such an attitude of contrition . . . the more convincing, too, since her arrival was unanticipated. Was it, though? She indulged in a fleeting perplexity, as if to diagnose from past performances the cause of this abject surrender.

When he realized her presence in the room, in spite of himself, a chill came over him. He had in mind, when this moment should arrive, to throw himself at her feet . . . and evacuate his emotions. He had imagined that when the door should open, and the miracle of his deliverance rend him, all the pent-up agonies of his shameful ways would bubble over and flood her in a glamorous spate of words. Now they stood face to face, each trying to pierce the veil which separated them. She was mute, impenetrable, unapproachable. And yet a passion stormed through her blood, took possession of her heart, and leaped with the turbulence of a freshet to the fastness of her lips. A wistful expression gathered between her eyes, like a low-hanging fog pressing against two arc lights. She no longer remembered that her soul had been smashed to bits on their Procrustean marriage bed; she was aware only of a gathering ache that clutched with tenacious fingers and hollowed her with groans.

Moloch had left his wife that morning the image of a hopeless slattern. Her tiny Cupid's mouth, which he kissed perfunctorily, had seemed a trap geared with invisible wires and pulleys that caused it to open and shut with a mechanical cadence that at once fascinated him and repelled. When the hinge moved, and the trap fell open, he could see the taut filaments of her geranium-colored tongue. It wagged like a poodle dog's tail, her tongue. It never ceased wagging. When the trap opened the tongue fell out and lapped against a full lower lip or slid reptilewise along a bank of lace-pearl molars. That very morning he had restrained an insane notion to leap at her and bite the damned thing out of her mouth.

Now he stood gazing helplessly at the tremulous corners of her pursed lips. He expected them to open and utter mysterious language. They did open. They parted sweetly on these words: "Jim Daly came to town. I just left him. We spent the evening together."

"Then you didn't go to the theater?" He was left openmouthed, speechless.

She expressed surprise that the news should affect him so strangely. If the long-heralded Messiah had made the long-promised terrestrial descent it could not have affected him more.

"Are you . . . *hurt?*" she asked.

He shook his head slowly, sorrowfully. He was too overcome even to throw out a monosyllable.

She flew on in a light, gossipy vein. . . . "I would have brought him here only he had to return on the midnight train. He sends you his warmest regards. It was just a flying visit . . . to see how we were getting along, he said." She paused. "Do you know, he acts as if he can't believe that I'm still married to you. I guess he's still waiting for me. . . ." She paused again, to study the effect of her words. Had she said enough?

"Poor Jim," he said suddenly. "I can't help liking him. He was a brick. . . . He was the one you should have taken, Blanche."

A mirthless laugh gurgled from her tiny Cupid's mouth.

"A pity you didn't think of that before. A fine time to tell me what a mistake I made."

He started to speak again. She was gazing at him in utter amazement.

"You remember the night we stayed at the Claridge Hotel . . . just a week before we were married? You remember telephoning your aunt the next morning from the hotel? You recall that

she told you Jim Daly was on his way to New York to see you
. . . that there was a telegram for you?"

"Yes, yes," she said, looking at him bewilderedly. "I remember everything . . . *everything,* very distinctly. I stayed at the hotel
all that day, and Jim met me there."

"He came to see you on a very important mission, didn't he?"

Blanche hesitated. "Ye-e-s," she faltered.

Moloch pressed on. He reminded her of the events that followed upon that meeting, their little banquet at the Café Bous-
quet, the discussion they carried on, the way Jim and he took to
each other immediately, the strangeness of that mutual admiration.

Blanche was getting impatient. "I know all that. What of it?"

"Well, after I took you home that night, and you told me you
had refused Jim your hand, I went back to the Claridge and went
to bed with Jim."

"You did?" she gasped. "You never told me that!"

He paid no attention to this exclamation.

"Yes, I went back to your lover and told him everything, I was
so touched that I volunteered to remove myself, and let him have
you."

"You told him everything?" she cried, ignoring the remainder
of his speech. "God, I detest you for that! Who gave you the right
to do such a thing? You're a brute! The idea of torturing him that
way . . ."

Moloch smiled. "I don't believe he felt tortured. He liked it—I
mean the dramatic qualities of the scene. He took a great fancy
to me. Really, we became excellent friends—just on account of
my actions, I believe. Oh, it was a regular Alphonse and Gaston
scene, all right. We never slept a wink all night."

"You think it quite a joke, don't you?" Her voice had become
hard and bitter again.

"No, I don't," he replied at once. "Of course, it does seem a
trifle ridiculous now. But at the time it was very real, very tragic,
for both of us. You must remember, we were genuinely in love
with you . . . then." (He was sorry he had added that "then.") "It

was no light resolution on my part to relinquish you. For once I was capable of forgetting myself and my own selfish desires. Perhaps it was because I wanted you so much that I could understand and share his agony. I'm sure he understood my motives. He realized that it wasn't just a bit of playacting. . . . What will you say if I told you that we shed tears over you? We lay there like a couple of schoolgirls, raving about you, gloating over your beauty, admiring the charm of your character, weeping about you as if you were some lost princess. . . ."

"And my figure . . . my beautiful breasts . . . what did Jim have to say to that?"

"Your figure? Your breasts?" He stared at her confusedly. At the same time he was aware that her figure had changed . . . for the worse.

"Yes," said Blanche, "I mean my body . . . since you discussed *everything.*"

He was taken back. He didn't know whether to ask her or not.

"You mean," he began timidly, reluctantly, "you mean that you thought I told him about . . ."

"Why not? You said a moment ago that you had told him everything."

"Blanche," he said, and his voice dropped, "do you mean that you believe I would say—? You thought me capable even then . . .?" It was impossible to get it out.

"Oh, God!" she exclaimed. "How can I believe you? You lie to me so. . . . Are you sure, Dion? Are you certain?"

He hung his head. He was ashamed of her, of himself, of the whole god-damned business of love and what it had brought them to.

Blanche went over to him impulsively. She threw herself in his lap, and begged him to forgive her. She realized now that she had been mistaken. . . . He said nothing. He let her talk. Blanche clung tight. She poured a flood of strange, tender words in his ear. It was a new kind of joy for her. He took down her hair and buried his lips in the soft silky mass that hid her face.

At last he spoke. His voice was soft and suasive.

"Tonight, dear . . . what did you tell Jim?"

"Not now," she pleaded. "Don't ask me now. Nothing is changed."

"But what do you think . . . about Jim, I mean?"

She crumpled up in his arms and closed her eyes that he might not see the tears which were streaming down her cheeks. "I . . . I don't know what to think," she murmured.

He pressed her no further. Her limbs were trembling violently. Thus the earth trembles when fear-crazed buffalo stampede. . . .

Gently he brushed the tangle of hair from her brow, and placed his tender lips upon her eyelids. Her peppery breath, like the odor of sandalwood, left him careening through a dizzy vortex. The room was a Pompeian fresco of sound and space. Through every spore and interstice of his palpitant flesh the elixir of her veins penetrated and drugged him. Outside, in the night, a whorl of glinting pinpoints studded the expensive dome of a ravaged universe. His thoughts, gushing like a geyser, fled quivering into the night. "Just love, just love," he repeated to himself, transfixed by the swell of her abdomen, which rose and fell like a sea.

"You do love me, then, Dion?" Her voice was a torn veil.

He answered with lowered eyes, blinded by the milky hues of her thighs.

Somewhere in North Africa the baobabs were rustling in the keen night wind. A wave of passion engulfed him as a Spahi is caught in a simoom.

The mask with which she met the world fell from her as a yashmak is lifted to admit the gaze of a lover. Her body became a lovely, sacred vessel, such as it once had been. The sweeping contours rose in velvet undulations. The skin was cool and chaste to the touch. It reminded him of a Cretan urn, diapered with splintered jewels, carved with handles of rare ivory.

All the lies, the counterfeits, the baseness of his past was transmuted by her love into a gospel of devotion. The parched infidelities, like a barren soil in which they had struggled and starved together, promised to blossom and flower under the rivulets of this reawakened passion. Deep down in the rich sub-soil of love hope took root.

A pale finger of light invaded the room upstairs. They undressed in tense silence, shy and oppressed by the heavy gloom in which the room seemed to float. In the dark nuptial loam which they had rediscovered their desires expanded and fructified. Scalding tears trickled down the white of his flesh and caressed him. They were her tears. They burned into the lymph and tissue of his organism until they were identified with the adulterous specters of forgotten loves. . . .

There were women he had known under the coverlet whose sloe eyes were Niagaras of repentance. Some had a stagnant beauty that exhaled a miasma which dulled the senses. Some fell into his arms like marble goddesses toppling from their pedestals. These were excited by the tremors of their fall. Some cowered like nuns under the twilight of their robes, surrendering themselves in a swoon to the desecration of his touch. Some fairly reeked of passion and whispered inflammatory words that left a sulphurous gleam in their wake. . . . No one was like another.

He felt his wife's grip tightening about him until it seemed that they must be welded together. All her fears, all her desires and hopes, were dissolved in one stupendous wrack of passion. An autumnal unison, beaten out of the shattering dissonances of their lives, fused the turmoil of their hearts.

16

THE MAELSTROM OF SUBTERRANEAN PASSIONS WHICH
sucked these two human beings under left their bodies strewn on
the bed like wreckage next morning. Moloch scooted off to work
without disturbing the prostrate figure of his wife. She remained
outstretched, her oval face lost in a wilderness of hair, her lips
slightly parted in an attitude of expectancy.

What had been accomplished? he asked himself. Was this to be
the beginning of a new life? The answer to this was lost in a
vague, scattered silence of the flesh. He felt like one who had
been encircled with drum-fires, whose very soul had been singed,
and was now curling up, scarred and shriveled, under the tunic
of his skin.

She's not the piece of wood I thought I had been living with,
he decided. The idea of identifying her with a piece of wood
intrigued him. He wondered if Jim Daly had found her very

wooden the night before. It was a vile thought, and he tried to suppress it, but think what he would he was seized with the notion that there was something unusual, if not suspicious, about her sudden, inflamed ardor. He tried the sequence of the dialogue which had precipated their reunion but his memory of words was no more than a white ash, powdery, opaque, and cool to the touch.

The rapprochment which they had established was not quite on a plane with the spiritual solidarity he had envisaged, he himself saw. Again kneeling before the low-cushioned chair, praying for the moment when Blanche should return and unleash his impetuous declarations. He had anticipated a studied silence, a withering glance, and expression of dubiety, perhaps even consternation. But he was totally unprepared for the vision of loveliness which had assailed him. The vision rose before him again, in all its phantasmal lure; it spread its wings about him and crushed him to the earth. The rich loam in which they had wallowed still clung to him. He shuddered ecstatically and made an involuntary movement as if to free himself from the cloying stains of the earth. . . . No one was like another. . . . Some there were who fell like marble godesses toppling from their pedestals.

He arrived home that evening, three quarters of an hour earlier than usual, in a somewhat disordered state of mind. Blanche was absorbed in the excitement of turning the room into an inferno with her bone-cracking pyrotechnic. He sat on the couch and listened to the massacre of the "Liebestraum."

Sensing the silent imprecations which her consort usually reserved for such compositions, Blanche abandoned her efforts and commenced tinkering with Stojowski's "Love Song." It was Stanley who had once said that Blanche ought to be restrained by law from committing this sacrilege. Stanley's Polish ear was limited to a narrow range of musical compositions, but within those limitations his judgment was precise and unfaltering. Whether it was because she had no soul for Slavic lyricism, or whether it was due to an innate sterility, it was a fact that in the realm of sentiment, of tenderness, of passion, she was lost. The flail-like automation strokes with which she belabored the instrument made every nerve in his body twitch with pain. She had taken to repeating a certain passage, breaking it up into its component measures, dissecting every chord, every arpeggio. Her bludgeon strokes fell with the methodic, senseless beat of a metronome. Every note was a fresh bruise. Moloch buried his head in the pillows to muffle the hideous din.

Lying thus, with eyes closed and ears partially stopped, he was besieged again by the insidious advances of her flesh. He remembered how he had left her in the morning, lying mute and exhausted, with half-opened lips. At the office, engrossed in the petty preoccupations of routine, this fresh image had been forgotten. He was pleased, consequently, when he arrived unexpectedly, to find her arrayed like a practiced coquette. In all the petty details which had to do with her personal appearance, such as the selection of her attire, the gloss of her nails, the arrangement of her coiffure, she had become suddenly (miraculously almost) attentive. This inordinate fastidiousness had extended so far as to embrace even the living room, which heretofore had always been a triumph of artistic neglect. The room now presented the peaceful, ordered charm of a virgin's sanctuary. The pleasant sensations induced by this complete metamorphosis were swamped by the unsuccessful blend of her washboard dynamics. The very mention of Liszt was sufficient to suggest to his mind the pleasures of the carousel, the imbecilic blasts of calliopes, *déjeuner sur l'herbe* with frankfurters and ants.

The melodies of these two love themes were telescoped, as if they were two express trains colliding in successive dreams. They became inextricably interwoven, forming a huge contrapuntal pattern that beat an insensible tattoo upon his frayed receptors.

The faces they brought with them to the dinner table were like burnt-out craters. They roused themselves intermittently to pass a bowl of vegetables, or exchange vapid comments concerning the flavor of the tea, or the state of the weather. He thought he read a declaration in her eyes that this surrender of the previous evening was merely a truce.

The reality which she dragged to the table made him conscious of a larger unreality that existed in a submerged state. This hidden disturbance floated through the room like the submerged bulk of an iceberg guided by unknown boreal currents.

He made a number of efforts to foster a flood of small talk. Blanche refused to be coerced. His words were tiny rills flowing into an ocean of silence. Finally he managed to rap out a polite, insincere query about her mother. It was seldom that he dared to trespass on these grounds. For some reason Blanche had put a taboo on "mother" talk. However, that individual was expected now in a day or two.

The word "mother" seemed a convenient lightning rod in the electric disturbance about to break.

"You find this a very exciting topic, I notice." It was Blanche opening the bombardment.

"Exciting . . . exciting? That hardly seems the word, Blanche. I don't understand you." He knew he was skating on thin ice. What the devil was she up to now? "You know I've always liked your mother," he said aloud, as though to convince her by these harmless words that he was merely repeating an idle assertion.

"I know how much you like. Well, she'll be here soon enough . . . you won't be disappointed."

"Now, Blanche, what's the meaning of this?" His voice betrayed an increasing irritation. Fine! They would be at it again in no time . . . hammer and tongs.

Since she said nothing to this he went on. It was imperative to defend himself, no matter what direction the attack came from. He was waiting to see "the whites of their eyes."

"So you haven't the slightest idea what I'm driving at? You sit there as though you expected me to tell you a pretty little fairy tale." She paused a moment. Then, agitato: "Why did you get home so early today? Thought she'd be here, eh? Couldn't wait till she arrived?"

He repeated the last line like a refrain. He glared at her furiously. "Speak out!" he bellowed. "Don't beat about the bush this way. Always these damned insinuations."

"Oh-ho! *Insinuations?* I do like that. You're annoyed, are you? Think perhaps I imagine things?"

"I think that you're capable of imagining anything." He no

longer cared what he said. He was utterly beside himself.

She kept fending him off, stinging him with light jabs, buzzing around like an insect. Her words fairly crackled. It was not so much what she said; it was the implications concealed behind every remark that made him raw and helpless.

"You think you can run off and leave me here alone every night, and then when you've had your bellyful and your conscience bothers you, you expect to come home and find me waiting here like a neglected mistress who is ready to fall in your lap for a smile or tender word."

This sentence, delivered all in one note, took the breath away from her.

"What has all that to do with your mother?" he asked, regaining his composure. (A mistake to revive the "mother" theme. He realized that at the moment it was out.)

"You'll find that out, too," she hissed. "It's high time you were informed of a few things. . . ."

"Look here," he blurted out, "just what do you mean by that?"

He observed that she hesitated, apparently reluctant, even in her rage, to disclose the rankling. When she had gained sufficient mastery of her emotions to formulate her thoughts with some semblance of coherence, she proceeded. At first he listened incredulously. A skillful detour that concealed the direction of her target almost convinced him that he had nothing to worry about, that she had missed her objective. But just as he began to feel wholly assured, a thorough disquiet overtook him and he was victimized by a premonition of impending disaster. "She's leading me by the nose," he said to himself. . . . "Leading me right up to the brink of the precipice." And sure enough she was. He knew every inch of the road they were taking. *"But how in God's name could she have kept it down so long? Could she really have known all the time and preserved this horrible pretense?"* For a moment he harbored the suspicion that she was feigning a secret knowledge, and that this torture had been premeditated with the purpose in mind of making him squirm and fidget until he himself blurted out the truth. . . . But he was wrong in this conjecture.

It was obvious that she knew everything. The picture was only too complete.

The tableau which she mirrored from him was of such a monstrous nature that—well, once the truth was out he no longer heeded her, his mount found it difficult to pierce the limits that hedged this piece of isolated depravity. . . . "My own mother—to think of it!" That phrase lodged in his brain like the knife of an assassin. His thoughts raced backwards and forwards over detail connected with the unhappy circumstances she had just related. He searched vainly for some crumb of justification. He ransacked his heart, scoured his conscience. There was nothing to cling to, absolutely nothing.

Yet there was this iota, let the people say what they would: this woman, this mother of Blanche's—had she ever acted the part of a mother? Was it not that which had emboldened him to look on her with offending eyes?

To understand what was taking place in Moloch's brain it is necessary to forget for a space this conjugal scene at the dinner table. Let us go back to the root of the disturbance. . . .

To begin with, when Moloch married Blanche there was little said about this prefix, mother. Blanche had been living under the guardianship of a maiden aunt. A year passed, and one day the two of them decided to go on a belated honeymoon. Blanche had pictured her parents as a gay, middle-aged couple, living a stereotyped existence in a little out-of-the-way hole somewhere in Delaware. She had only visited them half a dozen times since her childhood. They looked forward to spending a quiet leisurely time with these strange people who had brought her into the world.

Hardly were they forty-eight hours under the parental roof when Moloch's preconceived image of the mother was shattered. It required the services of no village gossip to make him realize that this middle-aged woman who greeted her daughter so affectionately was the talk of the town. Wherever they went, people turned and stared at her. . . . The father led a strange life, too. He turned up at mealtimes, spoke about his work or the latest political gossip, and disappeared. Moloch sized the situation up as best as he could and came to the conclusion that these fond parents had arrived at an open convenant permitting each to go his or her own way and no questions asked. There was not even a latent air of hostility between them. Whatever it was, the thing had been settled long ago, and the compromise, such as it was, seemed to work smoothly. . . . This trim, dapper little man, whose age one could only guess at, was certainly not a bad sort. Immediately upon their arrival he showed a great liking for his son-in-law and lost no time in introducing him to his circle of friends. Sometimes Blanche would accompany them, and then the dapper little parent fairly beamed at everyone, so proud he was to be seen with his daughter and her sensible young husband.

Blanche was totally at a loss to understand her mother's conduct. As soon as luncheon was over the latter busied herself with her toilette, a thoroughgoing, painstaking process. Moloch soon found himself lingering behind during this process, pretending to be absorbed in a book. Blanche's preparations to meet the public eye had never enlisted his attention. To be sure, Blanche had never learned to make a ritual of this art, nor had she ever appeared to derive a tenth of the satisfaction and enjoyment which her mother breathed when the task was consummated. Never before had he been made so aware of the intricacies of the coiffure, the subtleties of the perfumers' art, the mysteries of the bath. By degrees he got to look forward to these ample ministrations and, when the fatal "hope hour" approached, would hang about the house like a moonstruck calf. Blanche, of course, was quick to take notice of this sensual repast. Unable, however, to circumvent his newly acquired habit, she hid her discomfiture by locking herself in her room during the ordeal.

"Does she always act like this?" the mother asked one day when Blanche had retired to her room in a huff.

"More or less," he sighed.

"You ought to be out having a good time. You only live once, you know."

She stood before him in a shimmery negligee, careless of the avid glances which licked her robust body. It struck him that she never considered him as a man. What was it—was he just a raw youth in her eyes? Or was he too dull for her? (In his morbid moments he was able to convince himself that Blanche had made an old fogy of him.)

So it became a vital question with him—whether this woman regarded him as wholly unattractive. He made up his mind that he was going to find out. . . .

It was Blanche who remarked one day that there was something "enigmatic" about the woman. (Blanche frequently referred to her mother as "the woman.") "I can't see it," he replied, summing up for her various elements that created the woman's personality.

What he saw seemed plain and obvious enough. The woman was a Circe, unsung as yet by any Homer. There were many in the land, only people never recognized them until their infamies were screamed in ten-inch headlines. She was a type, such as one might find in a Greek legend, between the covers of a D'Annunzio volume, or in a Wagnerian opus. One might even find her in an eighteenth-century bordello. A home she has not; merely a rendezvous. Her age is a myth: she is neither youthful nor decrepit. Her features have the splendor and charm of an ancient ruins, mellowed and softened by the touch of time. The nostrils, well-grooved and carving a thrilling arabesque, when distended suggest faint caverns of joy. The head, slightly tilted and enframed by the lecherous twilight of the boudoir, presents a magnificent chiaroscuro. There may be just the barest suggestion of the coming of a Guadeloupe chin. Centered implacably, like a zither flaming with lust, is the gaping red maw. The artist in her fixes it by a staggering daub of vermilion. Her loose, sensual lips are never quite closed. They exist only to slake men's thirst, themselves remaining parched and seared. A crepuscular odalisque withal whose torso rises like a groundswell. Rondures like the contorted nocturnes of Michelangelo . . . certainly not the baleful, iniquitous curves of a Utamaro. Something begun by Praxiteles, and left for the moderns to complete.

Does this Circe seem *enigmatic*?

Anyway, the mistake that Moloch made was to listen to the siren's song. It floated out from the bathroom and affected him so that neither looks nor things abstract could quiet the forces secreted in his loins. The ceremony took place every day at the same hour. He had only to listen to her rain-shattered melodies—and he was lost.

It was the strangest honeymoon he had ever spent. He had taken with him a bride, and he had discovered a succubus. And now, after all these years of silence, he learned that his wife knew everything.

How did she know? He never asked her that. But when he contemplated the spectacle of this indignant creature, labeled "wife," who was capable of lying beside him night in and night out during all the years of their married life, who could walk up to the brink of the grave at childbirth, still with lips sealed, his soul revolted. All the malice and suspicion that she had accumulated during the years of their common strife he looked upon as nothing more than the venom of a poisonous reptile. For what, he wanted to know, for what could she have nurtured this slimy secret of their past?

He rose from the table gravely and demanded scornfully what else she held up her sleeve. "What else do you know? Out with it!" he cried.

"What else ought I to know?" she said ruefully.

He wavered a moment. Then he said firmly: "How much can you stand?"

The brutality of this remark undid her. She put her arms on the table and buried her sobs in them.

When he could stand it no longer he went over to her and put his arms around her soothingly. The table trembled with her grief. Once before, when she was in a state of nervous collapse (due to her fear of childbirth), he had seen her weep this way. There was something animal-like about it . . . reminded him of a squealing calf at the slaughterhouse when it gets its first whiff of fresh-spilt blood.

He was ashamed of what the neighbors would think. "Stop it, please, I beg you," he repeated, stroking her hair and finally getting down on his knees beside her. The gentleness of his voice only seemed to stimulate her tears. New reservoirs of emotion were tapped; her whole body rocked and sagged until the pain of it numbed him. He rose to his feet and waited stoically for the exhaustion which he knew would follow. He began to reflect about the situation philosophically.

Meanwhile, between hiccoughs and groans, she contrived to put in a few words. Her utterances were repetitious. They were chiefly interrogations, addressed to a remote and imperturbable deity.

"Oh God!" she wailed. "What have I ever done, what *could* I do to deserve this?"

He beseeched her to control herself. "You're hysterical, Blanche."

"Oh, why must I be humiliated in this way . . . always, always, always? Haven't I been a good mother, haven't I always been loyal to you?"

"Of course, Blanche . . . of course. There, there . . ." he whispered soothingly.

She flared up again. "You don't mean it, I know you don't. You'd say anything just to have me stop." She continued to weep copiously. He stood stone still, waiting, waiting for her to dry up.

He fell into a reverie as he stood beside the cowering figure of his wife. At his slightest touch she shuddered, gasped anew, and fell into a collapse. Queer thoughts were roving through his head. This man, Jim Daly, for instance, who was consumed with love for Blanche—how would he have managed things? Would he have made a mess of it, too? Was it not inevitable that with such a woman for a wife such and such situations would occur? Jim Daly was probably eating his heart out because he couldn't have this woman, Blanche. Another man, out in North Dakota, was in the same fix most likely. The two of them suffering agonies over the loss of this imaginary being. Yes—*imaginary?* Did the women they yearn for exist? Where was she? Surely it wasn't this abject, grief-crazed, tear-sodden creature hanging over the table like a raped virgin?

For all he knew she was yearning for them, too. He couldn't tell which was the favorite. She probably wanted them both. To tell the truth, he had a suspicion that she didn't know who she wanted, or *what* she wanted. She, too, was concerned with imaginary beings, with lovers who would fade, at the first touch of reality, into mythic monsters. He wished to God they would change places with him for just a little while. It was all nonsense, this raising a woman to the skies without knowing a thing about her. . . .

He thought of the letter Prigozi had sent him upon his wife's death. The words were graven in his memory. . . . "From the first time I met you I considered you a friend. To me that means but one thing; that nothing you ask of me is too much, that you are free, nay, more than free, to come and take unasked what I have to give . . . that no thought be hidden from you, and no secrets kept." And all the actions of this fantastic individual, for whom he had come to have such a strong affection, were but proofs that these assertions were not idle. Here was one whom he had not married, whom on occasion he had taken mean advantage of, and had mocked and treated slightingly; yet the little word "friendship" had taught him to behave in a noble, generous way. And to Blanche this man whom he called friend was nothing more than a disgusting little Jew who delighted in prying into other people's affairs.

He gave up thinking about it all. It was useless to reason with Blanche. She had her point of view, and he had his. He saw life as an adventure, perhaps a sordid one, but an adventure nevertheless. As for her, she was wriggling through life on her belly. No wonder she was afraid and disgusted. To her it could never be other than a crawling, stinking affair.

17

"... IN SOFIA I STARTED TO DO WHAT YOU CALL THE White Way stunt. You must not think, however, that I did this only for the fun of the thing or that I am by nature perverted, but here in the Balkans feelings towards such kind of things are totally different. You rise right away in the esteem of the people here when you keep a notorious and much-coveted 'grande cocotte,' or when you sit at a gambling table and stolidly rake in your gains and still more stolidly look at your money being raked in. Especially in Sofia I got the right dope as I took for a few weeks as my companion the most notorious woman here, who is called here *'la seule grande cocotte de Sofia'*—went with her to the fashionable bathing resorts, etc. Then I discarded her and took the prima donna of the Royal Opera here. After three months of this kind of life I had established just the right kind of rakish reputation to find grace with the public opinion, as I wrote you already, quite different from public opinion in the USA. I feel that I can retreat and start again a sober life.

"I give you all these details in order to show you how it is possible that I, who was only a couple years past scanning the street and apartment numbers in the neighborhood of the Flatiron Building with a bunch of telegrams in his hand and dressed up like a horse and wagon, can allow himself now to entertain prima donnas of the Opera. . . . Saturday night I had only one wish and that was that you could have sitten next to me. . . .

"The boss wants to be back in Roumania on the fifteenth as he is invited at the Cornation of the King and Queen of Roumania. I will join that event, too, and will have a third opportunity of renewing acquaintance. I have found a charming Roumanian girl here, which occupies most of my spare time. . . .

"My impressions about my native land were as you could realize not very definite. The only thing I can write you is that I felt as if I was in a big village. After having left the hustling, noisy New York: works the calmness of a town like the Hague and Scheveningen as a anesthetic. . . ."

Moloch crumpled the letter up and shoved it back in his pocket. It was the third time he had started to go through it. There were twenty-six pages to this letter, covering four continents, nine women, three royal families, ambassadors and potentates galore, innumerable quarts of champagne, coke dreams, camel rides, and two social diseases. But Moloch simply couldn't pull himself together. The escapades of his old friend Jacques Dun failed to stir him. If the Stock Exchange had been blown up he wouldn't have been stirred either. He was going about in a coma.

Blanche had risen early that morning, prepared his breakfast (an unusual thing!), and just as he was about to leave had informed him in a calm tone of voice that she intended to go away soon. She refused to say for how long. "I have no definite plans," she announced. "I'm just tired of it all. . . . I want to go off somewhere and think things over."

That afternoon she left with the child. She requested, in a note,

that he put the furniture in storage. It was impossible, she had
written, to say how long she would remain away. Perhaps she
wouldn't come back at all. She left no mailing address, though
it was quite likely she knew where she was going.

The strangest thing about this leavetaking was that it caused
him no unusual bitterness. As a husband perhaps he had a right
to show some resentment. He had none. That evening he came
home, moved about the house mechanically, and after he had
read her note several times came to the conclusion that as a
human being she had a right to make her own experiment, if that
was what she was doing. The loss of the child affected him most.
He realized then, more than ever before, how passionately he was
attached to her. What if he were never to see her again?

He waited a day or two before making any move, hoping that
Blanche would change her mind. He kept on the lookout for the
mail man. When the bell rang he would rush to the door, expect-
ing to see the two of them standing there with open arms. . . .
Three days passed; then four, then five. . . . Still no word from
Blanche.

Where the devil was she, and what was she doing with the little
one? Hell, this was no way to treat a grown-up man! If she had
found someone else, and she wanted to start all over again, why
didn't she let him know? He'd give her a clean bill of health. But
this damned suspense! God, she might have been crazy enough
to take the child and jump off a bridge . . . the two of them might
be lying at the bottom of a river!

He was getting ready to tear his hair out.

He adopted her suggestion and put the things in storage. He
tried to pull himself together. Maybe she was only giving him a
dose of his own medicine. . . . During the day, head over heels in
work, it was easier to banish them from his mind, but at night,
when he was perfectly free and might have gone gallivanting with
other women, he became moody and lost in melancholy reflections.

He was thinking about them a hell of a lot. . . .

On the tenth day he received a letter. She was writing him from
a little town in Massachusetts to let him know that the two of

them were well and would like to hear from him. There was a pathetic little bit at the end to the effect that she was running short of funds . . . she didn't want to ask him outright for aid, but if he cared to send her some she would appreciate it. He ran immediately to the telegraph office and wired her a tidy sum; then he sat down and wrote her a ten-page letter. He sent the letter special delivery.

Three days later he received another letter, thanking him for his great kindness and urging him to continue writing. She said nothing about moving on. There was no mention of plans at all. Through her letters there seemed to run a vein of quiet contentment. She wrote as one convalescing after a serious illness.

"Very well," he thought to himself, "let it go on. She needs to take stock of herself . . . get well again inside."

His own letters were carefully worded so as not to exert any undue influence. He tried to handle things delicately and avoid any semblance of pressure. It would be utterly foolish now, he reasoned, to implore her to do one thing or another. "Look after your health," he wrote. "Enjoy yourself. . . . Perhaps I've been a big fool."

Love he handled very gingerly, but if she had the least sense she could read between the lines that he fairly adored her now. The fact of the matter was, he was a very changed man during this vacation of his wife's. He had no eyes for any other women. At lunchtime he walked about the streets, peering into shop windows, wondering what to send them that would be particularly appealing. Several times he telegraphed flowers. He mailed books, too, and sent her candy and clippings from the New York papers which he thought would interest her. . . . In this way they were really drawing closer together than if they had been home lying next to each other, their thoughts a thousand miles apart.

This sort of thing went on for about two months, and still Blanche said nothing about returning. There was nobody else on the scene, he felt quite sure of that. By this time the letters that passed between them had become more outspoken. Blanche no longer made any efforts to conceal her affection; her letters were brimming with love, albeit there was always a tinge of sadness which he in his ecstasy attributed to her isolation. Once in a while, when he was victimized by a mood, he would sit down and send her a scorcher, but in the next letter he would make amends for his passionate utterances by confining himself to general topics or inquiring solicitously about her circumstances.

Then one day he received a large bulging envelope. (Why is it that people, when they are in love, place such extraordinary emphasis on the thickness of the letters?) He tore the envelope open greedily. A little bundle of photographs fluttered out and spilled over the desk. He seized them with trembling hands. Now he could no longer contain himself. His mind was made up. . . . It was about ten o'clock of a Saturday morning. He rushed to his lodging and packed his bag in a sweat. Then he took a taxi to the depot and bought a ticket. At the first stop he sent a telegram that he was on his way. . . .

"We have come into this world to accept it, not merely to know it. We may become powerful by knowledge, but we attain fullness by sympathy." The words of the poet—he had always accepted Tagore's prose as a beautiful thing in itself—now conveyed to his heightened senses a mystical import that veiled their fragility with a mask of profundity and solemnity. "We have come into this world to accept it!" What a clear, noble view! The evil and ugliness of life seemed far behind. Could a man grasp the significance of that thought, hold on to it like a rudder, what a sane course he might steer through the turbulent waters of life! He closed the volume of prose and stared with vacant eyes at the fleeting panorama. The brooks, the trees, the drab mill towns, the sodded, desiccated faces of the New England milieu were so many dreary items of a world that had lost its ecstasy. His lids shut down instinctively on the plangent realities of the world about him. It was a living world, a world of strife and sorrow, a distorted world that mocked the serene logic of the philosopher, the dignity and pathos of the poet, the security and aloofness of the heart of a spectator.

The train sped on through the miserable lands of the Pilgrims which he had blotted out. Hands he could not see pawed monotonously over the looms and lasts; women with flaccid breasts waited in dirty hovels for the whistle to blow that they might pick up the thread of life again; lean-visaged, hard-fisted Yankees were breaking their backs over stony potato patches, their souls as warped and twisted as the barren soil that nourished them; bloodless spinsters licked the spittle from their prattling lips, gooey with gossip, cancerous with hate and envy; village parsons, narrow and limited as their cabin'd confines, raised scrawny pious hands over the wickedness of a sinful people.

Somewhere in the midst of this cultural blight a mother and child were waiting for him. A lover was stretching out her arms, her breasts big with longing. He could see her heart exposed and bleeding, like the religious decoration on a alabaster virgin. ... "Dearest boy," she had written, "you are so thoughtful, so good to me . . . you mean so much more than you can ever realize. I want so much to make you happy. I do so want to prove to you the depth of feeling which I have for you—but I cannot! I want you always for just my own, but if I cannot have you— well, my happiness will be in seeing *you* happy. You dear, good boy—how I love you!"

The afternoon was pouring through the window of the train, touching his quivering lids with golden wands. The royal emissaries of the Lord were beckoning to his spirit; they bade him open his eyes and greet the pageant of the soil. At that moment he felt himself to be but an infinitestimal particle of a universe wheeling through the trackless space. He opened the volume which lay in his lap. A single paragraph sufficed. It was impossible to go on. . . .

"The prosody of the stars can be explained in a classroom by a diagram but the poetry of the stars is in the silent meeting of soul with soul, at the confluence of the light and dark, where the infinite prints his kiss on the forehead of the finite, where we can hear the music of the 'Great I Am' peeling from the grand organ of creation through its countless reeds in endless harmonies."

The deep, bituminous snorts of the engine were the echoes of a thunderous celestial music that rocked the town and its drowsy inhabitants. He clung ecstatically to the cushioned seat as the dripping, iron flanks of the monster grazed their way through the edges of the little Massachusetts town. The babble rising up out of the coach sounded to his ears like the frail, bleeding notes of a peaceful oblivion. His muffled flesh dimmed the roar of frantic trumpet calls. His soul was a broken shadow dancing over a precipice. . . .

For three days and nights they celebrated the marriage of the flesh. On the fourth day he could no longer put off his return. He was in jubilant spirits, his soul set free and soaring. Little Edda swayed unsteadily in her tiny bare feet and lisped in a quailing voice, "Goodbye, Daddy." In his absence Blanche had taught her to say a number of pretty things. The night of his arrival they had stood over her crib together and listened to the precious gurgling sounds issusing from her tired little throat. They were sounds no father could resist. How proud he felt over this tiny bundle of flesh, and a mist came over his eyes. What was there in life to equal this? "Excuse me," he said to Blanche, and rushed into the bathroom to hide his sobs.

Now he was bidding Blanche farewell, their hearts united in peace and love. She clung to him and drew him back inside the doorway for one final seal of affection. She whispered something in his ear. He blushed. Then the door closed behind him softly, like a curtain descending on an audience hushed and lacrimal. . . . His fingertips throbbed with the remembrance of her tinglish flesh.

When he had ridden a little way he opened his bag to look for some trifle and discovered to his great surprise a gift from Blanche. It was a small volume of Hamsun's called *Victoria*. In the flyleaf Blanche had traced this message;

"I am a grotesque written upon an old oak leaf vomited by a storm in late winter."

He swallowed this cruelly beautiful tale at one gulp. This berserker, with the heart of Strindberg and the neariness of Dostoevsky, lacerated his tender heart. He reviewed the closing pages of the book once more. What a monument to frustrated love, that last letter of Victoria's!

"Dear Johannes," she wrote, "when you read this letter I shall be dead. . . . O God, if you knew how I have loved you, Johannes.

"I have not been able to show it to you, so many things have come in my way, and above all my own nature. . . . If I got well again now I would never be unkind to you anymore, Johannes. How I have cried and thought about that! Oh, I would go out and stroke all the stones in the street and stop and thank every step of the stairs as I went by and be good to all. . . . My life is so unlived, I have not been able to do anything for anybody, and this failure of a life is to end now. . . . And today I was thinking— how would you take it, I wonder, if I came straight up to you in the street one day when I was nicely dressed, and did not say anything to hurt you as I have done, but gave you a rose which I had bought on purpose? . . . Ah, Johannes, I have loved you, loved only you all my life. It is Victoria who writes this and God is reading it over my shoulder. . . ."

He thought and thought and thought about this heartrending drama that was being enacted all over the world, wherever man and woman came together and whispered the piteous, tear-laden words that crushed them and raised them up and exalted them before God Almighty. He sat helplessly, blinded with tears, making himself small in a corner of the seat against the window. He wept for himself, for Blanche, for Johannes, for all the world . . . for all who have or ever will be touched by the insanity of love. The need to say something to Blanche, to call out to her, to get down on his knees and scream out his love, seized him by the throat.

Meanwhile Blanche was sitting in a little room in a squalid Massachusetts town; she was hypnotized by a sheet of blank writing paper soaked with tears. The pen rested in her hand, waiting for the tears to dry. She could not hear him screaming his love . . . he was so far away now, and the earth was so full of groans and wailing.

That night, when Dion Moloch reached his cheerless lodging, his brain was afire. He was determined to put an end to his vagabond days, to leave off the foolish role he had chosen, and strike out in deeper, unknown waters. He spoke aloud to himself. "What has my life amounted to? What am I living for?" He went on muttering to himself with clenched fists. "Do something—no matter how mad, no matter how terrible! Say something to the world: answer life with life. Strike out . . . free yourself from the clutches of a comfortable existence. . . ."

It was imperative to tell his thoughts to someone. With feverish energy he sat down and put his crazy thoughts on paper. He addressed them to his wife.

"Dear Victoria," he scribbled. "What have you done to me? I am naked and lost in a forest of pines. My heart is an Easter morning. What terrible, beautiful things are happening to me inside! Black rivulets of pain are pouring from the open wounds in my heart which your love cauterized only a few hours ago. This world is my world, my stamping-ground. I must run free, mad-hearted, bellowing with pain and ecstasy, charging with lowered horns, ripping up the barricades that hem me in and stifle me. I must have room to expand . . . vast, silent spaces to charge in so that my voice may be heard to the outermost limits and shake the unseen walls of this cruel universe. I must do something, dear Blanche, dear *Victoria*. . . . No longer can I go on as a cog in a wheel. Let me implore you to help, to save me from this daily degradation.

"Only now it has dawned on me what life can hold. I feel all life rising up in me, shouting Hallelujah!

"It is I, your husband, writing this. Not Johannes. Yes, I read your inscription on the flyleaf . . . "Something vomited by a storm in late winter." I prefer, however, to think of page 39, on which it is written:

" 'Ah, Love turns the heart of man into a garden of fungus, a luxuriant and shameless garden wherein mysterious and immodest toadstools raise their heads.' "

A GAUNT BARE OAK WITH BLACK-AND-PURPLE BOUGHS
threw a bold grotesque shadow on a neighboring wall. Moloch
thought of chesspieces he had seen in the museum, rugged Yakut
figures with horses like that crazy shadow.

He had returned to his room after posting the letter to his wife
and was now gazing idly out of the window wondering how to
while away the tedium of the brief interval before bedtime. The
profound silence weighed on him and drove his thoughts into
strange realms. He thought, for instance, of the austere and
vicarious devotions of the monks in the Buddhist lamaseries in
the Himalayas, where for centuries it has been the custom of
these recluses to get up in the middle of the night and pray for
all who sleep so that men and women all over the world, when
they awake in the morning, may be purified and begin the day
with thoughts that are pure, kind, and brave. He thought, too, of

that ill-fated genius Gauguin, who in the midst of his career had been reduced to the ignominy of pasting advertisements on the walls of the Gare du Nord. Gauguin had once said: "The duty of the artist is to affirm the dignity of life." Very well, then, was he prepared to go ahead and break his neck in order to affirm the dignity of life.

The dignity of life! The majesty of the phrase invoked a consciousness of suggestions forever denied the vehicle of words. The words were like a filament separating the palpable from the impalpable. They created the image of a sensuous world, a world beyond all expression or analysis, neither of the intellect wholly, nor of the senses.

He was seized with an inexplicable and overwhelming desire to rush down to the waterfront, to get down on his knees under the dilapidated elevator structure whose splintered limbs dangled and groped for the cold waters of the river. He wanted that very instant to be translated to the spot so that he might look above him, in dazzled awe, at the somber fretwork of the Brooklyn Bridge, that airy Titan's span over which a profilerous cortege shuttles with muffled scraping and the sizzling drone of an ocean of Vichy. He wanted to see the bridge lights flaring with cold luminosity, shedding fantastic naphtha gleams on the swollen tidewater deep below.

Time and again, in midnight mood, he had stolen down to the water's edge to throw open his nerves and arteries to the brutal splendid of this shadowy nocturne. Now, in his mind's eye, for a transient, fractional interval (during which a world may be born and die again), it loomed before him, bulk and shadow, a serrated cardboard megalith floating in eerie phantasmal configuration. Towers of steel and masonry arose—sea-forms glistering in moonfire and spume, shaking off through crest and spire their sea-trove of chrysoprase, chalcedony, sardonyx. A torpid, myriad-shaped dream demon wriggling in sea-foam and star-shimmer, spouting twisted gouts of blood and mud up into the blue-black vault above.

And in the midst of this seizure his mind suddenly raced back and presented him with the image of Hari Das lying on the freight siding, his beautiful brown body cold and stiff, pumped full of embalming fluid. The cold immobile lips had once boasted: "My highest pride consists in not-standing-on-solid-earth; the principle of my philosophy is the ultimate principle of the universe, which is NO-Principle. . . . I boast of my system being fluid, gaseous, capable of evaporating."

Golly, how Hari once could laugh! What ever made it possible for a man to laugh so heartily? He recalled a story he had told Hari once—it was about a corpse. It seems the undertaker had undressed the corpse, but forgot to remove the socks. Fancy shoveling a man under with a dirty pair of socks! Perhaps they had laid Hari out—he was only a nigger—without placing a clean silk hankerchief in his breast pocket. . . .

Midnight. The last act of *The Cherry Orchard* for Fulton Ferry. Battered hulks snoozing in velvet slips. Done with the sea, inviting corruption. The ferryhouse, crumbling in the shadows, more grim, more ghastly than Caesar's gutted corpse.

Farther on, up the quay, the *Troubador* lolls. She is just in from Curaçao, ten thousand bags of coffee in her hold. Her bottom is painted crimson, and about her tremulous white belly is an azure band. Hawsers and cables fix her gleaming prow to coppered stanchions that dot the pier and quay. Whirling constellations of stevedores transporting the odorous freight to the belching maws of warehouses a stone's throw away. Perched eerily above the vomit-hold, checkers are busily engaged working out the arithmetic of commerce. Queues of abbreviated motor trucks straggle through the blue calcium light over slithery, splintered planks. The wharf is alive with cranes, hand winches, bales, stumbling figures in blue denim, fat-bellied tuns, derricks, masts, and yardarms. A swirling, gurgling, full-crested tide leaves the mossy flanks of the wharves with glistering plashes of cabbage-green water. Bracing odors of tar and seaweed iodize the lungs. The *Troubador* squeals and grunts as she rubs the dock-timber like a boar in rut. Impervious and aloof, defaming the screaming silence of midnight flaps the Union Jack, wharf rat's symbol of power and greed.

Moloch's turquoise gigue of thoughts is stabbed by the pompom puffs of a locomotive. From far-off places come mysterious bursts of song that match the delirium of stone on the opposite shore. His vagrant fancies oscillate between the phantom horizons of the British Empire and the condition of his existence, which more than ever now appears like a tremulous causeway linking dream to dream. His soliloquies are squeezed through primitive angles of mast and boom, only to be flattened against monstrous skeletons of steel and concrete, plastered with false faces. A pleasant sensation invades the pit of his stomach as he watches the fling and sag of the *Troubador*. The water gives out rich, juicy sounds—better than an all-day sucker. The flooded stream rushes by, fuming and spuming, pushing and surging toward the sea. . . . Here one comes to rest, even as by the waters of Babylon. Here golden argosies are moored—great, shambling vessels, cheap as Woolworth baubles—their entrails steaming with rancid stoker-flesh. Shoving off in the morning for Valparaiso, Singapore, Sumatra, Rangoon, and Mozambique . . . And yonder, rising still and bright in the night, the slim, myriad-chinked palaces of the money-grubbers. Tremendous towers of vertigo that pierce the womb of night.

More than all the glamorous, ineluctable truths of the world beyond is the ineffable charm of somnolescence. The low, age-old edifices squatting at the water's edge were wrapped in thick, palpable gloom. Their stately desuetude, their sententious philosophic repose—all this mortuary splendor captivated and enthralled him. He felt that he was being carried away on a wistful catafalque to a purple-black, deeply poetic death. Frog-toots and sirens by the great black throat of the river.

"If one could only get away!"

He is tortured by imaginary fears of tomorrow. Midnight wears a surtout that conceals the bestial acromegaly of age. . . .

Leaving the docks behind, Moloch sauntered through a high-walled street that drops like a canyon below the terraces of Columbia Heights. The silence here was more ominous, more intense. It was a splendid place to get dirked. He walked gingerly in the middle of the street, fascinated by the queer iron stars on the sepulchral walls of the warehouses. Opposite the warehouses were tumbledown shanties and a string of boarded saloons.

Time was when the doors swung lightly, and hobnailed boots ground the yellow sawdust like pollen. Schooners brimming with suds left sparkling saucer-rings on the smooth, mahogany-stained bars. Hairy-chested apes, burned in the Red Sea to an eggplant glaze, used to dip their bristling mustaches in the cool, soapy foam. Their sinews flexed with snakelike ease, and the air was burnt with their foul, fornicating oaths.

Alas, those days have been confined and deodorized. The sweetish stench of wassail has evaporated like sweat. There are no good old drunken bums to slobber over anymore. The waterfront is as clean as a hound's tooth, and as morose as the grave. It is as safe here now as a patent medicine.

Drearily Dion Moloch turned away from this deserted street once stuccoed with saloons and crazy jerries. Above him were the dreary mansions of the rich. Within, sheltered from the fever and storm of life, were the brittle bones that were still too proud to betake themselves to the cemetery, where they belonged.

Looking down over a magical flight of steps at this fugitive backyard of Brooklyn, Dion Moloch cast his eyes once more over the rubble of shards heaped before him.

What was it, this grand view from the terrace? What did it reveal? A dump heap littered with rusty can openers, broken-down baby carriages, discarded tin bathtubs, greasy window shades, antiquated trunks, wheelbarrows, sewer pipes, copper boilers, nutmeg graters, and—animal crackers that had been partially nibbled.